Alice-Rose

Alice-Rose

Caitríona Leslie

Library of Congress Control Number: 2012915778
ISBN: Hardcover   978-1-4797-0588-7
               Softcover   978-1-4797-0587-0
               Ebook   978-1-4797-0589-4

To order additional copies of this book, contact:
Xlibris Corporation
0-800-644-6988
www.xlibrispublishing.co.uk
Orders@xlibrispublishing.co.uk
303717

CONTENTS

To my family, my husband Timmy and our children Tegan, Jack and Hugh, for affording me the time to write. To Edel, for her unwavering belief in Alice-Rose.

A place belongs forever to whoever claims it hardest, remembers it most obsessively, wrenches it from itself, shapes it, renders it, loves it so radically that he remakes it in his own image.

(Joan Didion)

Libby

CHAPTER 1

Meeting 'Her' Again

I T WAS ONE of those special, crisp, golden days of autumn. The air was heavy with promise, and I felt the knot of anxious excitement tighten in my stomach. I pushed open the tall cast-iron gates and began the long walk upwards, entirely alone except for bramble, brush, and briar.

I wondered about all the changes that I was sure to find and whether or not that day would deliver Alice-Rose into my future or consign her to the past forever. When courage almost failed me, one thing drove me onwards—the knowledge that a single glimpse of the old house would be enough to reveal whether or not we belonged together.

At last, I rounded the head of the avenue, and I saw it again, dignified and largely unchanged. Time and neglect had not prevailed; the heart of Alice-Rose was waiting for me. It was our time.

Alice-Rose, named after the daughter of the estate's original owner, was the place of my dreams, and on that morning two years ago, I felt a sense of belonging as strong as if I had been returning to my childhood home. It was the twenty-fifth of October. I remember the date clearly because it was my twenty-ninth birthday, and I was coming from my parents' house, having started the day there with a family breakfast.

While driving along the boundary wall of the Alice-Rose estate, heading in the direction of Ballyedmond, I saw a man preparing to erect a sign at the entrance up ahead. I was transfixed by the scene. Instinctively, I jammed on the brakes, giving no consideration to safety, my own or anybody else's. Luckily, the road behind me was clear, and I ground the car safely to a halt some six inches away from the man's shins. My near victim turned out to be Dan Bryant, a well-known estate agent from the locality.

Although Mr Bryant wasn't in the first flush of youth by any stretch of the imagination, he was still handsome. Besides his distinguished good looks, Dan Bryant was tall and solid and had all the appearance of someone who was doing well for himself. On that particular day, even while undertaking an exercise that involved no small amount of effort, he was flawlessly turned out in a pinstriped suit and a wool overcoat. I did, at the time, privately question the wisdom of his attire, but ultimately, I was more fascinated by the significance of his task than I was in his choice of clothing. Could it be that Alice-Rose was finally for sale?

'Is he selling it?' I asked abruptly, my thoughts spilling out in a way that managed to state the obvious and convey an attitude of absolute rudeness in one simple sentence.

I wasn't usually so blunt or so unfriendly, and I immediately regretted my approach.

'Hello,' Dan Bryant grunted, landing a blow of a sledgehammer to the post. 'Yes, she's on the market as of today, and *she's* a beauty!'

Despite his exertion, there was fervour in his voice and a little wistfulness, if I hadn't imagined it.

'I know,' I agreed, a little more warmly but with an assurance intended to convey to him that I knew 'her' worth.

'If I was a young man starting out,' he continued undeterred, 'I would do all in my power to buy her.' He spoke with conviction as he prepared to land the post another blow. '*But*,' he added, 'she's a place that needs a young family to bring her back to life.'

He looked directly at me as he said this, and his expression caused me to wonder what *exactly* he was thinking. Although I felt a momentary twinge of irritation at the personal nature of his comment, I was far too interested in the sale of Alice-Rose, to allow his unsolicited opinions to distract me from my quest.

'I must see *her* again,' I said, leaving Dan Bryant to his own assessment of what Alice-Rose might, or might not, need.

My heart was beating fast, and my head was buzzing as I tried to do the math, but deep down I felt certain that I was in a position to buy the place. I marched with determination up the curving avenue, diligently ignoring the butterflies dancing in my stomach. The lawns on either side were overgrown and tangled with grass and brambles so that the tall and ancient oaks appeared to scarcely have trunks. The very course that I stood on was growing narrower by the day as its borders threatened to engulf it. The post and rail fencing beyond the knotted mass of vegetation was broken and sagging and had the verdant hue of moss and mould. It was difficult to reconcile the shabbiness and neglect that lay before me then with the Alice-Rose of my childhood.

As I walked on and witnessed further the prevalence of nature that without intervention would eventually return Alice-Rose to an uncombed wilderness, I became filled with an even greater determination to succeed in my mission to buy it. When, at last, I rounded the curve of the avenue that brought face-to-face with the limestone beauty of the great house, I stood and looked for all of two seconds before turning on my heel to beat a hasty retreat.

Dan Bryant was about to get into his car just as I reached the gates, and I hesitated for an instant, slightly embarrassed by my earlier brusqueness. Then steeling myself, I called out, 'Mr Bryant!' He looked up, his surprise at seeing me so soon again quite evident. It occurred to me then that he had probably been trying to 'beat a hasty retreat' of his own. After all, who, given half a chance, wouldn't try to avoid a rude, crazy woman? Nevertheless, Dan Bryant was nothing if not professional, and he did not allow any trace of disappointment to show as he turned towards me, smiling openly.

'Yes, Miss . . . ,' he said, hesitating.

'Libby Finn, Mr Bryant,' I said, making no pretence at not knowing his name and extending my hand to shake his. 'But please call me Libby.'

We shook hands as he acknowledged that he had in fact recognised me. His handshake was dry and firm.

'I know your father well, Libby,' he said pleasantly. I waited for him to continue, but he didn't elaborate.

'I'm sorry I was so rude earlier,' I apologised, by then genuinely repentant for my earlier manner. 'I'm not usually so abrupt.'

Dan Bryant waved aside my concerns, but I felt obliged to explain myself.

'My only justification I'm afraid, is that I got a shock when I saw you putting Alice-Rose on the market.' The excuse sounded lame, even to my own ears.

Dan nodded in a gesture of understanding, but I knew that he couldn't possibly guess at the depth of my passion for Alice-Rose. I also imagined that he must have been thinking how easy it was to 'shock' me, and that I needed to get better control of my emotions if an everyday occurrence such as that one elicited such rudeness in me!

'I've always loved Alice-Rose, and I want to ask you some questions if I may?' I said, before thinking better of my presumption that Dan Bryant would stoop to be at my immediate disposal. 'I mean I need to make an appointment to see you.'

So far, the man had done nothing to offend me, and I had been abrupt to the point of insolence, not to mention having almost run him over!

'That won't be necessary, Libby, and *please* call me Dan,' he said, smiling at me in a way that could only be described as heart-stopping. I did actually think of Dan Bryant and heart-stopping in the same sentence despite the fact that the man was old enough to be my father!

'I could give you a tour now if you like,' he continued, 'even though it sounds like you already know the place very well. We can talk as we go.'

'That would be fantastic, Dan!' I shrilled, before he could change his mind.

I was overjoyed at being able to avail of an immediate tour of Alice-Rose, and I was hopeful that by the end of it I would know a lot more about a number of things, including what the owner's expectations were in terms of a price. At that point, I didn't even know how much of the property was for sale.

'I spent a lot of time up here with my father when I was a child,' I went on, attempting to shed some light on my personal interest in the estate.

'I *see*,' Dan said solemnly, but I could tell that he had some doubts. 'I hope you won't be disappointed, Libby. I'm sure some changes have taken place since then.'

'Maybe, but I intend to buy Alice-Rose if I can,' I said firmly. I didn't want Dan Bryant in any doubt as to what my intentions were.

'Not just the house,' I insisted, 'but *all* of it. Do you understand what I mean?'

'Yes,' he acknowledged earnestly. 'I think I do.'

I wasn't sure whether or not he was mocking me, but I didn't care; my only concern at that point was for Alice-Rose. As I watched Dan Bryant fetch a pair of wellington boots from his car, I found myself wondering if I could actually go out with a man who drove a Mercedes. I had always equated the make with the older generation, but suddenly I found myself reconsidering my long held view. These thoughts were followed by others that raised even more improbable questions. Did Dan Bryant wear pyjamas to bed? Was Dan Bryant still interested in sex? Just *how old* was Dan Bryant anyway?

My imagination was brought into check by the realisation that this man was in all probability married. I allowed myself a discreet glance at his left hand. Yes, there it was in all its glory, one large gold wedding band. I wasn't at all surprised, but, nevertheless, I had to admit to feeling more than a little disappointed. The aphorism 'the good ones are always taken' came to mind, and I was left feeling slightly deflated as I tried to remember who I had last heard quoting those particular words of wisdom. Probably Jules, I decided finally. Jules Mahon was my best friend and a reliable harbinger of all tales cautionary and wise.

'Hello? Libby?' Dan's voice broke deliberately into my thoughts. I had fallen into a state of reverie, the likes of which had become unfamiliar to me. I couldn't recall the last time I had speculated romantically about a man, but I knew that I hadn't done it since Max's death. I had to admit that it felt pretty good, and I felt alive in a way that I hadn't been sure I ever would again. I inhaled deeply and smiled unashamedly.

'Sorry, Libby. I thought you were miles away,' he apologised. 'I didn't mean to shout.'

Dan Bryant looked at me with a mixture of concern and slight bewilderment, and I realised that I had never before, in my whole life, felt such an instant attraction to a man.

'You didn't shout, Dan,' I said. 'I *was* miles away. But I'm back now. I'm finally back in the land of the living.'

An indisputable look of realisation crossed his face, and it became clear that, despite our very different appearances, Dan Bryant had mistaken me for my younger sister.

Starting up towards the house again with Dan Bryant by my side, I anticipated viewing Alice-Rose with renewed hope. I observed undeterred the neglect and decay that had befallen her with the passing of time. These things paled into insignificance when compared to the brilliance of sheer blue sunshine filtered through the branches of a giant oak or the glimpse of a perfectly rounded porthole on the gable end of a cut-stone barn.

CHAPTER 2

Alice-Rose: The In-between Years

TWO HOURS LATER, having finished our tour of Alice-Rose, I was back at Willow Cottage, a small two-storied farmhouse that had lain idle for an age at the far end of my parents' land. Some years earlier, they had undertaken its renovation, and thereafter it had acted as overflow accommodation for visitors to their home.

As one might have expected, when I returned for the unforeseeable future to Lough Glen, I fell between two stools. I was no longer the innocent child of my parents, nor was I their once fully fledged chick. When everything was taken into consideration, it was decided that Willow Cottage was the obvious solution to my accommodation needs. For my part, I was very glad of its proximity to home because I craved the reassurance of my parents' closeness, but I needed the separateness of 'independent living'.

One month after Max's funeral, I moved from Lough Glen House into the little farmhouse, and it became my sanctuary. I insisted upon paying rent for two good reasons: firstly, it gave me a sense of self-reliance, and secondly, I could well afford to! I set up the smallest of the three bedrooms as my office. It held my computer and most of the files and accounts of my small importing business. I was a one-woman show, specialising in the importation of American antiques. It was a niche market, and most of my clients resided in the United Kingdom and beyond.

After the morning's events at Alice-Rose, I found myself sitting before my computer scrolling down through my bank accounts. It would have surprised everyone, including members of my closest family, to know that I had accumulated just over five point three million euros in my relatively short life.

The bulk of this had resulted from an initial stake of five hundred thousand euros in various 'sound investments'. This lump sum had not been acquired through any wiliness or talent of my own, except perhaps that my character reflected that of an old and very shrewd relation, my grandaunt Lucy. At the tender age of sixteen, much to everyone's surprise, I inherited a jewellery shop in Dublin's southside inner city from my elderly relation. Why she chose to leave her property in its entirety to yours truly, we'll never know; I had only met the woman on a handful of occasions, but I must have made an impression, nonetheless!

Apparently, during one of our rare meetings, my mother's aunt decided to have a little fun with me. She suggested, in my presence, that my father was going bald and that he would 'soon be in need of a crown-topper!' To my five-year-old mind, Grandaunt Lucy, despite her seniority, had crossed the line because I adored every part of my father, including his nowhere near-balding head!

If the story is to be believed, I responded to her ludicrous suggestion by pulling myself up to my full height, before announcing to her, and to all listening, that she was nothing but an 'old witch'. Well, everyone present was quite sure that I had burnt my bridges as far as Grandaunt Lucy's affections went—it was well known that the woman could not abide a cheeky child! However, that being said, she must have made an exception in my case because Grandaunt Lucy, who was a spinster and childless, decided, for reasons unknown, to leave her estate to me.

When I got over the shock of my grandaunt's will and as soon as I could legally do so, I sold my inheritance. I didn't see myself ever having any use for a business premises on Fade Street.

Luckily for me, not everyone felt the same way about it as I did, and quite a few prospective buyers found the shop very appealing. This narrow four-storied building amassed a small fortune for me. When all of the fees and taxes were paid, I was still left with almost six hundred thousand pounds!

I duly gave my siblings a generous handshake and invested the bulk of what remained in banking and construction shares, something that one would be ill-advised to do today! Within a year, I had doubled my money, and I continued to gain ground for the next four years. I secured a place on a business degree course in University College Dublin, and it was here that I met my future husband, Max.

Max was studying physics, and although his family happened to be very well off, Max himself had very little interest in money. This was one of the many things that attracted me to him. Despite his parents buying him a car for his eighteenth birthday, Max preferred to cycle to college whatever the weather, and it was in a bicycle shelter that we first 'bumped helmets'. Casual chats as we struggled on a daily basis to find a place in the overcrowded shelters on campus led to less casual 'chats' in the Student's Union bar. 'Pillow talk' in my student accommodation inevitably followed soon after, and it didn't take me very long to realise that he was The One.

Besides having practically no interest in money, Max had other qualities that I found irresistible. He was handsome for starters; his thick mop of dark red hair was readily identifiable around the college grounds. His eyes were darkest grey, and they had a depth that was rarely found in the eyes of other guys his age.

My best friend Jules Mahon described Max as being 'terribly cerebral and just a bit intense'. I supposed that he was, but nevertheless, I found him compelling. I can't deny that Max's 'intensity' played its part in causing me to fall for him hook, line, and sinker; it extended quite pointedly in my direction and was effectively translated by his all-consuming passion in the bedroom!

But most of all, I found Max Kilbracken's appetite for knowledge and life hugely attractive, and it soon became clear that I too held a long-term attraction for this boy. My love, being the old soul that he was, saw marriage as being the next obvious step in our relationship, and neither of us viewed our relative youth as a deterrent.

Fortunately, our parents weren't overly concerned by our lack of life experience either. They themselves had married young, at a time when people did. Even so, we were relieved by their votes of confidence, and having them on board certainly made planning our wedding a lot easier. We married when we were both still only twenty-two.

Even in the very early days of our marriage, I was quite definite about my immediate ambitions. I was determined to set up my own business and to make babies, and not necessarily in that order. While I managed to achieve the first of these goals rather effortlessly, the second proved to be rather more difficult. For the three years and seven months of our short married life, Max and I tried valiantly to get pregnant. We made love once a day, twice a day, three times an hour, every second day, upside down, and inside and out! But regardless of our best efforts, I remained conspicuously non-pregnant.

Although Max was committed to 'the baby effort', he wasn't quite as focused on the goal as I was. While my levels of anxiety grew, he remained calm and reasonable. It was his considered opinion that there had to be a logical explanation for our failure to conceive, and his reasoning was simple—we were young, we had time on our sides, and we had resources.

We would get to the root of the problem and we would try our very best to fix it. If it turned out that we were unfixable, then we would adopt.

On *non-hormonal days,* I agreed with his line of logic, but there were dark days when I was convinced that we would remain childless forever. Max and I already had so much; being granted a child would mean that we had everything that we could possibly have hoped for. In a world where so many suffered so much at the cruel hands of fate, why should we be overindulged by the universe? My darling husband refused to entertain this line of thinking and referred to the countless examples of people who had somehow managed to *have it all.*

Unfortunately, we didn't have that much time in the end. We never did get to the root of our problem, and we never managed to have it all. Fate intervened in the cruellest of twists. One morning, while taking one of our first steps towards solving the puzzle that was our infertility, Max was knocked off his bicycle as he returned from Saint James Hospital, having just dropped off a sample of his semen for analysis. He was killed instantly, and I was left a widow at the age of twenty-six.

The sale of our mortgage-free home, the value of which had increased considerably since its purchase four years earlier, together with Max's half of a life assurance policy meant that I was taken care of financially. It seemed as if my sole purpose in life was to accrue money through the loss of my nearest, and sometimes not so dearest, relations. Needless to say, I didn't like it, not one bit. In fact, I despised it!

After Max's death, I had a knee-jerk reaction to my increasing wealth; I saw it as a block to my ever achieving lasting happiness. I had no objection to wealth per se, but I decided that I had more than enough money for the time being at least. I needed to simplify and reassess my life. I started by selling every last share that I possessed. Even this barely considered decision was to work to my advantage. Within months, there was a downturn in the economy and what had once been a very healthy share portfolio dwindled considerably for those who had relieved me of it.

CHAPTER 3

Life Without Max or Reason

B ACK IN WILLOW Cottage, as I stared intently at my computer
screen, I reflected upon the vagaries of life. I considered the fact
that Alice-Rose would probably not have been on the market then
had it not been for the national, and to a lesser degree global, economic
crash.

George Baxter had inherited Alice-Rose from his uncle Michael Stevens
over a decade previously and had held on to the place while continuing to
make his fortune in property development. I had often wondered why he
had never embarked on her restoration in light of the fact that he had all of
the necessary contacts to facilitate such an undertaking. Word had it that
the old place held little attraction for George, who was more interested in
mass productions than he was in class constructions, sentiments that I was
now very grateful for. George's apparent disinterest in Alice-Rose meant
that while the old place might have remained unappreciated, no irreparable
damage had been done to it.

The property's arrival on to the open market bore witness to the fact that
George's fortunes had gone the way of so many, and a lack of funds was by
then forcing him to part company from his neglected bequest. While on one
level, I sympathised with George's plight; the nurturing instinct in me relished
the prospect of having the opportunity to rescue his 'abandoned child'.

Alice-Rose was about to be advertised nationwide, and the notice
would reveal the appeal of her early Georgian residence, resplendent with
all its original features. It would detail the large stone farmyard, featuring
the lofted stable block, as well as the walled garden, all nestling on two
hundred and thirty-three acres of prime farmland. If I was to have any
chance of preventing the estate from going to auction, I had to make
George Baxter a serious offer from the start.

After much deliberation and consideration of similar properties and
their asking prices over the previous two years, I calculated that two point
nine million euro would be a fair offer and should by rights be enough to

clinch the deal. After all, the property had been neglected for a long time, including a number of years preceding Michael Stevens's death.

I picked up the phone and dialled Bryant and Bryant Auctioneers. I asked to speak to Dan Bryant and was disappointed to learn from his receptionist that he had already left for the day. However, the lady informed me that if my call was urgent, I could talk with the other partner in the business, Mr Paul Bryant; he was still in the office and would be more than happy to help me. Since my call was, in my opinion, of the utmost urgency, I readily agreed to this.

Paul Bryant, like his brother, was affable, and even over the phone, the similarities between them were striking. Once introductions were out of the way, I informed Paul Bryant that I wanted to make George Baxter an offer for Alice-Rose and that it would be my first and final offer. If he agreed to my price, then I expected that the property would be taken off the market immediately and that all legal documentation would be exchanged without delay. Because I intended to tell no one, not even my closest family, I stressed the need for absolute confidentiality in all matters until the deal was concluded.

I was more than a little surprised when twenty minutes later Paul Bryant rang back to say that George Baxter had accepted my offer and that he was agreeable to the estate being taken off the market that day. He was also in a position to tell me that even as we spoke Mr Baxter was in the process of informing his solicitors of the sale and that he hoped to have the papers to me by the end of the following week. Confidentiality was assured by all!

'Wow, things must be bad,' I said aloud, having first carefully ended the call. Two seconds later, I was jumping around the room, screaming with excitement, unable to quite believe the events of the day.

At some point in my euphoria, it occurred to me that I should inform my own solicitors and bank about my plans. Pouring myself another cup of coffee, which was by then more freshly stewed than freshly brewed, I once again picked up the phone and started dialling. The rest of the afternoon was spent 'in conference' with the various other parties concerned with my financial interests.

When all of the necessary phone calls were made, I looked outside and was disappointed to see that darkness was already falling. I had hoped to steal back up to Alice-Rose in daylight; I longed to look through the gates and to imagine how it could and would look in the future.

I pictured installing discrete lighting along the front and rear avenues, nothing showy, something tasteful and low-key in keeping with the 'old girl'. I laughed to myself as I imagined the spirit of Alice-Rose harrumphing in annoyance at being described as 'low-key'. Truth be told, there was nothing low-key about Alice-Rose in terms of its breathtaking beauty, but it was a dignified and tasteful beauty nonetheless. Despite the descending darkness, I grabbed my keys and headed for the door; I just had to have another peek through the gates before bedtime.

Returning to Willow Cottage later that evening, I decided to keep a low profile and phoned my sister Emma to decline the dinner invitation that she had extended earlier in the day. It wasn't easy to persuade her that there was 'absolutely no way' I could travel to Dublin that night to dine with herself and her boyfriend Mark. They had taken it upon themselves to invite one of Mark's work colleagues to dinner in order to make up a 'cosy foursome'. Personally speaking, I didn't think there was anything cosy about a foursome! If three was a crowd, then four was an even bigger crowd when two of the four people involved didn't know one another.

I hated set-ups because I always felt hugely inadequate at pulling them off, regardless of the occasions sometimes involving the nicest of people. Blind dates usually started off well enough but more often than not ended badly. As the evenings wore on, lips would invariably become loosened by alcohol, and I would end up feeling like I was being interrogated about the 'unusualness' of my situation, given my 'comparatively young age'.

Of course, the nature of Max's death did little to curb people's morbid fascination. Heaven only knows how excited they would have become had they known the purpose of that fateful bike ride, although I often suspected, judging by some people's enthusiastic probing, that our hosts had already covered that aspect of the story.

Emma was persistent in her pleas that I should join them 'just this once'. Augustus, as my prospective blind date for that evening was called, was apparently just my type. With a name like that, I really didn't think so! But his unlikely moniker was the least of my worries. The legacy of past dates that Emma and Mark had chosen as my potential suitors gave me far more cause for concern!

Remembering our most recent dining fiasco, yet another aimed at setting me up, I stood firm. Before ending the call, I light-heartedly suggested to Emma that it might, in future, be better to give me advanced notice of any matchmaking plans that she might have. I hoped that she would conclude from this that I was disappointed at not having been able to make that evening's dinner rather than being offended that I had declined her invitation. On the other hand, if Emma took my suggestion on board, it would give me due notice of any future schemes and allow me enough time to invent plausible excuses when necessary.

I ended the call, relieved to have successfully evaded 'capture'. The last thing I needed right then was to have to make polite conversation with one of Mark's chums. If Augustus was anything like his friend, then he was definitely not a candidate for my affections. While Emma might have considered Mark to be a catch, I was of the firm opinion that anyone who remotely resembled him was a definite no-go area. As far as I was concerned, my sister's boyfriend was one of the world's greatest bores!

Mark's lack of charm was not the only reason for my reluctance to re-enter the dating game that night. Although it remained unconfirmed, I couldn't dismiss the fact that I was in all likelihood barren. This in itself was reason enough to decline dates with randy young studs, who would ultimately want to increase the world's population with their superior offspring.

Although I was still only twenty-nine, and despite increasing efforts by many to relieve me of my independence, I rarely considered romance as being part of my future. I hoped to continue with my interests while satisfying any maternal urges with the prospect of future nieces and nephews.

Having freed myself up for the evening ahead, I wrapped up warmly and left the cosiness of Willow Cottage, heading for the bright lights of the local town of Ballyedmond. The town was only fifteen minutes away, and my pursuit was simple, I needed the makings of supper.

As I drove slowly through the town, the buzz around the streets and in the heavily festooned shops was palpable. The sky was clear and bright, and the smell of the first turf fires of the season filtered through my partly opened window. People were beginning to baton down the hatches for the winter ahead, and I remembered, not for the first time, how much I loved that time of year. The seasonal atmosphere, that was so apparent in Ballyedmond, inspired me, and I made a mental note to look for Hallowe'en fare in the shops.

When I reached the car park of my local supermarket, it was busy, despite the lateness of the hour, and I was forced to park at the far end of the lot. Making my way towards the rear entrance of the shop, I snared a trolley that had been abandoned to one side, and I noted its appearance as a sign of good luck in a 'find a penny, pick it up' sort of way.

Browsing the aisles, I stocked up on store cupboard essentials including the ingredients for lasagne. In the supermarket's fruit and vegetable section, I took my time selecting various items, including three large pumpkins, before finally moving on to the off-licence. There I chose six bottles of good wine, three white and three red, reasoning that I would make a five per cent saving by buying in 'bulk'. I didn't intend to drink them all at once!

Returning home laden down with groceries, I left the pumpkins on the doorstep at the front of the house. They could rest there until the thirty-first of October, whereupon I would attempt to carve them into some ghoulish forms before using the flesh in some recipe or other. My frequent trips to the States, the celebrator of all things pumpkin, meant that I had pumpkin recipes in abundance!

I set about preparing a beef lasagne, and after placing it in the oven, I did something that I occasionally did when I was alone, I poured myself a drink.

Carrying my drink into the sitting room, I settled down for a little pre-prandial foot-toasting by the open fire. I had barely wriggled my toes in appreciation of the flame's bright heat when I heard a car on the gravelled drive. I looked out of the sitting room window just in time to see my mother's silver Audi disappearing around the side of the house. An encounter with my mother was exactly what I had been trying to avoid!

My mother is like the *Columbo* of mother's; she can smell something 'cooking' a mile off, and I'm not referring to the dish that was cooking in the oven on that occasion! She would have become immediately suspicious once she saw the opened bottle of wine and would certainly have wondered what the occasion was that warranted my drinking alone. I put my glass down wearily and headed for the kitchen, determined to lie for Ireland.

Making my way across the kitchen floor in the dim under-unit lighting, I could see my mother's still pretty face peering through the glass panel of the door's upper half. She was wearing sheepskin and wool and looked cosy and well-groomed, but then she always did! Impeccable grooming was a skill that I had yet to master. I could step up to the mark when an occasion demanded it, but more often than not I fell somewhat short of Mum's exacting standards. I set those thoughts aside and opened the door to my mother.

No sooner had I done this, than another car could be heard driving on the avenue. Because of the darkness and the blinding effect of the car's headlights, we couldn't make out whose it was until it had pulled within the confines of the yard's spotlights. Then my mother, being the woman about town that she is, announced its identity to me with a considerable degree of astonishment.

'It's Dan Bryant's car!' she said, with as much incredulity as if the Popemobile itself had pulled into the yard.

'So it is!' I replied, trying to mirror her surprise.

We waited while Dan brought the car to a stop and got out. My mother called out a cheery 'good evening', and I attempted to send him discreet wide-eyed signals behind her back before saying, 'Nice to see you again, Mr Bryant. Did you decide on the writing desk after all?'

'Hmm . . .,' he started, clearly at a loss as to how to proceed. Then regaining confidence, he continued undaunted.

'Yes, Libby. I did. I hope you don't mind me calling so late, but I forgot to get your business card, and your number doesn't seem to be listed.'

I eyed my mother discreetly, but I was unable to tell what she was making of the situation, and so I returned my gaze to Dan. Luckily, this was all the encouragement he needed to continue.

'John's birthday is this weekend, and I was hoping to have it for him by then,' he said, leaving the conversation open to interpretation.

'Yes, sorry about that, Dan,' I apologised, continuing the charade with surprising aplomb. 'Come on inside, and I'll see what I can do.'

I turned to Mum with a *what can you do, business calls* sort of shrug, and after determining that hers was just a passing visit, I assured her that I would phone her in the morning, before bidding her a firm goodnight! She went rather reluctantly, clearly intrigued by the arrival of Dan Bryant on her daughter's doorstep at that hour of the night. If only she knew!

Dan

CHAPTER 4

Falling for Libby Finn

I WAS LOST IN solemn thought when Libby Finn entered my life. Finding myself outside the gates to the Old Stevens's Place had set me thinking about the wrongs of the past and wondering vaguely about the possibilities of the future.

I had received a call the day before from George Baxter saying that he wanted Alice-Rose put on the market immediately. George, who had inherited the place some ten years earlier upon his uncle's death, was hard-headed and dour and an unlikely heir to his kindly relative's estate. However, George was the single child of Michael's only sibling, so that it was bound to be either him or the local branch of the ISPCA that would benefit from his uncle's death. That being said, the opinion had often been expressed by many that Michael Stevens would have done considerably better to have left his worldly goods to the latter!

Personally, I didn't have an opinion. I took George as I found him, abrupt and to the point, and I never questioned the reasons for his manner. I agreed to handle the sale of Alice-Rose, assuring him that I would do my best to secure the highest price. First thing the following morning, one of his sons dropped the keys of the estate into the office, and George phoned soon after on the pretext of confirming that they had been delivered safely. However, it soon became clear by the ensuing conversation that the main reason for the call was to emphasise his need for the place to be sold as soon as was humanly possible.

My eldest son, John, who was by then working with us, was away on holidays so that it was just myself and my brother Paul who were left in the office that day. As the most junior member of staff, all posting and dismantling of signage was usually left to John, but under the circumstances, I decided to put the sign up myself rather than wait for his return.

I loaded a sledgehammer, a spade, and a for-sale sign into the boot of my car, making sure that my wellingtons were still there in case I needed them. I usually wore a suit to work, and that day was no different, except that on this occasion I was particularly formal in my dress because I had to attend a neighbour's funeral at noon.

I was sorely tempted to postpone the job at the last minute, mindful of my inappropriate clothing and not wanting to risk arriving late for the funeral. But remembering the definite sense of urgency in George Baxter's voice that morning, I proceeded somewhat reluctantly. Trying to inject some enthusiasm into the situation, I reasoned that the weather had been beautiful all week despite the lateness of the season and that the ground should be in good condition. All going well, I would easily make it back to Ballyedmond none the worse for wear and in good time for the church service.

My path converged with Libby Finn's, just as I was about to land the first blow to the for-sale sign. As I've said, I was lost in thought, remembering how I had always fancied the old place myself, but acknowledging the fact that even if it had come on to the market sooner, my wife would never have been in favour of buying it! The place was too remote and too old to have appealed to her love of all things urban and current.

Marie was the sort of woman who redecorated a room at least three times before she was happy with the end result. Even then, her contentment only endured until the next trend hit the high streets. Currently, the house was overdone with accent walls papered in various shades of purple and gold. Ornaments that might have had some sentiment had been exchanged for mass-produced vases that didn't contain any flowers. I didn't see the point. Family photos were replaced by large frameless, block-mounted portraits that seemed to scream, 'Look! *We* are the smug upwardly mobile.'

I had tried to express my outright dislike of these new soulless makeovers, but I was quickly put in my place with a derisive laugh.

'Darling,' Marie would say coldly. 'I leave money matters to you, so you should leave all matters concerning the house to me.'

In truth, I had often contemplated leaving the house to Marie, just leaving full stop. It was clear that we had reached a point in our marriage where material things had come to matter far more to my wife than I did, and I didn't know how much longer I could endure the charade that had become my life.

I felt alone and oppressed by an unshakable sense of duty to always do the right thing. The thought of tearing my family apart, such as it was, had always prevented me from leaving. In the end, it was Marie who left. Her sudden and untimely death from a brain haemorrhage left me alone in a show house that filled me with an abiding sense of opportunities lost.

So as I stood there, lost in the regrets of the past, my life took a sudden and unexpected change in direction. In fact, I was so engrossed in my own thoughts that it was only after Libby Finn had brought her car to a complete stop that I fully realised just how close I had come to being knocked to the ground! Then all of a sudden there she was, emerging from her old red Volvo, laughing and talking all at once, and she smacked me off balance more effectively than any car ever could!

Her hair was the rich dark colour of a well-ripened chestnut, and it fell over her shoulder in one loosely woven plait. Her eyes were chocolate brown, and it was as if they were dancing out of her head! Her smile was wide and generous, and it melted my heart. She was tall and had the appearance of slenderness, although her exact figure was difficult to judge because she was wearing an old oversized waxed jacket. She was also wearing a pair of green wellington boots, and she looked completely countrified and at one with her surroundings. At that precise moment in time, I wouldn't have been in the least bit surprised if she had reached into her car and pulled out a shotgun before announcing that she was off to do a spot of shooting.

As it turned out, Libby had her sights set on an entirely different target. She was direct and to the point, and I liked that about her; it was a refreshing change from the obsequiousness of most potential clients, especially the women! Our initial conversation was brief, to the point of leaving me wondering if we had in fact exchanged words at all. All too soon, I was gazing at her retreating back as she headed up the avenue towards the old house, oblivious to the fact that she was, for all intense purposes, trespassing.

I was stunned to find that our meeting felt like a stomach punch! It wasn't as if I wasn't used to meeting attractive young women; my children were of a similar age to Libby, and they frequently had their friends and 'love interests' visiting or staying over at the house.

I counselled myself to get a hold. Libby Finn was young enough to be my daughter, and I wasn't the type of man to go mooning after young women, no matter how beguiling they were! Besides which, she was just the type of girl who would have been perfect for one of my sons, both of whom seemed intent on dating young ladies who had very little to recommend them apart from their over-primped good looks. Yes, Libby would have been ideal for one of them! I resolved to finish the job at hand as quickly as possible and to leave before she returned. I could come back and lock the gate later. There was no fool like an old fool, and I wasn't about to make an idiot of myself.

I had been on the brink of achieving a clean getaway when I heard the return of footsteps, and there was no escaping Libby as I turned to see her hurrying down the hill towards me. She was clearly anxious to talk to me, and I gave myself over to her charms, deciding that the dead would forgive, and maybe even celebrate, my absence from the formalities that day.

For the next ninety-seven minutes, I relaxed in the easy company of this interesting and vibrant young woman. She was a dynamo of ambition and zest for life. She laughed easily, and her face never lost its radiance. Every step she took was like a spring towards a future filled with hope and promise so that it was difficult to believe that she had ever known a day's hardship.

As we walked together, it became clear that she knew every inch of the estate by heart and that it held wonderful memories for her. So much so, that by the time we returned to our cars, I wanted Libby Finn to have Alice-Rose almost as much as she wanted it for herself.

I didn't expect Libby to get her finances in order as quickly as she did. While I didn't know much about the antiquing business, Libby Finn's relative youth lead me to wrongly presume that her plan to buy the property was, in all probability, a pipe dream.

It seemed highly unlikely that one as young as Libby would have accumulated enough capital to secure a mortgage on the place, and I had wrongly assumed that Libby was counting on financial support from home. While her parents were certainly well off, I didn't envisage them handing over a wad of cash to secure the deal; property prices were falling rapidly, and one would have been paying over the odds for the land. The thought that Libby herself would have sufficient funds to buy the place outright never crossed my mind!

And so, as you can imagine, I was both surprised and disappointed when I returned to the office later that day to discover that Libby had already been in touch and had made an impressive offer on the place without any further help from me. In fact, I was more than disappointed: I was gutted! Would I have felt that way if it had been anyone other than Libby Finn? I had to admit to myself that I probably would not. Business was business, and any profit from the sale of Alice-Rose was going back into the same pot from which we all drew a salary.

It was as a result of that unshakable disappointment that I found myself driving out to Willow Cottage later on that evening. Negotiating the country roads in the dark didn't allow much time for reflection, just enough to recognise that I felt like a schoolboy on his first date. I kidded myself that the trip was a last-minute decision and that I was just stopping by to congratulate Libby and to wish her well with the place. There was no ulterior motive.

Despite every fibre of my being telling me that my visit was a bad idea, I didn't seem to care enough to turn back. Since meeting Libby Finn that morning, I had lost all sense of rightness and inhibition. I even considered at one point bringing a good bottle of wine with me! Thankfully, some good sense still prevailed, and I decided that bringing alcohol would have appeared premeditated and far too desperate!

And so I succeeded in convincing myself that mine was just a courtesy call and that after that evening I would leave it to Paul to handle the sale of Alice-Rose. If, in fact, I was suffering from some form of midlife crisis, a little distance between Libby and myself was all that was required to make my adolescent feelings disappear.

I tried to conjure up images of Marie in an attempt to dampen my schoolboy crush, and that pretty much did the trick! Thoughts of her mortifying disapproval brought me temporarily back to reality. By the time I turned on to the lane leading up to the small farmhouse, I had managed to successfully ditch my schoolboy's cap, and I was wearing my auctioneer's hat once more. However, the sight of somebody's car parked beside Libby's, as I entered the yard, knocked that hat right off again, and I was catapulted back to not knowing whether I was coming or going!

Libby had advised me that she didn't want anyone to know about her plans to buy Alice-Rose until the deal was sealed; therefore, I could not be seen to be calling in a professional capacity. I desperately needed to think of another excuse for my visit, and right there and then I couldn't, for the life of me, think of one, and it was too late to turn back. I had no option but to play it by ear and take my lead from Libby, presuming that was that she gave me one.

Seeing Libby and the 'someone', who turned out to be her mother, standing in the doorway brought me to my senses like no image of Marie ever could. Sarah Finn, who had to be in her fifties, was still a beautiful woman, and at a glance, she could have passed for someone much younger. I often bumped into Sarah at various community gatherings, and I always remarked upon her natural and unaffected beauty.

She was blonde in contrast to Libby's dark colouring, and she was somewhat shorter than her statuesque daughter. If Sarah Finn had been single or a widow, then she was exactly the sort of woman that I should have been seeking out, not her heart-wrenchingly lovely daughter. Taking stock of the two women, I came to the conclusion that as far as wooing Libby Finn went, I had definitely missed the boat . . . Libby had been born twenty years too late!

Libby

CHAPTER 5

I'd Rather Be an Old Man's Darlin'

I HAD TWO MAIN concerns when my mother announced that it was Dan Bryant's car on the lane that night. Firstly, would he let the cat out of the bag and presume when he saw Mum that I had changed my mind and told her of my grand plans to buy Alice-Rose? This was quickly followed by a far more alarming thought, had George Baxter reneged on the deal?

It was difficult to read Dan's face as he stood in the glare cast by the yard's halogen lamp, but regardless of the reason for his call, I didn't want Mum getting wind of any business dealings concerning Alice-Rose. I knew with certainty that she would try to talk me out of buying the old place, and I needed to remain focused.

I was so intent on coming up with a cover story for Dan's sudden appearance that it was only when we finally found ourselves alone that I remembered how God-awful attractive he was! After Mum had pulled well away from the house, Dan held out his arms in a gesture of apology and gave me an irresistible sideways grin that left me no choice but to presume that his wife existed in a constant state of simmering desire.

He was dressed more casually than before in brown cords, a button-down shirt and a charcoal grey sweater. He had swapped his polished black leather shoes for rather shabby-looking loafers. He was very tall, around six foot two or three, and he held himself well. His hair was thick and for the most part dark brown; his greying temples leant him an air of distinction. His skin was clear and it had the healthy, weathered glow of someone who embraced the outdoor life. Overall, Dan Bryant looked to be in excellent shape for a man of his age. Of course, his exact age had yet to be determined, and there didn't seem to be much point in doing that when there was a Mrs Bryant on the scene!

Okay, Libby, get a grip! I admonished myself inwardly. *You are a child compared to this man, and I am pretty sure that he would not be impressed by your silly nonsense!*

I did not usually give in to flights of fancy, and I had to remind myself that I was not the reason for his visit, Alice-Rose was.

'Sorry about the charade, Dan,' I said, motioning him to follow me into the kitchen's warmth. 'I was afraid that you might have been at a loss for words when you saw my mother.'

'I was,' he replied truthfully, stepping across the threshold before closing the door firmly behind him. 'I'm sorry, Libby. It was silly of me to just drop by like this. I wasn't thinking. I should have called first.'

I could tell that he was regretting his decision to come, and I didn't blame him. Having to lie to someone was never pleasant. However, while Dan might have been experiencing some regret, I was not. It was good to feel a pulse throbbing in my veins again, even if nothing could come of it!

'Paul filled me in on everything regarding the sale of Alice-Rose,' he continued. 'I happened to be in the area this evening, and I thought it would be a good opportunity to pass on my congratulations.'

I thought nothing of the fact that he had called by. I presumed that any one of his clients would have received the same courtesy.

'I hope the old place will be lucky for you, Libby,' he said finally.

'Thanks, Dan, me too,' I said, hoping that I hadn't bitten off more than I could chew.

'I was disappointed to have missed you when I phoned the office,' I added, wanting to apologise to Dan. 'I didn't wait for you because I felt I had to act quickly. Otherwise, someone might have talked me out of it.' The justification sounded more like an excuse, and I cringed inwardly.

'Of course, of course,' Dan said, dismissing any concerns that I might have had regarding auctioneering protocol. He was leaning against the kitchen's island unit, and he looked decidedly unconcerned about the matter.

'It all worked out well in the end,' he said lightly.

Dan's approach to the matter was meant to be reassuring, but for some reason, it made me feel even worse about how I had handled the situation. It wouldn't have killed me to have waited until I could speak to Dan before making an offer on Alice-Rose. In fact, it would have been good manners to do so in light of the time he had afforded me earlier that day. I continued to explain the reasons for my haste.

'Being a widow, sometimes feels a bit like being a child,' I said. 'Somebody invariably thinks they know what's best for you. I doubt that any member of my family would think that buying Alice-Rose is a good idea!'

'I know what you mean,' he said unexpectedly. His tone was sincere, and he spoke with an air of definite understanding.

'Do you?' I asked, unable to conceal my doubt.

'Of course,' Dan replied, obviously surprised by my question. 'I was recently widowed myself,' he explained. 'Sorry, I presumed that you knew.'

He must have seen my eyes steal another glance at his wedding ring because he hastened to justify its presence.

'I haven't felt that the time has been right yet to take it off,' he said, indicating the gold band on his finger. 'It's all a bit new I'm afraid.'

'God, Dan, I'm so sorry,' I babbled. 'I really had no idea.'

I was mortified by my own ignorance of his situation and astonished by his revelation.

'I confess that I did hear about your bereavement, but I was living in Dublin at the time. I wasn't sure which one of you it was,' I said. 'When I saw your wedding ring, I presumed that it was Paul who had been widowed. I am so sorry.'

He waved away my apologies and reassured me that I couldn't possibly have been expected to know his circumstances any more than he would have been certain of mine. On the one hand, I felt a ridiculous thrill upon learning that Dan was widowed. While on the other, I felt that all hope of any romance developing between us had been crushed by his admission that four years on, he still considered himself to be newly widowed.

Disregarding the ambiguity of his emotional status, I asked him to join me for dinner, and to my delight, he readily agreed. Despite his obvious appeal, I don't think that I would have had the courage to insist had he declined my offer. His apparent charm would have made it more difficult to do so without appearing to have had an interest in more than just his professional opinion! The evening turned out to be my idea of the perfect end to a busy day. Dan and I ate our dinner in the warmth of the kitchen. The lasagne was a hearty meal, perfect for dispelling Autumn's chill, and the Burgundy was aired to perfection. Dan was an interesting and amusing conversationalist who complimented my cooking and was content to pass an evening watching television. Unfortunately, as so often happens when someone is enjoying themselves, time flew by, and Dan was gone all too soon. As the credits for the last in the series of *A Victorian Farm* rolled, Dan 'rolled' too, and I was left with the unsettling feeling that the little farmhouse was far too big for just one.

CHAPTER 6

Engaging Emma

THE MORNING AFTER my 'dinner party á deux' dawned clear and beautiful like the one before, and I awoke filled with the wish that Dan Bryant had stayed for more than my Rachel Allen-inspired chocolate muffins. During Dan's visit, and long after his hasty departure, I had experienced a deep and certain longing, something that had become less familiar to me since Max's death.

While the intervening years since that fateful day had not been easy on many levels, for the most part, any overwhelming physical desires that I might have had, had been effectively dampened by the guilt that I felt over the circumstances of my husband's death. If it had not been for my relentless determination to get pregnant, Max would never have gone to Saint James Hospital that day. He would most probably still be alive and well, and still with me.

I missed Max so much and for so many reasons. He had been my best friend, my lover, and my number one fan. But on that morning, even I had to admit that the saying 'time heals all wounds' was proving to be true. I was slowly but surely discovering that the living are fundamentally selfish and that life *does* go on.

So when I awoke on that particular morning in the middle of a dream that featured Dan Bryant's imagined naked body instead of Max's beatific face, I dismissed the guilt and decided to enjoy the moment instead. However, the moment turned out to be so short-lived as to be practically non-existent when at the very point of realising the futility of regret, insistent knocking came to interrupt my daydreams.

Before I could react properly, the knocking stopped, only to be followed almost immediately by the sound of my mobile phone ringing. Even in my still-sleepy state, I figured that the two forms of communication had to be somehow linked. Picking up my phone from the bedside table, I jumped out of bed and heard my sister's clear, but rather anxious voice, speaking to me.

'Where in God's name are you, Libby?' Emma demanded.

Judging by her tone, there was definitely an implied blasphemous word in there somewhere.

'At home, where, as far as I know, I am supposed to be!' I answered, unable to refrain from sarcasm.

I hate sarcasm, and I couldn't agree more with whomever it was that first said that sarcasm 'is the lowest form of wit'. But in my defence on that occasion, I wasn't trying to be witty.

'But hang on,' I said lightly, trying to distract from my acerbic remarks, 'there's somebody at the front door. I'll just go and see who it is before calling you back.'

Emma never indulges in sarcasm, no matter how justified its use might be. Descending the stairs two at a time, I opened the front door to my sister's smiling face.

'Well, fancy seeing you here!' I said. 'Is there something wrong?'

I checked over Emma's shoulder for the ever-present Mark. He was conspicuously absent.

'No Mark today?' I observed, raising my eyebrows and trying hard to disguise my relief. I was half expecting that he would jump out from somewhere as one rarely saw one without the other. A dose of Mark was never pleasant at any time, but I imagined that it would have been doubly so first thing in the morning!

Mark Waldron was the kind of guy who liked to talk, which in itself is not always a bad thing, except that in Mark's case the subject of every conversation was himself! I use the word conversation loosely as this implies an exchange of words between two or more people; Mark was somewhat unique in that he needed only the odd nod or grunt from his captive audience to continue waxing lyrical about he, himself, and him!

'No!' gushed Emma in answer to my question. 'He wanted to come. He really did,' she said, pausing for effect before continuing. 'But I insisted that I wanted to deliver our news to you all by myself!'

Barely two sentences had been uttered, and already the red flags of dread were waving in my brain, but there was no time to think because Emma was not quite finished.

'*Especially* in light of everything that you have been through in recent years,' she said, her voice dripping sympathy. She paused deliberately once again.

Oh dear God, I thought, *this was not good, not good at all!* Emma worrying about my feelings, in terms of all that I had been through, could only mean one of two things: either Mark had asked her to marry him, or she was pregnant! Neither option filled me with joy as either way we were stuck with Mark! Emma was wearing her best *it will happen for you too* expression as she settled herself at the kitchen table and joined her gloved hands as if in prayer. She hadn't bothered to take off her coat; she had merely opened it as a mark of concession to the heat of the kitchen.

Under her immaculate cashmere coat, I could see that she was wearing a baby pink twinset, complete with a double strand of white pearls. Not for the first time in recent months, I found myself wondering what in the world had happened to her. Emma was my junior by three years, but she looked older than our mother! Her freshly highlighted blonde hair was cut in a sensible bob, and she was picture-perfect. It was as if she had just stepped off the cover of a 1950s edition of *Vogue;* there was not a single hair out of place! Although not as tall as our mother, she definitely resembled our mother in looks. She had Mum's fair complexion and fine features. Their eyes were the same deep blue, and she had Mum's small straight nose.

But that's where the resemblance ended. Mum would never in a million years have contemplated dressing in clothes that even vaguely resembled her youngest daughter's; she would have laughed at the very mention of twinset and pearls! Emma's clothes were more befitting of our grandmothers' wardrobes, just about! Emma's spinster-like sense of fashion was definitely down to Mark's influence; he was slowly but surely turning our 'Little Emma' into a younger version of his own mother!

There had been a time when Emma and I would laugh uncontrollably upon encountering life's small, unforgettable absurdities. Now we were never together long enough to encounter much of anything, ridiculous or otherwise. And even when we were, Emma was oblivious to life taking place around her. The days of Emma and I raiding the sherry bottle and indulging in gossip were long gone; she existed in the parallel universe of *Mark and Emma,* and nothing else seemed to matter. Since meeting Mark Waldron, Emma had become one half of an inseparable pair, and the old Emma had been gradually replaced by someone new and far less appealing.

I fixed a cheery smile on my face and enquired as to whether or not she would like some tea before telling me her news. Personally, I was in need of some sustenance. She declined, so I settled myself down opposite her and joined her 'in prayer'.

'*Oh, Libby*, I'm sure you've already guessed our news!' she whispered encouragingly.

I smiled harder. Should I go with the engagement or the pregnancy? It was difficult to say. So far, Emma wasn't giving anything away.

'I *think* I have a fair idea,' I said cautiously.

If her news didn't feature either of the presumed topics, I didn't want to go giving her any 'bright' ideas. Neither did I want to risk upsetting her if it turned out that what she was about to tell me was rather more mundane than what I had imagined. Emma didn't falter in her guessing game and continued to fix me with a gaze that left me no option but to continue.

'If it's what I think it is, then I'm thrilled for you both, and well done you two!' I said, still hedging my bets and hoping that Emma would finally crack.

I persisted in grinning enthusiastically while waiting for her to finally give in and tell me her news. Surely, if what she was about to tell me was as good as the smile on her face suggested, she wouldn't be able to keep it to herself for much longer. But Emma continued to sit in smiling silence, looking at me expectantly.

'Emma . . .,' I said slowly, as I became aware of a potential clue in the game. 'Is there a reason why you haven't taken off your coat and gloves? You must be boiling in there!' I added in reference to her excessive clothing. Still nothing!

'Let me take them from you, and *then* I'll let you know what it is I think you've come to tell me,' I insisted, hoping to finally 'crack the nut'.

And as it happened, it worked. In asking Emma for her coat and gloves, I had struck a chord.

'Oh, Libby, I knew *you* of all people would guess!' she thrilled, whipping off her coat and pulling the furry leopard print glove off her left hand. 'Da da!' she declared, presenting her ring finger, or in Emma's case her *rock* finger, for inspection.

The object that clung there was, in my opinion, the very essence of vulgarity and bad taste! I was surprised that I hadn't managed to spot it before then, bulging under her glove!

'Oh my God, Emma, it's . . . it's perfect!' I gushed insincerely, feeling slightly nauseated by the sound of my own voice. But what else could I have said? I hoped that my insincerity wasn't as obvious to Emma's ears as it was to my own. I refrained from adding *just like you*, fearing that that would have been an enthusiasm too far, even for Emma.

'Congratulations,' I continued. 'I'm so happy for you both.'

Again, I held myself in check and desisted from saying, *you deserve each other*, as they so obviously now did!

'When is the big day?' I enquired, desperately trying to determine just how much time we had left to try and stop the wedding from taking place.

Not that I really held out much hope of success. By that point, Emma and Mark were so close that it would have been practically impossible to have driven a wedge between them. And there again why should one have even tried? They were blissfully happy by all accounts, and surely that was all that mattered in the end.

The prospect of future family gatherings featuring their saccharine and self-satisfied union was beside the point; one couldn't always put one's own happiness ahead of others. That was just plain selfish, wasn't it? Yes, definitely yes!

Having talked myself into a more positive frame of mind, I was able to continue.

'I *am* really happy for you, Emma. I hope you have a very long and lucky life together.'

I tried to feel the words in my heart, and I consoled myself that I at least had the good grace to feel ashamed of my slowly fading disappointment.

'I know it's a little early in the day to start drinking, but how about a Buck's Fizz to celebrate the occasion?' I laughed self-consciously in anticipation of my sister's disapproval; I fully expected the new Emma to decline.

'Oh yes, please, Libby!' said Emma, the picture of girly innocence and daring. 'Mark's up at Mum and Dad's now, *asking* for my hand.'

She laughed, delighted by the idea of it, and I cringed inwardly for Dad.

'I said I'd meet him there at eleven, so that gives us plenty of time for a quick one.'

I found a bottle of champagne in the wine rack under the stairs, and set to work while Emma prattled away outlining their plans for the wedding. Needless to say, it was going to be a grand affair, and she hoped that Dad wouldn't be too shocked by the number of guests that they intended to invite. Personally, I didn't think that Emma and Mark could have come up with anything at that point that would have shocked our father . . . but I was wrong.

According to Emma's calculations, there would be just in excess of four hundred people on the guest list. Dad would go mad! Firstly, he would hate such an obscene display of excess by his own flesh and blood, and secondly, while he wasn't short of a few bob, he was hardly the Prince of Wales! If I knew my father at all, I knew that he would not be happy to go along with their elaborate plans. In fact, if Mark and Emma persisted along a path of vulgar extravagance, the bride might end up having to find somebody else to give her away!

Two Buck's Fizzes later and a slightly intoxicated Emma left Willow Cottage heading for Mum and Dad's. I feared for her wellbeing and cautioned her to postpone the number crunching with Dad until a later date. It was better to deal with one thing at a time, I advised. After all, besides our parents, there was still the rest of the family to tell, and Dad might 'panic in the excitement'.

Emma seemed to take this on board and agreed to leave discussing the actual wedding for another day. With any luck, I would get to Dad first and pave the way for Emma. He usually listened to me, although God alone knew what I could say to him on this occasion that would make any difference. Closing the door behind Emma, I wondered vaguely what the others would make of the announcement.

The rest of our family included three brothers. Philip, my junior by thirteen months, was a veterinary surgeon who worked alongside our father in the family practice. Philip, at that time, was dating the lovely Amanda, who was a warm and practical girl and the perfect partner for my brother! Amanda was a midwife in our local hospital, and I imagined that Amanda would be a wife of another kind before too long.

Emma came after Philip, and she was followed by two more boys, Tony and David. Tony was a medical intern, and David, the baby of the family by a number of years, was in his final year at the local Community College.

There was no doubt but that each of them would have their own thoughts on our sister's upcoming wedding. Nevertheless, even allowing for the possibility that Emma and Mark might secure some approval, I knew with certainty that we would be united in introspection as we pondered how it was that our once fun-loving sister had morphed into a stuffy young woman.

The sad reality of the situation was that Emma was a gifted musician and equestrian who had laid her talents aside to become the 'Stepford wife' of a domineering and insufferable bore. Soon after meeting Mark, she gave up teaching music, and her love of horses, to work in his investment business. Mark, who was Emma's senior by ten years, had managed to convince her that working as his personal assistant was her only chance of ever having a 'proper career'. I could only hope that that was not a decision that my sister would one day come to regret.

After Emma left, I made a batch of pancakes and indulged in a substantial breakfast in an attempt to erase the headache that was developing as a result of our early morning indulgence. Whereas previously I had planned on having a leisurely afternoon that would include some light housework and a trip to the local gym, that now seemed highly unlikely. An afternoon of endless phone calls was far more probable!

As predicted, my well-laid plans for that Saturday were foiled by Emma and Mark's announcement. By noon, it was clear that news of my sister's approaching nuptials was spreading rapidly throughout the entire extended family! For the most part, the responses were loyal, and only my father was brave and honest enough to express what the rest of us were really thinking.

'So the game's up? We're stuck with him!' he said in disgust. I hadn't the heart to dissemble.

'I'm afraid it looks that way, Dad . . . but at least *Em* seems happy,' I said, trying to ease the blow somewhat.

'There is some consolation in that at least,' he agreed.

My heart went out to my father. As a young girl, Emma had been his 'little princess', and as she grew, it became apparent that although she did not resemble him in appearance, she had inherited his love of music and his passion for horses.

Both of them were accomplished fiddle players, and some of Dad's proudest moments were those spent alongside Emma, entertaining family and friends at various gatherings. Those occasions had become virtually non-existent as a result of Mark's scathing disregard for my sister's talent, and she had become increasingly self-conscious and out of practice.

Over the years, my father had witnessed the subtle, yet persistent, undoing of his daughter's passions, and I knew how much that disturbed him. Nevertheless, his essentially gentle nature prevented him from interfering. Dad had stood back and hoped that Emma would come to her senses and realise what a vain, arrogant, and self-centred man Mark Waldron really was. Unfortunately for all of us, the waiting game hadn't paid off, and time had seen his darling girl committing to spend the rest of her life in the shadow of a man he could barely stand, let alone respect.

Dan

CHAPTER 7

No Fool Like an Old Fool

I REALISED VERY QUICKLY that calling to see Libby Finn had been a foolish mistake. She was more charming and more beautiful than I had ever imagined any woman could be, and she could cook! I spent the entire evening at Willow Cottage, struggling to convey unaffected ease in her presence, when all I really wanted to do was take her clothes off!

The main course wasn't over before I realised that this young woman, under different circumstances, could have been my soulmate, my one true love. Normally, watching a programme like *A Victorian Farm* was my idea of a good night in. Throw in a home-cooked meal, a good bottle of red, and a blazing log fire, and it was just about the perfect end to any day! However, factor in the irresistible, unobtainable Libby Finn into the equation, and the night was reduced to one of unutterable torture!

My voice caught on more than one occasion as I felt my ardour rising, and that wasn't usual for me! I had never had any trouble containing my 'emotions' before then, and I was horrified to find myself suddenly taken completely unawares. Luckily, I was able to put my erratic voice change down to a touch of laryngitis, and I hoped that Libby was sufficiently engrossed in her television programme so as not to notice *anything* else! Once the credits came on, I hastily excused myself and left a slightly bewildered Libby in my wake.

Driving away from the farmhouse, I resolved to put as much distance between myself and Libby as I could without drawing too much attention to myself. I would also start dating women of my own age! I hadn't given anyone a chance since Marie's death because the experience of a less than blissful marriage had left me reluctant to dip my toes in the potentially murky waters of a new relationship. I decided there and then that I was being overly cautious and that I should at least give other women a chance to dispel my misgivings. It wasn't as if I would ever be getting married again, so there could be no real harm in casual dating.

My neighbour and long-time family friend, Peggy Holmes, had recently asked me out, and I had vacillated. On the long, reflective journey home from Libby's, I made up my mind to call Peggy that night and to accept her invitation to Ballyedmond's Hunt Ball. Peggy was a wonderful woman by all accounts, and more importantly, she was exactly the type of woman that I should have been pursuing.

Libby

CHAPTER 8

The Cat Jumps Out of the Bag

THE DAY AFTER Emma's announcement, Jules Mahon dropped by for coffee. An accountant by trade, Jules was self-employed, and that morning saw her passing by Willow Cottage on her way to visit one of her clients.

Although I was well used to Jules's fly-by visits, there was something about her demeanour that morning that made me suspect that she had more than a quick cup of coffee on her mind. And as it turned out, I was right.

'Now, Libby,' she protested, in a tone intended to induce a sense of reason in me, 'don't say no before hearing me out.'

I immediately became suspicious and a tad uneasy. Any conversation with Jules that began with a request to 'hear her out' rarely ended well.

'Yes?' I hesitated, wondering how I would manage to wriggle out of whatever hare-brained plan Jules had hatched for us on this occasion.

'I got us a pair of tickets for this year's Hallowe'en Hunt Ball,' she said, a beseeching expression in her eyes.

'Really?' I said, relieved for once by the apparent simplicity of her plan. I looked for the catch. 'Is that it?'

'Yes,' she replied simply, yet clearly surprised by my response.

'When is it on?' I asked.

'I knew it! You don't want to go, do *you*?' she said, her voice rising as she fixed me with a look of complete exasperation.

'What do you mean?' I asked, genuinely bewildered.

'It's a trick! No matter when I say it's on, you'll have other plans!' she cried.

Clearly I had declined Jules's invitations once too often, and she had lost faith in me.

'I *just* asked when it was on!' I said defensively. 'Actually, I would love to go as long as it isn't this coming weekend.'

'Really? You'd *actually* love to go?' Jules almost squealed her disbelief.

'Yes, as long as it isn't this coming weekend!' I reiterated deliberately. That weekend was the official Bank Holiday weekend, and I had already made unbreakable plans.

'As it happens, it's the following weekend, the actual thirty-first,' Jules said, eyeing me doubtfully. 'I just can't believe you're actually interested in going!' she stressed.

'Well, it just goes to show that you don't know me quite as well as you might think!'

I was feeling put out by the fact that Jules thought I was so noticeably predictable.

Jules and I had been friends since our very first day together in primary school, and to the best of our knowledge, we had never really fallen out. We were like sisters; in fact, we were closer than most!

'You know, I had a whole speech ready,' she laughed.

'I can imagine!' I said, as haughtily and as witheringly as I could manage.

'I was going to cut straight to the guilt trip if you turned me down,' she confessed.

'I never doubted it!' I said, laughing despite myself. Jules had a PhD in guilt; in fact, nobody could do it better! People twice her age hadn't mastered it to the degree that Jules had.

'God, I can't believe it!' she continued. 'Does this mean that you are finally considering being *out there* again?'

Her question was delivered with an intensified look of hopefulness.

'Well, I'm not sure about being *out, out* there again,' I said cautiously. One thing that I didn't need was the overenthusiastic Jules Mahon, making it her business to find me a man!

'However, I will go so far as to say that my attention has recently been drawn to one possibility.'

I smiled intriguingly despite myself, and Jules leant towards me, hanging on my every word. I continued, unable to resist the temptation to draw my friend in, we lived for these moments.

'Nevertheless,' I said cautiously, remembering how improbable a match between myself and Dan Bryant was, 'I should add that the guy in question is probably, yes very probably, totally unsuitable!'

'Who is he?' she gasped, and I knew immediately that Jules was thinking *married man.*

'I really would rather not say for the moment,' I said resolutely, 'but I will say one thing for the benefit of your filthy mind . . . he is definitely not married!'

'Huh!' Jules said indignantly. 'For your information, I would never even have dreamt such a thing!'

'Really?' I said archly, and my expression demanded absolute honesty.

'Not really,' she conceded, shaking her head and smiling wickedly, 'I will admit that the thought did very *very* briefly cross my mind.'

'Your dirty mind,' I corrected.

'Yes, all right, my dirty mind!' she admitted.

'Your dirty, filthy, twisted mind,' I insisted.

'All right already! Don't shoot me for the love of God!' she implored, waving her hands above her head in mock surrender.

'Takes one to know one,' I conceded.

I poured myself another cup of coffee and adopted an exaggerated air of mystery before continuing.

'Suffice to say that I might enlighten you someday soon. In the meantime, you can just keep on guessing.'

'Hmm,' Jules said thoughtfully. 'But if the mystery man turns up at the Hunt Ball, then you have to at least let me know that he's there. Okay?'

'Okay,' I agreed.

Jules and I spent the rest of her visit planning a shopping trip to Dublin for the following Tuesday. If we were going to the ball, then we were going to be the *belles of the ball*, with sugar icing and a cherry on top!

Jules was a girlie girl, even when dressed in her professional best. She was a true redhead and had a figure to rival that of Marilyn Monroe. Her hair was long and curly, and whenever possible, she wore it loose. Jules was always perfectly groomed, spending a sizeable portion of her earnings on self-maintenance. She was vibrant and fun, and she had the wickedest laugh of anyone that I knew. Men loved her!

Jules was single by choice, having thus far failed to discover any maternal instincts other than to call her own mother at least once a day! She didn't see the need for a full-time boyfriend if one had no intention of settling down to have babies. Her carnal instincts, on the other hand, were not so undiscovered, and she had had a string of highly unsuitable boyfriends over the years, none of whom had been successful in taming her!

Although Jules quickly tired of many things in life, including the various men that tried to woo her, fashion was one of the few things that had yet to bore her. From the latest trend in hats to the most current essentials in footwear, Jules was a font of studied knowledge. If one was going shopping for glamour, then Jules Mahon was the best woman for the job.

I spent the weekend before the Hunt Ball in County Cork, attending an advanced cake-decorating course at a well-known cookery school. My love of gastronomy often compelled me to better my skills, and that particular course was so oversubscribed that I had been on a waiting list for well over a year. Hunt Ball or *no* Hunt Ball, that was one previous engagement that I wasn't about to break!

Although the course was more challenging than I had anticipated, I returned from the weekend refreshed and eager to bore the knickers off Jules on the drive up to Dublin the following Tuesday. Although Jules loved her food, she didn't appreciate blow-by-blow accounts of how to prepare the perfect soufflé! In truth, I didn't really obsess about food, but I loved to turn my enthusiasm up a notch or two, just to see the pained expression on my friend's face. It seemed only fair that if I had to endure hearing about the finer points of the latest smudge-proof mascara or kiss-proof lipstick, that I should be able to enjoy a little culinary torture of my own.

Jules arrived on the dot of eight o'clock on the morning of our trip to Dublin. The girl was sometimes tardy but never when it came to business or matters of retail. I didn't bother to offer my shopping accomplish a cup of coffee, knowing that she would be *chomping at the bit* and anxious to get on the road. Jules was dressed from head to toe in Tommy Hilfiger and was wearing a pair of the latest Oakley sunglasses in preparation for the drive.

Sitting into the car beside her, I also noticed that she was wearing a pair of brand new Nike trainers, not the tattered ones that she usually wore for driving before slipping into her six-inch heels. There was no doubt about it, the girl definitely meant business. We were going to shop until we dropped.

We headed off without delay. It was a glorious autumn's morning, and I was excited about the upcoming dance and eager to find something a little bit special for the occasion. As my thoughts drifted to Dan Bryant, I scratched *a little bit special* off my mental shopping list. I didn't want to find something *a little bit special,* after all; I wanted to turn up at the ball in a dress that would knock his socks off! I didn't want Dan Bryant to just notice me; I wanted him to *want* me.

Just over an hour and a half later, Jules had found the perfect parking space in the Browne Thomas car park. An ample supply of city centre parking was one of the many advantages of midweek shopping, and we headed, without delay, to Bewley's Café to get our first coffee-fix of the day.

Having skipped breakfast in order to be ready when Jules called meant that I was ravenous and in need of more than just coffee. A hearty meal was essential to set me up for the task ahead. With this in mind, I ordered a portion of pancakes with maple syrup and a side order of sausage. Jules tried to resist having the same calorific feast, but in the end, resistance proved futile, and breakfast was delicious!

After dining like kings, we headed to the Lancôme counter in Browne Thomas to get our make-up done. I usually felt self-conscience, having someone lavish attention on me, and more often than not I came away from these encounters fighting the urge to run to the nearest restroom to remove the mask that had been applied. But for some reason, I felt unusually relaxed that day, and I gave the girl carte blanche. In return, I was pleasantly surprised by the resulting effect, recognising for once a delicate accentuation of myself rather than a stranger in the mirror. I was so pleased, in fact, that I bought every product that Melissa, my newfound friend, had so artfully applied.

Jules, on the other hand, did not fare so well and ended up resembling some garish gypsy from a tragic opera. It suffices to say that we made straight for the Ladies, fully equipped with cotton wool, cleanser, and a bag full of cosmetics!

We were still empty-handed, as far as our party frocks went, three hours later, and we were becoming increasingly concerned and a little bit weary! We had one stop left on our list of possibilities as we headed to the top floor of the Powerscourt Town House Centre, and we hoped that we had unwittingly left the best shop until last.

We had. The place was heaving with any amount of irresistible evening wear. We left the Design Centre some time later, clutching two very large bags and giggling with delight and relief. Things were finally under control, and we spent the rest of the afternoon in relative leisure shopping for footwear and accessories, secure in the knowledge that we would indeed be going to the ball in style.

Jules and I had only stopped for one very brief coffee break since eating breakfast in Bewley's that morning so that by the time we arrived back in Ballyedmond, we were both famished.

'Fancy a bite in Mac's?' Jules asked, as we approached the town's main street.

'Why not!' I agreed.

Jules skilfully slid the Mercedes into the first available parking space.

Entering Mac's pub was like entering a womb. The lights were low, and the atmosphere was warm and welcoming. Business was brisk despite it being a week night, and I recognised a few faces as we passed through on our way to a small table at the far end of the bar.

Mary MacNamara, or Mary Mac for short, the owner's daughter, arrived promptly to take our order. It was obvious that despite her cheery disposition, she was under pressure. After Mary left, Jules continued to study the menu while I decided to freshen up before our orders arrived. I left Jules minding our table.

The trip to the Ladies was uneventful. However, while returning to our table, I somehow managed to collide with none other than Dan Bryant, who was making his way from the bar carrying two pints of lager.

'Oh, I am so sorry, Dan!' I choked, grabbing a paper napkin from a nearby table and attempting to wipe spilt beer from his sleeve. 'I was miles away!'

Yes, miles away, anticipating the sweet taste of Mac's home cooking!

'That's all right, Libby. No harm done,' Dan insisted graciously. 'Actually, I'm glad we ran into each other. I wanted to thank you again for dinner the other evening. It was very good of you. Could I buy you a drink in return?' he asked.

'Thanks for the offer, Dan,' I said, beginning to feel a little flustered by his proximity, 'but I'm here with Jules Mahon, and we've just ordered one.'

'Another time then,' said Dan, looking briefly around him and giving a wave of acknowledgement to Jules. Jules waved backed enthusiastically, and I was reminded that Jules knew the Bryants very well. As it happened, they were neighbours, living in the same housing development in Ballyedmond.

Dan hesitated before saying, 'Grand so, Libby. Enjoy your evening.'

With a little bow of his head, he turned to leave, and then thinking better of it, he turned back to me before saying, 'By the way, I'll probably be in touch with you by the end of next week about that other matter.'

'Okay,' I said, and with that he was gone.

I walked back to Jules, trying to compose myself on the way. Sitting down opposite her, I soon realised that I needn't have bothered.

'So Dan Bryant is the mystery man,' Jules remarked noncommittally.

'What?' I asked, surprised by her intuition but determined nonetheless to play dumb. Her raised eyebrows and the patient expression on her face made me relent.

'Is it that obvious, Jules?' I groaned.

'Only to me, darling,' she soothed.

'I know it sounds crazy, but I seem to have developed a terrible crush on the man,' I whispered across the table to her, strangely relieved to at last be able to discuss my little infatuation with someone.

'I'm not surprised!' Jules whispered back. 'Dan Bryant is very *crushable* in every sense of the word!'

'I feel like a *teenager* again,' I groaned, my voice full of anguished longing.

'To be honest, Libby, I didn't realise that you knew Dan well enough to form a crush. It's not like you to be swayed by looks alone.'

I was reminded of just how well Jules knew me.

'You two certainly looked very cosy together! Is your relationship business or pleasure?' she persisted.

'Business, Jules. Unfortunately, it's purely business,' I sighed. 'I'll tell you all about it when we get back to the house.'

Jules nodded, unconcerned by any property ventures that I might have had planned. Mary Mac arrived with our food, and we ate in a silence broken only by the occasional expressions of appreciation for our food.

Despite Jules not proceeding to barrage me with a million questions, I could tell that I had piqued her interest. In fact, it was her silence that was the most telling, and I knew that she wanted every last detail of my personal interest in Dan Bryant saved until we had absolute privacy. If I had anything even mildly salacious to reveal, then Jules wanted to be able to give full vent to her emotions. Otherwise the whole exercise would be a complete waste of time as far as she was concerned.

This should be interesting, I thought, suddenly nervous at the prospect of Jules's trawling through my own ill-defined feelings.

By the time we finished our meal, Mary Mac was nowhere to be seen, and the buzz in the pub had subsided somewhat. We made our way to the bar, and catching the owner's eye, Jules handed over fifty euros to cover the cost of the food and to include a tip. Paddy Mac gestured that we should wait a minute so that he could sort us out with change, but Jules passed him a wink and a wave, and we headed for the door. Dan was still drinking with someone at a small table near the exit, and both men raised their glasses in recognition as we passed.

We reached Willow Cottage fifteen minutes later, and I was glad that I had taken the time to set the fire in the sitting room that morning. Within minutes, Jules and I were snuggled up in the fireside chairs, cupping two glasses of wine and choosing to completely forget about our journey to Dublin. We had far more interesting things to discuss.

For the most part, Jules was enthusiastic about Alice-Rose and the potential for romance between Dan and me. On the one hand, Alice-Rose was anybody's fancy, and Dan Bryant was a very nice man. But on the other, Alice-Rose was an awful lot of hard work, and Dan Bryant was old enough to be my father! The fact that I was barely older than his grown-up children was something else that had to be considered.

Jules had a lot of insight into Dan's marriage to the late Marie. It seemed that while Dan was well liked by all, Marie had not been. Once Dan began making some real money in the auctioneering business, his wife began busying herself with the ladies of the area who lunched. Climbing the social ladder became her main focus in life, and she didn't care who she alienated on her way up.

Most decent people had found Marie Bryant snobbish and rude. Tradespeople avoided working for her as her over-exacting standards were impossible to meet. Jules imagined that Dan must have led a tortured existence in the years prior to his wife's death. By the end of our bottle of wine, we had come to the intoxicated conclusion that all in all I would be a much better companion for him. We didn't dwell on the fact that Dan hadn't given any indication whatsoever that he was even remotely interested in me. Where would the fun have been in that?

CHAPTER 9

The Hunt Ball

JULES STAYED OVER that night because we had a lot of speculation to get through, and besides speculation, between us we managed to get through three of the six bottles of Tesco's 'specially selected' wine! As a result of our overindulgence, we both slept late the following morning, reluctantly emerging from our beds to face what was left of the day. After breakfast, we rifled through the shopping bags that had been discarded in the front hall the night before. We were pleasantly surprised to find that the dresses looked just as good in the cold light of day as they had in the artificial, and deliberately flattering, light of the shop's dressing rooms. I felt a renewed sense of hope that Dan Bryant's affections might just be within my grasp, disapproving children or not!

Jules left in a hurry just before noon. She had an appointment scheduled with one of her clients later in the day, and according to her, she had a lot of preparation outstanding. I was reminded of the fact that I had a lot of work of my own to catch up on. There were pre-Christmas orders to be checked and a buying trip to Massachusetts for the following week to be finalised. I spent the rest of that day playing catch up on things that I should have been doing the day before.

By the time Friday afternoon arrived, I felt utterly exhausted, to the point of not really caring whether or not I went to the ball. I climbed reluctantly into the shower at four o'clock and felt marginally better when I emerged half an hour later. I remembered a little belatedly that Jules could always be relied upon to inject enthusiasm into any occasion, and true to form, she turned up on the dot of five, clutching a bucket filled with ice and a bottle of very decent champagne. I began to feel better!

Sandra from 'Ballyedmond's Hair and Beauty Salon' arrived shortly thereafter, and by the time she was leaving, almost two hours later, there was a decidedly giddy air reverberating around Willow Cottage. Our taxi arrived just before eight, and before we knew it, we were being divested of our coats by the doorman of Ballyedmond's main hotel, the Donnard Arms.

Although Jules and I had planned on arriving early to the event in order to avoid the main throng's influx, it was immediately apparent that we had miscalculated the level of support that the affair would receive. The hotel lobby was already buzzing with activity when we arrived, and there was a terrific atmosphere of revelry reverberating throughout the hall.

We bumped into several people who were well-known to us, and within minutes, we were ensconced among neighbours discussing everything from the price of cattle to the more intriguing question of who it was that had bought the 'Old Steven's Place'. I gave Jules 'the nod', and we excused ourselves from the group; I didn't want to eventually be seen as the 'cute hoor' singing dumb amidst their speculation.

I scanned the crowds but could see no sign of Dan Bryant. Jules was looking for Sean Commerford, an old beau from the area in whom she was beginning at that time to express a renewed interest in. I wasn't entirely convinced that there was any wisdom in attempting to revisit that particular relationship; I had never liked Sean and would not have trusted him as far as I could have thrown him. But maybe Jules knew better!

By eight fifty-five neither man had arrived. The gong rang for dinner on the dot of nine o'clock, and Jules and I entered the hall disappointed by the men's failure to show. Jules had even gone as far as making a tenuous arrangement with the 'gorgeous Sean'.

We were seated at a table for eight, with two people that we knew and four others. Jules and I were the only singles in our party, a fact that surprised neither of us; these events usually attracted the 'happily matched'. Overall, the night wasn't looking hopeful in terms of either of us finding romance, and it looked even less so when Jules noted the late arrival of the brazen Sean with an unknown blonde on his arm.

Jules nudged me discretely, and seeing the loved-up pair for myself, I squeezed her hand, conveying my wordless commiserations. Unfortunately, I was soon on the receiving end of a consoling squeeze of my own when a beaming Dan Bryant entered soon after with the pretty and petite Penny Holmes on his arm! Dan looked like a latter-day James Bond, and Penny wasn't doing a bad job of imitating the fabulous Pussy Galore!

There was nothing for it but to relieve the tension with a burst of laughter, much to the bemusement of the others at our table. Jules and I apologised for our apparent rudeness before readily accepting the Sauvignon Blanc that was offered by our passing waiter. The night could only get better!

And indeed, the night did improve considerably. The meal was well above the standards of the mediocre rations that are usually dished up at these events, and our dinner companions turned out to be friendly and amusing.

After our giddiness had subsided, we noticed that my parents were seated at a table on the far side of the room. In attempting to avoid divulging the details of my property deal to them, I had successfully evaded them to the point of having absolutely no idea of their short-term plans. This was a rare occurrence, and it felt oddly liberating. Catching Dad's eye across the room, I waved and motioned to him that I would see them after dinner.

Having realised early on in the evening that our best-laid plans had been in vain, Jules and I determined to let our hair down and to enjoy the occasion for what it was. We rarely attended an event of this kind, and it was a great opportunity to reconnect with neighbours and friends. The evening had the added bonus of giving something back to the community; the proceeds of the ball were being donated to the local rehabilitation centre.

Everyone, without exception, appeared to be in high spirits that night. Once dinner was over, the tables were pushed back to clear the dance floor, and the music started to play. The organising committee hadn't scrimped on the entertainment either, and the band was as good as any I'd ever heard. People eagerly took to the floor to the dolce strains of 'It had to be you'.

Many songs later, I was still on the dance floor, and having my toes crushed by my neighbour and non-dancer, Mr Michael Quigley, while we attempted a loose interpretation of a waltz. I was beginning to lose the will to live when Dan Bryant politely intervened and asked if Michael wouldn't mind allowing him to 'have the pleasure'. Michael took the interruption well and confessed that my toes had probably taken enough of a bashing for one night.

Dan had been far from my thoughts when the exchange took place so that I felt remarkably unselfconscious when he took me in his arms and guided me across the dance floor. The difference between dancing with Michael and dancing with Dan was like the difference between night and day: Dan was a *fantastic* dancer! I felt like I had been handed the keys to a Rolls Royce, having just driven a clapped-out banger with no power steering. Dan was competent and confident.

We didn't speak for the duration of the waltz, but when the band changed from a waltz to a foxtrot, Dan whispered in my ear, 'Come on,

Libby. Let's show them how it's done.' His words had the effect of an electrical charge, heightening my awareness of the situation. The subtle, yet oh-so definite, suggestion of something sexual in his voice made me suddenly conscious of the heat radiating from his body. I couldn't answer him, but I followed his lead.

Max and I had taken dance lessons early on in our romance, and we had loved to dance together at weddings and at parties. I had always considered Max to be a pretty good dance partner, but then I had nobody to compare him to. Dan Bryant left my husband well and truly in the shade. By the end of the foxtrot trio, Dan and I were the only people left on the floor, and a large crowd had formed a circle around its edge. When we stopped, the spectators wolf whistled and called for more. We had managed to impress the assembly.

'Tango anyone?' enquired Dan, totally uninhibited as he motioned the band to *give him a tango*.

One very long tango later, we graciously excused ourselves from the crowd, and Dan accompanied me back to my table before asking if he could buy me a drink.

'I'd kill for a glass of water, Dan. Thanks,' I said. I was completely parched from concentration alone.

Dan disappeared to the bar, and Jules quickly returned to our table to give me a 'subtle' dig in the ribs.

'Libby, you sly old fox, who knew *you* could dance like that?' she exclaimed, more than a little surprised.

'Not me!' I replied truthfully. 'That man could make a mannequin look good on a dance floor.'

'Hmm, you know what they say about a man who *can dance*, don't you?' implied Jules.

'No,' I said, 'but I have a horrible suspicion that you're going to tell me.'

Jules didn't get a chance to tell me the theory about men who could dance because Dan Bryant chose that particular moment to return to our table, bearing a large glass of mineral water.

'Jules, what can I get you to drink?' Dan asked, placing the glass before me.

'I'm fine, Dan. Thanks,' Jules smiled. 'I didn't quite manage to work up the same thirst on the dance floor as you two.'

Dan gave a little smile.

'You pair were quite the dancing queens out there!' she added playfully.

'Yes, we were, Jules, and thanks for noticing,' Dan replied with good humour. 'It's hard not to look good when you have Libby in your arms.'

I blushed furiously.

Turning towards me, Dan gave a little bow before saying, 'Libby, it was a pleasure, and I hope you girls enjoy the rest of your night.'

Dan gave a final nod to Jules before leaving us to rejoin his group. I could feel the blush spreading from my face right down to my chest, and I hoped that the effect his words and actions were having on me that night hadn't been quite so obvious to Dan.

'Oh my God, Libby, he is *so* into you!' gasped Jules.

'Yeah right, Jules,' I sighed, forcing myself to regain a semblance of calm. 'That's why he left me sipping water while he returned to schmoose the night away with Penny Holmes.' Unaware that Penny had already left for the night, I wondered briefly what she had made of our little performance.

'Much and all as I would love to concur with your verdict, Jules, I really don't think you're on the money this time.'

Jules just smirked.

'Cheers,' I said resignedly, raising my glass of water in salute. It would have been pointless to continue trying to contradict her.

Dan

CHAPTER 10

The Way She Makes Me Feel

A S I'VE SAID, I arrived home after spending the evening at Willow Cottage full of resolve. From that night on, I would desist from 'punching above my weight' when it came to the fairer sex. I dialled Penny Holmes's number immediately, determined to prove to myself just how serious I was about my new resolution.

Unfortunately, the minute I heard Penny's number ringing, I knew that I had made a huge mistake. I would have hung up before she had time to answer, but I knew that Penny would have been able to identify my number. I had no option but to go through with my plan. Nevertheless, it felt *all* wrong.

I was not interested in Penny Holmes; I had never been interested in Penny Holmes, and I never would be interested in Penny Holmes. While Penny was a lovely, attractive, and vibrant woman, she held no attraction for me. She deserved better than to be taken out on a date in an attempt to cover up a middle-aged man's desire for a much younger, and totally irresistible, girl!

But there was no going back on the deal; that would only have made matters worse. I didn't think it very likely that I would run into Libby at the ball; I was far more likely to meet her parents there. After all, it was more *our* scene.

The night of the ball arrived, and I called for Penny as we had arranged. I had never seen Penny looking lovelier, but I remained unmoved by her efforts. I was made of stone.

That being said, when I stepped inside the door of the hotel's function room with Penny Holmes by my side, my *stony* insides turned to jelly. The first person that my eyes unconsciously sought across the room materialised in splendid emerald green. *She* literally took my breath away! I gasped inwardly, and for a few seconds, I was lost to her, completely unaware of anyone else in the room.

The gentle pressure of Penny's hand on my arm brought me back to rude reality, and we made our way to our table which was situated close to where Libby's parents were seated. It was hopeless. Try as I might to concentrate on Penny and the others seated with us, my mind kept wandering back to Libby.

I had never seen a woman look as beautiful as Libby did that night. To say that she shone would be to compare her to a star, and no star had ever shone so brightly! I made several trips to other tables on the pretext of saying hello to people I knew, all in the hope of bumping into Libby or, at the very least, catching a glimpse of her. Several glances of her shimmering beauty later and I was worse off than before. My desire for her had been whetted, not satisfied! Once the dancing started, it was as if the men of Ballyedmond were conspiring to keep us apart. I watched helplessly as they jostled for her time and attention.

I had given up all hope of speaking to Libby when events took an unexpected turn. Penny developed a splitting migraine. She admitted that it had been threatening to strike all day but that she had been 'so looking forward' to the event that she hadn't cancelled despite knowing from experience that she probably should have. Penny apologised for the inconvenience but conceded that her only option was to cut the evening short and return home. I was relieved by the prospect of leaving early; being so close to Libby in Penny's company was proving tortuous.

But Penny wouldn't entertain the idea of me leaving with her. Instead, she insisted upon going home alone, promising that she would call me the following day. I felt my spirits soar at the realisation that now at least I had a chance of engaging with Libby. I forced myself to be patient and bided my time before seizing my opportunity.

After what seemed like forever, I finally made my way towards the music. Libby was dancing with Michael Quigley, a well-known farmer from the area. Michael was in his forties, and I would have put money on it that he was a confirmed bachelor until I saw himself and Libby dancing and laughing together. They appeared to be having a whale of a time; Michael certainly looked like he was enjoying himself!

I almost felt guilty for what I was about to do. Did I have the right to intervene? Libby had a few inches on Michael, and they were hamming it up on the dance floor. As Libby playfully twirled Michael under her arm, I looked around for motivation, and I found it in the several young men who were standing on the sidelines, just waiting to take Michael's place.

Reminding myself that all was fair in love and war, I cut in rather rudely before somebody else did!

Libby was surprised by my interruption; there was no doubt about that, but once I took her in my arms, she relaxed into the music, and it was if we had been dancing together for a lifetime. While Marie and I had enjoyed dancing, and towards the end it was one of the few interests that we had left in common, she didn't compare to Libby, who was accomplished beyond her years. I considered that some, who had witnessed my wife and I dancing together in later years, must have gotten the impression of a very happy couple, quite the opposite of the grey reality. And then I marvelled at the wonder of being completely in step with the girl in my arms, and I allowed myself to get lost in the moment.

After a while, I was able to fully observe Libby's breathtaking beauty. Once I made eye contact with her, I found that I was unable to look away, and I was charmed by how unselfconsciously she held my gaze. Her dark gleaming hair was swept back into a French knot at the nape of her neck, and she wore an emerald green gown that exposed her slim arms and shoulders. Four fine bands of velvet criss-crossed her upper chest, giving an impression of modesty and innocence. Her body felt slim beneath my hand, but the occasional brush of her breasts against my chest betrayed a bosom that was full and generous. Notwithstanding all of Libby's physical attributes, it was the laughter in her chocolate brown eyes, and her ever ready smile, that sealed my heart's fate.

When we finished our last dance, Libby laughed, delighted by the effect of our performance on the crowd.

'Christopher Leavy, School of Dance 2001,' she said, explaining her proficiency on the dance floor.

'Christopher Leavy, School of Dance, sometime in the late twentieth century!' I groaned, and we both laughed at the absurdity of the situation.

Christopher Leavy had been giving ballroom dance lessons in Ballyedmond for thirty-five years, and although he was a comical character, he was an effective teacher and one who was still pursuing his passion!

I tore myself away from Libby, and her companion Jules Mahon, sooner than I would have liked. There was no doubt but that the two girls would have been fun and entertaining company, but I was afraid of falling any deeper for Libby's charms, not to mention making an even bigger fool of myself than I had done already!

I decided that by retreating at that stage, I at least had some chance of passing off my enthusiastic dancing as a simple willingness to enter into the spirit of the occasion. Besides, I knew Jules Mahon quite well, and I got the distinct impression that she was wiser to my true feelings than I might have liked. I let my head take control of my heart, and I bade the ladies goodnight, withdrawing without a backward glance to the safety of my own group. I wasn't naive enough to think that I could escape completely 'unscathed' from my dancing episode with Libby; at the very least, I would have to suffer the rude good humour of my dining companions.

'You sly old dog!' and 'There's life left in the old dog yet!' were but a few of the *dog* references thrown my way for the rest of the night.

Reflecting on events later, I concluded that one dance alone with Libby Finn was worth the endurance of any amount of taunting. I fell asleep with a silly grin on my face and awoke the following morning with a heavy heart, certain that Libby and I had already shared our most intimate moment.

Libby

CHAPTER 11

Did I Dream that Tango in the Night?

T HE WEATHER THE morning after the Hunt Ball was in keeping with my hangover. The rain lashed against the windows of Willow Cottage, mirroring the sensation of my brain pulsating against my skull. At no point in the night had I felt overly intoxicated, but unfortunately mine was not a body that took an 'excessive' consumption of alcohol lying down. If I was ever foolish enough to exceed my safe limit of three drinks, I invariably suffered the consequences of my 'excess' the following day.

Luckily, the day was Saturday, and I had nothing much on. I had already managed to finalise plans for my trip to the States the following Tuesday, whereupon I would fly to Boston before making my way to my aunt's place in Eastern Massachusetts. I was looking forward to spending time with my relations and indulging my passion for antiquing while at the same time hoping to source some quality antiques for my rapidly depleting stock.

Once again, I marvelled at my good fortune. How many people got to indulge their passions while making a healthy profit from it? Christopher Leavy and I were a rarity! My business also afforded me the opportunity to travel and to link up with family and friends who I would otherwise have seldom met. I brewed a pot of coffee and wondered mildly how Jules had fared the night before. It was after three in the morning when I left the Donnard Arms, and at that point, Jules was deep in conversation with one of Ballyedmond's most eligible bachelors, Mr Noel Kinsella.

Noel was a local businessman, and although he was wealthy and well-regarded in the area, he was not typical of the sort of man that Jules usually went for. In the first instance, Noel was not very tall. In fact, he was on the stocky side, with a thatch of red hair to rival Jules's own, and Jules never, ever, went for a fellow redhead! She had an unreasonable dread of bearing a red-haired child. The fact that Jules wasn't even remotely maternal and had no intention of getting pregnant in the foreseeable future was beside the point. Jules cited the old adage of 'There's many a slip between the cup and the lip' as warning enough for her. She could not, and would not, give birth to a red-haired child!

Jules's abiding aversion was a constant source of amusement and puzzlement to me because I couldn't see how Jules had ever suffered as a result of her hair colouring. She had always been popular with both males and females alike.

Besides his physical appearance, Noel was not overly talkative and struck me as being the quiet, sensitive type, in other words not at all the type of man that Jules Mahon usually pursued.

After two mugs of strong black coffee, I took a long hot shower and dressed in my 'do absolutely nothing clothes'. Getting dressed made me feel almost human again, and I decided to make a start on packing my suitcases for my forthcoming trip to the United States. By four o'clock that afternoon, I was sorted and ready to go. Happy that I had at least achieved something during the day, I was about to nip into Ballyedmond to get a takeaway meal when I received a text message.

I was surprised to see that it was from Dan Bryant. *Business or pleasure*, I wondered eagerly. It turned out to be business. Dan was only inquiring as to whether or not I could drop into the office by the end of that week to run over some documentation, and *not* to ask me out on a date, as I had secretly hoped.

In all the excitement of the previous few days, it had completely escaped my attention that I would be out of the country when the sale was due to be finalised, and I presumed that it couldn't go ahead without me. I dispensed with texting and called Dan back immediately, hoping that he would be able to delay matters. For my part, I would try to exchange my flights for one the following day, and another that would get me home before close of business the following Monday week. Dan agreed, and I got to work rearranging my flights.

The week in Massachusetts could not have worked out any better. The weather was sublime and the downturn in the American economy meant there was an abundance of antiques available to buy. I had never come across such a selection of high-quality early American furniture at such reasonable prices.

My trip happily coincided with the arrival on to the market of an eighteenth century home within a half-hour's drive of my aunt's place; the house was crammed wall-to-wall with antiques! The owners were moving to a retirement village, and the sale of their home, together with most of their belongings, was necessary to fund the move. I was in the fortunate position of being able to make them an acceptable offer for the entire contents of the house and that business transaction alone justified my trip twice over. I spent the next three days taking photographic inventory of everything before arranging for the items to be packed and shipped back to Ireland. Sales had certainly slowed down back at home, in line with the downturn in the world economy, but I found that some people still had money for quality pieces.

Flying home from New England, I was surprised to realise that Dan Bryant had been very far from my thoughts, and I concluded that my *deep attraction* to Dan had been more of an infatuation than the *love story of the century* that I had imagined it to be. I decided that I had probably been feeling vulnerable when I met Dan and that, more than anything else, was what had contributed to my exaggerated feelings of attraction. I was bound to be feeling more emotional than usual around the anniversary of Max's death, that and getting a year older. The realisation was somewhat of a relief to me because I imagined that the last thing I needed at a time when I was about to embark on a major project was the distraction of romance.

Autumnal homecomings usually left me feeling wistful for the States; after all, nobody does Hallowe'en and Christmas better than the Americans! But back then, the prospect of owning Alice-Rose and making my new home there drew me back to Ireland like nothing ever had before! I pushed open the front door of Willow Cottage to be greeted by the heavenly smell of warm spices; my darling mother had left one of her home-made apple tarts in the kitchen in anticipation of my return.

Kicking off my boots, I moved the kettle on to the hotplate before heading upstairs to run myself a bath. When I returned home after long-haul flights, I usually went straight to bed, but that day was different, I had things to do! Returning to the kitchen a short time later, I flicked on my message minder and was greeted by several messages.

One was from Jules, apologising for not being 'available for comment' before I left for the States and urging me to call her the second I got back. Another message was from Emma, inviting myself and 'a friend' to their engagement party the following Saturday night. There were several messages from clients, anxious to place their Christmas orders and wondering when 'exactly' my website would be updated, and there was a message from Mum inviting me to supper that evening. Good old Mum, she could always be relied upon to feed the body as well as the soul!

The final message was from Dan Bryant, assuring me that all the paperwork was in order regarding the sale of Alice-Rose and informing me that he had arranged for a meeting of both parties for three o'clock that afternoon at his office. He hoped that I would be able to make it and asked that I confirm as soon as possible.

The sound of Dan's deep, velvety tones brought all the feelings of longing that I had confidently dismissed, flooding back, and I was hurled back to square one in the love stakes! *Oh foolish heart, what a fickle friend you are!* I thought, climbing the stairs and heading for the sanctuary of the steamy, lavender-scented bathroom.

When I emerged some time later, I was slightly alarmed to find that the clock on my bedside table read two-o-five! That didn't leave me much time to get ready, and I still had to decide on what to wear, and that was rarely an easy decision for any girl!

Underwear, a garter belt, and some silk stockings were the obvious starting point before giving my hair a quick blow-dry in the hope that I would get a chance to finish drying it before leaving for town. Rummaging quickly through my wardrobe, I found the navy pinstriped suit that I was looking for, and I matched it with a white silk shirt. Shrugging myself into the jacket of my suit, I stood briefly before the full-length mirror that was mounted on the bedroom wall.

'Not bad, Miss Jones!' I said aloud.

Living alone had, as one might have expected, brought many changes to my life. For one thing, I found that I talked to myself quite a bit more than I had done when Max was around! I hoped that I wasn't actually going mad. Further appraisal of my reflection confirmed that I was almost ready; all that remained for me to do was to slip into my black pumps and to finish off my hair.

I raced back to the dressing table and gave my hair another blast of the hairdryer before twisting it into a French knot. It was at that point that I remembered to apply some blusher, a quick brush of mascara and a little lipstick. I wasn't used to applying make-up, so I tended to veer on the side of caution; less *was* more, in my opinion. A pair of small pearl drop earrings completed the look.

I rifled the house looking for my 'flats', but they were nowhere to be found! Only after I had exhausted all of the possible hiding places did

I finally remember that I had left them at Mum and Dad's a few weeks previously. I couldn't have retrieved my shoes from home then even if there had been enough time because I would have been met by a torrent of questions as to why I was 'so dressed up on a Monday afternoon'! The only alternative left to me was a pair of six-inch heels; they weren't quite the look I was hoping for, but they were my only option.

Clutching my shoes and a handbag, I slipped into a pair of old loafers before heading downstairs, taking the steps two at a time. The untouched apple tart 'called' to me in vain; there was no time then for reflection over tea and Mum's home baking! I snatched my wallet from the kitchen counter and threw it into my bag before grabbing my keys and heading for the car. I banged the hall door on my way out just to be sure. Knowing how distracted I was that morning, I didn't want to be second guessing my security measures from the comfort of Dan Bryant's office!

CHAPTER 12

Sealing the Deal

THE PARTNERSHIP OF 'Bryant and Bryant' was housed in a large terraced Georgian house located in the main square of Ballyedmond, a heritage town that bragged another three such squares, albeit of lesser dimensions. Although the Bryant property adjoined its neighbour by an archway that lead to customer parking, I opted for on-street parking, a short distance away. Pulling a parking ticket from the glove compartment, I scratched the panel to display the correct time and date of my arrival, before shaking off my loafers and slipping into my heels.

As I approached the offices of Bryant and Bryant, I noted that the house was beautifully maintained. The sash windows were painted a rich cream, and the front door, which was standing ajar, was painted pillar box red. I took the limestone steps one at a time, narrowly resisting the urge to hike up my skirt and take a run at them; my heart was racing, and my hands were trembling slightly.

It was five minutes past three by the time Linda O'Reilly, the Bryant brothers' secretary, ushered me into the conference room. I imagined that it had been a drawing room in a former life and that it remained largely unchanged except for the addition of some modern-day furniture. The overall feeling in the room was light and airy, and I noted two oil paintings by renowned artists hanging discretely in the alcoves on either side of an impressive marble fireplace.

Dan Bryant greeted me warmly and ensured that I was acquainted with everyone present before gesturing me towards a chair; I shook everyone's hand before taking my seat. It soon became clear that I was the last one to arrive, and I began to feel a little self-conscience. All the men were dressed in suits as one would have expected, and the heavy scent of aftershave mixed with tobacco hung in the air. I thought I detected the almost indiscernible whiff of brandy too, but I couldn't be sure. However, there was one thing that I was certain of from the moment I entered the room, every eye was focused on me. I suddenly felt conspicuously female and, let's face it, rich!

'Good morning, gentlemen,' I said, sounding far more confident than I was feeling.

I settled myself beside Hugh Fagan of Dunne and Fagan solicitors. Hugh was a family friend and he had dealt with all of my legal issues to date. He gave me a reassuring smile and that made me feel significantly better. George Baxter's solicitor seemed decent enough; he stood and shook my hand firmly when we were introduced. How bad could the whole thing be?

As it turned out, the entire process was relatively straightforward, and that was largely due to the fact that there was no outstanding debt on the property. It seemed that George Baxter wasn't quite as reckless as some had imagined him to be, and less than two hours after my arrival, the deal was done. Gradually, one by one, people disbanded until there was only George and I left in the room. We regarded each other for a moment in awkward silence before George extended his right hand to shake mine and he proceeded to wish me luck with Alice-Rose.

'The old man always liked you, Libby,' George said magnanimously, 'he would have been pleased to see you getting the place.'

'Thank you, George. It's very kind of you to say so,' I replied, surprised by the man's generosity.

'*She* deserves to be taken care of, and I am in no doubt but that you are the right woman for the job!' he spoke with forced joviality, but I could tell that he was hurting.

'I'll do my best, George,' I said, 'and you must come and visit us anytime. Never be a stranger.' I meant it, and I think that George knew that I did. He nodded gravely before turning and striding purposefully from the room.

That brief, private encounter with George Baxter forced me to ponder his true feelings regarding Alice-Rose, and I concluded from his demeanour that Alice-Rose had meant considerably more to him than I had been lead to believe. I felt a brief, but real, sense of guilt over my good fortune.

'Is George gone already?' Dan Bryant's voice broke into my thoughts.

I nodded.

'I thought I'd invite you both to dinner,' he said, sounding disappointed.

While there had been coffee and biscuits served at the meeting, it was getting late, and I was beginning to feel very hungry. I hadn't eaten anything substantial all day, and the dreaded jet lag was beginning to strike with a vengeance.

'Yes, Dan, he's gone. I'm afraid,' I said, feeling deflated after the initial high of the deal. 'It's a nice thought, but I don't suppose dinner with me would have been George's idea of fun.'

'Hmm, I suppose you're right, Libby. I hadn't really thought it through,' Dan agreed. 'However, I'm sure George's hasty retreat is no personal reflection on you,' Dan spoke reassuringly. 'George would have had to sell the place to someone, and it might as well have been to you, for a fair price.'

What Dan was saying was most likely true, and it did make me feel a little better about the situation.

'That being said, I don't mind taking just you to dinner if you fancy it?' His tone was playful, and it worked a treat after the intensity of the previous couple of hours.

'Let's skip dinner, and I'll show you what I really fancy,' I said, in my head. What I actually said was 'I'd love that, Dan. I'm starving!'

Dan

CHAPTER 13

Going, Going, Gone!

I MISSED LIBBY FOR the entire week that she was away. Knowing that there was absolutely no chance of bumping into her was surprisingly difficult. I went to bed the night before her return and found that I was unable to sleep; my excitement at the prospect of seeing her again had reached epic proportions. Neither could I face breakfast the next morning, I was giddy with anticipation.

'This is ridiculous!' I said aloud to the cat sitting on the window sill outside. 'Libby is not for you, you old fool. Cop on to yourself!'

For once I was very glad to be alone in the house.

Even my secretary Linda commented on my mood.

'Are you *all right*, Dan?' she asked anxiously. 'You seem distracted,' she added helpfully. 'Can I get you anything?'

'I'm fine,' I replied confidently, trying to reassure myself as much as her. 'I just didn't sleep very well last night.'

That much at least was true. I had spent the night tossing and turning, snatching moments of dream-filled sleep where I made love to a very naked, and very willing, Libby.

'Any calls?' I asked, hoping against hope that Libby might have phoned the office.

'Just the one, from Caroline, she asked if you could call her back.'

'Thanks, I'll do that now,' I replied, glad of an excuse to do something other than think about Libby Finn.

Retreating into the privacy of my office, I dialled my daughter's number in Dublin. Caroline was my only daughter and the youngest of my three children. She was twenty-one years old, and she had been spoiled rotten by her mother. Nevertheless, she had turned into a fine young woman. In fact, all of our children had turned out rather well despite my late wife's best efforts. In the latter years, Marie had tried to instil a sense of superiority into them, but thankfully, by some unknown grace, her constant brainwashing had failed miserably.

'Hi, Dad!' Caroline said, her voice was cheerful and enthusiastic. 'How are tricks in Ballyedmond today?'

'Good, sweetheart,' I replied, feeling suddenly uncomplicatedly happy at the sound of my daughter's voice. 'How is life in the Big Apple?' I asked.

'Dad!' she exclaimed, feigning exasperation at my little joke. 'But since you ask, life is good, Dad, pretty good!'

Caroline was in the final year of a nursing degree.

'We're up to our tonsils revising for the Christmas exams,' she went on, giving a little groan more for effect than anything else. Caroline was a grade 'A' student, with a natural ability to learn. She rarely got stressed out over work of any kind. I wasn't worried.

'The reason I rang,' she continued, 'was because I was wondering if you would be free for dinner on Saturday evening?' Alarm bells, albeit little ones, rang in my brain. 'Todd's parents are over from the States, and it would be great if you could meet them. It really would, Dad.'

Todd was Caroline's latest flame, and in truth, he was a very nice guy. I could think of worse things than having him as a son-in-law. Meeting his parents, on the other hand, was an entirely different matter. It's not that I presumed that I wouldn't like them, quite the opposite in fact, but I always felt like 'billy no-mates' on these occasions, the odd lonely one out.

'That would be lovely, darling,' I said, conquering my instinctual reaction to offer any excuse as to why I couldn't make it. 'Just name the time and the place, and I'll be there.'

Caroline named a restaurant in the city centre, and we settled on meeting up for pre-dinner drinks in a nearby pub at 7.30 p.m. the following Saturday.

The morning dragged by. Everything was in order for the sale of Alice-Rose, there was no work left to be done regarding it, but I couldn't concentrate on less-pressing matters. I spent most of the morning playing solitaire on my laptop while taking the odd phone call, too distracted to concentrate on any real work. Lunch consisted of a sandwich and a mug of coffee taken at my desk.

Finally, it was ten minutes to three o'clock, and with the approaching hour came the first of those involved in the sale; Libby, however, was the last to arrive. She made her appearance at a fashionable five minutes past three. I was fully aware that the girl was beautiful, but when she walked into the conference room that day exuding svelte sophistication and sexiness, she was drop-dead gorgeous! Judging by the amount of throat clearing that took place upon her arrival, I'm certain that I wasn't the only man present that was moved by the sight of her!

I sat Libby beside her solicitor Hugh Fagan, while I took a seat opposite, next to George Baxter. I had wanted to sit beside her, but I had to remind myself of who it was that I was working for.

Taking my seat and glancing over at Libby, I realised that enough of her shirt buttons were undone to allow a generous glimpse of her bra. The whiteness of the lace, contrasting with the creaminess of her skin, was tantalising, and my few remaining hormones jumped into life, forcing me to indulge in a brief fantasy where I was on intimate terms with the bra in question and the breasts beneath. It was truly amazing how this unassuming young woman could fill a man with lustful longing, the likes of which he had been sure he would never experience again. Finally, regaining touch with reality and finding my voice, I handed the reins of the meeting over to George Baxter's solicitor.

The next two hours were spent in careful concentration because by that point I was fully aware that I was not my usual astute self in Libby's presence. No woman had ever had that effect on me before, and it was disconcerting to say the least! Indeed, it was quite worrying, especially in light of the fact that there wasn't a lot I could do about it! I consoled myself with the knowledge that my dealings with Libby were drawing to a close and that life would soon return to normal.

But did I really want it to? I didn't see how life could ever be the same again; Libby Finn had awakened something in me that I wasn't sure I could suppress, no matter how hard I tried.

The meeting passed quite quickly in spite of the fact that there were extra items to be dealt with that were not directly related to the sale of the property. Libby wanted to purchase some articles of furniture belonging to the house, provided that George Baxter was agreeable. The items included a grandfather clock that Libby remembered Michael Stevens saying had been in the house as far back as he could remember. The clock was no longer there; however, it was still in George's possession, and he was willing to part with it. The second item was a marble-topped sideboard with mirrored doors which was still in the house but for which George had no use. The other items were largely outside and included several large stone troughs and a pony trap. As the meeting concluded, I breathed an inward sigh of relief; I might finally get a chance to speak to Libby alone.

When almost everyone had gone their separate ways, I left Libby and George Baxter together while I returned to my office to get the keys to Alice-Rose. George had directed me to give the keys to Libby once the meeting was over and the papers were signed. This contradicted the usual practice of waiting for cheques to clear, and it was an unmistakable gesture of goodwill and trust on George's part.

I wasn't really surprised to discover that George had taken his leave before my return, and I knew that his departure presented me with a golden opportunity to invite Libby to dinner. Libby had already agreed to join me for something to eat when I remembered the large bunch of keys still in my hand. Handing them to her, I was in the enviable position of seeing the look of absolute joy that illuminated her face as she realised their significance. Pressing them to her breast, she laughed her toothy laugh, and taking my arm in hers, she marched me through the front door and out to her awaiting car. I was at once both calmed and excited by her easy touch.

'Dan,' she announced, 'dinner it definitely on me!'

Libby

CHAPTER 14

Alice-Rose: The Girl's All Mine

DAN AND I headed for Mac's. While there was no longer any need for absolute secrecy, I still had to tell my family about my latest undertaking, and I hoped that we wouldn't bump into any of them in the pub. We didn't.

Taking into account that we both had to drive home, Dan and I contented ourselves with two glasses of house red. Gently touching glasses, we toasted the future before ordering the dish of the day, beef bourguignon with celeriac mash and winter beets. This was followed by spiced apple crumble with vanilla cream and two large black coffees.

The conversation ranged from my plans for Alice-Rose to Dan's plans for semi-retirement. He had invested in a small farm some years previously and was hoping to start making some improvements to it. These included renovating a late nineteenth-century farmhouse and yard on the property. Leaving the cosy atmosphere of the pub some time later, we practically stumbled on to the street outside; we were drunk on rich food and as giddy as two kid goats.

'I want to see *your* place in the country, Dan!' I demanded, sounding more forceful than I had intended.

'*I'd* like that, Libby!' he said, not sounding at all offended. 'Maybe you could give me some design tips? How about next Saturday if you're free?'

'It's a date,' I said.

Dan declined my offer of a lift back to his office, saying that the walk would do him good. Taking my hand and wishing me well, he released me and strode off in the direction of John Edmond Square. I went in the opposite direction, heading back towards Lough Glen and my parents' house. The time had come to tell them about my most recent adventures in the property game, and my feelings were that of excitement mixed with apprehension. I wasn't entirely sure how either of them would feel about any of it, including my decision to keep them firmly in the dark!

Mum wasn't surprised by my arrival at Lough Glen House; she had, after all, invited me for dinner. Dad was just back from a call-out, and the appearance of any one of his children in his kitchen was always pleasantly reassuring to him. It signified that all was right with the world and that life's equilibrium remained intact. That being said, the news that I was the new owner of Alice-Rose came as a huge surprise to both of them!

Mum's initial reaction was one of absolute incredulity.

'I always knew that you loved that house,' she said, 'but I never dreamt that you'd want to buy it, especially now!'

Her words were open to all kinds of interpretation, but I took them to imply that she couldn't understand how upon finding myself alone in the world, without *chick nor child*, I would choose to rattle around in a big old house on my own. She had a point I supposed. Dad, on the other hand, was always the voice of reason, and he interrupted Mum's flow before she could say too much.

'Now, now, Sarah, I'm sure Libby is old enough to know what she wants,' Dad said reasonably. 'I think it's a great news, Libby! Alice-Rose is a wonderful old place, and I look forward to seeing her reincarnation.'

Thank goodness for, Dad! I was thankful for his seal of approval at least.

'Well done, Libby!' he continued. 'If you ever need any help, you know where your mother and I are.' Dad put a reassuring arm around my mother and looked purposefully at her before saying, 'Isn't that right, Sarah?'

'Yes, darling,' my mother said, softening visibly. She came towards me with open arms. 'It's wonderful news and very exciting too. You won't be very far away from us if you need anything. And as Dad says, we'll help you all we can, Libby.'

'Thanks, Mum. Thanks, Dad. I knew I could rely on you two!' I said, glad that everything was finally out in the open and that I could count on my parents' unconditional support as well as their love. Once I had them on board, all I had to do was get down to the business of bringing Alice-Rose back to life. That couldn't be too difficult, could it? With enough willpower and hard work, I was sure that I could achieve my goal and enjoy the adventure as it unfolded. And get to work I did, the very next day!

It was by then the eleventh of November, and I wanted to get as much work started around the place as was possible before people began winding down for Christmas. I, for one, would be very busy in the run-up to the holidays so that I needed to get the ball rolling without delay.

My first port of call was a local firm of tree surgeons. My brief tour of Alice-Rose had opened my eyes to the scale of her neglect, and I had some immediate concerns for the preservation of some of the estate's older trees. There was also a good deal of ground clearance to be done as well as bloodstock fencing to be repaired and replaced. I arranged to meet Dougie Power from 'Ballyedmond Tree Surgeons' in the afternoon of that first day.

Packing a light lunch and a flask of coffee, I left early so as to be able to take a quick look inside the house before Dougie arrived. Feeling the heavy bunch of keys weighty in my coat pocket, I started the old Volvo and headed for the rear entrance to the farm.

It was a pleasant surprise to find that the back gates still hung well on what appeared to be the original stone piers, and they swung open freely once the bolt was released. I secured them in place with two large rocks that lay to one side for that purpose before driving the Volvo up the lane, where parallel rows of deciduous trees mirrored their front avenue counterparts. Their branches were bare, but I seemed to remember that the planting included of a mixture of oak, beech, and chestnut. I drove along behind the house and straight under an archway into the farmyard.

The yard was a model example of all that a Georgian farmyard should be. The entire place was cobbled and consisted of four large blocks of stone buildings surrounding a central square. There were two lofted stable blocks and another large stone archway stood square to the one leading to the back lane. This archway, which was somewhat narrower than its comrade, led to a separate block that had always been referred to as the Coach House, and this building linked the yard to the main residence.

The Coach House consisted of three separate ground-level units. Wooden stairs-like ladders stood in one corner of each compartment and all led to one enormous attic space that ran the entire length of the block. This space had been traditionally used to store hay, and in his day, Michael Stevens had used the compartments below to store grain, anthracite and timber respectively.

I had many fond memories of Michael sending me to the 'grain room' to fetch a bucket of oats and bran for his favourite brood mare. The grains were kept in enormous wooden bins that were equipped with heavy hinged lids to keep rats and mice from helping themselves to the contents, and I often had to remind Michael of the fact that I was still only a child when more often than not I would run to the store only to find the lids firmly shut. Michael would invariably laugh before making some little joke or other about my needing to eat more 'hairy bacon' in order to build up my muscles. As a child, I never grew tired of his yarns.

I smiled to myself, recalling the memory. Michael had been more like a grandfather to me than anything else. Yes, I was home; I had finally come home. For some inexplicable reason, this place was in my heart. It was part of my past, and I had always felt a very strong sense of belonging here.

Pushing through the large gates under the archway, gates that safeguarded the house from the potential hazards of the yard, I made my way forwards, passing the large stone Coach House on my right. Those buildings were all empty then, but I paused to admire the splendour of the stonework and that of the structure's form.

I wondered briefly about repurposing the two smaller compartments and considered the possibility of converting them into living spaces with a view to renting them out to artists or poets for a nominal fee. Having others around would certainly liven up the place as well as diminish any feelings of isolation that I might encounter living in the big house on my own. With the idea of Alice-Rose as an artist's retreat taking shape in my imagination, I continued on my way towards the house.

There were three entrances to the residence: one of these was the front door leading to the main entrance hall. A side door led to the pantry and was accessed through a lean-to glasshouse that ran at the back of the Coach House. This door gave access to the house from the walled garden beyond.

The back door, the most important entryway to the house as far as I was concerned, was sheltered by a sizeable conservatory, and it was upon this that I gazed before entering the house for the first time in years. I hadn't entered the house with Dan Bryant; I had wanted to be alone for the most important part of the tour.

The conservatory, like the rest of the house's woodwork, was bearing signs of prolonged neglect, but that didn't worry me unduly. I knew that with enough time and effort, and let's not forget cold hard cash; all these things could be put right.

Letting myself into the conservatory, I stepped through a portal and was transported back to another time. Its floor consisted of the same cracked cement that had existed in my childhood, and the three limestone steps leading up to the back door were as rounded and as polished as I had remembered. I felt my heart swell with an all-consuming love for the place.

I hurried to unlock the partly glazed double doors at the top of the steps, trying to peer inside as I struggled with the lock. The glass was grimy, and I couldn't see through the gloom that prevailed within. Finally, releasing the lock, I stepped inside, and with a feeling of great expectation, I flicked the switch on the inside wall. Nothing!

The doors leading off the back hall were closed, and even with the back door open behind me, there was barely enough light filtering through to allow me to edge forward. I rebuked myself for having forgotten to bring a torch with me before pressing onwards, carefully inching my way towards the pantry door before using my full weight to force it open.

This made a small difference, but the back hall was still in relative darkness. Despite its considerable age, it had never been a dark house, and that hall had not been an exception to the rule as far as I could remember. Looking around, I found the cause of the problem. The shutters on the large window beside the back door were closed, and it soon became apparent that any windows in the house that could be curtained or shuttered, had been. I needed to let some light in.

The scarcity of sunlight, combined with the absence of heating, had left a permeating chill that didn't reflect the true sunny nature of the house. I struggled to release the shutters and, in doing so, succeeded in dramatically changing the atmosphere. The back hall was transformed from a room of gloom into a threshold of promise.

Standing in the hallway with the sunlight streaming in, I was able to look around properly for the first time. The slate floor was covered in a layer of dust and grime, and cobwebs hung liberally from every surface. Michael Steven's old boot box stood beneath the coat rail on the left, and I was surprised to see that the mahogany box, where he had kept his clothes brush, still hung on the wall opposite, its mottled mirror dusty and smudged. I lifted the hinged lid and found the brush; its polished oak and the horsehair bristle were in near perfect condition and had obviously lain there undisturbed since Michael's death.

Next, I made my way towards the large sliding door that led into the kitchen, and I found that it was almost fully closed. With no small amount of effort, I managed to slide it back just enough to allow me to squeeze through. I remembered that the door had always been troublesome and very noisy, but despite these obvious drawbacks, Michael had never seen fit to replace it; he had simply accepted them as being part of the house's character. I decided there and then that the sliding door would have to stay, albeit in a more user-friendly form.

Although it was only a very small one, nonetheless, I had made my first decision regarding Alice-Rose, and it felt good. I could only hope that the rest of my decisions regarding the old girl would be that easy. Standing in the huge kitchen, the winter sunshine filtering dimly through the filthy windowpanes, I sent a silent prayer to Michael Stevens, and to the universe afar, for guidance. And it appeared that Michael Stevens and the universe were in fact listening! No sooner had I uttered my supplication, than I caught a glimpse of something scurrying to my right. The message was loud and clear: I needed to implement some form of vermin control!

'Thanks, Michael!' I said, my laughter conclusively breaking the incessant silence that had, in later years, descended upon the house.

Looking around me, it wasn't difficult to see one potential contributing factor to the rodent problem. The kitchen sink was a mess of unwashed crockery, and kitchenware lay scattered around the countertops of the outmoded 1970s style units. George Baxter was obviously not the sort of man who cared about what other people thought of his housekeeping skills!

A time-worn AGA remained in place, central to the capacious room, but apart from it and the kitchen units, the room was bare. Two unadorned light bulbs dangled precariously from age-old lengths of electrical cord, and large sash windows, heavy with dust and a decade of grime, hung bravely in place as if awaiting rescue.

I crossed the room, making my way to the wall accommodating one of the kitchen's three windows. Using the sleeve of my coat, I cleared a small circle in the glass and gazed out into the walled garden. It was overgrown and forgotten. The series of lean-to glasshouses were on the verge of collapse, with much of the glass either entirely missing or cracked beyond repair. Once the work on the main house was underway, I would see about turning my attention to them; there was clearly no time to loose!

Turning back into the room, I noticed for the first time that the telltale signs of my unwanted visitors were in evidence everywhere! I could only hope that the droppings were that of mice and not of rats. I decided to go outside and call pest control before continuing my tour.

Returning to the kitchen a short time later, I proceeded on through to the sitting room where, unsurprisingly, I found the heavy velvet curtains drawn firmly closed. I flicked the light switch, but again nothing happened. It finally occurred to me that, of course, the electricity supply had been cut off and that getting electricity reconnected to the house was another matter that required my immediate attention. Shuffling my way carefully across the floor, I came to the first set of curtains and gingerly drew them back across the supporting brass pole, an action that I almost regretted. The cloud of dust that enveloped me was like nothing I had ever experienced before!

The vista from this window was shared by the kitchen windows that didn't look directly into the walled garden. Before me lay the remains of a broad gravelled path, now suffocated by weeds and the overspilling grass of the expansive lawn that hugged two sides of the house. I gazed beyond the gardens, up to 'the mighty hill' crowned by a tight four-strong ring of mature Scots pines. The Scots pine was my favourite tree, and it was my belief that the scene that sprawled before me rivalled all others. I knew that I had never seen one that I liked better! I released a long and contented sigh before returning my attention to the room.

The sitting room, like the kitchen, was largely empty except for the fireplace and the curtains. The floorboards were laid bare, and the large slate fireplace was in desperate need of a polish and the glow of a fire in its hearth. That which had been a charming feature of the room was now a mess of ash and the branches of a crow's nest that had fallen through and scattered on to the floor. The décor, that had once been cosy and welcoming, looked drab in the unforgiving sunlight; the abandoned bareness of the room accentuated the tattered wallpaper and the yellowing paintwork. Alice-Rose had lain empty for far too long.

I left the sitting room and crossed the wide front hall to the room that Michael had always referred to as the drawing room. It was a grand title for a grand room, and I had plans that befitted its potential splendour! I was in the process of opening the shutters there when the silence was broken by the ringing of my mobile phone; Dougie Power had arrived and was parked in the yard. I cut my tour of the house short and went to meet Dougie outside.

I had never met Dougie Power before that day, and the first thing that struck me when I saw him was his size. If ever a man suited his job description, he did! Dougie Power was a *tree* of a man, all six foot something of him, and built like a giant oak to boot! Even his name suited him; he did indeed look Powerful! I felt positively small in his presence and marvelled at the fact that I didn't recognise him from the area; he wasn't exactly the kind of man that one could easily forget!

During the course of our introductions, I learnt that Dougie was relatively new to the area. He and his Irish wife had made the recent move back from Inverness in order to take over the tree surgery business from his soon-to-be-retired father-in-law. Dougie had been working as a parkland manager in Northern Scotland and so was well qualified to take over the work.

Having acquainted each other with the essentials of our mutual circumstances, we decided to walk the estate in order to get an idea of the scale of the work required to get Alice-Rose looking her best again. Dougie had an easy manner, and the rest of the afternoon passed very quickly. He was a fountain of knowledge when it came to forestry and horticulture, and I felt reassured that I had happened upon the right man for the job.

By the end of our farm walk, it was clear that work on the land would be ongoing for the foreseeable future. By all accounts, the estate had been totally neglected since Michael's death, and it would take no small amount of effort to put it right. Night was falling by the time we made it back to our vehicles. Without an electricity supply, it was pointless to attempt any further exploration, and so I followed Dougie Power's jeep out the back lane and headed for home.

I hadn't thought about Dan Bryant at all that day; my mind had been full of plans for Alice-Rose. However, when I got back to Willow Cottage, there were several messages on the landline, and one of them was from Dan. Although he would love to get my opinion on his farm cottage and yard, 'unfortunately' he found himself snowed under by previous commitments! He requested a rain check and hoped that we would meet up 'sometime'. I presumed that that was his way of saying, 'See you around'.

Getting the brush-off from Dan didn't leave me feeling as disappointed as I might have imagined. After all, I was pretty busy myself! I thought about Dan Bryant as I got to task with lighting the fire in the sitting room, and I considered all the facts as I sat at the kitchen table, relishing every mouthful of a hot meal after a day spent in the cold. By the time it came to settling down by the blazing fire for the night, I had managed to convince myself that I was in fact relieved not to be meeting up with Dan Bryant anytime soon.

There was plenty of time to meet someone new if, in fact, that was what I wanted. What had I been thinking of anyway, falling for the first handsome face that had come along since Max? Or for that matter a man who was old enough to be my father? I put it down to a hormonal imbalance, a sudden rush of blood to the brain, or some other such nonsense. There was a mountain of work to get through before Christmas, and I didn't need *any* distractions, least of all that of a new man on the scene. Emma and Mark's engagement party would be distraction enough!

I spent a good deal of the remainder of that week in the pursuit of business and that included updating my website. Paula Nolan, who had designed and managed my website from its inception, was based in Dublin and was a joy to work with. Had I not been preoccupied with so many other things, I would have thoroughly enjoyed the exercise. I usually stayed over in the city on these occasions, taking the opportunity to meet up with friends in the evenings for dinner. However, once I had Alice-Rose to think about, I was anxious to finish up as quickly as possible and get back on the road to Ballyedmond without delay.

Three days' worth of work was squashed into two, and the end result was a little short of the perfection that I usually insisted upon. However, I wasn't unduly concerned, and I trusted Paula to tie up the loose ends. The pictures I had taken in the States had turned out well, and I was certain that the dimensions stated for each piece of furniture were accurate. As long as the customers could get a good idea of what each piece looked like and could reliably measure their spaces for fit, then the rest was window dressing.

Thursday was spent in the company of a building surveyor, who was a long-standing friend of my parents. While Jimmy Lynch himself was entertaining company, it was the fact that he had only good things to say about Alice-Rose that I found particularly gratifying.

The roof 'considering its age' appeared to be in quite good order and had provided the house with substantial protection through 'the neglected years'. However, Jimmy believed that the building would benefit in the long term by having the roofing timbers replaced, while the existing slates could be reused along with replacement slates where necessary. Although replacing the timbers wasn't the end of the world, neither was it ideal. Besides the extra work and expense involved, I was concerned that it would make starting the renovation weather dependent.

On a brighter note, there was no dry rot, which meant that all the original flooring and woodwork throughout the house was in excellent condition despite it having remained unoccupied for more than ten years. There was rising damp in one corner of the sitting room that would need attention, and it was no surprise that the house required a new heating system as well as rewiring, but everything else was cosmetic as far as the engineer could see. Inspection of the farm's outbuildings revealed a similar story: they were all structurally sound but would benefit from some maintenance work. Overall, the news was very good, and it was a relief to know that I hadn't taken ownership of a money pit.

The next day was Friday, and I spent the morning returning customer calls. Friday afternoons were usually set aside for order collections, and that one was no exception. As it happened, it turned out to be a particularly hectic one, and I didn't have Mum on hand to take inventory with me. Mum usually helped out if she was free, but she was having her hair highlighted for Emma's engagement party the following night so that I was reduced on that occasion to a one-woman show.

Consequently, I fell in the door at eight o'clock that evening with nothing on my mind except a hot bath and a large glass of whatever came easiest to hand! I wondered vaguely about the state of my own hair and came to the conclusion that whatever I managed to do with it myself the following evening would have to suffice!

Throwing my coat at the nearest hook on the hallstand and missing my target by a long shot, I left it where it lay and headed for the kitchen, where the phone had started to ring. In my haste to answer the call, I almost gave myself a partial appendectomy on the corner of the island unit and cursed long and loud before picking up the receiver to Jules.

Jules was checking on the time of Emma and Mark's party and wondered if I wouldn't mind making my own way there as she had decided to take Noel Kinsella!

'I'm sorry, Libby, but you know what they say,' she said without a hint of apology, 'three *is* a crowd!' I was too tired to care.

'Cheers!' I said to myself, opening the fridge and lifting what was left of a bottle of wine from the door. Jules was nothing if not honest, and the past had taught me that Jules could never be relied upon to stick to a plan. As it happened, I was just as happy to travel to the party on my own. I wanted to get back to Ballyedmond early on Sunday by direct route and not via some vague 'scenic route' that happened to take Jules's last-minute fancy! The fact that she had decided to bring Noel Kinsella to the engagement party had, however, come as somewhat of a surprise because it was most unlike Jules to bring an apple to an orchard!

Judging by her past performances where men were concerned, I would have expected her to leave Noel at home, simmering on the back burner, none the wiser to the fact that she was attending a party! Her usual modus operandi was to fob off any new boyfriend with the excuse of visiting her sick grandmother while she attended some social event or other alone, checking out the potential talent as she went. The fact that her grandmother enjoyed rude good health was of little consequence, very few boyfriends ever made it as far as meeting the woman! So the fact that Jules was bringing the most unlikely of boyfriends to 'the engagement party of the year' was indeed noteworthy!

Saturday dawned clear and sunny. Feeling fresh and rested after a dreamless sleep, I decided to make an effort with my appearance, after all. I phoned 'Hair Flair' in Ballyedmond to see if any of the girls were free to give a quick trim and up-style to my neglected locks. One of the girls happened to have a four o'clock cancellation, which suited me perfectly and gave me plenty of time to shop for a new outfit in some of the town's fine boutiques.

When it came to shopping for clothes in Ballyedmond, I favoured 'Tina's House of Fashion', which always stocked the latest styles along with some timeless classics. 'Tina' was a former classmate, and although he was christened Martin, he was known as Tina to everyone except his mother. While Tina had no transsexual tendencies, he was unapologetically gay and was the most entertaining by far of our circle of friends. In addition to the obvious inducements to shop with him, Tina always gave us a healthy discount, and he sold cutting-edge accessories and shoes!

Luck turned out to be 'a lady' that day because the first dress that I tried on fitted me perfectly and suited the occasion to a tee! It was a simple slash-neck mini with long bell sleeves, and the fabric was a pale shimmering gold that was heavy enough to allow it to hang flawlessly. The edge of the sleeves and the hem of the dress were trimmed with a thick band of brocade, and Tina coordinated the outfit with sheer stockings and gladiator-style shoes. Elaborate hoop earrings completed the look.

I left the shop upbeat and feeling entirely more prepared to enjoy Emma and Mark's party than I had at any time during the previous week. Later that evening, with my hair piled elaborately on top of my head and wearing my Tina-inspired outfit, I slipped into my long fur coat and headed for Dublin.

CHAPTER 15

Twosomes

I ARRIVED OUTSIDE MARK'S house that evening to find that it was lit up like Central Park at Christmas, with an abundance of fairy lights twinkling in the trees on either side of the path leading up to the large Georgian front door. The house dated back to 1810, and it had been close to derelict when he bought it at auction five years previously. I had to admit that Mark had done a superb job when he undertook its renovation, and undaunted, he had transformed it from a rat-infested dump into a home fit to be featured in the summer edition of that year's *Irish Architectural Monthly*.

I pressed the porcelain button at the centre of the brass doorbell and was surprised to find that I was actually looking forward to the night in spite of the fact that it symbolised the sealing of Emma's fate to a lifetime of pretension and social climbing. I had hardly pressed the bell when the door swung open to reveal a harassed-looking Mark, who certainly wasn't looking his usual calm and 'totally-in-control' self. That being said, his recovery was amazing! When he saw that it was me, his future sister-in-law standing in the doorway, he managed to effuse an extravagant, yet distracted, welcome in my direction as he glanced over my shoulder and hurried me into the hallway before quickly closing the door. He took the bottle I was holding and placed it without a glance or a 'thank you' on a table with a number of others.

It never ceased to amaze me how Mark and I, although never openly expressing our mutual disregard for one another, still managed to convey it quite plainly under a thin veil of social politeness. As Mark tried to hurry me out of my coat, I got the distinct impression that there was somewhere else that he desperately needed to be. Some perverse sense of wickedness directed me to delay my divestment, if only to witness Mark's predictable frustration. When he eventually wrestled the coat from my unyielding frame, I cautioned him to put it somewhere safe, giving him a conspiratorial wink before making my way towards the kitchen.

Turning back mid-stride to lift a glass of champagne from a tray on the hall table, I noticed Mark surreptitiously studying the label on the inside of my coat before making his way upstairs with it. I couldn't help but smile. For all his airs and graces, Mark probably wouldn't know fake fur from the real thing!

The party was getting into full swing in the kitchen, and I was pleased to see that quite a few 'blasts' from Emma's past were in attendance. I saw this as being a hopeful sign that Emma hadn't turned her back on everything that was good in her life. Mingling in the crowd, I was quickly reminded of how decent and likeable Emma's 'old friends' were.

A bunch of them were congregated near the patio doors, and I joined the group with a quick 'remember me?' All of them were gracious enough to at least pretend that they did, even though there was at least one girl that I couldn't remember ever having met before! We chatted amicably for a while before I excused myself to show my face to the girl of the evening, Emma.

I found Emma at the centre of some people that I didn't know. She was wearing yellow and looked radiant in a beautifully cut dress that complemented her slender frame and colouring to perfection. Although she was deep in conversation, I managed to catch her eye just to let her know that I was there but not expecting her to interrupt what she was doing. However, Emma immediately excused herself from the group, hurrying across the room to greet me as if I was the one person that she had been waiting for.

I found myself absurdly gratified by that small act of acknowledgement and wondered, not for the first time, where we had gone wrong. If memory served me well, Emma and I started drifting apart around the time that she first started seeing Mark. However, their meeting and subsequent relationship had coincided rather closely with Max's death so that I couldn't be sure which incident had actually precipitated the increasing emotional distance between us. I suspected that neither had helped.

Emma found the love of her life just as I was about to lose mine. Her awkwardness under the circumstances had never quite left her, although for my part I had never borne her any grudge. To be honest, the fact that Emma had met somebody had, at the time, largely passed me by. I was far too engrossed in the highs and lows, and the pressing practicalities of my own situation, to notice or even care about anybody else's! When I did eventually emerge from the all-consuming, self-centring fog of my grief, and had Emma's choice been wiser, I am certain that I would have taken comfort from her happiness despite the devastation of my own.

She stood before me that night, radiantly happy and completely at ease in her role as the soon-to-be Mrs Mark Waldron. The thought sent a sudden shiver of dread down my spine; it was as if someone had walked across my grave. I was being ridiculous. Okay, so Mark wasn't my cup of tea, but he wasn't exactly the 'Yorkshire Ripper' either!

'Emma, you look absolutely beautiful,' I told her, trying to shake off my sense of foreboding. 'I'm so happy for you!' I bleated, resolving to be more positive about their union.

I handed Emma the carefully wrapped present that I was still holding. Suddenly, Mark was by her side, and I had to admit that they did make a very handsome pair. Then Mark opened his mouth, and I was reminded that looks weren't everything.

'Well, Libby, what *did* you bring us?' Mark asked in a deliberate tone. 'Some small trinket from your travels, no doubt!'

He laughed and took the unopened package from Emma's hands. Emma blushed deeply and looked acutely embarrassed. This was a breakthrough. I had never seen Emma react to any of Mark's displays of bad manners before then. There was a glimmer of hope, a chink of light in the darkness. I felt joy.

Without further ado, Mark ripped open their engagement present and gave it more than a cursory glance. You could sense his mind working overtime as he examined the antique silver frame. How much was it worth?

'Oh, Libby, it's wonderful! You have such good taste!' beamed Emma. 'We will treasure it. Thank you!' My sister gave me one of her old 'Emma-esque' bear hugs and bestowed upon me a kiss of such affection that I immediately wanted to yell out, 'He's not good enough for you!'

'Yes. Yes, it's wonderful, Libby,' Mark grudgingly agreed. 'Can I get you something to drink?'

'A glass of Chablis would be lovely, thanks, Mark,' I replied, forcing myself to use the name that he had been christened with and not one of my own choosing!

While Mark went off in search of the wine, I noted the rest of our family's absence.

'I was sure I would be the last one to arrive,' I said to Emma. 'It took me ages to get the car going,' I explained, continuing to search the crowd.

'Mum rang,' Emma said, reading my thoughts. 'Apparently Dad got a flat tyre just outside Ballyedmond.' We both laughed at this.

Poor Dad, it could only happen to him! Our father was an erratic driver who preferred to gaze out over 'another beautiful field' than on the road ahead. This lead to a lot of punctured tyres for our darling father as he seldom managed to avoid the numerous potholes that lay in wait for him around the country roads of North Wexford. For the most part, he accepted his motoring misfortunes with good grace, but we both knew that Dad would be unimpressed with having to change a tyre on Mum's 'newfangled contraption'.

'Luckily, Philip and Amanda were following behind them and they stopped to help,' Emma said sympathetically. 'Oh, and Tony is coming tonight, and he's bringing a date!' she added with raised eyebrows.

'Oh,' I said, 'a date? An actual date? Wonders will never cease!'

Our younger brother Tony had never introduced us to a girlfriend, although we suspected that there were many! Gifted with a brilliant mind and looks to match, our brother grabbed life with both hands and lived it to the full. It would be fascinating to finally see what type of girl our brother was attracted to.

Sisterly bias aside, Tony Finn was as handsome a guy as anyone was ever likely to meet; he was tall and good looking in a 'fine man' kind of way. He had an infectious laugh and a very definite twinkle in his big brown eyes! All in all, it was safe to assume that Dr Tony Finn was probably the talk of Beaumont Hospital, at least as far as the unattached female cohort went. I imagined that he would probably roll up with some stereotypical leggy blonde.

A sudden commotion of excitement at the front door led us out into the hall to greet the tardy arrival of the rest of our family. Coincidentally, every outstanding member of the Finn clan arrived at the same time, congregating en masse in the hallway and talking over each other in their relief at having finally reached their destination. A short while later, Dad and Philip made their excuses and went to wash the grime of their labours off their hands.

With apologies for lateness and congratulations out of the way, we were finally able to regard the vision that had accompanied Tony to the party. Her name was Dr Dolly Twaddle, and I liked her on sight!

'I know, I know,' she laughed, as Tony proudly introduced us to his date. 'Deed poll was created for just such a name as mine!'

No doubt, ours were not the first ill-concealed smirks of amusement that she had encountered at the mention of her name. While we were all surprised at first by its comical sound, we were far more surprised when Tony leant in close and, without any pretence at humour, growled passionately into her ear, 'Why bother with deed poll when there are far easier ways of changing one's name!'

Dolly giggled like a schoolgirl with a crush and poked Tony playfully in the ribs; it was like a scene from *Carry on Doctor*.

Dr Dolly Twaddle was nothing like we had ever, or could ever, have imagined Tony's type to be. Emma and I admitted to each other later that we had expected Tony to bring along some intellectually dim, statuesque socialite. Ms Twaddle was neither. Standing five foot one or two at most, and definitely erring on the cuddly side, she was by far the shortest person at the party. Tony, on the other hand, was probably a foot taller than most!

However, what Dolly lacked in height she made up for in personality, and it didn't take us long to realise that Tony was on to a winner with this girl. Her genuine warmth, mixed with a fine academic mind, drew people to her. As the night wore on, it became clear that hers was a face that shone brighter and lovelier than most, and her mane of thick blonde hair, that was twisted into a long inverted plait, was the envy of every woman present. It was obvious that Tony was besotted with Dolly and that the lovely Dr Twaddle had herself fallen for his charms. We all liked her immensely and crossed our fingers that she might indeed be The One for him.

As the night wore on and I observed one happy couple after another, I found myself wishing that Dan was there. Jules, who had arrived later in the evening with Noel, read my thoughts perfectly.

'Dan, Dan, wherefore art thou Dan?' she whispered in my ear, handing me another glass of wine.

'Am I that obvious?' I complained quietly.

'Only to me, darling,' she said softly. 'After all, who else knows your dirty little secret?'

I gave her my best glare. She remained irritatingly unfazed.

'What you need, Libby, is to get back in the saddle, so to speak, with someone your own age.' She indicated the room full of eligible 'young things' with a discreet nod of her beautifully coiffured head. I groaned despairingly. *My* heart wasn't calling out to the masses, just to one man, one elusive man.

But Jules was right, and I had to admit it. There was no point thinking about Dan Bryant that night or any other night for that matter. Anything that had happened between Dan and me had happened in my head, and that was no use at all. I was in a house full of possibilities, and one never knew what a night could bring. I turned around to acknowledge the wisdom of Jules's advice and instead found myself face-to-face with my childhood sweetheart! How in the name of all that was good had he come to be there?

'Hello, Libby,' said the quiet gentle voice that belonged to another time. 'Jules just went to get herself a refill.'

'Peter Cunningham!' I said, finding my voice and realising that the man at the party, whose identity I had been vaguely trying to place, was none other than a boy I had gone to school with. Peter was smiling broadly, and we hugged as old friends do.

'You're all grown-up!' I said, finding myself somehow surprised that the passing of time had wrought so many changes in him. 'I thought you looked familiar, but I couldn't place you in this setting,' I babbled. 'You look great!'

The wine was obviously taking effect. Even as I spoke, I realised that I was being too incredulous to be wholly complementary. My astonishment implied that he hadn't always looked so good. He didn't speak, and the silence between us prompted me to go on.

'How are you?' I asked.

'Not as good as you look, Libby, if that's not too smarmy an answer?' he added quickly, blushing at his own impertinence.

'Smarm away, Peter!' I said laughing. 'You'd be surprised how little smarminess I get these days!' We regarded each other fondly before Peter recovered himself, saying, 'I was so sorry to hear about your husband, Libby.'

'Thanks, Peter,' I replied simply. There was nothing else to say. I had practised all sorts of replies to this sentiment over the years, but nothing sounded any better than a simple 'thank you'.

The two of us fell into easy conversation. The awkwardness that my 'situation' presented to most men did not seem to daunt Peter. He had heard about my marriage, and in turn about Max's death, through the grapevine. I, on the other hand, had somehow managed to remain totally unaware of events in his life since his family's emigration years before.

Peter's father had accepted a job in New York, just after Peter left school, and Peter was now working alongside him as a financial adviser. He had been invited to the party by Mark, whom he had only just met that day. Their connection was purely business. My curiosity was aroused as to why my future brother-in-law was in need of a financial adviser. After all, I thought doling out financial advice was *his* line of business.

Despite being intrigued as to what Mark and Peter's business dealings could possibly entail, I forced myself to feign indifference. Peter, for his part, was far more interested in talking about the old days, than he was in talking shop.

'It really is a small world!' I said, and immediately hated myself for rolling out the tired old platitude.

'Mark is marrying my baby sister, Emma,' I explained, checking his expression for any telltale signs of concern regarding that particular union. It was entirely possible that Peter knew something about Mark that the rest of us didn't. I could have sworn, but not on a bible, that he looked slightly uncomfortable as he absorbed the information, but then I could just have been reading into something that wasn't really there.

'I see' was his only response.

Peter had been two years ahead of me in school, and it had taken me completely by surprise when he invited me to his graduation dance. I remembered that I had been the envy of every girl in the school, including Jules! Not only was Peter Cunningham the head boy that year, but he was also an all-round nice guy, not to mention being very easy on the eye!

After Peter's graduation, we dated over the summer as best we could. Our relationship consisted of a couple of trips to the local cinema and countless stolen kisses on the avenue leading to our house. However, the fact remained that I was still only fifteen, and my parents were none too pleased about their daughter going out with an 'older man'. I wondered if they would feel any differently now that I was all grown-up. Peter had only been two years older than me and that had been bad enough. The age gap between Dan and I was considerably more! Somehow, I didn't fancy Dan's chances of winning my parents' seal of approval. I smiled, nonetheless, at the memory of our summer romance, and it was as if Peter read my mind.

'Ah, Libby, Libby, sweet fifteen and oh-so kissable . . .,' he murmured. 'You broke my heart. I hope you know.'

'You broke mine too,' I conceded, suddenly remembering the pain of first love.

Our trip down memory lane was interrupted by the arrival of Jules and Noel, who were actively trying to avoid the dance floor, and I was glad to

CAITRÍONA LESLIE

finally get a chance to meet them as a couple. Although I had met Noel before on a handful of occasions, I didn't really know him. It transpired that although Noel was quiet, he was not shy. I got the distinct impression of a man who knew his own mind and of one who was capable of handling Jules.

The party continued well into the early hours of the morning and ended with an exchange of phone numbers between Peter and myself and a promise to meet up before his return to New York. The deal was sealed with the briefest touch of our lips.

I left for Ballyedmond after brunch the following day minus my fur coat, which had mysteriously disappeared during the course of the night. I was upset by this because it wasn't the type of coat that could be easily mistaken for another. To add to the mystery, there wasn't another coat left behind in its stead, which lead me to suspect that a deliberate act of theft had taken place.

Ordinarily, I wouldn't have given the coat a second thought, but that particular coat was of huge sentimental value. Max had bought it for me in Macy's on Fifth Avenue during our last trip to New York, and now it was gone! I would have cried had I not seen the distress on Emma's face as she made the connection.

'Not to worry,' I said quickly. 'It's only a coat, after all!' Emma looked slightly less anguished, while Mark appeared to remain totally unmoved.

'Thanks again, you two, for a wonderful evening,' I said, ignoring the temptation to wipe the beginnings of a smirk off Mark's dough-like face. 'See you in Ballyedmond.' And then I left, hurrying down the garden path as if the devil himself was on my tail.

I waited until I had reached the privacy of my car before I burst into tears of sheer frustration and acknowledged the familiar sense of loss.

'For God's sake Max, did the coat *really* have to go?' I cried between gritted teeth, turning my anger on the only person that I knew would truly understand. And, of course, I also knew what his reply would have been—'Libby, it's only a coat!'

Playing his response in my head, I felt better and I slowly turned the key in the ignition. The car spluttered into life, and I faced it for home, letting the coat slip further and further away from me as I drove to the sound of Van Morison's 'Brown Eyed Girl'.

CHAPTER 16

Sometimes a Brave Heart Loses a Fair Lady

I REACHED HOME LATE that afternoon after leaving Emma and Mark standing together on their doorstep. The message-minder light was flashing on the phone in the kitchen. I dared to hope that there was a message from Dan. There was no message from Dan, but there was one from Peter Cunningham. He was returning to the States sooner than expected, and he was wondering if I would be free to meet him for dinner the following evening.

My frustration at never having received another message from Dan led me to jump at his invitation. After all, it wasn't as if I had a bevy of eligible bachelors vying for my attention. I rang him back immediately, and we arranged to meet in the bar of the Donnard Arms the following evening at seven.

I arrived in town the next evening fashionably late for my date with Peter. The church clock across the street from the hotel indicated five minutes past seven as I stepped out of the taxi. Peter was staying at the hotel and had asked if I could recommend a good restaurant in the area. I told him that I would take care of that end of things, and I had booked The Silver Olive for eight o'clock.

The Silver Olive was an outstanding Italian restaurant co-joining, and owned by, the hotel. Had it been the weekend, I would have been lucky to secure a reservation at such short notice. However, it being a Monday night, there had been no problem booking a table.

Entering the bar of the hotel, I could see that Peter was already seated at the counter. He had positioned himself so that he was facing the door, and he immediately rose to his feet as I entered. Peter was coolly handsome and well turned out in designer jeans and a tailored shirt. A jacket hung casually over the back of his bar stool.

Taking my hands in his, he kissed me warmly on both cheeks and complimented me on my appearance. After placing a drinks order with the barman, we seated ourselves at a small table beside a brightly blazing fire on the other side of the room.

Peter, by all accounts, was everything a girl could ask for. He was tall and handsome, and he was punctual. I speculated as to whether or not my desire for him could be reawakened as the dry martini slipped easily down my throat. I hoped so. *Maybe Peter wouldn't need that hotel room, after all*, I mused as I observed him sitting attentively before me.

I was very glad that I had made an effort to get dressed up for the occasion, and I felt reassuringly confident in my figure-hugging knee-length dress and stilettos. Jules was right; it was 'high time' that I got back in the saddle with someone my own age! Besides, I didn't think a little harmless flirting could hurt anyone, and I decided to allow myself to indulge in the long forgotten pastime.

Less than an hour later, it was as if a needle was being roughly scratched across the record that was playing in my head. Upon entering The Silver Olive, I was dismayed to find that Dan Bryant was already seated in the restaurant and with a beautiful woman into the bargain! My impulse was to retreat back to where we had come from and to order bar food instead. But any attempt at an escape was futile.

Henry, our maître de for the evening, took immediate charge of the situation and guided us without preamble towards our table. In doing so, he lead us in the direction of Dan and his companion who happened to look up just as we approached. I had little option but to stop and say hello.

Dan was friendly and charming as was his companion. The woman's name was Hazel. She seemed irritatingly at ease in Dan's company, and I was ill-prepared for the feelings of absolute hostility that arose within me towards her. I wanted the ground to open up and swallow me when I realised that any feelings that I might still have had for Peter paled into insignificance when compared to the feelings that this middle-aged man could awaken in me. Regaining my composure, I introduced Peter to the couple.

Dan made the connection between Peter and Ballyedmond immediately, and he admitted quite openly that he had gone to school with Peter's father! I wished he hadn't because I took it to imply that he wasn't remotely interested in impressing me romantically! For my part, I didn't care if Dan had gone to school with Peter's grandfather; he was still, by far, the most attractive man I had met in years!

Wishing them an enjoyable evening, the words nearly sticking in my throat, we excused ourselves and made our way to the table where Henry stood, patiently waiting to seat us. Fortunately, our table was well out of earshot of Dan and his companion, something for which I was very grateful. I had no interest in hearing Dan and his companion whisper sweet nothings to each other.

Although Henry had seated us at the other end of the restaurant, I was positioned in a way that afforded me a discreet view of Dan's dining companion, the lovely Hazel. Initially, I was heartened by the fact that she was probably a good deal older than me, but on reflection, I concluded that this wasn't necessarily a good thing. Between the forty-something Penny Holmes and the forty-something Hazel, I was beginning to think that Dan was only interested in the more mature woman. Was I mature? Obviously, I was not! Mooning over a man that had absolutely no interest in me when the man of any girl's dreams sat within reach was hardly the actions of a mature woman!

Upon finding myself in the same restaurant as the man of my most recent fantasies while sharing a table with a man that I realised could never compare, I wondered frantically what in the world I was going to do!

Well, first things first. I had to get through the meal and subtly recall all the flirtatious signals that I had sent Peter in the bar earlier. Unfortunately, an ingrained lack of patience in me meant that subtly didn't come naturally.

'What an idiot you've been!' I chastised myself, while frantically browsing the menu.

'Pardon?' Peter asked, glancing up from his menu. I had obviously spoken my thoughts aloud.

'Sorry, just thinking aloud,' I said vaguely, hoping that Peter would interpret my inability to stop frowning as my having a problem deciding on what to order. What had I been thinking? I had thrown all caution to the wind and behaved like a love-struck teenager whose hormones had gotten the better of her! And what's more, Peter could have taken only one meaning from my behaviour!

Yet there I was, practically in a cold sweat at the thought of what I had almost allowed myself to do. Despite the pickle that I found myself in, there was no doubting the fact that my hormones had been reawakened, and I took some comfort in that at least. Spring had come to my dormant desires, and I found myself wanting very badly to be taken to bed, but not by Peter, that much I did know! If Dan Bryant was otherwise occupied, I would have to cool my ardour until I found somebody that lit my fire with the same intensity that he undoubtedly did.

A waitress arrived to take our order, and a large jug of water was my first request, not to pour over my head, although the thought did cross my mind! To begin with, I had to lay off all alcohol; I needed a clear head to get out of the fix I had so willingly landed myself in.

'Red or white wine, Libby?' Peter asked with the exuberant air of someone who knew they were on to a good thing. I had to think fast.

'Actually, Peter, I'm afraid I'm going to have to refrain from any more alcohol,' I said, instinctively covering the wine glass that graced my side of the table. 'I have a terrible feeling that I'm developing a migraine.' I grimaced for effect.

Although my head wasn't feeling the best, I had never suffered from migraine; I presumed the pressure in my head was the direct result of guilt-induced stress. However, it's an ill wind that doesn't blow some good, and my muzzy head presented me the perfect solution to my dilemma.

I refrained from ordering the mussels in cream and garlic and chose a light salad instead; I didn't want to look like I was enjoying myself too much! Once I had thought of a plausible excuse for curtailing the evening, I relaxed somewhat and decided to exaggerate my symptoms towards the end of the meal. There was no point in allowing the evening to be completely ruined; we could at least enjoy each other's company over dinner. That was the very least that I owed him.

And that's exactly what we were doing when Hazel made her way to the loo. We had finished our starters and were deep in conversation when I noticed Hazel out of the corner of my eye. Under normal circumstances, I would have gone out of my way to give her a friendly acknowledgement, but these were not normal circumstances. Instead, I gave Peter my full and undivided attention. If I was annoyed that this woman had usurped me, she was going to be the very last one to know!

Of course, Hazel was blissfully unaware of my little charade, and on the way back from the Ladies, she deliberately detoured via our table. I had to admit that she seemed like a warm, friendly person, and under different circumstances, I probably would have liked her. Nevertheless, on this occasion, it annoyed me intensely to realise that she didn't appear to be even the least bit threatened by me. But then why would she have been? As far as she could see, I was spoken for, and not in the least bit interested in her dining companion.

Hazel didn't impose herself on us. She simply enquired as to how we had enjoyed our starters, saying how nice it had been to meet us both and wishing us an enjoyable evening before returning to her table. Dan took her reappearance as a signal to leave. He rose to his feet before helping her into her coat, and then they both left after giving us a final brief and friendly nod.

'Hazel is a very attractive woman, don't you think?' Peter commented after they had left.

'Yes, she is,' I replied grudgingly.

'Very attractive in a *Sigourney Weaver kind of way*,' he continued appreciatively. Enough already!

'I suppose she is, if you're the sort of man that likes an *alien*-type of woman,' I added, unable to stop myself.

It was totally out of character for me to behave like a bitch. In fact, I really don't have a bitchy bone in my body. I didn't like how I sounded.

'What?' Peter was clearly shocked by my tone.

'The films,' I explained. 'Sigourney Weaver made at least ten of them.'

'Oh right!' He laughed doubtfully.

'Sorry, bad joke,' I apologised. 'You're right. Hazel is a good-looking woman, and they do make a very attractive pair.'

And I had to admit that they did! Hazel was very tall and very fit looking. Her hair, which was cut short, suited her face, and she did bear a striking resemblance to the aforementioned actress. She was well-dressed in a beautifully tailored suit, and I couldn't fault the woman apart from the fact that she was stepping out with Dan. As they left the restaurant, I had noticed Dan putting a protective hand at the base of Hazel's spine, and I was reminded of the occasion when Dan had done the same to me and how intimate the simple gesture had felt.

With Dan and Hazel gone, I tried not to think about what they were doing in private. I distracted myself by digging into the Barberry Duck that had finally arrived on a bed of celeriac mash. It was predictably delicious, and I was reminded of all things delicious . . . like Dan. With the arrival of the Hazelnut Meringue, I had to remember that I was a woman with an impending migraine, and I forced myself to leave half of it behind. This did not go unnoticed by Peter or without comment from Henry, when he arrived to clear our plates.

'Everything to your satisfaction, Libby?' he enquired, gesturing towards the meringue.

'Yes, thank you, Henry. Everything was delicious, as always,' I said, feeling quite the fraud. 'I'm afraid I'm developing a migraine,' I added by way of explanation. It sounded more like a plan than a coincidence!

Henry arched his eyebrow disapprovingly, and I got the distinct feeling that he wasn't buying my explanation. However, on this occasion, much to my relief, Henry left us without further comment.

With Henry safely out of the way, I swung into action, displaying acting skills that I never knew I possessed. Within the space of fifteen minutes, I went from the picture of health to a woman transfixed by the unimaginable pain of a migraine. I had friends and acquaintances who suffered from the dreadful condition so that I was well versed with the accompanying symptoms.

It was indeed regrettable; I acknowledged to Peter, 'that tonight of all nights' I should suffer from one. And just when everything was going so well too! However, even though it was bringing our evening to a disappointingly premature end, I assured him that the only cure for a migraine was to return home to bed as quickly as possible, alone.

Peter was wonderful throughout, expressing both concern and understanding for what I was going through. I did have the decency to feel ashamed of my deception. That being said, there was nothing else for it! Peter and I were never going to work out and ending the evening this way bought me time, time to think of a way of letting him down gently.

Peter wished me a speedy recovery and promised that he would call me the next day before his flight. The briefest of kisses later, and I was safely ensconced in an awaiting taxi. I breathed an audible sigh of relief as I settled myself on the back seat for the unaccompanied journey home to Willow Cottage.

Remembering Jules's martyrdom to migraine and forgetting that I was not entirely alone, I exhaled an audible, 'Thank you, Jules!' This utterance did not go unnoticed and elicited an insightful comment from my taxi driver.

'I don't know who Jules is, but that chap *obviously* wasn't your cup of tea!'

Dan

CHAPTER 17

Bitter Pill

BY KEEPING BUSY night and day once the sale of Alice-Rose was complete, I had successfully managed to push Libby Finn to the back of my mind. In fact, I had blanked her out. My simple and naive logic had been working perfectly for a while. If I couldn't see her, then she didn't exist!

It was, therefore, more than a little frustrating to be reminded that we shared the same small town and that avoiding her would not always be possible. A lifetime had passed without us meeting, but suddenly, Libby was home to roost, and I couldn't go to my favourite restaurant without running into her.

Regular dining out featured quite high on my new game plan to keep busy at all times, at least until my 'Libbyitis' wore off. On the night in question, I happened to be enjoying a meal with one of the most entertaining women I know, my sister Hazel, when the evening took a sudden nosedive. Hazel was about to launch into an account of a play that she had recently reviewed for the *New York Times* when my concentration was shattered by the arrival of Libby Finn. That in itself was bad enough, but Libby was in the company of a good-looking man, and that made the situation close to intolerable!

Something about their body language and the way she was dressed told me that this man wasn't her brother. Libby was looking particularly appealing in a figure-hugging jade dress that showed off her figure to full advantage, and I was acutely reminded of my *fatal* attraction to her. To make matters worse, her companion was the son of a man that I had been in school with, albeit not in the same year. They looked right together, and I resigned myself yet again to the fact that metaphorically speaking, the horse that was a romance between Libby Finn and myself, had well and truly bolted!

As Libby talked enthusiastically about Peter's connection with Ballyedmond, I found my mind wandering, speculating that her lime green shawl was surely inadequate to protect her from the chill outside. It was, however, perfect for producing a substantial rise in temperature in any man in possession of a pulse!

As I watched it slide gently down her slender, beautifully toned arm, I resisted the urge to reach out and touch her creamy skin. And my thoughts didn't end there. I had to consciously will myself to reconnect with the conversation going on around me.

I was aware that I sounded a little too enthusiastic in acknowledging my acquaintance with Peter's father, but I was anxious to convey my recognition of the generation gap that existed between us. Realising that I had gone to school with the father of Libby's date was just another painful reminder of my advanced years compared to hers! When they left us, I found myself lost in thought, a fact that didn't go unnoticed by my dear sister.

'Penny for them,' Hazel said, leaning in close and gently touching my hand.

'Oh, I was just thinking of Marie,' I said brusquely, in an attempt to cover up my true thoughts.

'Ah,' she replied, and I knew that she didn't believe a word of it. If anyone was aware of the lonely nature of my marriage, it was Hazel.

A short time later, Hazel continued, 'They make a handsome couple, don't they?'

A knife plunged through my heart.

'Who do?' I said, feigning ignorance.

I knew immediately to whom she was referring, and she knew I knew.

'Libby and Peter,' she said patiently.

'Oh yes, them. I suppose they do,' I said, feigning disinterest.

'However, if you ask me . . .,' Hazel's tone was conspiratorial, 'that boy isn't going to get anywhere with the lovely Libby tonight.'

Now I was interested. Was Hazel throwing me a bone of hope?

'Really?' I said, looking up to see Hazel smiling indulgently. 'Why would you say that?'

'Because, my dear Dan, she obviously has feelings for someone else. And it wouldn't surprise me at all if that someone was you.'

I laughed a little too brightly before quickly dismissing the idea. Darling Hazel, she had always been my champion. She had seen through me and, realising my feelings for Libby, was now trying to console me. Changing the subject back to her cutting review of the Broadway play, I resisted the urge to burden her with my feelings. Our time together was precious enough; I didn't want our last evening to be spent in conjecture. And besides, we were both far too old for that. Hazel was due to fly back to Manhattan the following day. We would see each other again for New Year, and by then, all inappropriate longing for Libby Finn would be well and truly conquered.

Libby

CHAPTER 18

I Want to Be Alone

JULES CALLED BY the following day, phoning first to make sure that I wasn't busy 'entertaining' the gorgeous Mr Cunningham. I wasn't entertaining anyone, gorgeous or otherwise, so I was free for interrogation! I invited her to lunch; it gave me the perfect opportunity to test out my new recipe for apple and raspberry crisp! Jules was a sucker for all things sweet, so she was an excellent dessert critic.

I decided to start lunch with baked bruschetta, topped with a mixture of sun-dried tomatoes, goat's cheese, basil, and rocket. I would follow this with a dish of blue cheese and baked walnut risotto. Jules loved her cheeses, and I was really looking forward to having a good old natter with her. We hadn't had a chance to talk properly since the night of the Hallowe'en Ball, and a lot had happened since then.

Jules arrived looking the picture of consummate professionalism in a three-piece suit, complete with the requisite six-inch heels. Her hair and make-up was flawless, as always. Jules didn't do casual, at least not at my level. I felt a tad on the slovenly side with my long-sleeved grey T-shirt, turned-up skinny jeans, and converse trainers. A well-worn, but clean, striped apron completed the look.

I could tell the minute Jules arrived that her schedule had changed since our phone conversation. Her opening line was 'I've got exactly forty minutes, so spill!'

'Okay then,' I said, drawing in a deep breath before taking a run at a summary of the previous evening's events.

'All was going swimmingly well with Peter. Then we walked into 'The Olive' and came face-to-face with Dan Bryant and his date for the evening, the end!'

'Whoa! Just a minute!' exclaimed Jules. 'Rewind to the evening was going swimmingly! And what, pray tell, has Dan Bryant got to do with anything when you're dining with a dish like Peter?'

As I prepared to elaborate, Jules held up a quieting hand and removed her cell phone from her Christian Dior handbag before dialling a number.

'Hi, Niamh, Jules Mahon calling,' she intoned. 'I'm afraid I cannot make that appointment with Mr O'Leary, after all. Really, the notice was far too short, and I am extremely busy! If he would like to reschedule for another day, that would be fine. Thank you, Niamh.'

Well, I guessed that told Mr O'Leary!

'Business can wait,' she said, snapping the phone shut and reaching for the bruschetta.

This was certainly unusual! Normally, the only thing that would stop Jules in her tracks when it came to business was a splitting migraine!

'So, Libby, start at the beginning and don't leave anything out!' she demanded, settling herself down at the kitchen table.

By the time we were ready for my apple and raspberry crisp, Jules had been filled in on all the previous night's details. No iota of conversation was missed, and no detail of clothing overlooked. We even went through the previous evening's dinner and drinks menu!

Two generous helpings of fruit crisp later and I was left in no doubt as to what my dear friend made of the event and of me! The night, according to Jules, had the potential to be the perfect first date, and I had ruined it. I had a problem, a big problem!

I was mad, well and truly mad! One could not compare Dan to Peter and vice versa. I needed to get 'some sense' fast and realise that someone like Peter was far more suited to me from an age, as well as an *everything else,* point of view! Dan clearly had more sense than I had, judging by the age of his dining companion, and Jules reminded me unapologetically that Dan Bryant was little more than a fantasy that I had taken to playing in my head!

Then Jules cut straight to the chase as only she could.

'Libby, I hope the fact that you and Max were having trouble conceiving, is not the reason for all of this!' she said, without any attempt at sugar-coating.

'For all you know, the problem lay with him.' She paused to consider her words before continuing. 'I mean look at you! You are the picture of fecundity!'

I tried to interrupt at that point. As far as I knew, fecundity didn't have 'a look,' but Jules was having none of it! With a raised hand, she stopped my protestations and continued, 'And yet here you are, deliberately sabotaging the chance of a future with a wonderful man!' Jules was in full flight now.

'And for whom?' she continued. 'A man who is old enough to be your father, and one who is probably not interested in adding to the three grown-up children that he already has!'

I didn't try to interrupt any further. It was futile. Jules's initial acceptance of my interest in Dan Bryant had been obliterated by the appearance of the younger man on the scene.

'Libby, I cannot accept that you have given up all hope of having children. You were born to be a mother, and I believe that you will be one, someday. Stop following the geriatric route, and get back on the road that is most likely to bring you to where you want to go! When Peter calls, you make a date, and you follow through the next time. Okay?'

'Okay,' I replied meekly.

It was pointless to argue with Jules when she got like this. I knew she had my best interests at heart, but *my heart* was the problem. Never did the saying 'the heart knows what the heart wants' make more sense to me than it did right then. My heart wanted Dan Bryant. Yes, he was older, and it was true that he probably wouldn't want any more children, but those things didn't seem to matter.

Changing the subject quickly, I asked Jules about herself and Noel and how things were going between them. Apparently, very well! Not only had Noel asked her to go skiing with him in the New Year, but he had also invited her to attend his friend's wedding in Italy the following April. Surprisingly, Jukes had said yes to both!

As a rule, when it came to relationships, Jules never committed to anything more than two weeks away. She dismissed my suggestion that this relationship might be different to the ones that had gone before, but a little smile playing around the corner of her eyes led me to believe otherwise.

After Jules left, I decided to take a trip over to Alice-Rose in order to see how work was progressing on the grounds. Dougie had said that he would be able to start work there that week, and I felt confident that he wouldn't let me down.

Grabbing my coat, I headed for the car. Ten minutes later, I was still sitting in it, and it hadn't moved an inch! It seemed that no amount of coaxing it was going to work this time; the car was dead, well and truly dead. I had to concede that it was time to buy myself a new one.

I returned to the house to call my mother. She was the only person I could think of who might be free to bring me car-shopping the following day. Normally, she would have been but not on that particular occasion.

'Oh, Libby, I would love to,' my mother said, sounding crestfallen, 'but I offered to take Ruth shopping for an outfit for Bridget's wedding.'

Mum was referring to Ruth Meehan, our elderly neighbour, whose grandniece was due to get married at the end of March.

'Ruth and I finally settled on tomorrow, and I can't disappoint her. I'm sorry, darling.'

'That's okay, Mum. It's a short notice, I know,' I said, wondering what my next plan of action could be. 'Not to worry, I'll think of something,' I finished, sounding far more upbeat than I felt.

'Why don't you wait until Thursday, darling, and I'll bring you then,' she soothed, and I felt all of ten years old again!

'It's okay, Mum,' I said, regaining confidence. 'I'm sure I'll think of something, and if I'm really stuck, I'll wait until then. Say hello to Ruth for me, and I'll see you tomorrow, one way or another.'

Hanging up the phone, I gazed around the kitchen absent-mindedly, trying to think of a way around my problem. There really was nobody else to call; everyone was working. I could call a taxi, but somehow that didn't appeal to me. Then the idea came to me, I would cycle into town! It shouldn't take me too long, and the exercise would do me good. I could nip around quite easily to all the garages on my trusty old bike. I felt strangely empowered and very pleased with myself.

By then, it was beginning to get dark, and there wasn't any point in cycling over to Alice-Rose. Jules was heading to the cinema with Noel, and I was having another quiet night in by the fire. This in itself was not a problem; the problem was that I was starting to enjoy my own company far too much. If I didn't do something soon, I would become known as 'the old spinster, living on the hill' or something similar and probably far less flattering! I had to start making a greater effort to connect with old friends or alternatively make some new ones.

Most of my friends from college were scattered around the world. I had a couple of close friends still living in Dublin, but they had busy lives of their own. Jules was my closest friend from home, and we had a perfect balance of contact between us. We were always there for one another, but we didn't live in each other's pockets. I didn't want that to change. There was nothing for it but to start making a greater effort to expand my social circle. While making contacts was something that I was very good at doing in business, it was something that I was sorely neglecting to do in my personal life since losing Max.

CHAPTER 19

The Geese Are Getting Fat

I CYCLED INTO TOWN the morning after the demise of my car, and I embarked on a tour of all the local garages. It proved to be a fruitless exercise as I should have known it would be. The choice of vehicles was limited to say the least! It wasn't that I was particularly fussy, but there definitely wasn't anything I liked in Ballyedmond. I would have to look further afield.

The Volvo that I had been driving up until the day before was my very first car. Dad had bought it 'for a song' ten years previously, and the old girl had served me well. Dad had chosen wisely. But regardless of this, I didn't want to rely on Dad to buy all my cars for me. I wanted to start doing things for myself, and I wanted the car to be of my own choosing. In the meantime, I had the cheek to rent a small hatchback from one of those local garages!

Three weeks and much online research later, I became the proud owner of a brand new Landrover Freelander, complete with every conceivable extra. I did feel totally spoilt and self-indulgent, but I justified the extra expense by resolving to hang on to this vehicle for at least as long as I had hung on to the last! This undertaking went some way towards easing my social conscience.

Not only did I leave the forecourt that day with a new four-wheeled drive, but the deal also came with a date thrown in for good measure! It's amazing how close you can get to a man over the course of buying a car! I know, I wouldn't have guessed it either. But there I was, about to drive away from Midland Garages forever, when Simon McQuaid cleared his throat and enquired as to whether or not I 'might be interested in going for a drink sometime?'

I was so taken aback by his proposal that I hadn't time to consider my options or come up with a plausible excuse as to why I couldn't or wouldn't be interested in a date. Simon certainly wasn't unattractive by any stretch of the imagination, and he had been perfectly pleasant in all my dealings with him. Besides, hadn't I just decided that I needed to get out more? A perfect opportunity was being presented to me on a plate, so to speak, and it would have been unreasonable and defeatist of me to refuse. Looking at Simon McQuaid through the open car window, I decided to make it my policy from then on to give everyone, within reason, a chance, and I said, 'Yes.' Besides, Jules would have killed me if I ever admitted to letting such an opportunity slip through my fingers!

It had become obvious to me of late that Jules Mahon, being the good friend that she was, did not wish for me to go on mourning indefinitely. In fact, I would have even gone so far as to say that Jules did not want to be the best friend of a widow for much longer either, not when she had found someone who just might tame her. If Jules Mahon was going to be shackled by commitment, she wanted company! Bearing all this in mind, and being the considerate friend that I am, I embarked on a series of dates with Simon McQuaid, heir apparent to the throne of Midland Garages.

Simon kept me busy enough socially in the run-up to Christmas, and on the business front, the antiques trade was brisk. Despite the economic climate, some people still had money to spend so that by Christmas Eve, the storage rooms were looking surprisingly bare. I was thankful that the fruits of my last shopping trip to the States were due for delivery early in the New Year!

Besides business and leisure, the task of returning Alice-Rose to its former glory kept me more than gainfully occupied. Dougie Power started work on the grounds as promised, and by mid December, the estate was looking like a tousle-headed little boy who had just received his first real haircut. The transformation was dramatic; Alice-Rose was beginning to look all grown-up!

The spaces between the trees lining the front and rear avenues had been completely cleared of brambles and weeds, and the trees themselves had been rendered safe by having any dead or dangerously overgrown branches cut back. Despite the lateness of the season, the lawns had been given a 'high mow', and their overgrown edges had been treated with weedkiller. Their reseeding was a definite consideration for the following year.

We hadn't taken any chances with the fruit trees in the orchard, and although they were very overgrown, Dougie had recommended waiting until the following year before beginning to gently prune their elderly boughs. The beds in the walled garden had been extensively dug and treated to a good covering of well-rotted farmyard manure from the old cow byres.

CAITRÍONA LESLIE

Dougie Power and his team had accomplished a huge amount in a short period of time, and still there was a lot left to be done. He and I were forming a good working relationship, and in doing so, we were becoming friends. The man was a likeable character, being both good-humoured and hard-working, and I looked forward to working with him into the New Year and beyond. I imagined that I'd always need Dougie's expertise; Alice-Rose was beyond my capabilities alone.

When it came to the restoration of the house and yard, I had chosen an architect from a reputable firm in Dublin to guide me: 'Stackpoole and Mullen,' specialised in restoring Georgian properties. Austin Stackpoole was the senior partner in the firm, and he fell in love with Alice-Rose from the start, taking her under his wing like a child in need of mentoring.

For my part, like any doting parent whose child is being recognised as having special talents, I immediately took a firm and fast liking to the devotee. I do mean liking in the purest sense. If Dan Bryant was old enough to be my father, then Austin Stackpoole was old enough to be my grandfather! And even I, despite my newfound interest in the older man, had no intention of going there! Besides, I am sure that his good wife, Dora, would have had something to say about it if I had. Having met her on one occasion, she struck me as being a formidable woman!

After extensive research and numerous site visits, Austin drew up a strict set of guidelines for the restoration of the buildings before putting me in touch with the only contractors that he would personally recommend for the job, the brothers 'O'Rourke and O'Rourke'.

My first phone call to the offices of O'Rourke and O'Rourke was to be the first step towards the formation of a relationship that has lasted to this day. From the outset, I was left in no doubt but that the O'Rourkes were among the finest in their field. Their offices on North Great George's Street were housed in an impeccably restored early Georgian townhouse. Both brothers had studied architecture in Bolton Street before diversifying at the height of the Celtic Tiger into restoration work.

Paddy and Mick O'Rourke had serious dispositions and were, as far as I could tell, devoid of any sense of humour. Their names seemed oddly out of kilter with their demeanour. I remember thinking at the time that Patrick and Michael would have suited them far better! Judging by their attitudes, I presumed that they lived to work, and for my part, I found this assumption strangely comforting. I wanted the restoration of Alice-Rose to be taken very *seriously*.

I was informed by Paddy, the eldest and most serious of the two, that if I decided to avail of their services, they would commence work on the thirtieth of March. Taking into account how most builders operated in Ireland at that time, I imagined the date to have a built-in flexibility of at least a month or two.

Mr O'Rourke did not appreciate, or even recognise, my feeble attempt at humour when I playfully questioned the exact date. Perhaps he thought that I was questioning his integrity, but either way, Paddy O'Rourke advised me to be at my property at 8 a.m. sharp on that date—not the twenty-ninth and not the thirty-first of March but the thirtieth of March. They would find their own way there, thank you very much, and if in the unlikely event that they did encounter any navigational difficulties, *they* would contact *me*.

I left number 13, North Great George's Street, somewhat bemused but with the realisation that I had very little choice but to put my trust in the O'Rourke brothers. It would be interesting to see what the thirtieth of March would bring. Glancing back at their door, I hoped that the number thirteen wouldn't turn out to be a bad omen regarding the build. Then remembering the glowing recommendations that Austin Stackpoole had given these two men, I decided instead to draw comfort from the saying that thirteen was lucky for some. Hopefully, that 'some' would include me!

CHAPTER 20

Christmas Eve

S O, BETWEEN THE everyday running of my antiques business, occasional dates with Simon McQuaid and the work involved in getting the restoration of Alice-Rose under way, I didn't have very much time for reflection. Most evenings saw me collapsed in front of the fire, bowl of soup and sandwich in hand, too tired to think. Therefore, it wasn't surprising that it was late December before Dan Bryant and I crossed paths again.

Jules was hosting a Christmas Eve party at her house, and I was really looking forward to going to it. We had both been so busy that I hadn't seen much of her in the run-up to Christmas. Simon was in bed, sick with a dose of the flu, which meant that I would be attending the party alone. In truth, I didn't mind, and in fact, I was glad. It was becoming clear to me that while I certainly liked Simon and he possessed a lot of the qualities that I admired in a man, we were missing that certain 'je ne sais quoi'.

That vital missing ingredient in our relationship meant that I had declined from taking him to my bed while all the time hoping that my feelings would change. To be honest, it wasn't looking good. I had reached the point of being hugely grateful for viral infections such as the seasonal flu, which meant that contact between Simon and I could be legitimately restricted without anyone's feelings getting hurt. And I really didn't want to hurt Simon. He was an extremely decent and likeable fellow, but he just wasn't for me!

However, on the flip side, viral infections also meant that I remained 'attached' to Simon beyond the point of reason, beyond the point of having well and truly had enough! Even so, I wasn't callous enough to break up with him by text message or over the phone. I would just have to be patient and wait until I saw him again before gently 'disentangling' myself from the relationship.

Fortunately, there was the small consolation that Simon hadn't wasted any money on me during our brief courtship. Earlier in the week, I had spent ten minutes on the phone listening to him bemoan the fact that he had fallen ill just before he intended to do his Christmas shopping, and that included shopping for my Christmas present.

Alleluia! I thought to myself; this was the perfect opportunity to tell him that I thought it was far too early in our 'friendship' for either of us to be considering buying the other one a present. I hoped that my use of the word friendship would give him some indication of my true feelings, and for good measure, I reassured him that I wouldn't be wasting any time or money on him either. Obviously, I put it to him more gently than that, but I was sure that he got the message all the same.

On Christmas Eve, I decided to take a taxi to Jules's party and hoped that I would be lucky enough to get one back home again without too much bother. The journey into town was spent contemplating the good fortune that saw me attending the party alone despite Jules's best efforts. It had never been my intention to invite Simon to the party, but Jules had other ideas. She had taken it upon herself to call Simon at work and had extended to him the warmest of invitations to the event. I had been annoyed but helpless to do anything about it.

I paid the taxi driver and was turning to go into Jules's house when I heard footsteps behind me.

'Going my way?'

Dan Bryant's distinctive voice carried on the cool evening breeze. Oh joy! Oh rapture! It had crossed my mind that Dan might be going to the party, but I hadn't dared to hope, or to ask Jules for that matter, there was only so much derision a girl could take! I did, however, know that she was inviting some of her neighbours and Dan only lived three doors away from her. I had taken the precaution of crossing my fingers.

Despite wanting to assume the outward appearance of calm, I couldn't help but smile broadly. I was ridiculously glad to see him. I didn't quite know what this man's magic was, but it worked on me every time! He had such an easy, bashful charm and yet you got the feeling that he was in complete control of his life.

'Hello, Dan!' I said.

Drinking in the sight of him, I was reminded of how incredibly attractive he was. There weren't many men who aged as 'gracefully' as Dan Bryant.

'And yes, if you're going to the lovely Miss Mahon's, then I'm going your way,' I finished in answer to his question, gladness welling up in my heart.

We paused for a moment in silence, just looking at each other. And then I remembered *the other woman,* and I felt a sudden sense of loss.

'So, will Hazel be joining you later?' I blurted out, unable to contain my disappointment.

'Hazel?' Dan asked, clearly puzzled. He looked as if he was trying to remember who exactly Hazel was.

'Ah, Hazel!' he said, relaxing visibly as he recalled who she was and where I had met her. 'No, I imagine she will be celebrating the night in New York. But we'll meet up for New Year.' My disappointment must have been clearly etched on my face, judging by Dan's next comment.

'You do know who Hazel is, don't you?' Dan asked sharply. 'She's my sister, my twin sister.'

I felt as if metaphorical clouds had parted in my soul to reveal the most brilliant sunshine.

'No, Dan, I didn't.' I cried, laughing with relief. 'I presumed that Hazel was your girlfriend!' That was when Dan started to laugh too.

'Sorry,' I said. 'You just looked so right together. It must be the family resemblance.'

'Either that or the fact that we've known each other all our lives!' Dan said, still laughing.

'Speaking of people looking right together . . . how is Mr Cunningham?' I thought I detected a discernible edge to Dan's voice.

'To be honest, I haven't got a clue!' I admitted.

Peter had called quite a few times, but despite my promise to Jules that I would try harder with him, I knew it was hopeless. Peter, above all people, deserved my honesty, and so I had done my best to let him down gently. He admitted to being disappointed but seemed to understand when I told him that I didn't feel ready to embark on a new relationship. In saying that I thought Peter deserved honesty; I didn't mean that he deserved brutal honesty, more like the sugar-coated variety!

As Dan and I stood shivering in the lamplight, he began to fumble in the inside pocket of his topcoat, and after what seemed like an age, he produced a small neatly wrapped box that he handed to me.

'It's just a small house-warming gift, Libby, nothing special,' he said dismissively.

Dan turned his head away from me, so that I couldn't read his face. My hands shook slightly as I took the delicate package from him.

'Oh, Dan, you shouldn't have!' I whispered, but in truth, I was so glad that he had!

I didn't care if the box contained a ball of fluff; the important thing was that Dan Bryant had thought enough to buy me something. The irony of the situation wasn't completely lost on me. While I would not have welcomed a gift from Simon McQuaid, my official boyfriend at the time, I was totally bowled over by the prospect of a trinket from Dan.

Carefully removing the wrapping and placing it in Dan's outstretched hand, I opened the box. The glow from the street lights revealed a delicately crafted brooch in the shape of a Georgian house. It looked to be fashioned from silver and diamonds, and I was rendered speechless. I in turn kept my head bent, too moved to trust myself to look at Dan.

'I just happened to see it, and I thought of you,' he said, emotion registering thickly in his voice. 'I wish you all the luck in the world, Libby.'

Looking up at him with tears in my eyes, I touched his shoulder with my gloved hand and kissed him gently on the cheek. His skin felt warm and had the faint, lingering smell of soap. I found myself brushing his cheek with the back of my gloved fingers. I didn't just want this man; I was falling in love with him, and I knew that just as sure as I knew the following day was Christmas. Pulling back from Dan, I looked at him, willing him to kiss me.

'Libby . . .,' Dan said, his voice catching.

'Just kiss me, please,' I said. And then he did.

Dan

CHAPTER 21

Confusion Reigns

MY EXISTENCE BEFORE meeting Libby was undoubtedly more solitary than I would have liked. The kids had left home, and although family and friends were very good at including me on every list, I still felt on the fringes of life, just as I had in the years preceding Marie's death.

I had yearned for sustained romantic love in my marriage, but it seemed that once it left, it was never going to return. Meeting Libby had rekindled all those desires for emotional intimacy that I had carefully suppressed over the years. While I knew that I could never have Libby, I now had the problem of not being able to see past her for the fulfilment of those desires, and I felt increasingly helpless to overcome my infatuation. Just when I thought that my sense of isolation couldn't get any worse, I discovered that a life spent avoiding this girl was an even more painful undertaking than ever before.

Seeing Libby and Peter Cunningham together in The Silver Olive did little to dampen my ardour. Despite my feeble denials, I was relieved when Hazel expressed her opinion that there was nothing romantic going on between them. A few days after that meeting, I was strolling down Grafton Street when I stopped briefly to look at watches in Weir's window. There, nestled among the Rolex's, was the little brooch. I hesitated for only a moment before going inside to buy it. It was made from platinum and diamonds, and it cost a pretty penny, but I didn't care. It was the perfect gift for Libby, and I wanted her to have it. The jeweller gift-wrapped it carefully, all I had to do was find the perfect time to give it to her, without appearing too pathetic.

As luck would have it, I bumped into Jules Mahon a few days later, and she invited me to her Christmas Eve party, adding that Libby would be sure to be there. I found myself blushing under her gaze. Jules Mahon was shameless, and I was wholly transparent. She was on to me all right! The burning question was whether or not she was teasing me, knowing that I didn't stand a chance in hell, or was she giving me a nod of encouragement? I decided that I had no alternative but to find out for myself.

Therefore, Christmas Eve found me pocketing my small gift in anticipation of meeting Libby. I was determined to find an opportunity to give it to her, and as it happened, luck was on my side that night, for a while at least. I was deep in contemplation as I approached Jules's house when I spied Libby getting out of a taxi. She was wrapped from head to toe in warmest cashmere and looked as beautiful as an angel. I seized my opportunity.

Libby's reaction to my gift was better than any I could have hoped for. I hadn't become so removed from affairs of the heart that I no longer recognised when a woman was interested in me. Quite a few women had made passes at me since Marie's death, and even a few before, but this was the first time that I had ever wanted to respond.

I was filled with doubt about the wisdom of giving into our mutual attraction, and my courage failed me in the end. For some unfathomable reason, I resisted the urge to take Libby in my arms, and instead, I placed the chastest of kisses on her warm, fragrant cheek. I thought I saw confusion and hurt in her eyes the instant I pulled back from her, and I would have rectified my mistake immediately had it not been for a sudden and unwelcome interruption by Simon McQuaid!

However disappointed, I might have imagined Libby to be by my apparent lack of ardour; moments later, I was very thankful for my sudden absence of courage. I had been annoyed initially by Simon's unexpected appearance and at a loss as to know what exactly was going on. My irritation soon turned to misery nonetheless when it became painfully clear that Libby and Simon's relationship was not entirely platonic. I was such a fool, such an old fool! Libby was just being her usual friendly self when she kissed me on the cheek.

When I thought about it later, Libby's kiss was much the same as all the kisses bestowed upon me over the years by my own darling daughter. I, in my desperation, had read more into her gentle gesture and had very nearly made a complete and utter fool of myself! Yes, luck was indeed on my side that night; Simon McQuaid's timely arrival had prevented me from placing both myself and Libby in the most embarrassing of situations.

Libby

CHAPTER 22

I Don't Want This Bird That's in My Hand

I STOOD THERE, STATUE-STILL, waiting in eager anticipation of Dan's lips finally touching mine. Then he bent towards me and kissed me . . . on my cheek. It occurred to me then that the words that had been so vivid in my brain had never actually been translated into sound and that Dan was still unsure as to how I felt about him. I was about to take matters into my own hands, with the Dutch courage afforded to me by the glass of wine that I had consumed before leaving home, when a voice cut through the stillness of the night between us.

'Libby! Libby, hold up!' came that voice, the voice of Simon McQuaid! A voice that should have been, according to my calculations, safely tucked up in bed some twenty miles away! What in God's name was he doing here, and now of all times? Turning round to face back down the street, I saw a well wrapped-up Simon advancing on us.

Oh dear God, no! Somebody up there was having a right laugh at my expense! First, there was Peter, and now there was Simon! By the time I disassociated myself from Simon, Dan would surely have come to the conclusion that I was some kind of man-eater and that he was altogether better off without me!

Even if Dan was inclined to give me the benefit of the doubt, there was always the chance that while I was busy simplifying my love life, *he* would meet some gorgeous woman and forget all about me. I wanted to *roar* with frustration when Simon put a proprietary arm firmly around my waist before kissing me fully on the lips! Why had Simon chosen then of all times to behave like a caveman? One of the main reasons for my wanting to split from him was his apparent lack of testosterone. Most of our dates consisted of limp hand-holding sessions that culminated with a few brief and uninspiring kisses. In truth, I had begun to think that he was either gay or 'just not that into me'. However, judging by his performance that night, something in him had definitely *changed.*

Despite him not being a well man, his testosterone levels on that occasion seemed to be above average. Pulling away from him with as much grace as I could muster, in a vain attempt to salvage the situation, I was dismayed to learn that the two men already knew each other. Yes, apparently Dan's eldest son was going out with Simon's younger sister. And yes, we all agreed that it was indeed a very small world! Dan kept the niceties to a minimum before quickly excusing himself on the pretext of retrieving something that he had forgotten back at his house. He assured us that he would see us at the party later.

I knew instinctively that Dan wouldn't show up at Jules. But even so, I spent the entire night glancing towards the door every time it opened, hoping against hope that Dan would come as he had promised. I even managed to convince Simon that he was in no fit state to be out of bed, and I walked him back to his car just before eleven, assuring him that I would be fine and that I would call him the following day. Something was definitely having an aphrodisiac-like effect on Simon that night, and he pulled me lecherously towards him on several occasions between leaving the house and reaching his car; perhaps, it was the flu medication that he was taking. Luckily, the potential contagiousness of his condition excused me from having to have any mouth-to-mouth contact with him, and I bestowed a chaste kiss to his cheek before manhandling him into his vehicle.

I hadn't thought it possible, but compared to his performance on that occasion, the Simon of old was beginning to look a lot more appealing. Could Simon *do* happy medium? I didn't know, and, frankly, I didn't care. That was a day's work for another woman, or man, as the case might have been. Putting Simon, and his bizarre extremes of behaviour, firmly to the back of my mind, I hoped that somewhere from his house Dan was looking and that he would see me return to the party alone. I willed him to find the courage to come and get me. But he didn't.

By midnight, I had given up all hope of seeing Dan, and I called myself a taxi. On the journey home, I resolved to finish with Simon as soon as possible. At least then I would be free to find Dan and to make my feelings for him plain.

CHAPTER 23

After the Party

CHRISTMAS DAY AND Saint Stephen's day passed in a blur of eager anticipation. I was fervently *anticipating* giving Simon the heave-ho as quickly as possible before fast-tracking my romantic life to merge with Dan Bryant's! The night before had been a disaster, but at least I now had a pretty good idea that Dan was, in fact, interested in me. Perhaps with a little bit of gentle persuasion, he would come round to the idea of giving *us* a chance. The memory of Dan giving me the little brooch sustained me as I faced the task of breaking up with Simon.

I called Simon very briefly on Christmas morning only to learn that the previous evening's foray into the night air had proven to be a very bad idea. He was feeling worse than ever! There was some consolation in this at least because it meant that it was unlikely that I would have to see him again for the rest of the holidays. Although I was anxious to finish things with Simon, I didn't really want to do it over Christmas.

There was no huge urgency to break up with him over the following few days either, because I thought that it would be best to approach Dan sometime in January, when Christmas Eve was a dim and distant memory! Besides, Dan was bound to be busy with his own family over Christmas and hadn't he more or less said that he was going stateside for New Year?

The immediate Finn family spent Christmas at home in my parents' house, all except for Tony, who was working at the hospital for the entire Christmas period. He didn't appear unduly upset by the prospect, so we concluded that he must have had the delicious Dolly in attendance!

Mum and Emma definitely noted a change in my mood. Fortunately, I was able to pass my giddiness off as excitement over the acquisition of Alice-Rose and an eagerness to get the New Year started. And indeed, I was excited about the New Year but for reasons that they never would have imagined! Emma, in turn, was aglow with the confidence that I remembered being newly engaged brings; I didn't think anything would have been able to wipe the smile off her pretty face.

And so with everyone in the Finn family 'feeling the love', we spent a very happy Christmas together in contented anticipation of good things to come. For the first time since Max's death, my family didn't seem to feel the need to thread carefully in my presence. I imagined that they presumed that having bought Alice-Rose, I was finally looking to the future, or perhaps they sensed a real change in me. Whatever the reason, I was happy to be treated as irreverently as I had been in the past. I felt robust and unstoppable.

Christmas Day at home was always lively and lots of fun. The day started early with the requisite full Irish breakfast, followed by mass at ten o'clock. Once home, we all got stuck into the work because George, our neighbour, whom Dad employed to help with the farm, was always off on Christmas Day.

Emma and I tackled the equine side of things together, feeding the horses before mucking out the stables. After that, we rode out the horses that weren't being hunted the following day. The Saint Stephen's Day hunt was a huge social event in the area, and despite my inner conflict about blood sports, I inevitably mounted up with the rest of my family. The fact that we practically never saw a fox, let alone killed one, went some way towards assuaging my guilty conscience.

The men in the family took care of the cattle in the sheds. Dad and Philip inevitably had their morning interrupted by at least one call out. Most farmers checked their stock on Christmas morning, so a vet's chances of being called late on Christmas Day were less. For this reason, Christmas dinner was always served after six, our mother being the 'hostess with the *mostess*', putting weeks of preparation into the day's menu every year. In fact, she kept us all well fed throughout the day. No matter what time we entered the house, there was always soup and nibbles on the go.

As well as keeping her family fed, Mum also kept a number of neighbours well entertained over the course of the morning. Quite a few dropped by on the day to say, 'Happy Christmas,' before heading home to enjoy their own dinners. They invariably left feeling a good deal 'happier' than when they had arrived!

Christmas night always saw us collapsed in front of the television like most families. Occasionally, one of us would prise ourselves out of a chair and attempt to put together some of the jigsaw puzzle that lay scattered on the card table in the corner of the sitting room. A new jigsaw for the Christmas season was a tradition in our family, and it usually took the entire week between Christmas and New Year to complete it. This one was proving to be educational as well as entertaining and consisted of a very large map of North America in two thousand pieces. I had picked it up on my last trip to the States with the Christmas Holidays in mind.

Just like Christmas Day, Saint Stephen's Day was always very busy; everyone in the family bar Mum and Tony rode out with the local hunt on the day. Horses and hounds gathered mid-morning in the car park of Lough Glen's only pub to begin the chase at noon. The hunt was always well-attended; it was another opportunity for neighbours to meet socially and to catch up on local news. The day dawned grey and misty, but by midday, the sun had broken through the clouds, and everyone was in high spirits.

Even Mark Waldron's appearance on the scene, in the midst of the chaos, couldn't dampen the mood. In fact, we all took great pleasure in teasing him when he turned up for the event kitted out like a country gentleman; the fact that Mark didn't know one end of a horse from the other was exactly the point! He strutted around the car park beating his thigh with his crop while proceeding to make asinine judgements about all things equine. He didn't seem to notice that his own mount for the day was more like a well-worn armchair than a gallant steed. Scarlet was a small, fifteen-hand cob, and as children, we had all learnt to ride on her sure and gentle back. At twenty-one years of age, she was a veteran of the hunting scene and judged to be the perfect mount for my future brother-in-law.

Emma joined in the fun, teasing Mark and warning him about the mare's 'feisty nature'. Mark looked horrified to begin with, but he managed to recover himself well, attempting to distract from his obvious disquiet with his usual bluff and bluster. He assured us that he had, in fact, been taking riding lessons. He didn't see what all the fuss was about; there couldn't be that much to riding a horse, after all!

Sometime later, Mark was eating his words, and the dirt, when Scarlet got 'bored' on the chase. This was something that the old mare was wont to do on occasion, and unfortunately for Mark, the hunt on Saint Stephen's Day was one of those occasions. His first unseating came as he attempted to walk his mount through a gap between two fields where the well-worn hollow was flooded. If I was a betting woman, and of course to some extinct I am, I would have laid money on the mare walking through it. But apparently, there was still life left in the old girl, and she cleared it like a young steeplechaser, leaving a furious Mark sitting in the middle of it!

Mark's second undoing came at the end of the hunt when everyone was gathering back in the village car park. A stray hound ran in front of Scarlet, and she reared up just enough to allow Mark to slip gently over her hindquarters and land squarely on his backside in the middle of a group of sniggering spectators. Fortunately, only his pride was hurt on both occasions, but his unseating did provide a good deal of hilarity for all present! When all the animals were safely boxed, the merriment continued into the pub where soup, sandwiches, and the odd brandy were consumed with the relish that only a couple of hours in the bracing fresh air can engender.

The good cheer didn't last as long as we would have hoped. As a group of us were leaving the pub to return home, a local farmer arrived with some upsetting and unexpected news. Dan Bryant's daughter Caroline and her boyfriend had been involved in a serious car accident the previous day, and both young people had sustained serious injuries; they were in a critical condition in Tallaght Hospital.

The news was like a very dark cloud descending on an otherwise beautiful day. I imagined the agony that Dan must have be going through, and my initial reaction was to call him. But good sense prevailed, and I realised that under the circumstances, any contact from me would have been completely inappropriate. When it came down to it, a business relationship was all that existed between Dan and I; we had never quite gotten to the point of becoming friends. Calling him then would have been overstepping the mark, especially in light of Simon's display of affection on Christmas Eve; things were still too complicated to risk a further misunderstanding. Instead, I elected to drop him a note later in the week, empathising with him and letting him know that I was there for him if there was anything at all that he needed.

The unfortunate reminder of how one's happiness balances precariously on a knife's edge made me wholly aware that the matter of my tenuous attachment to Simon McQuaid needed more immediate attention than I had previously thought. Entertaining the wrong men for the wrong reasons had become a habit of mine of late and one that I was going to break without further delay. These half-hearted incursions into the dating game had led to nothing but confusion for others and moral discomfort for myself. I vowed from then on to be true to myself, and if others didn't like it, then so be it! What had I been thinking of acting against my better judgement?

Simon called later that evening. He was feeling a lot better and wondered if we could catch up the following day for lunch; there was something that he had to tell me. I could break up with him over the phone or I could do it face-to-face, but what would be the kindest? In the end, I decided that Simon needed to know as soon as possible that we didn't have a future.

'Simon,' I began slowly. 'I don't want to do the whole 'it's not you, it's me' thing, but the truth is I don't think that it's going to work out between us.'

'And you're not upset?' he asked incredulously.

'Of course, I'm upset,' I said cautiously, gently feeling my way around the subject while at the same time wondering where Simon was going with his particular line of questioning.

'*But*,' I continued, determined to finish what I had started, 'I think that it's better that we realise it now before we waste any more of each other's time.'

'Libby, you're the best!' enthused Simon, clearly not at all devastated by my revelations.

'I am?' I said, confusion flooding my brain.

'Yes!' Simon continued, 'I was dreading having to confront you, but it seems that you felt the lack of chemistry too.'

This was definitely *not* how I had imagined the conversation would go. I would have fully accepted this account of our relationship pre-Christmas Eve, but taking into account the events of that night, his response left me baffled!

'Truth is,' he continued enthusiastically, 'my last girlfriend, whom I never really got over, is back in Ireland, and she wants to give it another go.'

Silence; if ever there was a pregnant pause, this was one of them.

'Simon,' I said eventually, relief overtaking my initial indignation, 'go for it! I hope it all works out for you, I really do.'

Mine was an automatic response to his disclosure, but I was surprised to find that I really meant it. I was genuinely pleased for Simon. He wasn't The One for me, but he could be perfect for somebody else.

'Thanks, Libby, I'll never forget you . . . and Happy New Year!' he said, putting down the phone without even waiting for my reply. Simon was certainly eager to get on with the rest of his life; that much was certain!

'And a Happy New Year to you too,' I echoed down the dead line.

Hmm, well, that was certainly a turn-up for the books! It hadn't occurred to me that Simon might be hankering after an ex-girlfriend, why would it? I hadn't really known that much about Simon; our discussions hadn't been deep or meaningful, and it occurred to me that he probably wasn't even aware of the fact that I was a widow. That little dalliance had been a right royal waste of time, and I experienced a small sense of indignity that I had allowed the advice of others to persuade me to act against my better judgement. But overall, I was relieved that the *non-affair* was finally over. Invigorated by my newfound sense of emotional freedom, I went into Dad's office, and pulling towards me a sheet of paper, I began to write.

CHAPTER 24

Ready, Steady, Go!

T HE RESTORATION OF Alice-Rose commenced on Monday the fifth of January 2011, almost three months earlier than expected; maybe thirteen was my lucky number, after all! On the twenty-seventh of December, I received an early morning phone call from Paddy O'Rourke saying that the 'project' that had been lined up for the beginning of January had fallen through. His clients were unable to secure a loan to cover the cost of the work. I could tell that he was less than sympathetic to their plight; Paddy O'Rourke didn't strike me as the kind of man who would suffer fools gladly, and judging by the tone of his voice that morning, that was how he now viewed his ex-clients.

Listening to his brusque, no-nonsense approach on the other end of the line, I suffered a brief nail-biting moment of apprehension as I wondered uneasily as to what in the long run Paddy O'Rourke would make of *me*. Was it too late to change my mind about this particular contractor? And was Austin Stackpoole's glowing recommendation really enough?

It soon became clear that it was indeed too late to change my mind. Paddy O'Rourke more or less demanded an answer there and then as to whether or not I would be interested in commencing the renovation of my property earlier than planned. If I couldn't give him an immediate answer, then he would give the option to somebody else, which could in turn result in a delay to the original start date of my 'project'. Crossing my fingers and mentally crossing my toes, I bleated out an assent to an early start on 'the Georgian project'. *What other kind of project was there*, I asked myself.

Once I had agreed to the revised date, I relaxed and found that I could hardly wait for work to begin on Alice-Rose, and I couldn't wait for the distraction that the work would bring.

Dougie and I had already cleared out all the rubbish that had been carelessly left behind in the house. We had ripped out the 1970s kitchen units and had skipped them along with a selection of old clothes, threadbare curtains and various flea-ridden mattresses that had been left lying around. Curtain polls, old shelving, and any stray nails that had been haphazardly hammered into place around the house had been carefully removed and followed suit into the skip.

Every wall and ceiling had been gently brushed down, and the floors vacuumed to within an inch of their lives. I had refrained from cleaning windows for fear of causing more harm than good. The yard and other areas surrounding the house had also been tidied up in terms of clearing any rubbish that had been left lying around. Having achieved that much around the house within the limited time frame, I hoped that we had done enough to inspire Messrs O'Rourke to realise its full potential.

Mum, Dad, and Emma accompanied me to meet the builders on the first day of the build. We were on site at 7.50 a.m. sharp because I was acutely aware that tardiness on my part would not be appreciated.

'No sign of the boys yet,' I said, somewhat relieved to arrive and discover that the main entry gates to Alice-Rose were still closed.

However, as we rounded the final bend in the avenue, I saw to my dismay that the O'Rourke brothers were already waiting by the back door; their large red van parked neatly in front of the Coach House. They broke into uncharacteristically wide grins when they noted our approach, then carrying out an ostensive check of their watches; they replaced their grins with headshakes of mock disapproval. I was pleasantly surprised by their little display of humour—up until that point, I hadn't credited the O'Rourke brothers with having any!

As we spilled out en masse from Mum's car, a white Peugeot van pulled up and parked alongside us. Two men hopped out in full builder's attire and joined the gathering crowd. It emerged that the latest arrivals were Eamon and Declan, the remaining core members of the O'Rourke restoration team.

My first impression of Eamon was that he made Paddy and Mick look like professional comedians. However, over the course of the next six months, I formed a very different impression of the man, and I found that Eamon had one of the keenest and driest senses of humour of anyone that I had ever met. Besides having his sense of humour to recommend him, the quality of Eamon's work was second to none, being both consistent and meticulous.

Declan, on the other hand, was little more than a boy, full of boyish charm and enthusiasm. It soon became clear that at the ripe old age of twenty-nine, as far as Declan was concerned, I was already over the hill; he constantly compared me to his mother! I didn't know whether to be offended or flattered, so I chose the latter. After all, it would probably be the closest I would come to being one!

The introductions didn't take long, and the pleasantries that followed were perfunctory. It soon became obvious that the O'Rourke brothers were anxious to get on with the job, and I got the distinct impression that Paddy O'Rourke had not anticipated the 'welcoming committee' consisting of quite so many people. While my presence had certainly been expected, and indeed necessary, everyone else's was surplus to requirement. Once the niceties were dispensed with, I became the focus of Paddy O'Rourke's attentions, and all his remarks were directed exclusively to me.

My parents knew when to take a hint, and once they had succeeded in gaining Emma's attention, they left us to it. Emma and Mick O'Rourke had been deep in conversation, the younger O'Rourke brother taking the time to ask my sister what her impression of 'the old place' was and whether or not it would be to her liking! In less than two minutes, Emma had succeeded in getting one of the O'Rourke brothers to ask her a personal question? Wonders would never cease!

I found myself oddly distracted by Emma and Mick as I tried hard to focus on my own conversation with Paddy. If I wasn't mistaken, my baby sister was flirting outrageously with the builder! While I didn't particularly like Mark Waldron, my sister's behaviour struck me as being entirely inappropriate for an engaged woman. Glancing at Emma's ring finger for confirmation of her status, I was surprised to note the absence of 'The Rock'. Alarm bells started ringing before I could remind myself of the ring's enormity. Emma's ring was certainly not your average ring of engagement, and it was probably only for 'good wear'. Why anyone would buy such a ring was beyond me!

Sometime later, I found myself alone with the boys. I had fully expected to be leaving with my family, but it soon became clear that that wasn't going to be an option. According to Paddy O'Rourke, there was still a lot to be discussed and decided upon regarding the renovation, an architect's plans only went so far in his professional opinion. Seeing Mum's car pulling away from the house, I counted myself lucky to have parked my old bike in the Coach House; I aimed to nip home at lunchtime for a bite to eat and a summary of Mum's opinion of the builders. However, lunchtime with Mum was not an option either! It was 'vital' for some reason, best known only to Paddy O'Rourke, that I was around when the men came later that day to collect the AGA.

The 'AGA saga' didn't just end with its safe collection! Mr O'Rourke had his own theories about this mainstay of country living, and since the 'AGA collectors' didn't arrive until late that afternoon, Paddy had ample time to expound his theories about the sacred AGAs and their mismatched owners.

Paddy O'Rourke could see that Austin Stackpoole had the AGA down for reconditioning and conversion to oil, and he was fine with that. He conceded that two fills of anthracite a day, and the generation of countless buckets of ash, were not practical for someone like me. I was very curious to know what exactly he thought someone *like me* was like as I surreptitiously examined my chipped fingernails. I was not shy of an honest day's work as a week spent in the bosom of my loving, yet very hard-working family, had proven!

'Let's be honest here,' I dared to say. 'There are very few people that two fills of anthracite a day and copious buckets of ash would appeal to!'

Apparently, I was mistaken! Paddy went on to inform me that a fair percentage of 'true AGA people' still went for the solid fuel option.

'I see, and good for them!' I said between barely ungritted teeth.

It was beginning to look like our working relationship would prove to be even more of a challenge than I had first thought.

While Paddy agreed in theory with the conversion of the AGA to oil, he was not okay with having it re-enamelled. He thought the 'old girl' had withstood the test of time very well, all things considered, and that she would be altogether better off with just 'a good clean'. 'These re-enamelling jobs' were never as good as the original work, and besides, he didn't see why I didn't just go and buy myself a new AGA if perfection was what I was after!

Had I said anything about wanting perfection? I didn't think so! And frankly, with Paddy O'Rourke making so many assumptions about me, I was beginning to worry that I might never get the chance to express an opinion! A man who didn't mince his words was one thing, but a presumptuous man who didn't mince his words was a horse of an entirely different colour! I wasn't sure what to make of him, and I was, therefore, very alarmed to find that I might actually have been warming to his abrasive approach as I humbly took his advice, and 'Aggie' was spared the indignity of re-enamelling.

I didn't leave Alice-Rose until late into the evening on that first day as one task after another was raked through meticulously by the O'Rourke brothers. However, that endurance test did have an upside; Paddy and Mick didn't think that they would need to see me again for another three days! *Hallelujah*, I thought to myself, straddling the Raleigh and peddling furiously for home! Up until then, I couldn't have imagined anything more exciting than a day devoted to planning the house's restoration, and while it had been thrilling on one level, hunger and Paddy O'Rourke's disapproving manner left it falling somewhat short of my expectations.

Nevertheless, the day's experience left me certain of one thing at least; I was definitely bringing a picnic with me the next time! My stomach felt like my throat had been cut; I had survived the day by slurping water from the tap in the yard, while the builders ate their sandwiches in the van, the unspoken rule being that no girls were allowed. They didn't even offer me a cup of tea from their vast selection of flasks or a measly Marietta biscuit from any number of the half-finished packets that spilled from their lunch bags!

I would have asked Mum to bring me a sandwich, but she was gone for the day, looking at wedding venues with Emma, and takeaway services in Ballyedmond didn't begin until after 6 p.m. I plotted my revenge as my stomach gurgled furiously; the next time I called on the builders, I would bring a lunch fit for a queen, and I wouldn't be sharing it with anyone either!

Contemplating vengeance sustained me on the bike ride home. However, once I got as far as Willow Cottage, hunger took over, and I fed directly from the fridge! When my appetite was sated, I pulled a chair up close to the AGA, the *oil-fired* AGA, and wrapping my hands tightly around a mug of hot chocolate, I allowed the tensions of the day to drain from my body and from my mind.

Taking time out to reflect on the day's events, I had to admit that despite the strain of getting through the food-deprived day, I felt a sense of complete accomplishment. We had achieved a lot in those eight hours, and by the end of them, I believed that the O'Rourkes and I had gone some way towards developing a healthy respect for one another.

Leaning back in my chair so that I could balance my crossed ankles on the rail of the range, I exhaled a sigh of utter contentment. Paddy and

I weren't exactly a match made in heaven in terms of our personalities, but for some reason, I trusted him to do his best. After that, what would be would be! The deal was done, the work had begun, and it was now, to a large extent, in the hands of the Gods as to whether or not we would encounter any problems beyond our control. Having said that, I was, and always would be, of the firm belief that God helped those who helped themselves! All that was left for me to do that night was to 'help myself' up the stairs and into a hot bath . . ..

CAITRÍONA LESLIE

CHAPTER 25

One Less Dress

AN HOUR LATER, I emerged from the bath, sugared and spiced, and all set to devour every last detail of the latest *Country Living* magazine that had arrived in the post that morning. Having thrown myself on to the sofa in the sitting room, I settled in for an evening of simple and uninterrupted pleasure. Then the knocker on the front door rapped three times. It was Emma.

'Hi, Libby,' she said rather breathlessly. 'Just thought I'd call and see how you got on today with Mick and Paddy.'

She was clearly out of breath, and I glanced outside, checking for signs of Mark, before closing the door behind her. I hadn't heard her car.

'I ran here,' she continued, obviously seeing the look of puzzlement on my face.

She was leaning over, hands flat above her knees, working to regain a steady breath.

'That's not like you, Em,' I observed, 'out running, and not a Coq Sportif in sight!' Emma only ever wore designer brands, and what she was now *sporting* was definitely not designer or even current by the looks of it!

'Come to think of it, where did you get those clothes?' I asked accusingly. 'They look like the things I used to wear rowing in college!'

'I know!' Emma said, smiling from ear to ear. 'They are yours! Mum saved them in case you ever needed them again.'

'Good old Mum,' I replied dubiously, surveying the arrangement of worn and out-of-date sports gear in front of me.

I made a mental note to give our mother my full permission to bin any items of my old clothing that she might have been saving for me!

'Anyway,' Emma continued, 'I decided that I'd jog over here, and I asked Mum if she had anything suitable for me to wear. As it turned out, she did, so here I am!'

'Those shoes aren't mine, are they?' I asked incredulously, wondering how Emma had managed to run the distance in my size sevens.

'Lord no! The trainers are Mum's,' she said laughing.

'Well, that's a relief!' I said. 'We can't have you breaking a leg before your big day!'

'No,' she said flatly as if I had reminded her of a something unpleasant that loomed before her.

But what was I supposed to say? Emma had, after all, taken the week off work to scope wedding venues and to find that all-important bridal gown.

'Anyway, I haven't jogged all this way to talk about boring old weddings!' she said jocularly. 'Let's talk about your day, and I'll fill you in on mine later.'

Boring old weddings and *let's talk about someone other than the royal-we that was Mark and Emma;* well that was certainly a turn-up for the books! Come to think of it, Emma hadn't mentioned much of the *royal-we* of late.

'Okay then,' I said, moving towards the kitchen and the *AGA for fakers.* 'Let's brew up, and I'll fill you in on *the boys*!'

Emma and I spent a lovely evening together talking about literally everything, everything that is, except boring old weddings! It wasn't that I didn't try to talk about the wedding or that I steered the conversation away from the subject, quite the opposite in fact. But the more I tried to talk about the forthcoming event, the more Emma wanted to talk about other things—anything, in fact, except her wedding!

And, of course, the less Emma wanted to discuss her wedding, the more I wanted to. Humans are complex by nature, and as the evening wore on, I was beginning to feel quite paranoid. Was memory serving me correctly? Had Emma actually asked me to be her bridesmaid, or had I somehow presumed it? Maybe she was feeling uncomfortable talking to me about the wedding because she had asked someone else to be her bridesmaid.

I was relieved when we parted on the understanding that she and Mum would pick me up the following morning to go shopping for a bridal gown and a bridesmaid's dress. I knew the bridal gown was for Emma, and I didn't think that I was being too presumptuous in thinking that it would be me, rather than mum, who would be trying on the latter.

The rain the following morning was torrential, it certainly wasn't a day for turning ones thoughts towards a sunny June wedding! Notwithstanding the inclement weather, Mum and Emma arrived just after the pre-arranged time of 9 a.m., and we headed off in the direction of Enniscorthy.

The bridal boutiques of Enniscorthy were our first ports of call on a very long list of possibilities, and we decided to fortify ourselves at Rose's Café before starting our tour. We were fortunate enough to find a parking space right outside the door, and since the weather showed no signs of improving, we made a dash for it through the pouring rain!

The café was quiet when we entered the premises just after 9.45 a.m. There was a young girl and an older woman behind the counter, and another girl was busy clearing away breakfast remains from some of the tables. We ordered tea and scones from the counter before taking a table by the window. From there, we had a bird's-eye view of the scene outside. The rain was easing off, and some who had taken shelter from the showers were now taking advantage of the break in the weather to make a run for it.

Looking out on to the street, whilst enjoying the quiet, cosy atmosphere of the little café, I deliberated as to what colour of bridesmaid's dress Emma would choose. I hoped, despite the fact that it was a June wedding, that she wouldn't put me in anything pastel. I would look awful in pastel; I was too tall and too dark. If Emma insisted on going the pastel-route, I would end up looking oddly cast as the foil to her blushing bride.

Lost in contemplation of the worst-case scenario where Emma chose a dress of mint green to showcase my wares, my thoughts were suddenly and alarmingly interrupted by the sight that met my gaze! Coming towards us on the opposite side of the street, and clutching the hand of an attractive woman, was someone who closely resembled none other than Mark Waldron! I glanced quickly at Mum and Emma to see if either of them were looking, terrified of the effect that it would have on Emma if indeed it did turn out to be her beloved Mark. Luckily, Emma was facing opposite to me, and both she and Mum were deep in conversation.

Reassured that my concentrated study of the scene outside was going unnoticed, I resumed my watch, craning my head ever so slightly in order to get a better view. As the couple got closer, I was able to make a positive identification of the man just as the pair turned into the hotel across the road from where we were sitting. I drew in a deep breath and tried to refocus my brain. What should I do? What *could* I do? What were the chances of catching Mark Waldron having an affair in Enniscorthy of all places? What was he thinking of? Didn't he know enough to know that one was not supposed to 'poop,' so to speak, on one's own doorstep! I didn't have any answers to the myriad of questions swirling around in my brain, but I knew that I had to try and steer Emma away from sudden and crushing humiliation. I would leave figuring out how to deal with her fiancé until later!

I was completely shocked by the situation that I found myself in. While Mark wasn't my favourite person in the world by a long shot, I would never have had him down as a cheater! For pity's sake, he was possessive of Emma to the point of smothering all self-expression from her! Surely, that wasn't the behavior of a man who wanted to conduct an affair?

Could I possibly have misunderstood the body language between Mark and this other woman? Maybe she was his sister? No. Mark didn't have any sisters. Perhaps the woman was Mark's cousin? This was highly unlikely unless she was of the kissing-cousins variety. I was certain that the body language between the pair had been that of lovers. Again, I wondered as to what Mark could have been thinking of when he decided to conduct a liaison practically under his fiancée's nose!

Pushing all questions to the back of my mind and assuming, with great difficulty, a 'normal' disposition, I turned my attention back to the conversation taking place between two of the most important women in my life. If Jules had been present, then the circle would have been complete.

'Libby darling,' my mother said, addressing me warmly, 'I was just asking Emma why she hasn't asked Sinéad to be a bridesmaid along with you.' Sinéad was Emma's equivalent of Jules.

'It would even things up nicely since Mark is having his two brothers,' my mother reasoned. 'You wouldn't mind, darling, would you?'

'Lord no, I think that's a great idea, Mum!' I said, focusing. 'After all, Emma, you, and Sinéad were practically joined at the hip growing up.'

'Yes, Libby, *were* being the operative word,' responded Emma rather grimly. 'For your information, I did ask Sinéad Prender if she would do me the honour of being my other bridesmaid, and she said no.'

'She said no, just like that? No explanation?' I asked incredulously.

'Oh no, she had an explanation all right!' Emma continued, hurt and bitterness evident in her voice. 'Sinéad explained that she 'loved' me too much to stand by while I . . . let me see now, how did she phrase it? Oh yes, threw my life away on a complete plonker!'

'She didn't!' I gasped, feeling a tad inadequate all of a sudden. Why had my courage failed where Sinéad Prender's had prevailed? Honesty was the mark of a true friend, and I applauded her silently, making a mental note to buy her a large gin and tonic the next time I bumped into her in Mac's.

CAITRÍONA LESLIE

'I see,' said Mum; neither of us could say a word either in defence of Mark or in accusation of Sinéad. The air hung heavy between us as the elephant in the room waited to be mentioned. Eventually, Emma broke the silence.

'The terrible truth of it is that she's right!'

What? Were my ears deceiving me? Had Emma actually agreed that her beloved Mark was a plonker? There had to be some mistake! Did my heart dare to hope that my sister had eventually seen the light? Mum and I were rendered speechless as we waited for Emma to continue.

'Don't worry,' she continued calmly, 'I'm not expecting either of you to jump to his defence. Let's face it, Libby. You never liked him.'

'Well, in *my* defence,' I said hastily, still not entirely comfortable with the idea of being brutally honest about Mark, 'I really didn't give him too much thought in the beginning.'

I tried to choose my words carefully. I paused, reflecting on Sinéad's courage. The thought of her daring and the memory of Mark holding another woman's hand made me realise that the time for honesty, and not of the sugar-coated variety, had arrived.

'But you're right, Emma,' I continued more forcefully. 'Once I made the effort to get to know him, I didn't like him. The only thing in his favour was that he seemed to be crazy about you even if it was to the point of suffocation.'

'And you, Mum?' Emma demanded, turning her full attention on our mother. 'How do you really feel about Mark?'

Head bent and looking rather sheepish, our mother admitted that she only tolerated Mark for Emma's sake and that on the whole she found him to be an 'insufferable bore'.

We held our breath as Emma digested our admissions.

'I hate to have to admit it so late in the day, but you're both completely right!' she cried, tears of frustration welling up in her eyes. 'The only question now is how do I get myself out of this horrible mess that I've gotten myself into?'

I was astonished by Emma's outburst, and my astonishment didn't end there. Mum was the next to speak.

'Well, Emma, if you're really serious about ending it with Mark, I do know of one way you could do it that would leave you totally in the clear.'

'Really, Mum? How?' asked Emma doubtfully, yet clearly intrigued by what our mother might have to say.

'Well, darling, you could go over to that nice hotel across the street and ask Mark Waldron what it is he is doing with that other woman. I saw him going in there with a rather average-looking brunette ten minutes ago, and somehow, I don't think that she was his sister!'

'You're kidding me?' spluttered Emma; the shock of what she was hearing caused a jet of tea to escape from her lips. 'If he's doing what you think he's doing, then all I can say is . . . *thank you*, Miss Brunette, I am free!'

Despite Emma's recent revelations of dissatisfaction with her fiancé, I couldn't believe my ears. Girl finds out that boy is cheating on her and she goes into celebration mode? It seemed highly unlikely! But apparently, Emma's reaction was genuine, and she exuded relief and eager anticipation as she prepared to make her next move.

'Wait here, this shouldn't take long,' she said, rising from her chair. 'In fairness, it never does with Mark,' she reflected, gathering her bag and her coat before leaving us with a quick wink.

Left alone, *Mother* and I looked at each other across the table.

'That was *too* much information,' Mum said, her face remaining deadpan. The woman never ceased to amaze me!

'Yes, Mum, I agree,' I said quickly, 'but don't you think we should go after her, just to make sure she's okay?' I was beginning to question the soundness of Mum's advice to Emma.

'Emma can look after herself or at least it's about time that she started to!' Mum said. 'Mark won't do anything stupid, and I doubt very much that Emma will either. Relax, darling. She'll be back in no time!'

I thought about this, and in the end, I could only hope that Mum was right. There really was no point in us going after Emma and muddying the waters any further; I imagined the scene would be ugly enough without any help from us.

'You sly old fox!' I said finally, unable to think of anything else to say. 'I didn't think that you had spotted Mark. You certainly didn't show any signs that you had.'

'Less of the 'old' please!' Mum scolded. 'And as for not showing any signs of having spotted the rat, I almost choked on my scone!' We sat in silence for a few minutes, pondering recent events. Eventually, I could stand it no longer.

'I wonder what will happen. Maybe we should follow her over there just in case?' I suggested once more.

'No,' Mum said firmly. 'Emma can handle it herself, and I think we should just leave her to it. She'll come back when she's ready.'

'Okay,' I said, bowing to Mum's superior judgement. 'We better have another pot of tea then while we're waiting,'

Twenty minutes later, Emma returned, a look of triumph on her face! Having toured the reception and bar areas in the hotel and finding no trace of Mark, Emma decided to investigate the bedrooms. A discrete knock on one of the many bedroom doors brought a semi-naked Mark running in eager anticipation of room service. Needless to say, Emma was the last person that he expected to see, and he realised immediately that the game was up. Like the true coward that he is, he stood aside meekly, allowing her to enter the room and confront the naked brunette relaxing in bed, her modesty discretely shielded by a bed sheet.

The naked brunette turned out to be none other than his riding instructor. How original! Emma had bumped into her once before when the woman was leaving Mark's house, my sister having returned 'home' early from a trip to Lough Glen. *Cora*, as the woman was called, had apparently just popped in to reschedule Mark's riding lesson!

Faced with the absolute truth of her fiancé's relationship with the other woman, Emma could think of very little to say to either of them except to comment on the fact that it was no wonder that Mark was such a bad horseman if *that* was his idea of practice! She observed that he might have fared better on Saint Stephen's Day, had he taken Cora to the hunt and ridden her around the fields of Lough Glen, instead of the put-upon Scarlet. Then she left them to it with her dignity intact.

'Oh my God, you cannot imagine the relief it is not to have to play the doting girlfriend any longer!' Emma said, resuming her seat and pouring herself a lukewarm cup of tea from the pot on the table.

'What was I thinking, agreeing to marry Mark Waldron?' she pondered aloud, emphasising every word purposefully by slapping her forehead with the heel of her hand.

'If I ever, *ever*, turn into a moron again, could you *please* have Dad put me down?' she demanded, before taking a long drink from her cup.

'But, Emma, when did you have a change of heart?' I asked, unable to suppress my curiosity. 'You seemed so happy over Christmas!'

'You'll probably find this hard to believe, but the minute I said yes to his proposal, I knew I had done the wrong thing.'

'Really?' I was incredulous.

'Really!' said Emma. 'Then I got carried away with the ring, and everyone wishing me well, but deep down I knew it was all wrong.'

Mum and I looked at her dubiously, struggling to believe that anyone could continue a charade for as long, and as convincingly, as Emma had done.

'I felt completely bereft after the engagement party,' she said. 'I had to finally admit to myself then that I never felt completely happy when Mark and I were on our own.' Emma finished the last of her tea before continuing.

'Anyway,' she sighed, 'I made up my mind before I came home for Christmas that the wedding would not go ahead, and that made me feel a whole lot better!' Emma paused again; I bit my tongue and willed her to get on with it.

'However, I hadn't quite figured out *how exactly* I was going to end it, and then this morning, life threw me a lifeline. Now I feel nothing but relief that I'm finally free. I'll figure out the practicalities later.'

Mum and I instinctively reached out to each other and to Emma, joining our hands to connect séance style.

'What about this other woman? Aren't you upset by that?' I asked, wanting to be certain that Emma had remembered *everything* before she decided that she was definitely okay. I didn't want her having an emotional meltdown on her own, later.

'I'm not overjoyed by it,' Emma conceded, 'but the fact that condoms were *Mark's* chosen method of contraception goes a long way to allaying any fears I might have about sexually transmitted diseases.' Emma blushed bright red.

'Sorry to be so graphic, Mum,' she apologised, squeezing our hands and smiling awkwardly at our mother.

'That's all right, darling,' Mum said gently, 'I'm relieved to know that. The possibility of Mark's *indiscretions* endangering your health *had* crossed my mind.'

I looked at Mum; she did look visibly relieved by Emma's latest disclosure.

'What do you want to do now?' I asked Emma, in an attempt to distract from the subject of her sex life and unsure of what else to say.

'I think that we should head home!' Mum said.

'Head home?' squeaked Emma, looking absolutely horrified by Mum's suggestion.

CAITRÍONA LESLIE

In a gesture of renewed energy, Emma released our hands and drew herself up into a very straight sitting position.

'Not on your Nelly!' she exclaimed. 'I don't know whether either of you have noticed, but I've been gathering cashmere and pearls for the last couple of years, and I need a change!' Ironically, Emma happened to be wearing both that day.

'Come on, you two,' she urged, 'you've got to help me find myself again, starting with a whole new look!'

It turned out that Emma really wasn't kidding! We headed for Dublin, and some two hours later, we entered a major department store in the city centre, where Emma proceeded to revamp herself from the skin out! At seven o'clock that evening, and being the very last people to leave the store, we returned to Emma's car for the last time, having made several trips back and forth to it during the day as our purchases accumulated. The car was by then full to capacity.

Squashing ourselves into the small remaining spaces, we declared the day to have been the best that any of us had spent in a very long time. Emma was upbeat and radiant, and Mum and I were somewhat incredulous that she could bounce back so effortlessly from the morning's events. Regardless of her feelings for Mark, it could not have been easy finding her fiancé in bed with another woman. Needless to say, Mum and I had spent the entire day covertly watching for some crack in her upbeat disposition. It never appeared.

Now here we were, the three of us as giddy as schoolgirls, and suddenly, it just didn't feel right to end the day by going home. Emma was the first to suggest going for a drink when we got back to Ballyedmond, and I seconded her proposal, advocating that we should go for a meal while we were at it. However, Mum was not to be outdone and insisted that we throw caution to the wind and stay the night at a country house hotel that was on our route home. It was to be her treat, and we didn't need any persuasion! Revving up the engine like a professional rally driver, Emma made fast work of exiting the multi-storied car park, and soon, we were leaving the city lights behind, heading for the Wicklow countryside with nothing but rest and relaxation on our minds.

That night we indulged in the fine cuisine that was on offer at our hotel. After dinner, we withdrew to the hotel's bar for a nightcap before retiring to bed. I don't think any of us remembered our heads hitting the pillows, and sleep came easily despite the excitement of the day's events.

The following morning, Emma and Mum booked themselves in for full body massages while I treated myself to a session of reflexology. Taking into account the fact that my nails were in a pretty dreadful state as a result of the ongoing work at Alice-Rose, I briefly considered having a manicure. However, the prospect of having to endure Paddy O'Rourke's knowing smile, if he ever observed my freshly painted nails, was enough to convince me otherwise. Any outward displays of pampering would have to wait until after the work on Alice-Rose was finished.

While we were at the hotel, we also succeeded in making appointments to have our hair done. The girl at reception made our bookings for 12.30 p.m., and the morning passed in blissful, pampered relaxation before arriving at the hair salon that afternoon. Once there, Emma decided that her new image was in urgent need of a new hairstyle. Between us all, we decided that the girl should bite the bullet and 'go short'. Two and a half hours later, we left the beauty salon with a very different Emma!

Her hair was cropped at the nape of her neck but left quite long at the front. A T-bar of blonde highlights had been added to her already blonde tresses, and the overall effect was very cute in a boyish sort of way. Her new hairstyle transformed Emma from hick to chick!

Arriving back at Willow Cottage later that evening, I invited Mum and Emma to join me for one last coffee. Mum declined on the grounds that she was anxious to get home to 'the men', and Emma reluctantly declined on the grounds that she was driving Mum!

'I don't know how I'm going to break the news to Dad,' Emma sighed heavily, as she waited for me to exit the car, 'he was really fond of Mark . . . .'

Mum and I looked at each other, wondering if Emma could really be serious.

'Gotcha!' roared Emma, practically exploding with the effort of keeping a straight face. 'Dad will probably crack open the champagne when I tell him the news. Let's go, Mum. I can't wait to see his reaction!'

After the women left, I spent the next hour sorting through my purchases from the previous day before drawing up a shopping list. While my wardrobe had certainly been replenished, my cupboards were bare, and I needed to stock up on groceries. If I was going to inspect progress at Alice-Rose the following day, I was definitely bringing something to eat!

Before heading for the supermarket, I checked my answering machine for messages and was completely elated to discover that there was one from Dan. Standing by the window, gazing at the first of the emerging snowdrops, Dan's deep and unintentionally sexy tones broke the silence.

'Hi, Libby, Dan here,' his message started, as if I needed telling. I felt my heart beating faster, and what a wonderful feeling that was! The quickening of a heartbeat, in response to the one we desire, reminds us that we are wonderfully alive.

'I'm just home, and I got your letter,' Dan continued, his voice faltering slightly. 'I really appreciated getting it, and I'll try to get in touch with you again soon.' That at least was something I supposed hopefully.

'I'm heading to the hospital shortly,' the message continued. 'Caroline and Todd are both out of danger now, but they still have a long way to go.' There was a long pause before Dan went on. 'Anyway, kiddo, take care and thanks again.' The phone clicked, and he was gone. The message had been left the afternoon before.

Why, oh why, hadn't I been there? And why couldn't he have called that night instead? I pushed these thoughts to the back of my mind, choosing to replace them with positive ones of serendipity. The hands of the universe controlled my destiny, and Dan would be worth the wait!

Dan

CHAPTER 26

Cancel Christmas

T HE BOYS AND I hung around the house on Christmas morning, waiting for Caroline and Todd to arrive so that we could make our way together to the Donnard Arms for lunch. Justin, 'the middle child', was home from Scotland for the holidays. He had qualified as an architect the year before and had secured a job with a Glaswegian firm the month before Christmas. My eldest son John had come over from his apartment on the other side of town to join us for breakfast. We were all in good spirits, and we weren't unduly worried by Caroline and Todd's late arrival because Caroline had phoned when they were on their way to say that they had been late leaving Dublin and that they wanted to drop by Marie's grave with some flowers before meeting us at the house.

In fact, I was just about to give Caroline a call to see where they were when the Garda car pulled up in front of the house. I could see that it was Sergeant Maguire from the station in Ballyedmond, and I knew instinctively that something bad had happened to one, if not both, of them. *Please God don't let her be dead*, I prayed, rushing to open the front door.

Fifty minutes later, we were entering Tallaght Hospital, having received a Garda escort the entire way. Caroline and Todd were in surgery having sustained serious injuries in a head-on collision that so far hadn't claimed their lives; both were in critical condition. I found myself for the first time, in a very long time, communicating on a very real level with my wife. The fact that she happened to be dead was neither here nor there. If anyone in heaven would plead on behalf of these two young people, it was Marie, and she wasn't one to take *no* for an answer!

Besides numerous fractures, Caroline had suffered a ruptured spleen which had to be removed. Todd had multiple fractures to his right femur and five fractured ribs as well as a broken wrist. Thankfully, neither of them had sustained any head injuries. The medics were cautiously optimistic that as long as Caroline and Todd didn't develop any complications, their chances of making full recoveries were good. There was always the dreaded risk of antibiotic-resistant infection and that concerned me greatly! The truth of the matter was, that at that point, Caroline and Todd had a very long way to go before they would be completely out of the woods.

John, Justin, and I took turns holding vigil by their bedsides. Todd's parents arrived within twenty-four hours of hearing about the accident; they were met by the Gardaí at Dublin Airport before being escorted directly to the hospital.

Understandably, they were exhausted, and having feared the worst, they were immeasurably relieved to find that their son was alive and out of immediate danger. I thought Todd's mother would never stop crying after she saw her son for the first time. His father was somewhat more restrained, but one could tell from his pallor that the events of the last twenty-four hours had taken their toll. I knew how he felt.

Christmas was effectively obliterated, and between us all, we spent the next three days keeping round-the-clock vigil by their bedsides. Besides their physical injuries, when Caroline and Todd eventually regained consciousness, they were psychologically traumatised by the crash which resulted in the death of a young man. According to eyewitness reports, Todd was driving on the correct side of the main approach road to the town of Ballyedmond when his car collided with a car coming from the opposite direction on the wrong side of the road. It was later revealed that the driver of the other vehicle was on his way home from an all-night party and had a significant level of alcohol in his system. He wasn't wearing a seat belt when he was thrown from the car, and he died at the scene.

By some miracle, Todd and Caroline had survived but had little or no recollection of events post impact. Days passed in a blur of white coats. My sons and I took a room in a nearby hotel as did Todd's parents. Food consisted mainly of canteen dinners, vending machine coffee, and Chinese takeaways. It felt like we existed in a parallel universe to the rest of humanity. I developed a genuine empathy with those for whom this kind of existence had become a way of life because of chronic illness and through no fault of their own.

Eventually, Caroline and Todd showed real signs of recovery, and we checked out of the hotel and moved back home to Ballyedmond. It felt good to return to some level of normality. Eleven days had passed, and my housekeeper had seen to it that order was restored to the house that had been abandoned and periodically 'ransacked' over the course of that time. The Christmas tree, together with every other visible reminder of the festive season missed, had been discretely tidied away.

Pushing open the front door on that January evening, our senses were pleasantly tempted by the smell of home cooking. Mrs Farrell, God bless her soul, had left a casserole in the oven. The boys and I didn't hesitate to drop our bags inside the hall door, before making straight for the kitchen. We were ravenous for something that resembled real food, and Mrs Farrell's casserole didn't disappoint us!

Later on that night, I noticed a pile of letters sitting on the hall table, but by that point, I was too beat to be even remotely interested by their contents. I decided that having waited that long, they could wait another day for my attention; I'd look through them the following morning. Morning turned into afternoon, and it was after midday before I awoke, thankful that I had managed to sleep so late. I had been suffering from chronic fatigue since the accident, and that was the first time in a long time that I had felt anyway normal upon waking.

In fact, it had gotten to the point where I was beginning to wonder if I would ever feel normal again. Was middle age finally catching up with me? Was functioning in a state of mild confusion as good as it was ever going to get for me? Thankfully, that first morning back home after the accident saw me glimpse the first signs of hope that my life would eventually return to normal. And that was a welcome relief.

I made my way down to the kitchen and put a pot of coffee on to brew while I set about preparing a generous helping of scrambled eggs on toast. There was no sign of Justin, so I presumed that he was still in bed; I knew that John had returned to his own apartment the night before.

I retrieved the neglected post from the hall and laid it on the kitchen table so that I could go through it at my leisure over breakfast. There were one or two letters and cards for Justin and the odd late Christmas card for myself. However, one envelope in particular caught my attention as I carefully designated the post into various piles. It was a long narrow envelope of good quality paper, and it was addressed to me in a very precise and rather artistic script.

I checked the envelope for any identifying name or address of sender, but there were none. I put the letter carefully to one side and decided that I would open it first. When all the post was sorted, I retrieved a steak knife from the drawer and sat down before inserting it under the flap of this one envelope and drawing it back carefully. The letter was from Libby Finn.

'Dearest Dan,' the letter went, 'I am searching for the right words to open with, but none come. I must therefore simply say how sorry I was to hear about Caroline's accident. I am not sure when you will receive this note, but I hope and pray that when you do, things will have taken a turn for the better for your darling girl.'

'I can only imagine your anguish. Rest assured that you are all in my thoughts and prayers. Dan, if there is anything I can do for you at this difficult time, anything at all, please don't hesitate to call me. Kindest Regards, Libby (Finn).'

It was a simple note, and yet I felt that it was the most intimate piece of correspondence that I had ever received. I wanted to be in Libby's thoughts, *and* I wanted to be her 'dearest'. As for what she could do for me, suffice it to say, that it didn't involve preparing a home-cooked meal . . ..

After first forcing myself to sort through the remaining post, in an effort to clear my head, I then tried to phone Libby, desperate for some level of contact with her. She was not at home. I was bitterly disappointed, and I wondered what she was doing and who exactly she was doing it with. It was only at the point of returning the phone to its cradle that I remembered that Libby did, in fact, have a boyfriend, and I felt my newfound hopes crushed by the boulders of reality.

As luck would have it, I was soon distracted from my wallowing by the arrival of John and Justin. Unbeknownst to me, they had arranged to play an early round of golf down at the local club, leaving their old man to sleep in peace. I, in my naivety, had been tiptoeing around the house all morning for no reason.

I had never personally been a fan of golf, believing it to be the sport of the young and the elderly, people, in other words, who had time on their hands. Taking recent events into account, I wryly considered that it was perhaps time that I thought about renewing my membership. My late wife had insisted that we join Ballyedmond Golf Club at a time when we were becoming 'upwardly mobile', and she had become quite an accomplished golfer in her time. However, when she died, I had allowed our membership to lapse. I presumed people thought that I had done this out of a sense of loss, but the truth of the matter was that the game bored me to tears, and I couldn't stand the hole by hole 'post-mortems' that took place after every game. A grey and uninteresting future loomed ahead of me; I was fifty-two years old and already considering that my future lay in golf!

Back in the kitchen and in the process of making a fresh brew, I listened vaguely to the conversation that my sons were having; my thoughts having by then turned to Caroline and Todd. I was intending to head back to Dublin that day to visit them, and I had to phone Linda at the office before I left to let her know that I'd turn up for work the following morning instead. I was about to leave the kitchen to make the call when I thought I heard John mention Libby's name. If they were discussing Libby Finn, then I needed to hear what it was they had to say! I retreated back into the kitchen and, grabbing the pot of coffee, sat down at the table to listen, as nonchalantly as possible, to the conversation taking place.

'So the lovely Libby Finn is back on the market?' Justin remarked, a little less casually than I might have liked.

'It would appear that she is! And 'lovely' isn't the word that I'd use to describe Libby Finn!' John sniggered like an overgrown schoolboy.

'Why wouldn't you?' I croaked, unable to stop myself interrupting the conversation, despite fearing graphic revelations. Libby Finn was preoccupying my waking moments more and more with each passing day.

'Well, Dad, have you *seen* Libby Finn recently?' Justin asked earnestly, deep furrows appearing on his forehead.

'Not recently,' I lied.

'Well, *she* is hot! Red hot!' he declared, in a tone intended to convince me, beyond any shadow of a doubt, of her attributes. I didn't need to be convinced. While Justin made knowing faces to his elder brother, I felt a growing sense of discomfort.

'Well, she was definitely a nice-looking girl the last I saw of her, I'll give her that,' I said, not wanting to appear too out of touch with reality, yet desperate to keep my little crush a secret.

'*Nice-looking girl?*' Justin spat, throwing me a look of disbelief mixed with a generous helping of disgust.

'*Nice-looking girl?*' he repeated for effect. 'Dad,' Justin continued in an exasperated tone, 'Libby Finn is now *a* woman! All woman, if you know what I mean?' He made an hourglass shape with his hands and threw in a wolf whistle for good measure!

I was getting increasingly uncomfortable with where the conversation was heading, but Justin hadn't quite finished.

'And let's be honest,' he expounded further, 'the Widow Finn is not only all woman, she is a *b-e-a-u-t-y!*' His pronunciation of the word beauty was drawn out and exaggerated and implied a world of lustful longing!

I was already sorely ruing having asked any questions at all regarding Libby, but once I had, there was no going back. The Widow Finn? That was the first time I had ever heard anyone refer to her as that, and the name did not suit her! It made her sound like a preying mantis! She was a beauty all right, and a widow too, but those things alone did not define, Libby! She was gentle, generous, and wonderfully self-unaware, and I dreaded to think of what other 'insights' these hormonal nitwits, that I happened to love dearly, would come up with! John sniggered in agreement with Justin, and I tried not to imagine the nature of the thoughts in his head.

Then Justin said, 'Oh yeah, Dad! Didn't I hear that you gave her a twirl round the dance floor at the Hallowe'en Ball? Surely, even you must have noticed what a doll she is!'

A twirl? Twirling was for old fogies, and I wasn't one of those, quite yet!

'Well, yes,' I bluffed, flustered by the memory of that encounter. 'I did think at the time that she was a rather lovely young woman . . . and a very good dancer too!'

'*Rather!*' John mocked my use of the word and gave me a conspiratorial wink. I hoped the wink was meant to convey camaraderie and was not his way of saying, 'I'm on to you, you sad old man!'

'Anyhooo . . .,' John continued in a more normal tone, 'whether you think she's *hot or not*, Libby Finn is back on the market, as far as I know!'

'As far as you know . . . what does that mean?' I asked, throwing caution to the wind. The boys probably had me down as a non-runner anyway.

'All I know,' said John patiently, 'is that on Saint Stephen's Day, Simon McQuaid gave Libby Finn the elbow, and after that I don't know anything at all. For all I know, someone else has taken his place!'

My heart began to pound in my chest, and I felt the blood rushing to my face with disappointment and outrage: disappointment that Libby had not been the one to ditch Simon McQuaid, and outrage that he had dumped my beautiful Libby!

'Simon McQuaid broke it off with Libby?' I exclaimed in disbelief.

Had the man taken leave of his senses? What kind of man broke it off with a woman like Libby? A gay man was the only possibility that sprung to my mind!

'Well, truth be told, I think he wanted to get in there before she did,' John said lightly. 'Apparently, there had been no real *action if* you know what I mean?' John made insinuating facial expressions before continuing. 'Long story short, he saw the writing on the wall and decided to save face by inventing the return of an old girlfriend. Apparently, Miss Finn fell for it.'

'Hmm,' I said, not daring to say anything further on the matter. Hope had been restored, and my blood pressure slowly returned to normal levels, for all of two seconds. I had thought the subject closed when Justin threw the cat among the pigeons by pronouncing, 'Let the games begin!'

'And let the best man win!' John said, echoing his sentiment.

I was left wondering what *exactly* they meant. I could only hope that neither of them had any intention of throwing their own hats into the ring. That would really be the end of it! I had no intention of going up against my own sons in an attempt to win Libby's affections! At least John was accounted for romantically as long as he didn't decide to ditch Simon McQuaid's sister any time soon. And as for Justin, he would soon be winging his way back to Glasgow, hardly leaving him enough time to woo the 'Widow Finn'! I resolved, there and then, to throw my own hat firmly into the ring, just as soon as Caroline and Todd were on the mend. I could only hope that when that happened, it wouldn't be too late.

Libby

CHAPTER 27

Lost and Found

I HAD INTENDED TO pay a visit to Alice-Rose the day after our overnight stay in the Wicklow Spa Hotel; I was anxious to see how work was progressing. However, my plans were foiled when Emma phoned late the night of our return to say that Mark had been in contact and that she needed me, if at all possible, to accompany her to Dublin the following day to collect her belongings from his house.

Despite my initial disappointment at yet another day passing without seeing Alice-Rose, I readily agreed. It was Emma's hour of need, and I couldn't, and wouldn't, let her down. Besides, I was relieved to see that Emma was following through on her decision to break from Mark. Notwithstanding the hurtful and degrading nature of events that accompanied their split, I had harboured reservations about the strength of Emma's resolve; when all was said and done, she had invested a lot of time and effort in their relationship.

Not only had she been emotionally dependent on Mark, she was financially dependent on him too. He was her employer as well as her lover, and Emma would require a double helping of courage to see her through the break-up. Deep down, I had feared that he would talk her round and that she would find it in her sometimes too-generous heart, to forgive him. All that fighting talk could, in the end, have turned out to be the bluff and bluster of a wounded ego.

On the drive to Dublin the following day, Emma filled me in on the conversation that had taken place between the erstwhile lovers. I was way off the mark when it came to assessing Emma and Mark's relationship; Mark had not pleaded for her forgiveness and had barely had the decency to apologise. He was, according to himself, relieved to have been caught and planned on marrying Cora as soon as possible. To add insult to injury, Cora was pregnant, so the truth would have had to come out sooner rather than later.

I waited for the tears of outrage and humiliation. They never came. Emma sat beside me composed and unmoved. Eventually, she noticed me looking at her expectantly, bewildered by her lack of a reaction to what I would have considered to be pretty devastating news. She straightened from her semi-slouched position and levered the seat to a more upright angle. Then she looked me squarely in the eye before giving me a reassuring grin.

'I know it must seem like I'm in shock, and you're probably concerned that I'm heading for a delayed reaction,' she admitted, 'but the truth is, I have been very unhappy for a very long time.'

'Honestly?' I asked, seeking reassurance.

'Honestly,' she said.

There followed a long silence during which she must have read all of the contradicting deliberations that were still going through my head.

'I know what you're thinking, and I don't blame you,' she said gently.

'What am I thinking?' I asked, too quickly and a shade too brightly.

'That I gave a very good impression of being happy? That I could have fooled you?' she probed, reading my thoughts perfectly.

'Well, yes, if I'm being truthful,' I admitted. 'You had me convinced that you at least were happy in your relationship with Mark.'

'I was fooling myself,' she said candidly. 'After Max died, I compared my situation to yours, and I managed to convince myself that I should have been grateful that my boyfriend was, at least, alive. I know it doesn't make any sense now, but at that time, Mark was still pretty decent. The transition to the over-controlling Mark didn't happen overnight, and it was very subtle. By the time I realised that he had changed, it was too late. I had gotten myself well and truly stuck playing the adoring girlfriend that he and his family expected me to be!'

'But, Emma,' I couldn't help but say, 'you were positively glowing the night of your engagement party! And you did seem very happy over Christmas . . . .'

'I was happy the night of the engagement party because I had all my family and friends around me,' she explained patiently, 'and I had a little help from Jack Daniels!'

Emma wasn't much of a drinker at the best of times, so her admission of having indulged in strong liquor to get through a situation spoke volumes in terms of how desperate she must have been.

'After the party,' she continued, 'and after everyone had left, *especially you*, I knew that I couldn't go through with it. I finally admitted to myself that I was miserable and that I had become someone that I didn't like very much!' She paused to comment on a passing scene before continuing. 'Seeing you, and how happy and content you were, made me realise that being on my own for the rest of my life would be infinitely better than spending it with someone that I didn't even like.'

Emma stopped, waiting for me to respond, and believe me, I thought long and hard before I did so.

'Emma, I'm not altogether sure that I'm flattered by your assessment of my situation,' I said with mock indignation. 'I certainly hope that my destiny isn't one of abject solitude, and I wouldn't go planning on us becoming the Brontë sisters just yet! I am, however, happy that my present 'lonelytude' inspired you to ditch a man who is, quite frankly, not fit to wipe your boots! Thankfully, he is now dead to us, my dear sister, and we shall never speak his name again!'

I stuck my nose firmly in the air and looked imperiously ahead, just managing to narrowly miss a pothole. Emma roared with laughter and slumped back in her seat more relaxed than I had seen her since the break-up.

The trip to Mark's house was uneventful. That is to say, the collection of Emma's things was uneventful. We arrived at the house just after eleven o'clock, and Mark was nowhere to be seen.

Mark Waldron was nothing if not efficient, and one might even say eager, in dealing with the situation at hand. Stacked neatly against one wall of the hall were nine square packing boxes which had obviously been purpose bought for the job. They contained all of Emma's belongings and were labelled as accurately as possible in terms of what each contained. An exhaustive search of the house by Emma, while I commenced loading the lighter of the boxes into the jeep, revealed that Mark had been thorough in his work; Emma did not find as much as a toothbrush that had been overlooked.

When everything was loaded, Emma turned her attention to an envelope that was propped against a lamp on the hall table. It was addressed to her. The envelope contained a brief letter and a cheque for twenty thousand euro. The letter indicated that the twenty thousand euro was in lieu of a redundancy package and that if Emma cashed the cheque, it would be taken as evidence of her agreeing to the end of their business, as well as personal, relationship. He requested that she sign a contract to that effect—the contract was lying open under the lamp. Emma put both the cheque and the contract in her bag. Then Emma wrote a brief note of her own to Mark, stating that she would only sign the contract if it was passed by her solicitor and only after the cheque had cleared. We left, pulling the front door firmly closed behind us.

We had hardly gone a mile down the road when Emma remembered that she hadn't posted her keys back through the letter box. I suggested that she mail them back to Mark, but she was adamant that he would deliberately misconstrue the delay as her wanting to preserve contact, and she didn't want to give him that satisfaction. Finding a pub car park a little further down the road, I turned the jeep around, and we were soon back at Mark's house.

Mark and Cora had obviously been watching our movements from somewhere nearby because we arrived back just as they were putting their own key in the front door. Under the circumstances, this wouldn't normally have given us reason for surprise or comment but for the fact that Cora was wearing my missing fur coat! Mark had taken my fur coat and had given it to his mistress! I could not believe it! It was a new low, even by Mark's standards!

Emma's hand flew to her mouth in dismay and disbelief, her other hand still clutching the house keys. I took the keys from her and said very quietly, but decisively, that I would deal with the situation. I marched up the front path and wordlessly handed the keys to Mark before turning my still outstretched hand to Cora. She looked at me blankly, clearly unaware of the situation. I suddenly felt very sorry for her and even more relieved for Emma.

'The coat,' I said stiffly, 'that's my coat you're wearing.'

'I don't think so!' she said snootily, and suddenly I didn't feel sorry for her any more.

'I think you'll find that it is,' I said resolutely.

'Mark?' she demanded, as it began to dawn on her that I wasn't joking.

Mark looked extremely uncomfortable and just nodded, indicating that she should give me the coat, which she eventually did, a look of complete confusion and humiliation transfixing her face. I took my coat and without further ado marched straight back to my awaiting vehicle; my nose held at a lofty angle, a look that was by then nearing perfection!

Poor Emma was waiting for me, a look of absolute mortification still clouding her pretty face. After banging the driver's door firmly shut, I declared that I hoped 'my poor coat' had not contracted fleas from 'that woman'. This set us both off laughing, and we headed for home considerably more light-hearted than when we had left it that morning.

CHAPTER 28

Getting Busy With the Builders

WHEN WE GOT back to Lough Glen House, I helped Emma to unload the boxes and stack them in our childhood bedroom. It was hers alone now, but she didn't seem upset by the fact. In light of Mum having greeted us with a high tea of epic proportions, I wasn't too surprised. I could think of worse things than 'regressing' to the taste of our mother's home cooking!

We feasted in the kitchen on a banquet of egg-salad sandwiches, and an array of Mum's home-made bakes—Sarah Finn loved to avail of any opportunity to get busy with the oven! On that particular afternoon, she laid on traditional scones served with double whipped cream and home-made raspberry jam, followed by lemon meringue tart and her famous double fudge brownies.

Emma and I tucked in and proceeded to regale our mother with the saga of the fur coat, tears of laughter rolling down our cheeks. Somewhere, somehow, I felt that my darling Max was in on the joke; he would have been highly amused by the whole affair! That coat was a keeper all right, and I knew that no matter how tattered it got, it would always have pride of place in my wardrobe.

I left home shortly after seven, and even though I would have loved to have taken a quick detour via Alice-Rose, I knew that it would be pointless; it was by then completely dark outside. I would wait and collect Emma early the following morning as planned, and we would take a look at it together. It was nice to have Emma around, and I was determined that we would regain and maintain the closeness that we once had. I thought that her expression of interest in my new venture was her way of trying to do the same. On the other hand, it might just have been a ploy to spot the talent that was Mick O'Rourke. Either way, I was definitely feeling the sisterly love.

I picked Emma up before nine the following morning, and we headed on to Alice-Rose. Emma struck me as being a little giddy, but then I supposed that that was to be expected, given her newfound 'freedom'. The main entrance gates to Alice-Rose were locked, so we continued on up the road before turning off it to approach the house by the back avenue. But I was disappointed to find that these gates were also locked, and I wondered why the boys hadn't made it to work that day.

Making good use of my passenger, I handed Emma the spare key for the padlock and got her to open the gates. Then we drove onwards towards the farmyard before getting out. From there, we could see that the builder's vans were parked in the courtyard, after all, parked to one side of four industrial-sized storage containers. I felt an unexpected sense of overwhelming relief! I really had no desire to start chasing builders, especially ones that had come highly recommended. If they let me down, then what hope did I have that others would behave any differently?

Opening the yard gate, we went in search of the reason for the O'Rourke brothers' increased security measures, and it quickly became apparent. There were quite a few extra workmen around and most of the windows had been removed, to be replaced by plastic sheeting, and the roof slates were in the process of being numbered before being carefully removed for storage in wooden crates. The house was far more exposed and vulnerable than it had ever been before; the fixtures and fittings would probably fetch a pretty penny as architectural salvage if they managed to find their way into the wrong hands.

In hindsight, I was ill-prepared for the level of 'transformation' that had taken place around the house. Transformation suggests a positive change, but I couldn't decide whether the change that greeted us that morning was good or bad, it was just dramatic. All the internal doors had been removed from their hinges, and they were nowhere to be seen. I was afraid to ask what had happened to them and chose instead to presume that they had been sent away to be dipped. I prayed that they wouldn't fall apart in the process as I felt the first pangs of panic take hold.

Besides the removal of the doors, the very floor that we had once stood upon was nowhere to be seen, and instead, we were left standing on dirt. The sandstone flags had been laid directly on to a bed of clay! My heart began to pound. What had I done? They were dismantling Alice-Rose, and I had given my permission. A house that had stood proud and true for over two hundred years was now in the process of being demolished! Why couldn't I have just installed a new boiler and given the place a lick of paint like any sensible person? Several of Jules maxims sprung readily to mind . . . more money than sense! A fool and his money are easily parted! Etcetera, etcetera!

I vowed to cancel my subscriptions to all country home style magazines with immediate effect; they were the cause of all of this! I had taken a perfectly good house and had turned it into a bomb site on the strength of their 'expertise'. I felt nauseous. I needed to find somebody who could reassure me, and I needed to find *him* quickly!

I turned around to vent to Emma, but she had disappeared. I headed for the sitting room and then on to the drawing room, where I found Emma and Mick O'Rourke deep in 'conversation'. I didn't have time to think about this now not-so-unexpected turn of events; to put it bluntly, I was desperate to find the organ grinder and not the monkey. Rather too sharply, I asked Mick where Paddy was, only to be told that he was probably lifting the last of the sandstone flags in the pantry. Anxiety heaped upon anxiety! I made my way towards it, my heart beating a military tattoo in my chest.

Once there, I found Paddy O'Rourke on his knees, crowbar in hand. As you can imagine, the sight of the heavy iron tool did little to reassure me, if anything, it made me feel a whole lot worse! Wasn't a crowbar associated with acts of violence? My mind was racing, and I fought the urge to scream. I couldn't remember the lifting of Alice-Rose's metaphorical skirts being part of the plans! But then at that point, I couldn't really remember anything except that I had allowed these people access to her hallowed chambers.

My mind was in overdrive as I tried not to think about what other acts of destruction might be awaiting my 'approval'; there was still a great deal of the house that I hadn't yet seen. Why, oh why, had I stayed away for so long? Hadn't my father always said that it was the owner's eye that fattened the stock and that a stranger's care lays on a hair? In other words, don't entrust your affairs to anyone else. And yet I had given virtual strangers carte blanche when it came to something that was much more than a possession, Alice-Rose was my dream!

'Paddy!' I said, too quickly and too loudly to sound even remotely friendly. My tone was hostile, and I knew it even before I saw the startled look on his face as he turned towards me.

'Sorry,' I continued, holding up an apologetic hand, 'I didn't mean to startle you.'

His face relaxed, and he got to his feet.

'Hello, Libby,' he said in an even, *almost* friendly tone. 'Is anything the matter?'

'Well, Paddy, it's just that I'm feeling a bit uncertain . . . seeing the windows taken out, the roof off, and the floor uprooted has left me questioning the wisdom of all of this . . ..' I stopped, looking around me helplessly, unsure of how to continue.

This was not like me. I was usually so sure of myself and my decisions. Why was I suddenly questioning everything that myself and Austin Stackpoole had gone over countless times? The only reason I could think of was that I didn't personally know the O'Rourkes, and so far I hadn't managed to establish even the most superficial of working relationships with either of them. The fact that I had skipped town, in a manner of speaking, for three days, hadn't helped matters either! Renovation of the house was progressing more rapidly than I had expected, and now it was too late to call a halt to work that was irretrievably underway. That being said, my unplanned 'leave of absence' couldn't really have been helped. I concentrated my mind, drew in a deep breath, and continued.

'Paddy,' I said, forcing myself to be calm and reasonable, 'I'm sorry that I've been missing for the last three days, but I didn't expect the work to progress so quickly.' That was an understatement!

'It's shocking to be honest, to see it laid bare like this . . ..' I waved a helpless hand about me, feeling like a fish that had been unceremoniously dumped on the bank of a river and was now fighting for every breath.

'I'm overwhelmed,' I admitted, 'and frankly, I'm frightened that it's all moving too quickly and that it will never be the same again!'

'It never will be,' he said calmly, too calmly for my liking. This wasn't his 'baby'; this wasn't his dream. This was just another job to Paddy O'Rourke! We looked at each other, and I felt my strength returning with the anger that Paddy O'Rourke's cavalier attitude sparked in me.

'What exactly do you mean?' I demanded.

'I mean what I say. Alice-Rose will never be the same again,' he reiterated, but this time in a tone adopted to explain the obvious.

We continued to appraise each other until I eventually won the staring competition.

'Alice-Rose will be immeasurably improved, and I can guarantee you that you will not be disappointed,' he said, softening somewhat. 'I give you my word that it will be returned to you unharmed and considerably the better for wear.'

I like to think that Paddy's change in attitude stemmed from his realisation that I was not a woman to be messed with, and not from any dread that his usual caustic approach might trigger a bout of hysteria in the 'wreck' standing before him!

'I'll hold you to that, Paddy,' I said firmly, and I meant it. 'I'm back now, and you can expect to see me most days from here on in.'

Hallelujah! I'd finally managed to stand up to him! Despite myself, I had allowed Paddy O'Rourke to intimidate me from the very start. I had gotten the distinct impression during our first encounter that the man didn't particularly like women, or at least not 'this woman', and I had allowed him to overawe me. I vowed that from that moment on I would paint my nails 'Jungle Red' and wear skirts up to my backside if I felt like it! I was paying the piper, so I would be calling the tunes, and Paddy O'Rourke's misogynistic tendencies could go to hell! I held my ground and waited for his response. You could have knocked me over with a feather when it finally came.

'That's great, Libby.'

Was that it? No lecture about getting in the way or leaving the experts to get on with the job? Just a simple 'That's great, Libby'? And my surprise didn't end there.

'Now, I can see that you're a little *uneasy* about everything that's taken place in your absence, so why don't I go through everything that we've done so far, with you? We can refer to the plans as we go.'

Paddy looked at me, and I could see that he'd been through the same scenario countless times with other clients. It was probably best to nip any doubts that arose in the bud as swiftly as possible, better for Paddy and better for the client. Whatever the reason, I was just glad of any opportunity for reassurance, and I jumped at it.

'Paddy, that would really be great,' I said. My voice was heavy with relief and gratitude.

Although there was so much more to Alice-Rose than the house alone, nevertheless it was at the very heart of the place. If the house was destroyed, then Alice-Rose would never be the same again, and therein lay the real cause for my concerns. However, a short time later, after almost having had a seizure at the sight of her 'destruction', I was feeling much happier about everything that the builders were undertaking.

The sandstone flags, like the roof slates, were being carefully numbered and would be replaced in the exact same position over a damp-proof course and a new underfloor heating system. Any flagstones that had to be discarded, and Paddy assured me that there were very few, would be replaced with matching ones that would be carefully cut to size. I would never know that the floor had been touched save for the warmth underfoot.

In the kitchen and the adjoining sitting room, two doorways would be made where windows now resided. This would allow access to a new Georgian style conservatory that would wrap itself around two sides of the house. Paddy reassured me that all the wood from the original shutters would be incorporated into the new panelling and that it would blend perfectly with the existing woodwork.

As well as the internal doors, a third of the house's windows had been painstakingly removed, together with some of the frames. Any frames that were in good condition were left in situ. The windows and frames had been carefully packed and sent to a company in Dublin that specialised in restoring period windows and doors. The rest of the windows would be removed in due course and would follow suit. The company guaranteed that all the original glass would be preserved where possible. Since very few panes were either missing or damaged, Paddy expected that the cost of replacement glass would be minimal. Triple glazing would be achieved by the installation of a system of removable storm windows similar to the ones used in homes situated in much colder climes. The system would have minimum impact on the original windows but would still achieve maximum effect in terms of heat conservation.

Once satisfied that 'my ship' was indeed in safe hands, I left Paddy, removing the last of the sandstone flags, and went in search of Emma. I found her where I had left her, deep in discussion with Mick O'Rourke. It would have been obvious to anyone with an eye in their head that there was a *degree* of attraction between the pair.

'Hello again,' I said as casually as I could. 'How are things with you, Mick?'

'Very well, Libby, thanks,' he said, rising to his feet from a kneeling position. He had been in the process of removing some of the floorboards in the drawing room.

'The house is coming along well, don't you think?' he continued enthusiastically.

If I had been given the opportunity, I would have agreed, but Mick wasn't finished enthusing.

'I really like Emma's new haircut, don't you?' he went on. Emma had the good grace to blush, and I ventured a response.

'Yes, to both your questions, Mick,' I said. 'Work on the house is definitely progressing, and Emma does indeed look amazing!'

I was amused by his sudden openness and by Emma's uncharacteristic bashfulness. I wouldn't have immediately paired these two together, but something was definitely hanging heavy in the air between them. The three of us chatted for another few minutes before Mick insisted that it was time that he got back to work.

In truth, I was more than relieved by his assertion because I was beginning to feel like the third wheel. Emma said goodbye, adding a coy 'see *you* tomorrow'. Her disclosure left me feeling slightly concerned; how much work would Mick achieve if Emma's distracting new 'hairdo' was going to appear on-site every day? She must have read my thoughts, and as it turned out, I needn't have worried, because Emma informed me on the journey back to Mum's that Mick was going to collect her after work the following evening and bring her for 'tea'.

'How sweet!' I cooed, feeling just a little bit envious.

'I know!' she agreed, relaxing back into her seat and kicking off her shoes. It seemed that Emma was totally unaffected by recent events of her heart and was ready and eager to move on. This in turn left me wondering when events of my own heart would get a move on. I pondered the road ahead and considered a giant oak in my father's field as we drove by. The sight of it restored my peace of mind. There was nothing like the magnitude of an ancient oak to put life in perspective. It had stood the test of time as I could. Life had its own rhythm, and I felt reassured that all would be well in the end.

Everyone was out when we got back to Lough Glen House. Ignoring the appeal of joining my sister to pick over the contents of Mum's ever bountiful fridge, I left her, heading back to Willow Cottage with the intention of getting to grips with some long overdue paperwork and a weeks' worth of laundry!

CHAPTER 29

Wedding Belles

I WAS ELBOW DEEP in 'whites' when Jules arrived unexpectedly at the little farmhouse, expensive-looking bottle of champagne in hand. She looked relaxed, happy, and the picture of good health. If I wasn't mistaken, she had shed a few pounds! Jules was never what one would call overweight; she had curves in all the right places, but perhaps her curves got a little too curvy on occasion. That day Jules was looking almost svelte!

'Look at you!' I said, unable to disguise my surprise at, and appreciation for, her newly toned figure.

'You like?' Jules asked in her finest Italian accent, twirling in the small doorway of the equally small utility room.

'I like!' I laughed, gazing up at her from my kneeling position in front of the washing machine.

'I'll just go and open this in the kitchen,' she said imperiously, pointing to the bottle of champagne. 'Do come and join me when you've finished slaving over a hot machine.'

Something big was definitely going on with Jules, and I suspected that Noel Kinsella had something to do with it!

I managed to curtail my curiosity just long enough to finish loading the washing machine, before following her into the kitchen. Jules was already standing by the AGA. She proffered me a glass, brim full of champagne, as I entered, and she was grinning from ear to tanned ear, like the proverbial cat that got the cream! I took the champagne with surprising eagerness, considering the earliness of the hour. I hadn't had any 'quality time' with Jules in a long time, and I had a sudden urge to indulge in a boozy conversation with my oldest and dearest friend. I was in luck because Jules had a lot to discuss!

Although Jules was not yet sporting the latest in designer jewels, Noel had in fact asked her to marry him!

'So soon?' were my first astonished words.

'I know!' said Jules. 'That's why I told him I'd have to ask you first before I could give him an answer.'

'You didn't?' I gasped, not believing a word of it.

'I most certainly did!' she insisted. 'After all, who better to ask for advice on this matter than the queen of true love herself?'

I gulped down the rest of my champagne in response to this analysis of my character.

'Hit me,' I said, holding out my glass for a refill, 'I think I'm going to need it!'

Jules did as she was told, and she joined me in a second glass.

'Look, Libby,' she reasoned, 'you married Max when you were both practically children, and that turned out brilliantly, despite everyone's misgivings.'

I turned a quizzical eye, with a glint of devilment, on her.

'There were misgivings?' I queried archly.

'Oh, Libby, you know what I mean! You were both so young, so in love, so madly in love! Some might have doubted that it could last . . .,' she finished weakly, realising too late the fatalistic implications of her words.

I suddenly felt bad for having deliberately put Jules, the most loyal of friends, in such an awkward position. Her abject horror, as she realised how potentially ill-chosen her words were, was plain to see on her face. Her helplessness at not being able to take them back was even more painful to watch.

'Sorry, darling,' I said, going over and giving her a reassuring hug. 'I was just teasing. I knew what you meant.' Her face relaxed, and she gave a sigh of relief.

'As it turns out, you've come to the right place if it's affairs of the heart that you want to discuss. I *do* just happen to have one of those, a heart that is!'

The afternoon saw the champagne finished, and the kettle boiled countless times. Jules regaled me with accounts of Noel and their first Christmas together; she waxed lyrical about their skiing holiday in Italy. I had fully expected that Jules would embrace the après ski aspect of the holiday but presumed that she would spend the mornings in active pursuit of sleep rather than attempting to conquer the slopes. I was wrong. My dear friend assured me that she was up at cock's crow every morning with her 'beloved' as he taught her the rudiments of skiing before progressing on to more advanced moves.

'Indeed!' I growled suggestively, and Jules howled with laughter.

CAITRÍONA LESLIE

In the end, she produced her digital camera with the footage to prove her improbable claims, while admitting that Noel and she, despite their gruelling ski schedule, had also found time to perfect their 'horizontal ski manoeuvres'. In fact, Jules declared skiing to be the ideal holiday and was even considering making it an annual event. And finally, Jules wanted to reassure me that if she did decide to say 'I do' to Noel that it would probably be an October wedding; they didn't want to run the risk of clashing with Emma and Mark's big day. After all, I would be acting in the capacity of chief bridesmaid on both occasions!

'Where once the bride, now always the bridesmaid!' I quipped, before realising that I had completely forgotten to tell Jules about Emma.

Listening to the unexpected turn of events in my sister's love life, Jules expressed astonishment and relief in equal measures. It came as no surprise to learn that Jules had not been overly fond of Mark Waldron either, but she had remained tight-lipped about her feelings out of a sense of loyalty to our family. A few moments passed before it occurred to her that Emma might find news of her engagement upsetting.

'Oh no!' she gasped, 'I've only just realised that I can't possibly say yes to Noel, not yet at any rate! How would an announcement like that make poor Emma feel?'

I hadn't gotten as far as telling Jules that Emma was undoubtedly coping well and had already set her sights on a new 'horizon'.

'If it's meant to be between Noel and me, we can wait another while,' Jules said unconvincingly, looking abject despite her best efforts.

'Poor, Jules,' I said sincerely, 'I know with certainty that Emma wouldn't want you to put your plans on hold for her sake.'

Jules took some convincing, but I eventually managed to persuade her that she should proceed with her plans as if Emma had never been engaged, and by that stage, we were both ravenous!

'Let's go to Mac's,' I suggested.

'Great idea,' agreed Jules, 'I could eat a horse!'

I went upstairs to change into something a little less tatty and left Jules to call a taxi. When I descended some considerable time later, Jules was pacing the kitchen impatiently.

'What on earth were you doing up there?' she questioned. 'It's not like you to take so long getting ready!'

'Sorry, dodgy tummy,' I said, feigning discomfort.

'If that's the case, I wonder if you should really be going out?' she said sympathetically.

'I feel fine now,' I reassured her, reaching for my coat. Jules had retouched her make-up and was looking 'flawlessly finished'.

The taxi was already waiting outside, and we headed for town and the welcoming atmosphere of Mac's. We were light-headed from the champagne consumed earlier but mostly from hunger and excitement. As we neared the middle of the pub, I was pleased to see that a small group of Jules's and Noel's family members had gathered, including their parents, and more importantly, Noel himself! It had taken a little ingenuity and some deception on my part, but I had managed to organise the little posse at short notice. Jules smiled bashfully at Noel as he stretched out his hand to take hers.

'You can ask me now,' she said gently, and a look of deep love and affection passed between them.

Getting down on one knee before the locals of Ballyedmond, Noel Kinsella declared his love for Jules Mahon before all. He then 'begged' her, with her father's permission, for her hand in marriage. The entire pub stood in silence and waited, with bated breath, for her reply. After much feigned consideration, for the benefit of all watching, Jules eventually said yes, and the party got under way! As news of their engagement spread, more friends and family members called in to wish the happy couple well.

I was on my first beer of the evening when I noticed the O'Rourke brothers taking seats at the far end of the bar. They were looking somewhat bemused by all that was taking place around them, so I went over to say hello and to fill them in on the cause of the celebration. While Mick was entertained by the tale, Paddy was clearly not.

'That man made quite a spectacle of himself over that girl. I hope she's worth it,' he said without humour.

I was taken aback by his remarks and offended into the bargain! The guy clearly had a monumental chip on his shoulder.

'So, Paddy,' I said, a lot more casually than I was feeling, 'I take it you don't approve of men making fools of themselves over women?'

Despite my best efforts, my tone betrayed my true feelings.

'It doesn't matter what I approve of. Forget I spoke,' he said brusquely.

Normally, I would have let the matter drop. After all, why should I care what this man did or did not think? But for some reason, I did care, and I couldn't let it drop before one last say.

'I will,' I said. 'But before I do, would I be right in thinking that you would never consider making a spectacle of yourself over a woman? Even a good one?'

'Let's just say, never again, and leave it at that,' he said grimly.

But he couldn't leave it at that either, and despite himself, he continued further.

'I notice that you haven't taken the plunge yourself. It can't be for the want of offers!' he said, looking pointedly at my ring finger. The man was an ass, and I didn't even know why I was bothering, but I just couldn't let it lie.

'You're wrong there, Paddy,' I said. 'I took the plunge, and what's more, I made the offer! And it was worth every last *spectacular* moment.'

This wasn't strictly true, but I was determined to make a point.

The look of astonishment mixed with embarrassment on his face said it all; he hadn't in his wildest dreams expected me to come out with a statement like that one! I felt an immediate sense of freedom from the resentment that I had felt towards him only a few moments before. Perhaps the sullen moodiness of the man, that was Paddy O'Rourke, would think twice before he jumped to any more conclusions about people that he didn't even know. Whoever the woman was who broke Paddy O'Rourke's heart, I was sure that she had had a lucky escape! Any man that could suck the cheer out of the atmosphere like this one could was best avoided at all costs!

'Anyway, gentlemen, I must get back to the party,' I said levelly as Mary Mac arrived to take their order. 'Enjoy your meal.'

I rejoined the party, which was getting more raucous by the minute. Jules noticed my return and came over to join me, leaving her 'dearly beloved' deep in conversation with his future father-in-law.

'Who were those men you were just talking to?' she whispered conspiratorially. 'Anyone interesting?'

'Eh, that would be a no!' I said, looking past Jules in an effort to attract the barman's attention. I needed another drink.

'Really?' I could tell that she wasn't convinced.

'Not really,' I conceded. I knew Jules wouldn't let the subject drop without getting to the bottom of it.

'I forgot you haven't met them yet,' I continued. 'Their names are Mick and Paddy O'Rourke. They have the building contract for Alice-Rose.' I could hear the detachment in my voice.

'Gosh, Libby, it doesn't sound like you have that relationship quite figured out yet,' Jules said with some degree of insight. 'How are things going on, up at Alice-Rose? I've been so wrapped up in myself that I've neglected to ask you about the biggest thing that's happening in your life.'

I knew that she felt genuinely sorry, but there was absolutely no reason for her to feel that way. I did remember the all-consuming distraction of true love and even that of the not-so-true.

'Don't be silly, Jules,' I said, 'everything is going great up there! If I seem a little distant, it's because it can all be a bit overwhelming at times.'

'I can imagine,' she empathised. She had *no* idea.

'I don't know how you manage it all,' she said unexpectedly, leading me to believe that she might have had some idea of the task's enormity, after all.

'At least you have a couple of *hunks* to feast your eyes on while you struggle with your decisions!' She laughed, giving me a playful dig in the ribs.

Nope, it was just as I had first suspected. The girl was clueless!

'Come on, let's get you a drink,' she said, heading towards the other, less crowded, end of the bar, 'you look like you could use one!'

I followed slowly in her wake. A couple of hunks? The girl must have had a lot more to drink than I thought! While I might have given Mick a pass, since Emma at least seemed to find him attractive, Paddy, on the other hand, was far from a hunk in the 'fine thing' sense of the word! To be a 'fine thing', in my opinion, you had to have a personality, and on that front, *he* was sorely lacking! Paddy O'Rourke was a hunk, all right, a great hunk of sour resentfulness mixed with condescending self-righteousness! But then I had to remind myself that Jules was only surveying the outward package. If it was just looks you were into, then I supposed he had a certain amount of appeal, and that he might engage the interest of someone with *no brain*!

Okay, Libby, I thought, *enough is enough!* It wasn't like me to be so harsh. After all, hadn't I just been critical of Paddy O'Rourke's presumptuousness? I didn't know the man's personal history, and as long as he did the job I was paying him to do, I shouldn't sit in judgement of him. I made a mental note not to rock the boat again with Paddy O'Rourke unless it was absolutely necessary. The sooner the job was finished, the sooner I could forget about clashing my personality against his.

I awoke early the following morning, feeling surprisingly good despite the revelry of the previous night. Jules phoned sometime later to say that she

CAITRÍONA LESLIE

was suffering from the 'mother and father of all hangovers' and wondering if I fancied indulging in a little post-mortem of the previous night's events. I was happy to oblige because it really had been a great night!

Jules and Noel had planned on going to Dublin that day to buy the engagement ring, but Jules had cried off on the grounds that she needed to be in the whole of her health for that particular mission. They were going to buy the ring on Monday instead, and she wanted me to join them in Shanahan's on the Green for dinner afterwards. The thought of dressing up and dining in Shanahan's after a day spent in the company of the O'Rourke brothers was very appealing! And besides, my New Year's resolution was to grab every social opportunity that came my way. While I hadn't totally given up on Dan, I didn't intend to spend my days and nights gathering cobwebs while I waited for him to get back to me. I could have a good time and still wait. Getting out and about would make the waiting go all the quicker.

The rest of the weekend was spent getting to grips with paperwork. While I had been out the day before, a fax had come through and had lain waiting for me on the bedroom floor; my shipment of furniture was due to arrive from the United States into Dublin Port the following Wednesday. Hallelujah! I had been fielding quite a few enquiries from would-be clients regarding the stock's arrival date, and many of those were now in the process of making their second round of calls to me. I didn't like to keep clients waiting; it was bad for business. I emailed Paula Nolan to let her know that she could launch the updated website the following weekend.

I spent Sunday evening baking. This was something that I always indulged in when I was feeling nervous or bored. Nerves were the main reason for this particular session of baking therapy. Monday morning was going to come all too soon, and I had to admit that I was dreading the awkwardness that would inevitably accompany meeting Paddy O'Rourke again.

My mind raced with a million self-recriminations. Why had I bothered saying anything at all to the man? Why couldn't I have just let his bad humour pass? And why, oh why, had I insisted on making an already awkward working relationship even worse? Of course, I knew there was no point lamenting what had taken place in the pub between Paddy and me, but I should have known better all the same!

CHAPTER 30

The Thaw

I ARRIVED AT ALICE-ROSE at around 9.30 a.m. the following morning, shamelessly bearing the fruits of the previous evening's labours along with a pot of that summer's rhubarb and fig marmalade. On route, I had detoured via Ballyedmond to pick up a tray of freshly brewed coffees and a pint of cream from the Gourmet Deli on Main Street. This peace offering would either be met with gratitude or hostility. Either way, it would leave us both knowing where we stood.

Bending into the boot of the Landrover to retrieve the neatly packed box of food and beverages, I was startled by a voice.

'Can I help you with anything, Libby?' Paddy O'Rourke's quietly spoken question broke the stillness of the morning air.

'Oh, Paddy! Sorry, I didn't hear you coming. You gave me a bit of a fright,' I said unnecessarily, a blind man would have seen me jump.

'I think I have it,' I said, turning back into the vehicle and pulling the box towards me.

'Here, let me get it,' Paddy said, gently manoeuvring himself between me and the box.

'Thanks,' I said, feeling a bit of 'a girl' because the box hardly weighed anything. 'It's just something for your coffee break,' I explained.

'That's very good of you, Libby, especially in light of my rudeness on Friday,' he said rather unexpectedly. 'I'm sorry. I've become a grouch of late. It's a bad habit.'

'Forget it, Paddy. I should let things go. Not *letting* things go has become a habit of my own. Truce?' I asked.

'Truce!' he agreed, smiling.

Nice smile, I thought, as I watched Paddy's retreating back.

However, I didn't get a chance to think any more about Paddy's smile once we entered the house. While Paddy went in search of the others, I laid out the food on a wall-papering table that had been set up in the kitchen to serve as their dining table. Conditions inside were cool but not unbearably cold; stackable stools were scattered here and there, leading me to conclude that the boys had migrated from their vehicle's dining quarters.

A few minutes later, Paddy appeared back in the kitchen with the rest of the gang. Without fuss, or further ado, they all tucked in, and it was gratifying to see that every last morsel of food and drink was consumed with relish. Eamon even went so far as to express the wish that his wife 'could cook like that', while Declan declared that the only thing his 'ma' could cook was toast, and she even managed to burn that a lot of the time! Mick was obvious in his enquiry as to whether or not Emma enjoyed cooking, and Paddy admitted that they 'could get used to this'. I learnt quite a bit about the men that morning, more than I had in the entire time since they had started work at Alice-Rose.

I learnt that Eamon and his wife were childhood sweethearts and that they were still mad about each other despite the distraction of six children ranging in age from eight to twenty-two. It was always the quiet ones!

Declan had no girlfriend 'yet', and that was a very big yet because he was busy working on it. Besides, his 'ma' didn't want him to get tied down too young; she thought it was better to experience the carefree nature of the single life before 'getting serious'. *Good advice*, I thought, even though, strictly speaking, I hadn't followed it myself.

I learnt that Mick had qualified as a national school teacher before finally deciding that architecture was his real passion and following in his big brother's footsteps to Bolton Street. That, I never would have figured!

And finally, I learnt that Paddy was both a qualified architect and an accomplished pianist.

'You're kidding me!' I laughed, as Mick revealed the extent of his brother's talents.

'I kid you not!' Mick said, arching his eyebrows and nodding his head vigorously. 'Paddy could have gone the concert pianist route!'

'Then I think that it's Paddy who should consider taking Emma out!' I said laughing. A look of bewilderment crossed their faces. 'She may not be much of a cook, but she's one hell of a musician!' I explained.

'Really?' exclaimed Mick, now even more impressed with the girl than he had been already.

'Really!' I said.

When the coffee break was over, it was time to get back to business, and Paddy took me through the house one more time to discuss some minor details. While we were talking, Paddy mentioned that he would be taking a trip to an architectural salvage yard in County Cork the following month. He offered to bring me if I fancied going along for a look. He didn't have to ask me twice! I had been born to trawl through such places; in fact, there was almost nothing I liked better! Paddy promised to remind me about the trip closer to the time, and I left the men elbow deep in dust.

And so began a pattern that would last for the best part of the restoration. Most working days saw me dropping in on the builders around 9.30 a.m., bearing some small offering of goodwill. Besides allowing me to keep abreast of events taking place at Alice-Rose, my new routine also meant that my baking skills improved greatly as I experimented with one recipe after another. A critique of my latest creations became the highlight of my day. Phrases like 'not as good as yesterday' or 'the best so far' were anticipated with bated breath. Most of the time, the speed with which the food was consumed was the truest indicator of my food critics' opinions.

For the most part, humour in 'Camp Alice-Rose' was good. By far, the most gregarious of the men was Declan. Youth engendered in him a natural curiosity and an openness, which I found both appealing and refreshing. Gradually, he began to make fewer references to the fact that I reminded him of his mother, and I began to feel more like an indulgent older sister. Eamon remained contemplative for the most part, but every so often, he would deliver an insight that, I knew, would remain with me until the grave.

Mick and Paddy were similar in lots of ways, and in time, it became clear that they were also incredibly close. However, Mick possessed a more devil-may-care attitude compared to Paddy's almost constant state of seriousness. In fact, I was relieved on the days that he was merely serious as some days found him downright dour. On those occasions, breakfast was brief, and our chats about the ongoing work briefer still.

Jules constantly teased me about 'the builders', wondering mischievously as to whether or not I had succumbed to any of 'their charms'? She stubbornly refused to believe that they held absolutely none for me!

'Libby, Libby, Libby,' she would drone. 'You forget that I've seen the O'Rourke brothers for myself, and *I* know fine things when I see them!'

'And so do I!' I retorted one evening, completely frustrated by her persistence.

'Mick is fine, but Paddy can be very hard work!'

CAITRÍONA LESLIE

'My dear girl, the fact of the matter is Mick is fine and Paddy is finer still!' she insisted suggestively.

'Oh, for God's sake, you just will not be told, will you? The man has as much charm as a garden gnome! If you don't believe me, just ask Emma,' I said, hoping that Emma might add some weight to my argument.

'Libby, don't you know me at all?' Jules replied witheringly. 'Of course, I've asked Emma! She happens to think that Paddy O'Rourke is a very passionate man, perfect, in fact, for you,' she finished triumphantly.

This last statement genuinely amused me.

'Perfect for me? She has got to be kidding! That girl has porridge for brains since she broke up with Mark!'

I felt myself getting annoyed; it occurred to me that I was feeling justifiably aggrieved because nobody was supporting me in my affection for Dan. Then I remembered that Emma didn't even know anything about Dan and that she was only trying to be kind. Truth be told, she wasn't far off the mark as far as Paddy O'Rourke's character went either; I imagined that Paddy was passionate, about his work at least. I suddenly felt very guilty.

'Sorry, Jules. Emma didn't deserve that,' I apologised. 'She's right,' I conceded, 'Paddy is passionate.'

'Aha!' said Jules triumphantly, sensing some sort of breakthrough.

'*And,*' I continued resolutely, '*I'm sure* that if I was two hundred years old and built of stone that I would stand a very good chance of gaining his attention!'

I looked at Jules. She had her mouth open, ready to speak, but I was determined to have the last word on this occasion. I held up my hand to silence her before continuing.

'However, I am neither of those things, and besides which, I am not interested in the man, never have been, and never will be! Can't we just leave at that?' I pleaded.

'If *you* say so, Libby,' Jules said, in a tone that was clearly meant to appease me but which ended up infuriating me instead. Only the passing of time would convince Jules of the truth, so there was no point in protesting any further.

'I do!' I said, hoping that that would be the end of the matter.

On a brighter note, work on Alice-Rose was progressing steadily, and I was soon seeing real changes. While Paddy O'Rourke might not have been the chattiest person in the world, he was a stickler for detail, and a perfectionist! Every aspect of the renovation was meticulously reviewed and improved upon where possible, and nothing was left to chance. I was soon in no doubt as to why Austin Stackpoole had unreservedly recommended 'O'Rourke and O'Rourke'; they hadn't come cheap, but ultimately, I was getting value for money.

CHAPTER 31

Spring in the Air

JANUARY CAME AND went, as did February. I didn't have any contact from Dan during that time, but I wasn't unduly surprised by this. I heard through Jules that Caroline had suffered complications and that Dan was spending as much time with her as he could. Mum always said that good mothers put their children before everything else, and I supposed that good fathers did the same. For my part, I would be patient and immerse myself in other things.

As luck would have it, other things were in plentiful supply. On the home front, early mornings were spent up at Alice-Rose, assessing progress and making, for the most part, minor decisions. On the business front, trade in American antiques continued to be brisk despite the overall scarcity of money in the economy. Filling orders and sourcing potential suppliers occupied most of my late mornings and early afternoons.

As if all of that wasn't enough to keep me busy, being Jules's bridesmaid turned out to be a career in itself! Any spare time that I had was spent trudging from one bridal shop to another. I was appalled to learn that one couldn't just turn up in a bridal shop any more, it was necessary to make an appointment weeks in advance for the more desirable ones and even then you were strictly 'on the clock'. Jules turned out to be a very indecisive bride in the end, in fact I think it's fair to say that she turned into a 'bridezilla' of sorts. The girl would proceed to try on one gorgeous dress after another only to end up in a state of confusion and near hysteria by the end of the allocated hour. This in turn would necessitate the making of another appointment, which could mean a delay of anything from three days to three weeks!

Finding the perfect dress wasn't the only headache involved in organising a traditional wedding. Jules assured me that although she loved Noel dearly, he had dreadful taste in nearly everything except women, and what's more, he even had the good grace to acknowledge his own failing! For this reason, he was more than happy to leave the entire wedding arrangements to his soon-to-be blushing bride, content in the knowledge that her taste in all things was impeccable! However, this investment of trust had an adverse effect on Jules; she started, for the first time in her life, to doubt herself! Unfortunately, this is where I came in.

Next to herself, Jules accorded me with the best sense of style of anyone she knew. Flattering and all as this display of confidence in me was, it brought with it its own set of problems. Suddenly, Jules couldn't choose an envelope without first presenting me with an extensive range so that I might choose the final one!

I soon began to feel like I was the one getting married, and I didn't even like where the plans were going! The pressure to take 'the pressure' off Jules was immense, and I began to feel myself cracking under the strain as a month went by without us achieving anything! At the rate we were going, I would be remarried before Jules!

Noel expressed an interest in helping to choose the venue for the wedding reception, and Jules readily agreed. His involvement was bound to take the strain off us both. It didn't. My sense of relief was to be short-lived as Jules's doubts raised their ugly heads again, this time about her and Noel's ability to make a sound decision as a couple. Once more I was engaged, albeit in strictest confidence, to give my final seal of approval. As it turned out, on this occasion, Jules's doubts were well-founded.

We left Ballyedmond at 12.30 p.m. on 'wedding-venue-inspection day' under the pretext of going shopping. This was a plausible cover; shopping trips had become an even more frequent fixture of Jules's calendar than before, and I was her regular accomplice. I was, however, becoming a more reluctant collaborator with every passing week! That being said, I was more enthusiastic about that trip than I had been about some of the others. As far as I was concerned, Jules and Noel had decided on a venue, and it would just be a case of me throwing in a few well-timed 'oohs' and 'ahs' to give it the final seal of approval. When that was done, Jules and I could have a slap-up lunch together while continuing to applaud the soundness of their choice.

Jules had told me nothing about the place beforehand; she wanted it to be a complete surprise. It was. I was 'completely surprised' when an hour and twenty-five minutes later we were still on the road, with yet some distance to go! I bit my tongue and said nothing despite the ache in my stomach, and the dawning realisation that no matter how spectacular the place was, it could never be a runner, not if she didn't want to lose half of the wedding party along the way!

Besides the distance, as far as I could see, the hotel was at the end of a road to nowhere! Eventually, as we bumped along yet another treelined country road, Jules jammed on the brakes and came to a grinding halt at a truly magnificent gateway. She glanced at me for signs of approval before turning the car on to the drive. I think she was looking for a reaction to match the spectacle of the entrance, but I had passed that point a long time ago! I could just about muster the will to straighten up in my seat and crane my neck towards the horizon where I hoped food was being served.

Another ten minutes, and several cattle grids later, I finally caught my first glimpse of Castle Reddan. It looked magnificent, all right, in a mediaeval sort of way. Jules, with a final burst of enthusiasm, accelerated, and we soon pulled up in the gravelled forecourt of what appeared to be an authentic castle, complete with turrets!

There were none of the usual signs of life around Castle Reddan that one would expect to see around a hotel. Even taking the time of year into account, the place still seemed remarkably quiet. It had been drizzling on the journey up, or down, as the case might have been. By the time we arrived, I really had no idea where we were or what direction we had come from; I had completely lost my bearings. As Jules turned off the ignition, the heavens opened, and we were incarcerated in the car for another fifteen minutes by a torrential downpour.

Normally, I might have enjoyed such an experience, but by then, my legs were getting restless, and I was starving! I had eaten nothing since breakfast in anticipation of lunch around 1 p.m. Jules glanced at her watch and announced that it was twenty past two and that she hoped Mr Yeats wouldn't be too much longer.

'Who's Mr Yeats?' I inquired innocently.

'The caretaker,' replied Jules.

'The caretaker? Don't you mean the hotel manager?' I demanded, beginning to feel decidedly uneasy. True, the absence of any signs of life had been noted and dismissed as perfectly normal for the time of year, but then, as I studied the place through the pouring rain, I realised that there was no sign of human life whatsoever, and a shiver ran down my spine!

'This place *is* a hotel, isn't it, Jules? I mean this isn't some sort of do-it-yourself wedding venue, is it?'

Jules picked up on the panic in my voice and tried to pacify me as best she could.

'Wait until you see it inside, Libby. It's very well maintained and completely authentic!' she insisted enthusiastically. I did not respond.

'There's even a company who specialises in weddings, and other events, at these *distinctive* venues. Mr Yeats promises me that our every need will be catered for.' I was lost for words. I could not respond.

'Mr Yeats also assures me that *these people* can transform the place, giving us a day to remember!' she continued bravely.

I would reserve final judgement until I had met Mr Yeats, but having seen Castle Reddan from the outside, and now dreading what I might find on the inside, I was not hopeful that the man would, or even could, dispel my concerns.

Just as the shower cleared, a teal blue Morris Minor pulled up alongside us, and Mr Yeats made his appearance. It would be putting it mildly to say that the man did not immediately instil confidence in me, but I managed to close my mouth firmly while repeating carefully in my head, *you must keep an open mind, you must keep an open mind!*

Mr Yeats had all the appearance and 'charm' of Leonard Rossitor in Rising Damp, only less appealing, if that's possible? His clammy hand shook ours loosely in quick succession before he turned to skip nimbly up the stone steps leading to the front door of the castle. Sweaty hands were never a good sign! You could tell a lot about a man by his handshake, and I allowed myself the luxury of remembering the first time that Dan Bryant had shook my hand. His handshake had been firm and dry and warm, the handshake of a man you could trust!

I turned my attention back to Mr Yeats, who was by then fumbling feebly about in his pocket for what eventually turned out to be an enormous key. I already hated the place, and this man wasn't helping! As Mr Yeats scrabbled with the immense front door, I wondered what exactly Jules and Noel had been thinking of when they decided upon this place? Was Jules's madness spreading to Noel? Surely, they couldn't be serious? Then it came to me, Jules was playing an elaborate trick on me. That could be her only possible explanation for bringing me to a place like this; she was having a laugh!

Finally, Mr Yeats freed the lock and, with great effort, pushed the huge door open to reveal a gloomy and cavernous interior. The walls were hung with several large tapestries, and the furniture was heavy and dark as befitted such a place.

'Imagine it with log fires and hundreds of candles!' urged Jules unconvincingly. Despite my initial instinct to shout 'fire, fire', I decided to go along with Jules for the fun of it and to see where her little charade might take us.

'I can!' I said with great enthusiasm; although try as I might, I was having great difficulty picturing the transformation.

'It will be so romantic by candlelight!' she said.

'Are you considering a winter wedding, Jules?' I asked innocently. Jules threw me a quizzical look. At that point, Mr Yeats intervened.

'This building, flooded by candlelight, looks stunning in winter or summer.'

'Well, that's certainly reassuring,' I said, 'and it gives Jules and Noel lots of scope when it comes to planning their *big* day.'

'*I know*,' said Jules in a tone that implied that she couldn't quite believe their luck.

'What date were you planning on Jules?' I asked.

'Well, as luck would have it, Mr Yeats says that the recession has freed up a number of openings over the summer *and* autumn so that basically we can have our pick of dates between now and Christmas!'

'Really?' I said, my voice dripping sarcasm.

I wasn't at all surprised by the revelation.

And the 'good luck' didn't end there! Because of the number of cancellations that had occurred 'in response to the recession', the castle hadn't been maintained to its usual 'high standards'. This meant that Jules and Noel would either have to clean it themselves or hire somebody else to do it for them! Jules seemed unfazed by this, and Mr Yeats continued to hold forth for the next forty minutes, turning every recession-enforced restriction into a golden opportunity for Jules and Noel! Eventually, I couldn't take any more of Mr Yeats *or* Castle Reddan.

'Jules,' I said firmly, 'I'm starving, and I can't think straight. Let's go and get something to eat, and then you can have my honest opinion.'

Jules looked at me doubtfully, and Mr Yeats eyed me suspiciously. I was the fabled fly in his ointment.

'Come on!' I said, even more firmly; my tone brokered no argument. Jules said a quick goodbye to Mr Yeats before following me out to the car. I wasn't able to utter any words of farewell to the man because I didn't trust myself to speak.

'So is that a yes?' Jules asked as we drove away.

'Don't say a word,' I said quietly, staring straight ahead. 'I need to eat first, and after that, I'll be in need of a stiff drink.'

'Could I hope for *a maybe*?'

I remained tight-lipped. I still didn't trust myself to speak. I knew Jules was acting out of character since the engagement, but this goose chase was the final straw!

'Where do you want to eat?' she asked after ten minutes of driving in silence.

'I don't care, Jules. The first place that looks like it might have a slice of bread will do,' I said, and I meant it.

'Okay, okay, I get the picture,' she said in a tone that indicated that she was beginning to fight back.

I knew Jules so well; her manner at Castle Reddan had already indicated that she knew that the idea of hosting the wedding there was ridiculous! When exactly she had experienced this epiphany was anyone's guess, but one thing I did know for sure was that Jules always had a hard time admitting when she was wrong. Having had time to think and anticipating my response, she was getting ready to justify her madness, and there was a part of me that couldn't wait to hear what she had to say.

Thankfully, we eventually came to a beautifully maintained village that boasted two pubs on opposite sides of the street to one another. Both displayed signs indicating that they served food all day. The evening was getting on, and the bad weather, combined with the time of year, meant that although it was not yet four o'clock, it was already getting dark. Jules pulled into the car park of one of the pubs before saying, with the air of someone who had reached their pre-planned destination, 'Ah, here we are!'

'Here we are, indeed!' I said, but not too unkindly.

After all, Jules was my greatest friend, and I did love her. I made a mental note to tell her so before shattering her dreams of a wedding fit for a queen at Castle Reddan. Jules locked the car, and we headed for the back entrance of the establishment.

We had chosen well, and the pub turned out to be a veritable oasis, a haven in the wilderness! After a prompt and friendly welcome from one of the waitresses, we were seated and presented with menus. The 'specials' were written on a blackboard that the waitress brought to our table. Due to our mutual states of starvation, it didn't take long for Jules and I to decide on our order. Ten minutes later, I was tucking into seafood chowder, while Jules feasted on mussels in garlic butter.

CAITRÍONA LESLIE

'I know "we're" driving, but let's indulge in a glass of red just the same,' said Jules, obviously sensing an improvement in my mood since the arrival of the chowder.

'Why not!' I agreed cheerfully.

The pub was dimly lit and cosy. The décor was traditional in style, and it looked like it probably hadn't changed all that much over the previous hundred years or so. Business was brisk; recession or not, people still enjoyed eating out. The waitress arrived with our wine, and Jules did the taste test.

'Perfect!' she announced happily.

The lady filled our glasses, and Jules didn't hesitate to raise hers, while I paused for a moment before raising mine.

'To the best of friends!' she said.

'To the best of friends!' I echoed, relieved that she hadn't proposed a toast to Castle Reddan.

The rest of the meal passed pleasantly, and we chatted about Jules's forthcoming nuptials, avoiding the awkward subject of the wedding reception! We both seemed to understand that that was a conversation that would be best held in private. After dinner, we left the welcoming warmth of the pub, carrying our half-finished bottle of wine with us.

'We'll finish this at home,' Jules said with a smile, raising the bottle by way of explanation.

'You bet! It was quite a fruity little number,' I said, feigning pretension.

'Just like us!' laughed Jules, and it was good to hear her laugh.

It had reached the point where Jules was so preoccupied by wedding arrangements that she rarely seemed to be enjoying herself; a state of affairs would have to change!

We arrived back at her place just after seven, and Jules kicked off her shoes and headed for the kitchen, swinging the wine bottle as she went. I went into the sitting room and took the liberty of lighting the gas fire and pulling the curtains before dimming the lights to create a cosy atmosphere.

I loved Jules's sitting room; the décor was so different from anything I would ever have attempted, being the latest in contemporary designer chic from floor to ceiling! Expansive suede couches resided either side of the white marble fireplace; glass-topped tables dotted the plush carpeting. It was clutter free and absolutely spotless! Her bespoke shelving was crammed with impressive hardbacks, ranging from architecture to zoology, but despite the endless choice of literature, I settled for the latest edition of *Hello* that I found neatly arranged on the oversized coffee table.

Jules arrived back five minutes later, carrying a tray that held two glasses of our remaining dinner wine along with a freshly opened bottle of red. Jules placed the tray on the table between us before offering me one of the glasses. I took the wine and steeled myself for the inevitable interrogation that would follow, as prepared and as determined as she was to have my say.

'So,' Jules said, seating herself opposite me and adopting an air of nonchalance, 'I take it that you don't approve of Castle Reddan?' She wore an expression that said *I don't even know why I'm bothering to ask when I already know what your answer will be*!

'It's not a question of whether or not I approve, Jules. As long as you and Noel are happy with Castle Reddan, that's all that matters.'

I knew that Jules wouldn't be expecting this approach. When Jules was in the wrong, she preferred to respond from a position of self-defence; it gave her a better footing when it came to seeking the moral high ground. My attitude left her powerless. Jules didn't say a word but stared into the fire and took a sip of her wine. Eventually, I ventured the obvious question.

'Jules, you and Noel did agree on Castle Reddan together, didn't you?' I took another sip of my wine.

'Of course, we did!' she replied quickly, but her tone was defensive. Now it was my turn to play the waiting game. I picked up *Hello* and resumed flicking through its pages, feigning total engrossment. Eventually, Jules couldn't stand the silence any longer, and she relented, qualifying her answer with a delayed and sheepish 'sort of'.

I took my time. She stared in my direction.

'Sorry, Jules,' I said eventually, looking up from the magazine, 'I'm afraid I was far away in the Mediterranean. What did you say?'

'You heard me, you wagon!' came her quick reply.

'Actually, I couldn't quite believe my ears, so I thought I'd better check before venturing to comment,' I replied coolly. Jules and I were old pros when it came to verbal fencing, having indulged in the sport together since childhood.

'So,' I said, 'Noel does not approve of Castle Reddan?'

'Well, it's not that he doesn't approve . . .,' she hesitated, and I knew then the kind of vague, defensive conversation that Jules had planned for us. However, after the day that I'd had, I knew with absolute certainty that I couldn't endure an evening of beating about the bush!

'Okay, Jules, spit it out! And I want the unvarnished, no-nonsense version of events that lead to *you* considering Castle Reddan as a possible venue!'

'Okay! Okay! You got me!' she admitted, yielding faster than I would have expected. 'I talked Noel into going for Castle Reddan.'

'But why?' I asked confounded.

'I don't know!' she said helplessly, looking vulnerable and, for once, completely out of her dept. I suddenly felt very sorry for Jules as I realised that I hadn't really been there for her. Sure, I had tagged along on all the shopping trips and indulged her indecisiveness, while all the time imagining myself far, far away in 'Alice-Roseland'.

When it came to what Jules had really needed, I had completely failed her. At a time when Jules had needed firm advice, I had taken the 'softly-softly' approach. Well, the hour had 'cometh' and so had the woman, so to speak. I could no longer shirk my responsibilities as Jules's chief and only bridesmaid, it was time to act!

'Jules darling,' I said, in the same tone that my mother uses when she's endeavouring to instil a sense of reason into a situation, '*this* is not just *your* wedding! And it is, after all, just a wedding!'

'But it's supposed to be the most important day of my life!' she pleaded, her voice heavy with the weight of responsibility that such knowledge imparted. I also knew that she was finally allowing all of her pent-up emotion and anxiety to bubble to the surface.

'Jules, I think we both know that that simply is not true. It's *one* day, albeit a very important one, out of a lifetime of days. The main thing to remember is that you love and are loved. That's all that matters. Okay?'

'Okay.' Jules smiled, and I could see that she was beginning to relax.

'Now let's take control of this *baby*, and organise a day that everyone will enjoy and remember. All right?'

'All right,' she sighed. I could tell that with a little determination, and a lot of hard work, things would eventually come right in the end.

That night turned into a very long one, where much was discussed and settled upon. We decided to free up as much time in the immediate forthcoming weeks as was possible in order to finalise the wedding arrangements. Neither of us relished the prospect of things being left until the last minute, and time was already running out. We forewent the temptation to consume the second bottle of wine in favour of clear heads while we set to work drawing up a comprehensive to-do list. Copious cups of coffee kept us going into the early hours of the morning, and I finally fell into bed content in the knowledge that we had at least broken the back of Jules's decision-making.

It transpired that Noel had shared all of my concerns about Castle Reddan and a few more besides. While my main concern was its remote location, fearing that while half of the guests might lose their way, the other half would surely lose their will, Noel's concerns were primarily financial. He didn't mind spending money, but he wasn't convinced that even a large injection of cash could put Castle Reddan to rights for their big day. Noel had proposed the more beguiling Ballyedmond House; it was within walking distance of the church, and it was available for weddings. I thought Ballyedmond House was an excellent and sensible location, but Jules dismissed it out of hand on the grounds that it could only seat one hundred and thirty guests.

'That's what marquees are for, Jules!' I exclaimed, astonished that the ever-efficient Jules hadn't thought of the obvious solution herself.

'Of course!' she said, slapping her forehead with the palm of her hand. 'Why didn't I think of that?'

'Heaven only knows,' I laughed, 'but at least we've thought of it now. Come to think of it, you were much better at organising my wedding than I was. Love must melt our brains!'

'I did have a little help from your mother!' Jules reminded me.

In truth, it had been a joint effort on both their parts because I had been elbow deep in exams and could just about spare enough time to go for dress fittings. Jules had taken charge of sending out the wedding invitations, insisting in the process that she should write each guest's name in calligraphy. That was no small undertaking, considering the fact that Jules had never learnt calligraphy and that it hadn't turn out to be as easy as it looked! However, true to form, Jules mastered the art, and our invitations had looked all the better for her gallant efforts. She had also taken charge of the mass booklets and the church duties in general, including organising the organist, the wedding singer, and the flowers!

While Jules and Mum had worked hand in hand on my behalf, I was very much on my own when it came to planning Jules's big day. Jules's mother, Felicity, although a loving mother, had absolutely no interest in event planning unless the event involved a horse!

Felicity preferred family occasions to be presented as a fait accompli. The only preparation for any celebratory event that she thoroughly enjoyed was shopping for a new outfit; I don't know why I hadn't thought of enlisting her help sooner, she would be the perfect accomplice when

CAITRÍONA LESLIE

it came to finally choosing Jules's wedding gown! Ballyedmond, to that day, had never seen a more beautiful bride than the girl formerly known as Felicity Rafter. I took no personal offence to the widely held opinion despite the fact that I too had been a Ballyedmond bride. Nevertheless, I was determined to take up the gauntlet on my best friend's behalf, and I felt confident that Jules, in the right dress, could give her mother a run for her money!

A major pre-wedding oversight came to light as I waited for a cab to bring me home that night from Jules. Idling by the window, whilst keeping a lookout for the taxi's approaching headlights, I casually enquired as to whether or not Jules and Noel had remembered to register their intention to marry with the state.

'Intention to marry?' Jules cried in dismay, her emotions still quite close to the surface despite the earlier pep talk.

'I didn't realise that you had to tell anyone of your intention to get married!' she insisted, jumping up from the couch. 'I thought you just whizzed it by the priest and away you went!'

Detecting the rising hysteria in Jules's voice, and fearing an undoing of all the good that had been achieved, I hastened to reassure her.

'Jules, you have loads of time. You only have to give the State three months' notice. It's still only February.' Jules looked visibly relieved.

'I'll do that first thing in the morning. Where do I start?' There was a steely note of determination in her voice.

'If memory serves me well, you can get a registration form from the Health Board.' I tried to sound convincing, although I was not at all sure of my memory's reliability. At that point, my taxi arrived, and I bade Jules goodnight, promising to meet her for lunch at Mac's the following day to begin executing the next stage of our plans.

I slept through the alarm the following morning, and I awoke with a start, knowing that the men would be expecting something for their morning break; I didn't want to disappoint them. I quickly mixed and kneaded two loaves of soda bread, placing them in the oven before heading for a quick shower. I made a mental note to tell the O'Rourkes that I would be gone from the scene for at least a week. I needed to get as much of Jules's wedding organised as soon as possible; otherwise, I ran the risk of being snowed under with wedding duties just as work on Alice-Rose was nearing completion, and that was the very last thing that I wanted!

Wrapping the loaves in greaseproof paper and placing them in a basket along with a pound of butter and a pot of Mum's raspberry jam, I left Willow Cottage and headed for Ballyedmond to pick up a round of coffees. It was raining heavily the whole way into town, but the downpour eased off just as I pulled into the car park at the back of the deli. I took advantage of the break in the weather and dashed inside.

The shop was busy despite the relative lateness of the hour, and I made my way to the back of the winding queue. I was deep in thought, surveying the tempting contents of the chilled display cabinet, when somebody tapped me on the arm.

'Penny for them,' said a familiar voice.

I turned around to find Dan Bryant at my elbow. He was holding a lidded paper cup in one hand and a folded newspaper in the other, and he looked tastier than anything else on offer! I was momentarily lost for words.

'I was just on my way out when I spotted you,' he said by way of unnecessary explanation. 'I've been meaning to call you.'

'Have you?' I asked too eagerly, not realising until that moment just how much I had wanted him to! Deep down, I had been feeling forsaken despite knowing the reason for his apparent abandonment of me.

'Yes, Libby,' he said, looking at me in a way that reassured me that he meant it.

'Good,' I said simply, hoping to convey as much feeling in that one simple word as he had in two.

We chatted for a while about Caroline and Todd, and about Alice-Rose, before I reached the top of the queue and wished that I hadn't. I didn't want our meeting to end.

'I don't suppose you have time to come with me to see what's been happening up at Alice-Rose?' I asked.

I could hear the pleading tone in my voice, and I didn't like it. I had developed a good system for coping without Dan, and I didn't want one brief encounter to undo it.

Glancing at his watch, Dan smiled and said, 'I do!'

We drove out to Alice-Rose in virtual silence. I don't think either of us could quite believe our luck at finding ourselves together again so unexpectedly. We commented on non-personal things as we drove past neighbours' fields and houses, but inside, I was a maelstrom of emotion.

CAITRÍONA LESLIE

I wanted to pull off the road. I wanted to feel Dan's hands and mouth on my face and on my body, while at the same time I wanted the perfection of our 'non-union' to last forever. Dan didn't reach out and touch me, and I wondered if he ever would. It was blissful torture!

We arrived at Alice-Rose unified only in spirit. Paddy was emerging from the back door of the house when we arrived, and he greeted us more warmly than I would have expected. I introduced the two men to each other, not quite knowing how to describe Dan to Paddy; after all, I still didn't know for certain how Dan felt about me. I ended up introducing Dan as 'a friend and the auctioneer who handled the sale of Alice-Rose'. Paddy graciously offered to accompany us on a tour of the house, and we accepted; to decline would have been impolite. I didn't really mind, I was quietly optimistic that Dan and I would have all the time in the world to be on our own there very soon.

We explored downstairs first and were on the return of the main staircase, heading upstairs to inspect the rest of the work, when Dan's mobile rang. It was obvious straightaway that the news on the other end was not good; Dan's face bore an expression of absolute defeat as he ended the call.

'I'm sorry, guys,' he said quietly. 'I'm going to have to go. That was Paul, my brother,' he added by way of explanation to Paddy. 'He's had some sad news from our sister in the States. Her husband has died suddenly, and we have to get out there as soon as possible.'

My heart sank. It was one crisis after another! Would Dan and I ever have the emotional space to get started? As we made our way back downstairs with Dan, Paddy and I didn't know what to say, or do, other than to express our heartfelt sympathies. I would have offered to drive Dan back into town had I not already known from the call that someone was collecting him at Alice-Rose. It transpired that Paul Bryant was driving in the vicinity when he had placed the call, and he was already waiting outside when we got to the back courtyard. I had forgotten that Paul would have known the layout of Alice-Rose just as well as Dan did since he had also been involved in the sale. Dan and I bade each other a hasty goodbye, with not even a handshake passing between us.

'That's too bad,' Paddy said, as the car pulled away from us, heading back down the front avenue.

'Yes,' I said, wondering yet again when, if ever, Dan and I would get started. Our prospects didn't look promising that day; it was as if the universe was working against us, determined at all costs to keep us apart.

'Let's have some tea, Libby. You look like you could use a cup,' Paddy said kindly, and I wondered if he knew how I felt about Dan.

'Thanks, Paddy, that would be good,' I sighed, relieved that someone was taking charge of the situation. I felt intensely disappointed and suddenly tired by the effort involved in trying to maintain a relationship that was, at best, ill-defined. I followed Paddy back inside to the tea-stained mugs, and the primus stove set carefully on the slab of stone that 'Aggie' had stood upon for decades.

Paddy took charge of brewing a pot of tea and insisted that I sit down. It was nice to be waited on, and I saw a domesticated side to the man that I hadn't thought I would. It didn't take long before I was presented with a steaming mug of tea and a plate that held the last buttered and jammed slices of my soda bread. We picnicked in silence for a while before I broke it by commenting on the fact that Paddy appeared to know his way around a kitchen.

'Well, I can boil water, and that's always useful!' he laughed. 'Let's just say that I'm not in any danger of starving!'

We chit-chatted about cooking, and I learnt that there was nothing Paddy liked better than putting his cooking skills to use, in the great outdoors. The word *loner* came to mind as I listened to his fascinating accounts of life in the wild. He had been on several hiking trips to far-flung places such as Alaska and Nepal; it was obvious from listening to him that he was passionate about nature and concerned about the mark that man was leaving on the earth. However, none of his escapades seemed to involve companionship of any kind, at least none that he mentioned. He was quiet and serious, but occasionally, I caught a glimpse of a smile and I was reminded that a smile could light up a face.

After 'tea and sympathy', we recommenced the tour that had been interrupted earlier. We inspected the entire house most mornings despite the fact that more often than not the work was concentrated in one particular area. Paddy seemed to appreciate Alice-Rose in the same way that I did, often referring to it as 'this special place'. I supposed that he felt passionately about every one of his projects, but I was grateful nonetheless for his careful consideration of mine. As I was leaving, I mentioned to him that I wouldn't be around much for the next week or so.

'I've got a wedding to plan,' I said, by way of explanation.

'I see,' he said.

CAITRÍONA LESLIE

I thought that I detected a note of alarm in his voice, and I remembered that Paddy didn't seem to approve of love, never mind marriage. I felt an absurd need to explain.

'Not my own, I hasten to add!' I said, laughing self-consciously. 'The couple whose engagement you witnessed that night in the pub. Jules is my best friend.'

'Ah, yes,' he said, his face appearing to relax.

'I'm the bridesmaid, you see. Well, technically I'm the maid of honour!' I continued nervously. 'Anyway, apparently, I'm a crucial part of the planning!'

I was babbling, and I didn't know why, although I had been aware for some time that Paddy O'Rourke often had this effect on me. I sometimes thought that it was because of the fact that he was a man of such few words and that it was for this reason alone that I felt an irrepressible need to fill the space between us. The urge to babble was especially true when it came to discussing things that I knew Paddy had absolutely no interest in. I forced myself to be quiet.

'We'll miss you,' he said.

'Will you?' I asked, quite surprised and a little bit thrilled, I have to admit, by his disclosure.

'Of course,' he said, without guile, 'we'll have to bring our own breakfast from now on.'

I looked at him and felt incredibly wounded; my willingness to feed them was all that this man saw in me.

'Okay then,' I said simply, my voice catching. I was rendered numb, and I was unable to think of anything else to say. I turned to go.

'Libby,' he said softly, touching my arm gently, 'I'm sorry. I was joking. We'll miss you, and not just for your incredible cooking.'

He was smiling that wonderful smile again, and I thought to myself how perfect this man could be for somebody. Somebody else.

'Thanks,' I said, relieved that my other attributes were somewhat evident, after all. We looked at each other, and suddenly, I felt that inexplicable need again to fill the distance between us with idle chatter.

'I'll be back cracking the whip before you know it,' I joked and immediately regretted it. Why couldn't I just remain quiet? Paddy didn't have a problem with silence and neither did I, most of the time!

'I have no doubt about that,' he said, and the spell was broken. I felt at a loss. I had done it again. I had broken a tenuous connection that had been formed between us. What was I so afraid of?

'I'll be bringing my home bakes with me to soften the blows,' I said more gently.

'We'll look forward to it,' he said, smiling.

I left Alice-Rose feeling better about myself and about the man who was restoring my most prized possession. Paddy and I had almost formed a real connection, and if nothing else, I knew that our next meeting would be friendly and on equal terms. I also harboured a real hope that the awkward silences that I insisted upon filling would in time become a thing of the past. At the very least, that day's site visit meant that I could relax and concentrate on Jules, knowing that Paddy and I had parted on good terms.

CAITRÍONA LESLIE

CHAPTER 32

The Wedding Planner

T HE FOLLOWING WEEK passed in a blur of paper and lace, Jules having swiftly dealt with the 'boring parts' of the wedding arrangements the morning after our goose chase to Castle Reddan! Having successfully registered her and Noel's intention to marry with the State, and encouraged by her achievement, she proceeded to check the availability of the church and the priest before booking Ballyedmond House for Saturday the twenty-fifth of June! These initial accomplishments empowered Jules, she became a woman on a mission and one that I was very happy to follow and support! That week saw us decisively organising marquees, flowers, cakes, and menus, complete with matching invitations and thank-you cards. We were unstoppable!

Some aspects of the plans were more effortless than others. For example, Dad had inherited a vintage Jaguar several years previously which meant that we didn't have too far to go to find the wedding car. It had even been used for our wedding, and I could only hope and pray that Jules's marriage lasted substantially longer than ours had. That being said, if one regarded happiness over longevity, as most people did, then I couldn't have wished for more!

I thought briefly about Dan Bryant and chastised myself for my foolishness. There I was considering a relationship with a man who was, for all intense purposes, a fantasy! I had allowed a few brief encounters to fuel my imagination when I should really have known better. Nothing meant anything until someone had nailed their colours to the post, and regardless of mitigating circumstances, that was something that Dan Bryant had so far conspicuously failed to do!

With everything accounted for except the bridal party's clothing, Jules and I, together with Jules's mum, hit the bridal boutiques with a vengeance; we were three women on a mission!

'My dear girl,' Felicity announced imperiously at the start of our quest to find the perfect gown, 'if you cannot be the most beautiful bride that Ballyedmond has ever seen, you can at least be the third!'

'The third?' Jules enquired, confused as to how her mother had come up with that particular placing.

'Well, darling, you are in the unenviable position of having Libby and myself as forerunners!' She sympathised with her daughter, while at the same time directing a mischievous wink in my direction.

'I *see*, Mother,' said Jules with a sigh. 'I hadn't thought of that, and *thank you* for reminding me! I only hope that you pair aren't out to handicap me in order to keep your placing!'

'Never, darling, never!' insisted Felicity. 'Libby and I have only your best interests at heart! We want to see you crossing the finish line with flying colours, so to speak.'

'Hmm,' replied Jules, 'flying colours, indeed!'

Felicity Rafter-Mahon, having come from a long line of horse trainers, often expressed herself using racing terminology. Felicity's father, and his father before him, had Gold Cup and Grand National winners, to name but a few triumphs, to their credit. One of her father's more famous horses had even been called 'Felicity's Girl' in her honour.

Shopping with Jules and Felicity proved to be more fun than I'd had in ages! Jules would try on one gown after another to Felicity's running commentary—too long! Too short! Too plain! Too fussy! Too horsey!

To be fair, while her comments might give one the impression that she was impossible to please, Felicity's opinions were always on the money, and Jules knew it! Jules arrived out in one particular dress to be greeted by 'My God, Jules, you want to look a vision, not a sight!'

And so the search continued.

Too high! Too low! Too small! Too big! To finally . . . just perfect! In the last boutique, of a very long line of boutiques, at the end of a very long day, we found The One. Our search was brought to an abrupt and definite conclusion the minute we saw Jules emerge from the fitting rooms wearing the gown and trailing two beaming assistants. They knew it too.

'Goddamn it, girl, you might just pip us at the post! What do you think, Libby?' demanded Felicity, bursting with pride at the sight of her youngest child, and only daughter, standing before her. I looked at Jules and then at Felicity, and then we both started to cry. Jules looked amazing!

The dress was a perfect fit, and there was nothing more to be done except to allow Felicity to pay for it before heading back home.

We returned to Ballyedmond and the innate grandeur and elegance of the Mahon family residence, which was set among one hundred and seventy acres of lush farmland on the edge of Ballyedmond town. The relatively new housing development, that counted Dan Bryant's home among their exclusive numbers, was nestled to one side of the entrance gates.

'Libby dear, Leo and I were offered an obscene amount of money for six acres, so much in fact that we felt obliged to take it!' Felicity explained on one occasion. 'With seven children to see to, I knew that all things considered, dear old Daddy wouldn't have minded.'

No explanation was necessary, I assured her. Hadn't Jules explained it all to me when she was handed the keys to the most exclusive house in the development as a twenty-first birthday present! As for 'dear old Daddy' not minding, that was a reference to Felicity's father and to the fact that he had presented the farm to Felicity and Leo, as a gift, on the occasion of their wedding some forty years earlier! Socks and jocks didn't feature on the gift lists of the Rafter-Mahons!

Felicity Rafter was a 'well-bred' Church of Ireland woman, whose family was very well-off and *very* proper! She had trained as a nurse in Mercer's Hospital in Dublin and had put quite a few men through her hands before falling head over heels for Dr Leo Mahon, a 'well-bred' Roman Catholic.

'Well, Jules, to be perfectly honest, Mummy and Daddy were horrified when I broke *the news* to them,' she had once confided in me, referencing her parents' reaction to the news that their daughter was dating a Catholic. 'And it has to be said that Leo's people were none too thrilled either!' she had continued. 'In *those days,* you were expected to marry "your own", *if* you know what I mean?' I did.

'Anyway, Leo and I were determined to be together, and that was that! What Felicity wanted, Felicity got, and *they* just had to make the best of it!' She laughed as if to say, *plus ça change.*

Forty years and seven children later, Felicity and Leo were still following that line of thinking, 'making the best of it' and doing rather well! The pair had worked hard to make a success of their marriage and the legacy that had been given to them. Leo had built up a successful ear, nose, and throat practice in Waterford, whilst Felicity had carried on the family business of breeding and training winners. There wasn't a racing pundit in the country, or in the United Kingdom for that matter, who wasn't familiar with the name Felicity Rafter-Mahon!

'Being given the farm by Mummy and Daddy meant much more to me than the farm itself,' Felicity would say on occasion. 'While I knew Leo and I would do all right regardless, their *gift* showed that they approved of me and more importantly that they *approved* of Leo, and that meant everything!'

Felicity's privileged background allowed her to speak of being given a farm of land, which happened to include an enviable period residence, as others would speak of being gifted a china tea set! It had to be said, however, that despite their privileges, the Mahons were hard-working and generous, and they had instilled the same work ethic in each of their seven children.

Matt, Jules's eldest brother, ran the stud farm with Felicity. Mark, another brother, had a small chain of organic butcher shops, which netted him a very respectable turnover judging by the size of his family. His wife was expecting their eighth child, and there was no indication that this would be their last. Davey and Tim Mahon were fraternal twins, and they alone had followed their father into the field of medicine. Davey had just been made a consultant paediatrician in one of the main paediatric hospitals in Dublin, while Tim was a cardiologist in Cardiff. Patrick Mahon was an undertaker in the town, and James Mahon was a turf accountant. Felicity liked to boast that Leo and she were 'neck and neck' when it came to the number of their children who had followed in their respective footsteps!

Once we were safely back from our shopping trip and ensconced in the comfort of the Mahon residence, Felicity bustled with life and good humour, rousing her husband from his fireside chair and the latest copy of *Immunology Today*.

'Leo darling, we're back, and we've found the gown! Do leave that down and come and join us in the kitchen for a glass of champagne!'

Leo looked lovingly over the rim of his spectacles at his wife and retired both his spectacles and the journal to the fireside table before following Felicity into the kitchen. He was well-used to his wife's energetic approach to life and adored her for it.

Once all of us were gathered in the large kitchen that Nora, the Mahon's housekeeper, tried to keep in order as best she could, we toasted Jules and Noel amidst rosettes and racing calendars. We had barely caught our breath

CAITRÍONA LESLIE

when Felicity announced that she had spotted the perfect dress for me in one of the many boutiques we had visited.

'For heaven's sake, Mother, why didn't you say something at the time?' demanded Jules, rolling her eyes to heaven upon hearing her mother's admission. 'Can you even remember which one it was, out of so many?'

'Darling, I *couldn't* say anything at the time in case it gave you the wrong idea,' Felicity explained.

'What *sort* of wrong idea?' her daughter asked, her voice laden with suspicion.

'Well, that you might want something like it,' replied her mother, as if that explained everything, which it didn't!

'And just what would have been wrong with that? I am the bride, after all!' insisted Jules, becoming exasperated by her mother's vagueness.

'Ah, but *you* are the blushing bride, my dear,' insisted Felicity. 'The dress I have in mind for Libby is a little too sexy for a bride. We don't want *you* marching up the aisle in something that will leave the vicar wondering where on earth he should look, now do we?'

'*Priest*, Mother, *priest*!' reminded Jules, beginning to get the picture and softening her tone somewhat. 'Remember? You did baptise me Catholic.'

'Yes, darling, I am well aware of the fact and have often regretted that decision I can tell you!' exclaimed her mother. 'It never occurred to me at the time that I would be depriving you of a whole sector of potential suitors!'

'By that, I take it that you mean the clergy, Mother?' Jules sighed.

'Well, obviously, Jules,' she replied. 'There's nothing wrong with marrying a clergyman, you know . . . theirs is a job for life! And that's not something to be sniffed at these days, I can tell you.'

'Indeed,' agreed Jules, warming to the subject.

'Anyhow, I digress,' insisted Felicity, refilling everyone's glass as she continued to hold forth. 'Priests aren't even allowed to marry, so they definitely could do without the temptation of being greeted by your breasts hanging out!' We all stood around in mock horror, waiting for Felicity's next 'shocking' statement.

'Libby, on the other hand . . . well, it's high time she got back on the horse. The girl *can't* remain celibate forever, you know!'

'Yes, Mother, I do know that, and in case you hadn't noticed, 'the girl' is in this room as we speak,' pleaded Jules, throwing an apologetic glance in my direction.

'Don't mind me,' I said.

Leo and I allowed a look of amusement to pass between us. This type of conversation was not unusual between Felicity and Jules, their verbal conflicts a constant source of amusement to family and friends.

'Anyhow, the dress that I have in mind for Libby would make a saint turn sinner, without in anyway upstaging you, darling,' assured Felicity.

'Well, that's all right then,' said Jules, feigning gravity. 'Heaven forbid anyone should upstage me on the day, and that includes *you*, Mother!'

She gave a pointed look in Felicity's direction.

'I hope that you'll have some dowdy little number lined up for yourself come the twenty-fifth of June!' retorted Jules good-humouredly, knowing full well that Felicity Rafter-Mahon could never do dowdy.

'No worries there, Jules,' Felicity beamed. 'I've borrowed a super little outfit from Nora that I'm having altered for the occasion!'

At this, we all howled with laughter. Nora Gillespie, whilst being a one in a million housekeeper, had absolutely no interest in clothes, and it showed! Any money that came Nora's way was invested in her garden and her grandchildren. Fashion was a 'non-runner' in Nora's world. Besides Nora's humble wardrobe, she probably weighed twice as much as Felicity and was a good six inches shorter.

'Thank you, Mother! I'm sure that you'll look perfectly lovely in it!' pronounced Jules through stifled laughter.

'You're welcome, darling,' said Felicity solemnly.

Two hours later, when the Mahons were graduating on to spirits, I was relieved from joining them by the timely arrival of Jules's eldest brother, Matt. He had been checking on an expectant mare in the yard and had called in to say goodnight. I declined the invitation to stay over and begged a lift home from him. He was going in my general direction, and I knew that he wouldn't mind going a little bit out of his way. Matt graciously obliged me, understanding that compared to his family's capacity for holding their liquor, I was an amateur.

On the drive home, I enquired after Matt's wife, Fiona, and their son, William. I had never met more adoring parents, and it was obvious that William was the centre of his parents' world. William was about to turn eight, and he was an only child. I had always presumed that having just one child had been their choice because William had arrived into the loving embrace of his parents exactly nine months after their wedding. It never occurred to me that fertility might be an issue.

CAITRÍONA LESLIE

Therefore, I was surprised when Matt revealed to me that night, in the confessional-like atmosphere of the car, that they had been trying for another baby since William was six months old, trying without even a hint of success. The couple had attended some of the top fertility specialists in the country, and they had been unable to find anything obviously wrong with either of them. Matt and Fiona had tried various fertility drugs and two cycles of IVF in a desperate bid to conceive, but all to no avail. My heart went out to them.

Having experienced the heartache of infertility myself, I could fully empathise with their desire for a second child, a sibling for their beloved son. I suggested complimentary therapies, citing various articles that I had read which quoted the success of such approaches. They had tried them all. I left Matt that night wishing him and Fiona the best and promising to include them in my prayers to the universe. As was my habit, I followed through on my promise of prayers by lighting a candle in the kitchen that night. If there was a God, then surely he could grant this most reasonable of requests?

CHAPTER 33

Sitting Pretty on the Shelf

THE FOLLOWING DAY was Saturday, and I decided to spend the day getting to grips with my neglected housework, not to mention the numerous emails that were awaiting my attention. So far I had resisted the temptation to employ my own 'Nora'. The very idea of having a housekeeper at Willow Cottage was an alien concept. There was only me; surely, I could manage my own housekeeping? Besides, when I had the time, I actually enjoyed housework; I found it relaxing. You could switch off your brain, and there was a sense of achievement at the end of it. I likened housekeeping to giving your home a well-deserved massage.

I was knee-deep in my 'house massage' when Mum phoned that afternoon, ostensibly inviting me to dinner that evening. Emma was having some friends over, and Mum thought that I might 'enjoy the party'. Those were her very words! Mum mentioned that she would be 'helping' Emma in the kitchen and that translated roughly as follows: Mum would be doing all the cooking, while Emma took most of the credit! I presumed that Mum had disclosed her 'contribution' to the evening in order to encourage me to attend the party. While Mum was a wonderful cook, Emma was not.

'Anything I can bring, Mum?' I asked, fully expecting that my mother, as usual, would have everything in hand and would decline my offer of help.

'Yes, thank you, Libby, I was hoping you would ask,' replied Mum rather too quickly. I nearly fell off my chair! Mum asking for help was not a good sign. By the time Mum had finished listing all of the things that she would like me to bring 'if it wasn't any trouble', I was convinced that my mother was in fact dying!

'Are you okay, Mum?' I enquired, suddenly beginning to worry about the state of my mother's health.

'Fine, Libby, why do you ask?' she replied indignantly, as if totally oblivious to the fact that she was acting out of character.

'Well . . . you don't usually ask for help,' I replied honestly.

'Really, darling? I'm sure that's not true at all!' came her reply.

'Okay then, Mum, if you're sure there's nothing's the matter, I'll see you at seven,' I said, hanging up the phone and staring at it as I considered what might be going on with my mother. Maybe she was just getting older . . ..

I abandoned cleaning and laundry in order to tackle the long list of things that Mum needed doing for that evening. Under normal circumstances, I quite enjoyed a challenge, but that day, I felt myself breaking into a sweat just thinking about all the things that I had to get done before seven o'clock that evening.

Mum had asked for ciabatta, sourdough balls, French onion soup, profiteroles, and a coffee cake, 'if it wasn't too much bother'! For anyone else, it would have been, but not for Mum! Mum was selfless to a fault, and if she found herself in the position of needing to ask for help, then it had to be for good reason, and I would not fail her!

I carried out a manic examination of my cupboards, while all the time cursing my younger sister's selfishness. It was high time that Emma learnt how to cook, and failing that, it was high time that she earned enough to pay for caterers! An inventory of the contents of my kitchen cupboards revealed that, by sheer chance, I had all of the necessary ingredients. With any luck, and a little help from the Gods, I might even manage to shower before dinner. Mum rang again at five o'clock to see how I was getting on and to ask if I could bring along some elderflower cordial if I had any of the previous year's stock remaining. I had. I ended our conversation abruptly and got straight back to work.

By a quarter to seven I was almost finished, I just had to add a dusting of icing sugar to the profiteroles before heading upstairs for a shower. I emerged from the bathroom at five past seven and hoped that Mum was running late too. If I hurried, I could make Lough Glen by 7.30 p.m.

At 7.27 p.m., I was sitting in my car, about to drive away while leaving the fruits of my labours, sitting neatly stacked, on the kitchen table in Willow Cottage! When I did eventually pull up to the rear entrance of my parents' house, I noticed that there were only two extra vehicles parked in the yard. Was I early, or was everybody else late? I felt mild panic rising within me; two cars hardly made a party, and I hadn't noticed any extra cars parked at the front of the house. Considering the parked cars carefully, I identified one of the vehicles as belonging to Noel Kinsella and the other looked vaguely familiar too. I presumed that it belonged to Mick O'Rourke.

I armed myself with the large saucepan containing the French onion soup and hoped that there were more than three people attending the party, because *I* was dressed for a party! When I thought about it, Mum had been very vague about who was coming and about the numbers. Therefore, I had erred on the side of caution and had prepared enough for a small army!

I began to doubt myself. Perhaps Mum had said that dinner was *for* eight, instead of at eight. Whatever the truth of the matter was, I had no time to worry about it then. Climbing the short flight of steps to the back door, I heard voices coming from inside, and just as I was about to leave the saucepan down on the top step, Mum opened the door and peered out.

'Libby! At last! I was afraid I had asked too much of you!' Mum said, without any hint of apology in her voice. Again, not very Mum-like.

'Fetch the rest of the stuff, then come and join us,' she said, taking the large saucepan of soup from me before turning back into the house.

I felt like the caterer! I was just thankful at that point that my mother had managed to refrain from closing the door in my face! Bending back into the Landrover to retrieve the rest of the food, I heard a discreet cough behind me. And I knew that cough!

'Paddy!' I almost choked on my surprise as I turned to see Paddy O'Rourke standing beside me. 'What on earth are you doing here?' I gasped.

'Your mother insisted that I come. Sorry,' he said, looking at me apologetically.

'Oh, don't apologise!' I said quickly, realising how rude I must have sounded. 'It's good to see you. I'm just a little surprised, that's all. Sorry for being so rude.'

'Here let me help you,' he said, taking the stack of containers from me.

Unloading food together was fast becoming a habit of ours.

'Thanks. I'll get the door,' I said, grateful for the darkness that hid my blushes. How could I have been so rude? Emma was going out with his brother for goodness sake! There had been every chance that he would be invited. Closing the Landrover's door and hurrying ahead of Paddy to get the now-closed back door, I regained a level of poise and accompanied him into the kitchen where Mum was busy preparing some nibbles.

'Thanks, darling, you are an absolute angel! I don't know what we'd do without you on these occasions!' Mum praised, far too generously!

I cringed in Paddy's direction, and he had the cheek to wink at me in return.

CAITRÍONA LESLIE

'You two run along into the drawing room, Dad's in there with everyone,' Mum continued, brushing us both aside with a flick of her tea towel. We did as we were told.

I was beginning to feel increasingly uneasy. There were very few vehicles outside, and there were no 'extras' hanging about in the kitchen as was usual at parties, and Sir Galahad, aka Mr Paddy O'Rourke, had been sent to 'rescue' me. What was Mother playing at?

Entering the drawing room, my worst fears were confirmed, and it was just as I had begun to suspect. Standing by the blazing fire were my father and Noel Kinsella, dressed very sensibly in casual shirts and V-necked sweaters. Over at the far wall stood Mick and Jules, admiring my mother's latest work of art. She had recently taken up painting as a hobby and was proving to have quite an eye for it. 'Everyone', as Mum had so generously put it, turned out to be a cosy little group of couples, with the notable exception of yours truly and Paddy O'Rourke. I could have happily strangled her!

The smell of 'a rat' was pungent in the room, and I reached for a glass of Chardonnay from a nearby table and drank deeply. I would definitely be staying the night because I already knew that I wouldn't be able to get through the evening's 'ménage a huit' sober. The evening had been Mum's idea all along, not Emma's. Mum was obviously showcasing my cooking skills for the sole benefit of Paddy O'Rourke! Oh, the embarrassment, and oh, the shame!

I avoided eye contact with Paddy. It must have been blatantly clear to him, and to everyone else present, what my mother was up to! *Damn, Dan Bryant,* I thought furiously, he should have been making a greater effort to contact me, instead of leaving me idling on the shelf unspoken for! Without any outward signs of a romantic association, I was at Mum's, and every other do-gooder's, mercy! I definitely needed the fortification of alcohol to see me through the 'party', while I forced myself to adopt a devil-may-care attitude.

Two glasses of wine later and the alcohol began to take effect. I felt sufficiently relaxed to divest myself of the heavy wool coat that was acting as my body armour on that occasion. It was warm in the drawing room, and the coat was absolutely unnecessary. I knew that I couldn't keep it on forever, but I was loath to take it off in light of the limited number of people present. When I had thrown on my clothes in haste that evening, I had unwittingly gone for sexy. I was unhappy with my choice even at the time, but I didn't have time to change, and I had hoped that in a crowded room I would go relatively unnoticed. Therefore, I was completely underdressed for that evening's little affair, underdressed in the sense of not having enough clothes on!

Taking one last glance around the room before finally parting company with my heavy outer garment, I was reminded that all was just as I had feared; in comparison to everybody else present, I was practically naked beneath my coat! Shrugging myself out of it, as nonchalantly as I could, I consoled myself with the thought that I would strangle my mother very slowly after everyone went home. I concentrated hard on not wincing out loud as my sexy *little* halter-neck dress was revealed to the room, and yes, *little* was the operative word! What had I been thinking?

'Oh . . . my . . . God . . .,' a voice whispered.

At first I thought that, despite myself, I had unconsciously groaned my silent supplication. Then I realised that the low groan was of approval and that it had come from Paddy O'Rourke, who was standing to my left. I glanced at him and bit my lip nervously.

'Too much, I know!' I whispered. 'I was in an awful hurry, *and* I was expecting a bigger crowd. I don't normally overdress or . . . or underdress like this! Just pretend you can't see me.'

'Are you kidding me?' he laughed. 'In case you haven't noticed, Libby, I am a man!'

Now that he mentioned it, I hadn't. I never really considered Paddy O'Rourke and base animal urges in the same cerebration. He was normally so serious and involved in his work that I presumed he operated from a higher plane than the rest of us mere mortals.

However, I had to admit that he was looking pretty handsome that night; he was clean for a start! Not a trace of dust or dirt to be seen in his thick 'dirty blond' hair! He was tall, at least six foot three, and he wasn't carrying any extra weight. Paddy was wearing a crisp white button-down shirt over jeans, and he had ditched the herringbone-tweed sports coat that he had been wearing earlier. His eyes were slate grey, and he had a very distinctive Romanesque nose. He wasn't pretty-boy handsome; he had a good face, a man's face. It would probably be safe to assume that most single women, and the mothers of those women, would pick Paddy O'Rourke out of a crowded room as someone worth considering as potential husband material.

CAITRÍONA LESLIE

'You'll have to poke my eyes out with hot sticks first!' he continued good-naturedly under his breath. His voice broke into my thoughts, and I suddenly felt relaxed.

'Let's just play along with your mum and see what happens. I'll take my lead from you,' he whispered, behind fisted cough, letting me know that he knew the set-up and that he was prepared to have a little fun with it. I would never have guessed before that night that Paddy O'Rourke had such a wicked side to him!

We sat down to dinner. Emma was 'playing' the hostess, while Mum was 'playing' the maid. My sister seated me between Paddy and Jules, and I had reserved hopes that the night might just turn out to be okay in the end. However, it didn't take long before Mum was unabashedly quizzing Paddy about his love life. Paddy remained vague and unforthcoming. That was my signal.

'Have you been to The George lately, Paddy?' I enquired casually—The George being one of the main gay bars in Dublin. Paddy smirked to himself before adopting a deadpan expression.

'Not recently, Libby, no,' he said.

'The George? Is that a pub?' enquired Mum, completely unaware of where the conversation was leading.

'More of a club, Mum,' interjected Emma helpfully, shooting us both 'daggers' across the table. She knew what we were up to, and she wasn't having any of it! That one question pretty much saved the night for us. All but Mum knew that her little matchmaking plan had been rumbled. Emma and Jules, together with Mick and Noel, worked tirelessly for the rest of the night to take the heat off Paddy and me. We in turn were able to sit back and enjoy a wonderful dinner and some entertaining conversation, none of which referred to the idea that Paddy and I might 'make a lovely couple'.

When all the guests had gone home at the end of the evening, and Emma and Dad had gone to bed, I tackled Mum about her elaborate matchmaking plan. She was in the process of putting the finishing touches to the kitchen clean-up when I asked her what exactly the night had been all about.

'Whatever do you mean, Libby?' she said, feigning ignorance. She was good; I'd have to give her that.

'You know very well what I mean, Mum,' I said patiently. 'Anyone with half a brain could figure out that tonight's little gathering was some sort of set-up designed to get myself and Paddy together.'

'Okay, darling,' she said, briefly ceasing from her chores, 'I'll admit that in arranging the dinner party tonight. I had some ulterior motives regarding you and Paddy. I think that you and Paddy O'Rourke could be perfect for one another. You'd see it too if you'd only open your eyes.'

'Open *my eyes*, Mother?' I said, indignation welling up inside me. 'I meet *that man* practically every day, and I know him far better than you might think *you* do. Paddy O'Rourke and I are polar opposites!'

'Polar opposites?' It was my mother's turn to be indignant. 'You're not polar opposites! If anything, you're too alike!'

'Look, Mother,' I said quietly, already beginning to regret having started the conversation. '*I appreciate* your interest. I really do. But *you're wrong* about this, and besides, I'm actually interested in somebody else.' The minute the words were out of my mouth I regretted them.

'Oh, *don't* tell me you're referring to your little infatuation with Dan Bryant!' my mother hissed, her unfamiliar tone one of exasperation and anger. It was obvious that she did not want anyone overhearing that particular slice of our conversation. I was shocked that she knew about my feelings for Dan; I'd only told Jules, and I knew that whatever else, Jules could be relied upon to keep a secret.

'Well, yes, as it happens, but how did you know?' I hissed back, forgetting to add that it was *not* an infatuation as she had so witheringly put it.

'Because *anyone* with an eye in their head the night of the Hallowe'en Ball could see that there was a measure of chemistry between you. You were dirty dancing for God's sake!'

She spat the last sentence out as if it was something truly distasteful.

'We were *not* dirty dancing! And doesn't the fact that there's chemistry between us count for anything?' I whispered urgently, hoping to appeal to her romantic instincts.

'Oh, for God's sake, Libby, I can't believe that I have to point this out to you! It's not chemistry that keeps a marriage alive. It's common ground, and lots of it!' she whispered back.

'Common ground and chemistry!' I said, lost for an effective retort.

'He is literally old enough to be your father! Trust me, darling, he will never make you as happy as Paddy could,' she said, softening slightly.

'Anyway,' I said defensively, 'I'm not sure that I ever want to get married again. I think once was probably enough.'

I didn't really believe this; I knew what a wonderful blessing a happy marriage was. But I wasn't going to admit it to my mother, at least not that night.

'Besides,' I continued, 'since it looks like I can't have children, I don't think even 'the wonderful Paddy' would be impressed by that *minor* detail from my curriculum vitae. At least Dan has children already, that's a plus from where I'm standing.'

'Libby, I don't want to fight with you. You're a grown woman. I have to remember that and let you get on with things as you see fit. After all, you've done a pretty good job so far.' Mum hugged me and kissed me warmly on the cheek. 'I want only the very best of what life has to offer for you!'

'I know you do, Mum,' I said, hugging her back soundly. 'Let's forget we ever had this conversation.'

'Okay, darling. I think I'll go to bed now. I'm more tired than I realised,' she said, and I knew that she was more upset than she was letting on. We kissed each other goodnight, and we headed to bed, parting company on the return of the stairs. I went in one direction to the guest bedroom, while my mother headed in the other.

Sarah

CHAPTER 34

No Matter How Good the Cut, a Thread Always Remains of the Apron String

THE LATE NIGHT conversation with Libby did little to allay my concerns for her. While I would always worry about my children, that was a fact of life, at that time, I was worrying on the double for Libby. She was such a sweet and good girl, and she hadn't deserved any of the bad stuff that life had seen fit to throw at her. When Max died, I didn't know what to do! I was helpless to make things better for her. It was sheer agony having to watch her suffer so keenly and to not be able to reach out and make her pain disappear. It was only then that I fully realised that Libby was no longer my little girl but a fully grown woman who had ventured beyond the safety of my arms.

In the aftermath of Max's premature death, I was immensely proud to witness the strength of character portrayed by my eldest daughter. She bore her sorrow with dignity and without any hint of self-pity, although I knew very well that she privately endured very dark moments of despair. As time passed, I began to feel ever more satisfied that Libby would allow herself to love, and to be loved, again. I truly believed that she would eventually acquire the life that I knew she yearned for, a life that included marriage and children.

In fact, I was quietly confident about our Libby's future right up until the moment Dan Bryant took her into his arms on the dance floor of the Donnard Arms. I knew then that we were in trouble. I recognised burning desire when I saw it, and I understood it. My marriage and my children were the result of burning desire but not of burning desire alone, and I now feared more than ever for my daughter's happiness.

I held nothing personally against Dan Bryant. As far as I knew, he was a very decent man, and I had wished him nothing but good luck after the death of his wife. Having known Marie Bryant from various fund-raising events over the years, the man had my full sympathy; his wife had been a shrew of a woman if ever I had met one! Marie was the kind of woman who gave all women a bad name. In fact, I was surprised to find that she hadn't managed to turn her husband off woman for life! But since she hadn't, I was more than ready to acknowledge that Dan, like Libby, deserved a second chance at happiness, just not with *my* beloved daughter. I hadn't endured the pains of labour to see my firstborn child settle for a man who had already lead the life that ultimately I wanted for her.

So when I met Paddy O'Rourke on that first day at Alice-Rose, he was like an answer to an unspoken prayer. Here was a chance for Libby to have it all, and even if Paddy O'Rourke didn't turn out to be The One, he might prove to be just the distraction needed to make her forget all about Dan Bryant. I bided my time, and I grabbed my opportunity when it arose.

Unfortunately, Libby appeared determined in her pursuit of 'the older man', and I went to bed after the party certain that I had failed. There I remained, tossing and turning beside my darling Jack, until dawn's dim light witnessed my eventual fall into restful slumber.

CAITRÍONA LESLIE

Libby

CHAPTER 35

It's an Ill Wind

MONDAY BROUGHT GUSTY gales and rain in bucketfuls. It was almost the seventeenth of March, and it was typical of the weather that prevailed at that time of year. I was thankful that the roof at Alice-Rose was now weatherproof, even if the rest of the house was somewhat compromised by the ongoing building works. Jules rang Willow Cottage early in the morning. We hadn't planned to meet, but one of her clients had cancelled his appointment at the last minute, and she was free for the rest of the day. She wondered if I would consider one last shopping expedition in an effort to get my bridesmaid's dress sorted once and for all. I groaned inwardly; I wasn't sure that I could endure another day of retail torture.

'Please, Libby?' Jules pleaded, sensing my hesitation. 'Just think that after today, you might never have to set foot in a shop on my behalf again!'

'Okay, Jules, you've convinced me! What time should I be ready for?' I asked, hoping that I might have time for an extra forty winks. I had been on my computer until all hours the night before, catching up with orders and queries, and I felt exhausted.

'Well, if you would just let me in, I could brew you a cuppa while you get ready,' she said sheepishly.

I went to the landing window and looked out. There was Jules, phone in hand, dressed, judging by what little I could see, in full business attire, safely ensconced behind the wheel of her BMW three series. I hadn't heard her drive up and park practically in the front hall! I must have been dead to the world!

'Are you sure you wouldn't like to park just a little bit closer?' I laughed, waving down at her. She waved back, relieved, I suppose, that I was at least smiling.

'Have you seen the weather?' she retorted unapologetically. 'I could drown if I had to make a dash for it!'

Forty minutes later, we set off to begin retracing our steps from the week before. The rain hadn't eased off. I predicted that the evening news would feature reports of widespread flooding, and I questioned the wisdom of undertaking any unnecessary travel in such severe weather conditions; visibility was poor, and road conditions were bound to be treacherous. I cautioned Jules to take her time, and for once, she agreed without so much as a squeak of protest.

We had decided before leaving the house that we would begin our search in the boutique where Jules had bought her wedding dress, presuming that we would be most likely to find a suitable dress there. However, despite the considerable range of bridesmaid's dresses, we came away empty-handed. Although there had been quite a few dresses that would have complemented Jules's dress beautifully, those same dresses did very little to compliment me.

Jules's dress was very old-worldly and would not have looked out of place in a photograph taken sixty years previously. It reminded me of those worn by brides during the second World War, by whose sides stood handsome young men in uniform. It was made of palest cream satin, with a well-fitted bodice, and its skirt was full length and generously cut. It accentuated Jules's curves perfectly, while at the same time a veil of fine lace completed the outfit and lent the future bride a becoming air of innocence.

Unfortunately, the bridesmaid's dress that had been bought in by the shop to go with that particular wedding gown looked completely wrong on me. And while I was quite happy to look a frump on the day, Jules would not hear tell of it!

'I've heard of girls choosing their least attractive friends as bridesmaids while proceeding to put them in the most awful frocks in order to make themselves look better' Jules pronounced gravely. 'And *I can* see how one might be tempted to do such a thing. *However*, since I have bravely chosen the most beautiful girl in town to be mine, I am *not* going to run the risk of her outshining me on the day, despite the wearing of a God-awful dress! We must persevere, Libby,' she said, brokering no argument and guiding us out of the shop and onwards in our search.

Five bridal shops and seventy-three miles later, and in the words of U2, we still hadn't found what we were looking for. I was beginning to despair at the thought of having to give up yet another day to 'the search' when we ended up finding exactly the right thing in the most unlikely of places!

CAITRÍONA LESLIE

It was approaching closing time when Jules and I trudged down the main street of yet another country town, deflated and footsore, and resigned to the fact that our day's efforts had been in vain. We were beyond even the briefest of glances in a bridal shop window, regardless of how promising it looked. Our search, at that point, was for somewhere to eat before we started on our long journey back home.

I was silently debating my food cravings when I spotted the sort of country fashion shop that my mother loved. Given the fact that it was not a bridal shop, and therefore held no expectations or associated pressures for us, it was easy to persuade Jules to have one last browse of the day.

Downstairs, the shop accommodated a small selection of men's suits and wedding hire, together with woman's casual wear. The floor was manned by a pleasant-looking middle-aged woman and a rather gaunt, but friendly, elderly gentleman. Discovering quite quickly that there was nothing to interest us on the ground floor, we made our way upstairs for a quick look, certain that our visit there would be as brief as it had been downstairs.

Much to our surprise, downstairs did not reflect the glamour that awaited us here; the rails were positively bulging with a remarkably tasteful and selective range of ladies occasion wear. A very stylish young woman stood behind a cashpoint, pen in hand, her impeccably blow-dried head bent over paperwork of some kind.

Despite the fact that I was essentially all shopped-out, I undertook a casual browse of the rails, leaving Jules, who was following slowly behind, to her own devices. It appeared that Jules was even more shopped-out than I was, and rather than browse, she was content to pass the time in conversation with the girl who had lifted her head in greeting just as she mounted the last step of the stairs.

'I think I've got *just the thing* for her,' I heard someone say, but I didn't know at the time that they were talking about me.

'I'd say your friend's a perfect twelve, would I be right?' I heard that same someone ask rhetorically.

'You would!' Jules answered from somewhere close by, and there was a definite quiver of excitement in her voice.

I thought that I had left Jules back at the till. I glanced around quickly to find Jules and the girl right beside me. I was bemused. Jules introduced me to our shop assistant whose name turned out to be Kay. It didn't suit her, but she didn't seem to notice and neither did Jules. That being said, I soon got the impression that given enough time in this girl's company, and the name Kay could grow on you.

Kay apologised for startling me and suggested that we follow her; she had a dress in mind that 'just might suit' us. No offence to Kay, but at the time I seriously doubted it, it seemed highly unlikely that she would manage to pull a rabbit out of the hat for us at that late hour. After all, we had trudged through the puddles and the rain, to all the designer shops in the region, and had not unearthed as much as a possibility! On what must surely be one of the wettest days on record, it would be unbelievable to conclude our search in a small and unassuming country clothing shop.

We followed Kay to the back of the shop floor and through an archway into a smaller room, a room that was packed tightly with every imaginable style of evening wear! It was an Aladdin's cave of designer treasures! Kay made straight for the sale-rail, and at that point, my heart sank; Jules later admitted that she lost heart at that point too. If what Kay had in mind for me was on the sale-rail, then it couldn't be wonderful; otherwise, why hadn't it been snapped up already? The sale season was well over, and sale-rails at that time of year generally only held the dregs.

'Ah yes, here it is, the bargain of the century!' Kay said, pulling something from the far end of the rail. Jules and I held our breath while I shut my eyes in anticipation of the 'awfulness' that I was about to be presented with. I heard Jules gasp, and I knew immediately that it was a gasp of pleasant surprise.

'Oh my God, it's exactly what we've been looking for!' she exhaled.

I was really surprised by her comment. I hadn't realised that we had known 'exactly' what we were looking for. In truth, I felt that the crux of our problem lay in the fact that we had absolutely no idea as to what we were looking for! I stood corrected.

'Try it on, Libby! Fast as you can and put us out of our misery!' Jules implored. Her hands were joined and touched her lips as if in silent prayer. I took the dress which was carefully shrouded in clear protective plastic. It was a dress of sheerest golden silk, and it did indeed look beautiful. I forced myself not to get too excited, remembering that looks could be deceptive.

Five minutes later, I emerged from the dressing room to spontaneous and joyous applause. I have to admit that, from the moment I felt the dress slide over my body and come to rest lightly on my frame, I knew that we had found the perfect bridesmaid's dress for me. I sashayed up and down the floor, enjoying my moment of glory at the centre of such a small, but appreciative, audience.

Kay asked for my shoe size, and less than five minutes later, a girl from the shoe shop, three doors down, arrived with a selection of gilded sandals in size forty. They were expensive, but we really didn't care.

As it turned out, Kay was right about the dress, and it did end up being the steal of the century! It was part of the previous year's stock and had been reduced from five hundred and fifty-seven euro, to a mere fifty! We couldn't quite believe our ears. Apparently, although many had tried the dress on, it hadn't fitted anyone as well as it fitted me. Kay was of the opinion that the original price tag discouraged people from taking on the extra cost, and risk, of alterations. We could not believe our luck and practically ran out of the shop before anyone had a chance to reconsider the price tag.

'Goodbye, dress!' Kay called down the stairs after us.

We made straight for Jules's car, complete with bargain-basement dress and very expensive heels! We didn't delay, even forfeiting the opportunity to eat in our eagerness to return home with our 'prize'.

Our first port of call was to Felicity and Leo's. Jules couldn't wait to show my dress to her mother.

'Mum should be suitably impressed,' observed Jules as we entered her parents' house by the front door. We weren't prepared to run the risk of an encounter with an overenthusiastic pooch in the back yard, or of brushing the dress off dung-covered wellies in the boot room. Entrance via the front door was a rarity, and we were counting on the element of surprise to ensure a safe and, more importantly, clean arrival. Jules went in ahead of me and secured all doors leading off the seldom used drawing room.

'Get changed in here, Libby,' she said, drawing the blinds on the expansive windows. 'I'll go and fetch Mum and anyone else who happens to be around.'

I wasn't particularly looking forward to being made a spectacle of so early in the evening, but I knew that protest would be futile. I quickly shrugged out of my clothes and slide into the dress before stepping into my newly acquired sandals, and still there was no sign of anyone. I tiptoed over to the fireplace, where I surveyed the state of my hair in the overmantle mirror.

The reflection that greeted me was less than perfect. The March winds had left me looking decidedly tousled, and not in a good way. It would have been obvious to anyone that mine was not the deliberate 'just out of bed look', it was much more of an accidental 'dragged through a bush backwards' style! I rummaged in my handbag and found my hairbrush and some extra hairgrips. Years of experience meant that within minutes I had accomplished a fairly elegant up-style, and I was finally ready to greet my public.

My 'public' turned out to be Felicity and Leo together with Matt Mahon's wife Fiona and their son William. I felt very self-conscious as everyone present, without exception, expressed their complete and absolute approval of our choice.

'You'll be the most beautiful bridesmaid in the world!' sighed eight-year-old William, much to everyone's amusement.

'Thank you, William, but you know technically, I'll be Jules's maid of honour,' I said, trying to portray some modicum of humility.

'Maid of honour? There's nothing honourable about that dress, my dear girl!' snorted Felicity, before turning to the others for confirmation of her pronouncement.

'I'm afraid she's right, Libby,' agreed Leo in a more gentle tone, 'I don't think there will be a man present that won't want to dance with that dress!'

'Well said, Leo!' agreed Felicity.

'You look absolutely beautiful, Libby,' said the gently spoken Fiona. 'I don't think you could have found a more perfect dress!'

'Thanks, Fiona,' I said, grateful for her reserve. 'Can I get dressed now?' I asked hopefully. 'And while I'm doing that, will somebody please rustle up a large pot of very strong tea?'

'Coming right up,' said Leo, bustling William and himself out of the room and leaving us ladies alone to discuss the intricacies of fashion.

The following day, Tuesday, dawned bright and breezy. I awoke refreshed and clear-headed, secure in the knowledge that the wedding of the year was all but organised. My bridesmaid's dress hung in Jules's large, state-of-the-art wardrobe so that I didn't even have it to look after it. It was in Jules's care now, and I wouldn't have to think about it again until the morning of the wedding! My wedding duties concluded for the time being; I couldn't wait to get as far as Alice-Rose, and to see the latest developments that had taken place!

Packing a basket with freshly baked apple turnovers and two large flasks of hot milk, I headed for the house and the sights that awaited me there. The driveway leading to Alice-Rose looked particularly pleasing in the early spring sunshine; the newly repaired fences and neatly trimmed hedges allowed one to view the fields beyond more easily than before. The giant trees towered over the lawns that hosted a riot of daffodils beneath their stately boughs. My heart soared with the sheer wonder of the transformation that had been achieved in such a relatively short period of time.

The rear entrance to the house looked pretty much the same as before, apart from the arrival of yet another storage container. Eamon and Declan were outside mixing cement when I arrived, and they seemed happy to see me.

'Hello, stranger!' Eamon called out, as I alighted from the Freelander, food basket in hand. Declan smiled and stood to prop himself up on his shovel in eager anticipation of a chat.

'Hello to yourselves!' I called back, making my way towards them.

'The foundations for the conservatory are in!' Declan announced, delighted with himself.

'And the dwarf wall is nearly finished!' added Eamon.

'Well, I'll just have to force myself to go inside and inspect all that hard work!' I sighed, genuinely delighted by the warmth of their reception.

'Have ye time for a cuppa?' I asked, holding up the picnic basket by way of encouragement.

'We'll just finish mixing this load, and then we'll be in,' assured Eamon, pointing to the cement mixer. The men resumed their task, and I made my way around the storage containers and up the time-worn limestone steps to the back door.

Entering the house, I listened carefully for any signs of life within. I had forgotten to ask Eamon and Declan where exactly Paddy and Mick were, although I knew they were somewhere in the vicinity because their van was parked outside. I got as far as the kitchen before I heard their voices; they were coming from outside the far wall. I followed the sound through the newly knocked-through doorway into the space that would become my new conservatory. The foundations were finished, just as Eamon had promised, and the dwarf walls were nearing completion so that I was able to image quite clearly what the finished proportions of the new space would be. They were more impressive than I had dared to hope! Hearing my footsteps, Paddy and Mick turned to face me.

'Hello, stranger!' were the first words that greeted me from Mick.

Paddy just smiled as if awaiting my response.

'That's the second greeting of that nature that I've received already this morning! I'm not that much of a stranger, am I?' I asked.

'Not at all,' reassured Mick, 'it's just that some of *us* were expecting you yesterday and were a little disappointed when you didn't show.'

'Hmm,' I said, playing along. 'I wonder if a basket of buns had arrived on the doorstep, all by themselves, would you have been half so disappointed.'

They both laughed at this, and we stood in silence surveying the work until I couldn't contain my excitement in any longer.

'It's wonderful, boys! It's really wonderful!' I exclaimed, holding my arms out in a gesture of amazement. 'I never dreamt that the conservatory would be half as impressive as this! I'm so glad that you talked me into it, Paddy.'

'I knew you'd like it, and in fairness, I can't take all the credit,' he said modestly. 'I got the idea from a house that we restored in County Kildare last year,' he continued. 'It's similar to yours, and we decided at the last minute to add a wrap-around conservatory to it.'

'*As you do!*' I interjected, amused by the idea that something of that magnitude could be entertained as a last-minute decision. Laughing, he acknowledged the apparent absurdity of the scenario before continuing.

'Anyway, the owners insisted, after all the work was finished, that out of *everything* the conservatory was the best investment of all!' I could tell by his enthusiasm that Paddy was warming to his subject.

'You won't really be able to appreciate the difference it will make to how you live until it's finished. Just think. You'll be able to enjoy that wonderful view three hundred and sixty-five days of the year!'

As Paddy spoke, he pointed up the hill, towards the place where the Scots pines stood sentry.

'It's rare to find a view of such uninterrupted beauty,' he commented, turning to look deep into my eyes in a way that left me more than a little disconcerted.

'Indeed!' agreed Mick heartily, breaking the spell.

'I know. I *do* feel *very* lucky,' I said, wondering for the first time who it was, that I was trying to convince.

'Actually, I'm glad you came by today,' Paddy continued lightly. 'I was going to call you anyway to see if this Thursday suited you to have a look around that salvage yard that I was telling you about.'

I hesitated trying to remember the conversation. All the recent wedding talk had temporarily erased my ability to immediately recall anything that wasn't related to Jules's wedding.

'If it doesn't, we can make it another day,' continued Paddy, sensing my hesitation.

CAITRÍONA LESLIE

'Sorry, Paddy,' I said, remembering the plan and warming once again to the idea. 'My mind has been so consumed by other things that it took me a moment to remember what you were talking about,' I explained. 'Of course, I'd love to go!' I said, and I meant it.

At that moment, I couldn't think of anything I'd rather do.

'They have some sandstone flags that I thought might be worth a look,' continued Paddy enthusiastically. 'They might marry in well with the ones here.'

'Great,' I said, amused by his unconscious marriage reference.

'Are you sure that Thursday suits you?' he asked, completely unaware of my amusement.

'Actually, I can tell you now that Thursday suits me perfectly,' I assured him. 'It hasn't been easy, but I think we finally have everything under control. I'm all yours!'

I looked at the O'Rourke brothers who were looking at me somewhat quizzically. Clearly, I was making very little sense as far as they were concerned.

'Jules's and Noel's wedding,' I said by way of explanation. 'Apparently, it's the maid of honour's duty to oversee everything—well, this maid of honour at any rate!'

I paused only long enough to draw breath before continuing.

'Lord knows, I didn't put half as much effort into my own wedding,' I informed them, before adding a definitive 'none in fact!'

I was reminded of Paddy's babble-inducing effect on me, so rather than stop, I continued on.

'Maybe I will the next time!' I said brightly, desperately trying to dig myself out of the hole that I had dug.

For some reason, my last remark caused Paddy to turn bright pink and left a smirk as wide as Christmas on Mick's face.

'Anyway, enough about me,' I stammered self-consciously. 'All I really meant to say is that I'm definitely free on Thursday.'

There was relief all round as I brought my jabbering to a halt. Paddy and I decided upon the arrangements for the following Thursday before I made a hasty departure and headed for the hills. Literally!

Walking through the fields that surrounded Alice-Rose, I decided that one of the things that I was missing on these excursions was the exuberance and companionship of a dog. I would have to look into getting one, now that I was a woman of the land.

Another, and far more pressing concern in that regard, was the restocking of the farm. George Baxter had cleared the fields and sheds of cattle prior to the sale, and now that spring had sprung; the absence of any form of livestock on the land was becoming more obvious. While Dougie Power's help would be invaluable when it came to stock-proofing the fences, I would need an expert to purchase the stock. My father used a man by the name of Kevin Mitchell to buy cattle for him, and Dad was pretty fussy when it came to the quality of his animals, so I decided to call Kevin later that evening to ask him whether or not he might be interested in doing the same for me.

CHAPTER 36

Blame It on the Oysters

P ADDY AND I arranged that he would call for me at Willow Cottage at seven thirty on the morning of our planned excursion. I offered him a bed for the night before, but he had insisted that getting up an hour earlier than usual would make no difference to him, and if outward appearances were anything to go by, he wasn't kidding. Opening the door that morning, in answer to his gentle knock, I saw a man who looked as if he had just enjoyed the sleep of the dead and was now fit for any challenge that the day might bring. All six foot something of him stood tall and relaxed in work boots, combats, checked shirt, and waxed three-quarter length coat. Paddy O'Rourke looked extremely well-scrubbed and terribly attractive, for somebody else. I was, after all, still holding out for Dan.

Cork, which was a considerable distance away, was our destination. While I didn't object to the journey per se, I couldn't help but wonder, in the wane light of morning, whether or not a more local salvage yard might have done just as well.

We approached the outskirts of Waterford City an hour later, having spent most of the journey in relaxed silence as we listened to the radio and to Ivan Yates as he debated the state of the nation. At the first roundabout on the outskirts of the city, Paddy turned to me with a slight smirk and a nod towards the back of the jeep.

'Did *we* forget the picnic?' he asked.

The *royal we* turned to him and informed him that I had indeed stuffed a couple of ham sandwiches, along with a bottle of cold tea, into my pockets before leaving the house! Therefore, if Paddy could just find a safe spot on the side of the road, we could pull in and have our refreshments.

Paddy laughed out loud at this before telling me that he had a better idea as he turned the jeep in the direction of the town centre. It was clear that Paddy knew the town well, and soon, he was parking the Landrover in an underground car park close to the shopping district. One short stroll later, we were sitting in a small café that served everything from the traditional 'full Irish breakfast' to 'eggs benedict New York style'.

The café was buzzing at that hour of the morning, and we commented on our luck at finding an unoccupied table by the window. We browsed the menu in comfortable silence, neither of us asking what the other one was considering. Much and all, as I hated to admit it, Mum did have a point; Paddy and I seemed to have some interests in common. My stomach rumbled, reminding me to give my full attention to the menu that I had been absent-mindedly surveying. I settled on my old favourite in the end: pancakes and maple syrup with a side order of sausage. Paddy took a chance and ordered the 'eggs benedict New York style', although neither of us knew exactly what that meant.

Our orders arrived promptly, accompanied by a very large pot of strong, steaming-hot tea. I was in heaven, and by the looks of Paddy, he wasn't far behind me. Closing my eyes with satisfaction as I swallowed the last morsel of pancake, I wondered aloud as to whether or not life could get any better. I was gratified when Paddy agreed that it probably couldn't.

We were back on the road heading south, shortly after eleven. Over breakfast, I had casually made an offer to take over some of the driving from Paddy, fully expecting that he would decline my proposal. It had been my experience that most men hated being in a vehicle driven by a woman, but it appeared that in this regard, Paddy O'Rourke was not like other men, and to my astonishment, he readily accepted my offer. I supposed that there had to be a catch as I felt my hand close around the keys that had been casually thrown to me across the jeep's bonnet; the rest of the journey to Cork would probably be the equivalent of a driving lesson.

As it turned out, I had completely misjudged Paddy O'Rourke, and I couldn't have found a more relaxed passenger! He chatted away about the history of Waterford City, a road map of Ireland lying partly open on his lap, and that was before we had even left the car park! I eventually managed to interrupt his ruminations to ask for directions, which he gave rather vaguely, waving his hand casually over the general area of the map as he did so. Laughing, I took it from him, and after a quick scrutiny of my own, we headed in the direction of Youghal in County Cork.

I had very fond memories of Cork City; Max and I had spent a weekend there shortly before his death. One evening, we had gotten quite inebriated in Cooney's Pub and ended up not being able to find our way back to the hotel, even though it was only five minutes away, in the opposite direction to the one we took! Eventually, we ended up hailing a taxi, but the driver refused to take us on the grounds that it would be quicker for us to walk. I must have been smiling to myself as I remembered our time in Cork because my thoughts were interrupted by Paddy offering me a penny for them, just as Dan had on one occasion.

'Oh, I was just remembering my husband, and how he loved cities,' I said casually. I didn't feel sad; one couldn't feel sad and think about Max at the same time.

'You must miss him very much,' Paddy said sympathetically.

'Yes, I do,' I agreed, thinking not for the first time how different my life would be if Max was still alive. 'But I have wonderful memories of him, and that helps.'

'It must,' he agreed.

'How about you? Have you ever been in love, or should I ask how many times?' I enquired lightly.

'Just the once,' he said quietly.

'I take it that once was enough?' I ventured tentatively.

'For now at least,' he admitted. 'I'm afraid that my heart doesn't seem to have the wonderful powers of recovery that most men's do.'

'I'm sorry,' I said.

'Don't be,' he said lightly. 'I think I'm finally getting over it.'

I hoped so. His reaction in the pub to Jules's engagement and his general air of sobriety led me to believe that having his heart broken had been a particularly hard learning curve for Paddy O'Rourke. Whatever had happened, I wondered if this man would ever learn to trust again.

'I've never had my heart broken,' I remarked quietly, 'but one thing I do know for sure is that the right person is worth waiting for.'

The minute I had spoken the words, I regretted them. I couldn't have thought of anything less banal to say if I had tried, and I felt certain that Paddy O'Rourke would come to exactly the same conclusion. What kind of nitwit admits to never having had their heart broken and then proceeds to dole out advice to the broken-hearted? It was akin to a celibate man preaching about the joys of sex!

'I'm sure you're right,' Paddy eventually said without reproach. 'I'm just not sure there's a woman alive that could put up with me.'

His last observation was made lightly, and I was gifted with one of his heart-warming smiles. My sense of relief was immense as I realised that I really didn't want to hurt Paddy, but I did want to lighten his mood.

'A woman you say?' I observed playfully.

'Yes, what should I have said?' he asked, slightly confused and clearly beginning to question the political correctness of his remark.

'So you're not gay?' I asked, keeping my face as straight, and my voice as non-committal, as possible.

'God, no! You didn't think that I was did you?' he asked, his voice full of concern.

'Anything is possible. How about asexual?'

I couldn't resist from continuing the teasing tone of the conversation.

'Asexual! For heaven's sake, Libby, what gave you that idea?' he gasped, his voice was heavy with exasperation.

'I'm joking, Paddy,' I said, fearing that I had carried 'the joke' too far and remembering that I didn't actually know this man well enough to be indulging in a Jules-type conversation with him.

'To be honest, I've never considered your sexuality either way, but I have no trouble in believing that you are indeed heterosexual.'

'Thank you, I think!' he said, frowning slightly in my direction, before breaking into a grin.

'You're welcome,' I said, feigning excessive magnanimity. 'Anytime you need your confidence boosted, you know who to call.'

'If you don't mind, I'll consider all of my other options before making that call!' he laughed, and I knew then that things were all right between us.

The rest of the journey passed in a mix of easy silence and light conversation. Paddy was something of an enigma. For a man who appeared to require total control in his working life, he was surprisingly relaxed in other ways. When it came to getting us the rest of the way to Cork, he had total confidence in my ability to drive and navigate all at the same time. At one point in the journey, he even fell asleep and awoke quite unconcerned. However, he did apologise for nodding off and confessed to having a habit of falling asleep in the passenger seat.

Paddy's relaxed approach to my driving was a new experience for me. In general, I found that most men presumed that women were missing the 'driving gene'. Even Max, whom I had considered to be laid back in most respects, had been an impossible passenger! In the end, I never drove anywhere in his company, preferring to let him get on with it and avoid the confrontation that would inevitably arise. My father and brothers were guilty of the same offence against women, only they took a different approach.

Where Max adopted a defensive position as a passenger, gripping the sides of the seat and applying constant pressure to an imaginary brake, my father would set up a running commentary, pointing out every potential hazard along the way. My brothers were the worst offenders; they insisted on declaring near misses where in fact there were none. Paddy O'Rourke, on the other hand, was the perfect co-pilot. He concurred with every driving decision, good and bad, and was relaxed enough to fall asleep, leaving a 'helpless little woman' like myself in sole charge of a 'dangerous piece of machinery'.

Luckily, the directions that Paddy had been given were clear and accurate, and we reached our destination without difficulty. The reclamation yard was located in the countryside, some twenty-five miles the far side of Cork City, and was situated in the grounds of an enormous early Georgian mansion. It was an absolute treasure trove of architectural salvage that spilled out far beyond the yard itself to surround the entire house. The first items of interest that caught my eye, as we approached the main residence, were two huge stone spheres resting at either side of the steps leading to its front door.

'I want them,' I said, to nobody in particular.

'I know,' said Paddy.

'Too much?' I asked, wondering if I had sensed a note of reprove in his voice.

'Perfect,' came his reply.

It soon became clear that when it came to high-quality scrap, Paddy O'Rourke and I were in simpatico. We moved through the yard in unison. Side by side, we silently passed the palates of reclaimed brick to get to the crates of salvaged slate and flagstones.

From there, we went into the sheds that held stacks of reclaimed flooring. The oak floorboards that were needed to replace some of the more worn and broken ones at Alice-Rose were easily located. Paddy urged me to err on the side of caution, and I decided to buy every single one, the reasoning being that even if they weren't used in the house, they would be useful when it came to converting the lofted accommodation in the stable yard. I liked how Paddy was thinking; he had foresight and the interest to recognise all of Alice-Rose's potential.

We were just at the point of leaving the vast sheds that accommodated the reclaimed flooring when Paddy spotted something partially covered by a shabby grey tarpaulin. He lifted the corner of the covering to reveal a huge block of neatly stacked parquet flooring; I could tell immediately that he was having a 'light bulb' moment, and I waited a while before venturing to speak.

'What have you got in mind?' I asked.

'Well, you probably won't go for it, and I'm not even sure how much is here . . .,' he paused infuriatingly, clearly thinking through his plan.

'Try me,' I said, trying to disguise my impatience.

'If we could get enough of this,' he said, gesturing to the oblong blocks of thick solid wood, 'it would look amazing done in a herringbone pattern.'

'What other kind of pattern is there?' I asked rhetorically.

I could see where his line of thinking was going, and I liked it.

'How many rooms are we talking about, and do we even know how much we need?' I asked, anticipating a potential problem.

'I was thinking the sitting room, drawing room, study, and hall,' he said deliberately. 'All the other downstairs areas will be covered by the sandstone flags, apart from the front porch, which has the original porcelain tiling, and we don't want to change that.'

I smiled at him, and he looked at me quizzically as if to say, 'What?'

'Nothing. I just like your enthusiasm,' I said in answer to his unspoken question.

'Anyway,' he continued, 'besides paying for itself over a lifetime, in terms of durability, I think it would look unbelievably beautiful in the space and would really give the old girl a sense off va-voom!'

'*Va-voom*, you say?' I said, stroking my chin in a gesture of consideration.

'*Va-voom*!' said Paddy, playing along.

'Well, when you put it like that, Alice-Rose, quite simply, must have it!'

'Besides, we can save on the cost of the replacement boards,' Paddy continued, covering all the bases, 'we won't need them now.'

'Great,' I said, genuinely thrilled at the prospect of the parquet flooring. I had often *lusted* after it in magazines but had never considered it as an option for Alice-Rose, only ever thinking of preserving the existing fixtures and fittings.

'So we're agreed?' he asked.

'Agreed!'

With that, Paddy whipped out a floor plan of the house, and after what seemed like impossibly quick mental calculations, he came up with the figures. It turned out that we needed a whooping sixteen hundred square foot of flooring and that didn't allow for wastage. Although Paddy didn't know how much was in the lot that stood before us, he was certain that there wasn't nearly enough; he doubted if there was even enough to do the front hall.

As if on cue, the yard's owner came into the shed to ask us whether or not we needed any help. We did. As luck would have, the block of flooring that we stood beside was the overflow of a larger stock, the bulk of which was being stored in the main house itself. The wood had been salvaged from a bank in Manchester that was facing demolition to allow for the expansion of a shopping mall; to the best of his knowledge, there was in excess of three thousand square foot of it in total. Paddy and I did an instinctive high five; we were in business!

The owner of the yard, sensing, I suppose, that we were more than just tyre kickers, offered us some refreshment. We broke for tea and used the time to hammer out some deals, including a price for the huge stone spheres at the front of the house. The proprietor's idea of refreshments was decidedly underwhelming, consisting of two cups of weak tea and half a packet of digestive biscuits, delivered with a flourish befitting high tea at Buckingham Palace. Paddy and I supped in silence for the first few minutes, both of us unable to meet the other's eye for fear of convulsing with laughter.

Three hours later, having finished our tea and an extensive trawl of the remaining yard, we had seen everything and had acquired all that was needed to complete the work on Alice-Rose. We made the delivery arrangements and bade farewell, before pulling away from the grand old mansion, heading back in the direction of Cork City. While we had satisfied a hunger of the soul, a diet of tea and biscuits did little to sustain the body, and by then, we were in desperate need of some real food.

At the first roundabout, Paddy took the turn-off for Kinsale, reasoning that in the long run it would be quicker than going into Cork City. We arrived into the town, one well-known for its gastronomic delights, hungry and weary. At that point, I really wasn't too fussy about where we ate; Paddy however, had other ideas. It turned out that he was a veteran of the town, and it was his belief that if we were going to eat, then we might as well try to make it a pleasant experience. With this end in mind, he guided us to a small seafood restaurant on the main street called Cockles and Mussels.

'Original,' I said, surveying the sign doubtfully.

I had to admit that it didn't look very promising from the outside, and hunger was stripping me of my sense of humour.

'Ah, the cooking eclipses what the sign lacks in originality,' Paddy hastened to say, seeing the shadows of doubt cross my face.

'In a good way?' I asked hopefully, forcing myself to appear more cheerful than I felt.

'In a very good way,' he reassured me.

He looked at me with what was fast becoming his trademark smile. I wondered briefly why it was that I was suddenly noticing it more and more? Surely, he had always had it! However, I decided that I'd have to think about that some other time; right there and then, I could only think of food.

Despite the time of year and the apparent lack of bustle around the town, the little restaurant was doing a very respectable trade. There were a few empty tables dotted here and there, but on the whole, the place was busy. The maître de seated us close to one of two open fires; it appeared that two houses had been knocked through to create a roomy space that still retained an atmosphere of intimacy.

A waitress arrived soon after with our menus and a wine list, featuring some very respectable vintages. Paddy offered to drive home if I wanted to indulge in a glass or two over dinner.

'Are you kidding me? Where would the fun be in that?' I asked, finding the prospect of drinking alone decidedly unappealing.

'I suppose it isn't much fun drinking alone,' he agreed.

Then I had an idea.

'It's getting very late, Paddy, for either of us to consider driving home, drunk or sober,' I observed, looking at my watch which was registering 7.35 p.m.

By the time we'd get finished eating, it would be close to 9 p.m., and then we'd have to face a long drive home after a very long day. In hindsight, we hadn't fully considered the logistics of the 'day trip'. Regardless of abstaining from alcohol, neither of us could be safely expected to stay awake behind the wheel under the circumstances. Paddy's earlier admission that he had a tendency to nod off in the passenger seat didn't fill me with confidence either, even if one could be guaranteed that that was the only time it ever happened. We had other options, and I felt it was time to start considering them.

'Why don't we stay over at my expense, and then we can both enjoy a glass or two?' I suggested.

CAITRÍONA LESLIE

I had no idea how Paddy would react to my suggestion, but it seemed like the obvious solution given the lateness of the hour and the length of the journey home.

'And you wouldn't mind?' he asked.

Paddy appeared surprised by my proposal. It occurred to me then that the same thought had crossed his mind but that he had dismissed it out of hand, wrongly presuming that I would not have been keen on the idea.

'Of course not, provided we can secure a bed for the night,' I said without thinking.

Paddy raised an eyebrow in my direction.

'Or two!' I added laughing. 'You *know* what I mean!'

'Okay then, providing there are a couple of rooms available at the hotel, we'll stay. And I'll pay my own way, thanks all the same. I'll just go and check,' he said, rising from his chair.

Ten minutes later, Paddy returned giving me the thumbs up before settling back down into his seat. He had booked two rooms in the local hotel. We were sorted.

'So, what's good to eat?' he asked, adopting the easy manner that I was becoming increasingly familiar with.

However, I still couldn't quite reconcile the 'lovely Paddy' of that day with the Paddy that I was used to meeting at Alice-Rose. Sure, I had glimpsed this side of him at my mother's dinner party, but I had been too self-conscious to fully enjoy it. The following day, we had resumed our civil, slightly distant, employee-client relationship, as if the night before had never happened. I liked this Paddy much better!

'Well, everything by the looks of it!' I replied, turning my attention back to the menu in my hand.

'Let's have a drink while we consider our options,' he said.

We ordered a mid-priced Chardonnay, which turned out to be incredibly delicious to our parched palates. After further study of the menu, Paddy allowed me to order first. I chose oysters with sauce mignonette for starters, followed by a ragout of seafood.

'I was afraid to order the oysters in case you got the wrong idea,' Paddy joked. 'But they do sound delicious, and since you're having them, I think I'll join you.'

Paddy turned to our waitress who was surveying us indulgently, clearly presuming that we were a couple.

'Make that two oyster starters, and I'll go for the grilled sea bass with beurre blanc for my main course,' he said, before closing his menu and handing it back to the girl.

We thanked her, and she headed for the kitchen.

Paddy refilled our depleting wine glasses, and we toasted finding the perfect sandstone flags, and after that, we toasted the parquet flooring, and so on. Paddy spoke enthusiastically about Alice-Rose, and I was gratified and flattered by his fulsome praise of her. As the wine loosened my inhibitions, I became conscious of the fact that the conversation was based around issues that mainly concerned me. I braced myself and ventured to ask Paddy about himself.

Paddy and Mick O'Rourke were the adopted sons and only children of Emily and Desmond O'Rourke. Their father was an architect, who continued to run a successful business in Dublin despite the downturn in the economy; it was his father's greatest wish that Paddy would, in time, take over the concern. As it stood, Paddy ran approximately thirty per cent of it, in between co-managing the brothers' restoration company with Mick.

Paddy's mother was a talented musician, who taught in the Royal School of Music, as well as coordinating various musical events nationwide. Amazingly, Paddy had been gifted with the talents of both his parents, and still the burning question remained as to whether nature or nurture was the biggest factor in determining a child's developmental outcome. Since Paddy had never traced his birth parents, he could only presume that in his case nurture had prevailed.

Paddy dated a girl called Alyson throughout his days in college; they met on their induction day in Bolton Street College of Technology and had remained steadfast in their commitment to one another for the remainder of their time there. However, Paddy had been blindsided on the night of their graduation when Alyson confessed that she no longer loved him. She thought, as did her family, that they were too young to know what 'real love' was; she wanted a break from the relationship in order to be free to date other people. According to Paddy, he was devastated. He couldn't contemplate the idea of Alyson dating others guys before possibly returning to him; the relationship was over for him the minute the suggestion was made. I admired his strength of character.

Ten years on, and he still hadn't found anyone to restore his faith in love and commitment. He had grown-up in a secure and loving family, and despite the hurts of the past, he still hoped to someday meet someone special and to have his own family. He admitted that adoption held no appeal for him, putting it down to the fact that he himself was adopted.

'I just want my own flesh and blood,' he said simply and unashamedly.

Despite not being adopted myself, I completely understood where he was coming from. I reminded myself that Dan Bryant already had his own 'flesh and blood'.

'I don't think I can have children,' I said simply, brushing away the apologies that I knew Paddy would feel obliged to offer with a wave of my hand.

For some reason, I felt the need to reveal this delicate and very personal piece of information to him. I imagined it popping up in conversation between Emma and Mick someday, and I didn't want those facts getting back to Paddy second-hand. I didn't want his pity, delayed or otherwise; there were worse things than being infertile.

'It's fine, honestly! Believe me I completely understand where you're coming from. It's the most natural thing in the world to want your own child,' I said, and I meant it.

'Max and I wanted children very badly,' I continued before Paddy got a chance to interrupt, 'or at least I did! We were so young. I don't think Max really thought about it too deeply. However, he was fully committed to my vain attempts at conception!' I laughed, trying to inject some lightness into a very serious subject.

Paddy didn't say a word. I presumed that he was too embarrassed to speak, and besides, what was there to say? I began to wish that I hadn't chosen that particular moment to reveal the most personal details of my life, but since I had, I had no choice but to continue.

'It wasn't to be and I've finally come to terms with it,' I said a tad too stoutly to be truly convincing. 'But I'm determined to be, at the very least, a wonderful aunt,' I added a little more convincingly. 'We might even share nieces and nephews someday!'

I was relieved then to see that Paddy was at least grinning.

'Anyway, now that I've vomited that disturbing piece of information on to the table, let's raise a toast?' Paddy held his glass to mine, and our fingers brushed briefly.

'To everlasting love and to babies,' I said quietly and without a flicker of doubt.

'To everlasting love,' Paddy said gently, holding my gaze.

Then he did something totally unexpected: he reached out and took my hand, and sensing an element of pity in his gesture, I felt obliged to reassure him.

'I'm okay, Paddy, honestly. I do have hope, and nothing is ever certain.'

'Okay, Boss,' he said gently and waved in the direction of our passing waitress. 'Let's order another bottle to celebrate the end to a perfect day.'

Another bottle of Chardonnay later, and we both agreed that enough was enough. We were tired, and our tolerance for alcohol was substantially diminished despite a sumptuous dinner. I just wanted to crawl into bed and get a good night's sleep, and I had no doubt but that Paddy wanted to do the same. I allowed Paddy to pay the bill on the understanding that I would cover the cost of the hotel. He agreed.

A short while later, we were taking the lift to our rooms. As the lift ground to a shuddering halt on the second floor, I stumbled against Paddy, who caught me lightly by my shoulders. Our eyes initially locked in amusement, but this amusement was quickly and unpredictably replaced by the recognition of a mutual desire. Paddy kissed me hesitantly, and I drew him to me in an attempt to steady myself because I had begun to shake with the strength of my longing.

Before that night, I hadn't known that one's sexuality could manifest itself so overtly. Perhaps I had lead a very sheltered existence by most people's standards, but I was amazed to discover that my sudden 'attraction' to Paddy O'Rourke was like nothing I had ever experienced before! He responded to my needs with a visceral passion of his own. His lips sought mine with a possessive ferocity that left me feeling weak at the knees while his hands urgently explored my body. We had already passed the point of no return.

We struggled to regain the outward appearance of self-control as we searched for one of our rooms in order to achieve the sexual fulfilment that we both craved; we were aware that most people wouldn't appreciate finding us in such a position of extreme compromise! Giggling uncontrollably in response to finding ourselves in the most unexpected situation, we eventually located Room 113, and scanning the access card, we pushed open the door to reveal what looked suspiciously like the honeymoon suite! The room was occupied by a very large four-poster bed, and there were fresh, long-stemmed roses standing in a large crystal vase! I wondered briefly about the room rate, but to be honest, I would have willingly sold my soul to the devil for that room! Paddy was more circumspect as the door closed behind us; he wanted reassurance that I knew what I was doing and that I wanted it.

'I'm . . . not sure,' I said, suddenly worried that this man might not want to make love to me, after all.

Then I saw the look of agony that clouded his face, and I knew that he needed me every bit as much as I needed him.

'Could you kiss me just one more time?' I whispered seductively into the corner of his mouth.

He did. And I was sure.

In between fevered kisses and fumbled disrobing, we managed to establish the unlikelihood of pregnancy or the transmission of sexual diseases. I had only ever slept with my husband and had failed to get pregnant during three years of copious, unprotected sex. For his part, Paddy's last girlfriend had only ever allowed 'safe' sex; he didn't describe her as being a control freak exactly, but she was careful, and I silently applauded her circumspection while proceeding to throw all caution to the wind!

Paddy was a passionate and considerate lover. I marvelled at the tautness of his body and the gentleness of his touch that left me quivering on the brink of ecstasy before plunging me into the depths of sexual fulfilment. Two and a half years as a widow had left me 'hungrier' than I had realised. By morning's dawn, we were entirely spent; we fell into a deep and contented sleep, still entangled in each other.

However, despite remembering at the last minute to hang the Do Not Disturb sign on the door, I neglected to put my phone on silent, and as a result of this, our slumber did not last as long as I would have liked. Less than two hours after falling asleep, we were awoken by its persistent ringing, the annoying sound emanating from my handbag which had been flung to the far corner of the room the night before. Paddy drew me closer to him and buried his head deep between my shoulder blades.

'Don't answer it,' he mumbled sleepily.

'I have to,' I replied. 'It's probably Mum.'

He reluctantly released his hold, and I struggled out of the tangle of limbs and sheets to answer it. I had completely forgotten to enlighten my parents of my change of plans for the previous night, and now I imagined them to be sick with worry at my failure to return home. By the time I managed to get out of the bed and wrap myself in one of the complimentary robes that had been consigned to the floor the night before, the phone had stopped ringing. However, it resumed almost immediately, the caller's persistence causing me to answer the phone instinctively without first checking their number. If I had checked, I wouldn't have answered it, and things might have worked out differently.

'Hello?' I said, with as much equanimity as possible.

Mum didn't usually contact anyone before 10 a.m., so I knew that she must be really concerned about something if she was calling me at that hour. But it wasn't Mum.

'Hello, Libby,' came the somewhat distant voice, 'it's Dan here. I hope I didn't get you out of bed. I know it's early over there.'

He sounded tired, and all at once, I felt like a complete trollop! My heart sank to the floor, and I was immediately wracked with an enormous sense of guilt. Why had he taken so long to call me, and would it have made any difference even if he had? I would never know.

'Hello, Dan,' I said, feeling a lot less enthusiastic than I would have liked.

The warmth of my response was wholly compromised by Paddy's close proximity and by the memory of the previous night's activities. Ten feet away from me lay my lover, and my *love* suddenly felt much further away than the three thousand miles that separated us. My night of carnal pleasure had come at a very high price. At twenty-nine, in the cold March light of morn, I was experiencing, for the very first time in my life, feelings of complete and utter shame.

I glanced back at Paddy, lying in the jumbled mess of hotel sheets, and I winced inwardly. What had I been thinking of? I had no romantic interest in Paddy O'Rourke, and he had none in me. We had no future. Sure, we liked each other well enough, but that was hardly grounds to behave like animals and succumb to our basest instincts. Once would have been bad enough, but it had been more than once and I had to shamefully admit to myself that I had enjoyed every, last, delicious minute of our night together. Dan had never crossed my mind.

I kept repeating the phrase *it's not like me* in my brain, in a vain attempt to restore a sense of normality and to salve my increasingly guilty conscience. I felt sick. I indicated to Paddy that I would take the call in the adjoining sitting room, waving a reassuring hand in reply to his mouthed concern as to whether or not anything was the matter. The enormity of the mess that I had created crashed over me in heavy, nauseating waves. I had created a situation that made the chances of securing a long-term relationship with either man highly unlikely.

Safe in the privacy of the suite's sitting room, I felt slightly more relaxed and was grateful for whatever hand of destiny had landed us in such lavish accommodation. Had the circumstances been different, I would have taken it as a sign from above that all was right with the world and that Paddy and I were the beneficiaries of some sort of universal blessing. However, in light of Dan's ill-timed phone call, I concluded that the Gods were indeed smiling, at my expense.

Despite, or perhaps because of, the maelstrom of emotions that were churning within me, I went into survival mode. I hoped that I would be able to convince Dan that I was happy to hear from him, and I vowed never to lose control, in that way, again. Somehow, I would make it up to him; I reassured myself that he was the right one for me now, just as Max had been the right one for me then; Paddy, on the other hand, was the right one for somebody else. Turning my attention back to Dan, I crossed my fingers and concentrated.

As it turned out, Dan was having a particularly difficult time since his brother-in-law's death. Despite all evidence to suggest that Hazel could cope with anything that life had to throw at her, she did not deal well with the loss of her husband. At the time of Dan's phone call, three weeks after her spouse's death, she was still 'in a state of shock'. Dan had hoped to be back in Ireland by that weekend, but it was beginning to look as if it would be at least another couple of weeks before he would be in a position travel. I breathed a sigh of relief.

Being the gentleman that he was, he brushed over his own concerns and took the time to enquire as to how renovations were progressing at Alice-Rose, even expressing his regret that he was not around to see them. The conversation ended with Dan urging me to 'take care' of myself and reassuring me that he would let me know the minute his plans for departing New York were finalised.

I finished the call, pressing firmly down on the 'end call' button. I wondered wryly if, by 'taking care' of myself, Dan meant that I should take a lover in his stead. Somehow, I didn't think so. Would I ever be able to look Dan Bryant squarely in the eye again? Last night had been an unmitigated disaster, and I had no one to blame for it except myself. I braced myself and returned to the suite's bedroom, excuses as to why I couldn't 'come back to bed' already forming in my head.

I needn't have bothered. The super king-sized bed was empty; the sheets were stripped and lay folded in the middle of the mattress. If Jules, or any of my girlfriends, had told me that their lover had folded the bed linen before leaving a hotel room, I would probably have concluded that the lover was a little too in touch with his feminine side. However, remembering 'Paddy the lover' from the night before, I knew that the folded linen had nothing to do with any feminine urges that Paddy might have had and everything to do with him drawing a line under our night of lovemaking. I felt a mixture of relief and regret as I set about gathering my clothes together while I waited for Paddy to finish his shower.

I didn't know what to expect from Paddy when he emerged from the bathroom, but whatever I had imagined his attitude would be, I was not prepared for his warmth and compassion. I supposed that I must have looked a little 'hung dog' as I sat on the bed, in my oversized robe, anticipating his return. I certainly didn't feel a million dollars as a mixture of guilt and tiredness flushed through my body. By that point I just wanted the day to be over as quickly and as painlessly as possible.

'Hello, you,' Paddy said warmly as he emerged looking strong and refreshed from the shower.

He was, as was to be expected, unshaven, and this gave him a rugged, yet somehow more vulnerable, appearance. My unfaithful heart couldn't help but skip a beat.

'Hello,' I bleated, knowing that my face betrayed the complete and varied range of my emotions; I had always been an open book.

'You look tired,' he said sympathetically and without any hint of irony or innuendo. 'A shower will help. When you're finished, I'll meet you downstairs for breakfast,' he said, picking up his keys and leaving me to ponder my fate.

Sometime later, I emerged from the bathroom, feeling somewhat better. Even taking a shower in the same one that Paddy had used seemed like a further act of intimacy, but I had no choice. To say that I scrubbed myself in shame might be slightly overstating the case, but I was certainly meticulous in my ablutions that morning. Not for the first time I marvelled at the power of a shower to invigorate the weariest of minds and bodies, the extensive range of luxury toiletries that graced the bathroom's shelves also played their part.

Having washed, scrubbed, and moisturised my entire body using a range of products that would have satisfied the Queen of England herself, I felt considerably better about facing the day and the men ahead. I dressed quickly and ran the dryer over my hair, before pining it high on my head using whatever few hairgrips I could find lying scattered around on the floor. I applied a little eyeliner, some blush, and a hint of lipstick. The last thing that I wanted after the *gymnastics* of the night before was to look like a painted lady! Satisfied that I had achieved the outward appearance of a respectable young woman, I headed downstairs.

Paddy was sitting at a small table at the far end of the dining room. He was drinking coffee and reading the morning papers, and he looked the picture of relaxation. There were no obvious signs that he was suffering from any emotional turbulence of his own. Men rarely did, I supposed.

Paddy rose to his feet when he saw me approaching and waited to help me into my seat before retaking his. I noted that chivalry wasn't dead to Paddy O'Rourke with a bittersweet sense of satisfaction, and then I remembered that Dan would have done the same. Fifteen all.

Paddy sat down and indicated to a glass sitting on the table, explaining that he had 'taken the liberty' of getting me some orange juice. I could see that he had either eaten breakfast very quickly, or he had waited for me before having his own.

'Thanks. Just what the doctor ordered,' I said. 'Have you eaten?'

'Not yet,' he replied, 'I thought we'd eat together.'

'Thanks for that. I think it's going to have to be a full Irish for me today,' I said, laughing weakly.

'I think you're right,' said Paddy, signalling a passing waiter to our table.

We ate mostly in silence, neither of us quite knowing what to say to the other. Over breakfast, it emerged that Paddy had already settled our hotel bill, so we left afterwards without delay; there was no luggage to be organised, just my handbag, Paddy's wallet, and my burden of guilt.

Paddy took over the driving without discussion, and for that, I was grateful. I couldn't have faced getting behind the wheel. He assured me in passing that he felt fine and that I should try and get some sleep on the journey home; that would certainly be one way of dealing with any awkwardness that now existed between us. I didn't think that sleep was possible, yet I woke up some time later on the Waterford bypass.

'I'm so sorry, Paddy. I didn't mean to nod off and leave you to drive without company. I'm sure you're tired too,' I said. 'You must think I'm completely selfish.'

'I know you're not selfish, Libby,' he said, and I knew that he meant it. 'Honestly, I feel fine, and I don't mind. I would have done the same.'

'Well, pull over at the next service station and let me buy you a coffee at least,' I said.

'Okay, let's do that,' he said agreeably.

We stopped at a service station, the far side of Waterford City; I went inside to get two large coffees while Paddy filled up the tank. I had wanted to cover the cost of the diesel, but Paddy insisted that he could write a good deal of it off against tax. I hadn't the energy to argue with him, and much and all as I wanted to, I hadn't the nerve to enquire as to whether or not the cost of our hotel room was also tax deductible. I paid for the coffees. Some ten miles later, and fortified by half a cup of strong black coffee, my courage finally held up, and I broached the conversation that I thought we would eventually have to have.

'Paddy,' I said quietly. 'About last night . . ..'

'It's okay, Libby,' he said gently. 'We don't have to have this conversation.'

'We don't?' I wondered where exactly he thought I had been going with the conversation. Come to think of it, I hadn't really known myself.

'Libby, I know that last night was a once-off. What happened between us was dictated entirely by the unusual circumstances that we found ourselves in,' he said.

I presumed that he was referring to our mutual state of sexual starvation and not to the fact that we ended up in an elevator together. On the other hand, two red-blooded people, starved of 'love and affection', should probably avoid being confined together in a small space! Note to self: ask Paddy to play sardines when we get home.

'Yes,' I said, suddenly not at all sure that I meant it.

'Let's say no more about it and pretend that it never happened,' he said, not unkindly.

'Okay,' I said, feeling a lot less relieved than I would have expected.

Paddy was offering me a clean slate and absolution from my guilt, and I wasn't altogether sure that I liked it! Where I should have felt grateful, all I felt was irritated! Had I been that unremarkable that he didn't feel the need to fight for my affections? Then I remembered something that I rarely ever forgot: even if I had been the world's greatest lover, I was still barren, and that fact would reduce my appeal considerably in the eyes of most men!

I wasn't prone to bouts of self-pity, and I wasn't going to start indulging in them at that point, but I did have one last question before I dropped the subject with Paddy for good.

'Paddy?'

'Yes?'

'Do you dance?'

CAITRÍONA LESLIE

'God, no! Whatever made you ask?'

'Nothing, forget I asked.'

I made a quick mental note. Thirty-fifteen to Dan Bryant. Game over. Almost.

The rest of the journey home passed in virtual silence. It wasn't awkward; we were both just exhausted. You can't put in a long day, followed by a night of unremitting lovemaking, and expect to be full of beans. Add in an early start, followed by a long drive home, and we were both lucky to be able to keep our eyes open, let alone partake in conversation of any kind. Finally, after what seemed like an eternity, Paddy pulled on to the drive leading to Willow Cottage. It was mid afternoon.

'Coffee?' I asked, my voice lacking any enthusiasm.

'Please,' he replied, his 'enthusiasm' matching mine.

In the short time that it took us to reach my kitchen, coffee didn't seem like a good idea any more.

'Let's just go to bed,' I said wearily.

His face didn't register surprise. We were both past that.

'The spare room is made-up, and it's got its own bathroom. Help yourself.'

'Are you sure?' he asked, probably a little taken aback by the level of hospitality on offer, considering everything that had happened the night before. I nodded wearily before continuing.

'I just don't think I can stay awake any longer, and it's definitely not a good idea for you to get back behind the wheel.'

'If you're absolutely sure, then I'd really appreciate it! Thanks, Libby,' he said, looking more like a tired little boy than anything else. My heart softened. If I had to pick somebody to be reckless with, then Paddy O'Rourke seemed like as good a choice as any.

'You're welcome,' I said, smiling.

Paddy was right, the sooner we forgot about the events of the previous night the better.

'Now get to bed!' I scolded gently, leading him up the stairs and pointing him in the direction of his room before firmly closing the door of my own.

As I leant back against it, quietly relieved that we had gotten to that point, I heard the door of the guest room click closed. *That's it,* I thought, *the end of our little adventure where nobody got hurt.* With that thought in mind, I crawled between the sheets and fell soundly asleep.

I woke up several hours later, sticky and disorientated. It was dark outside, and the house was quiet except for the tick of the alarm clock beside my bed. Finding my bearings, I turned over so that I could peer at the clock's fluorescent face. It said ten minutes past eight. I had been in bed for almost five hours.

Fighting the temptation to stay there for the rest of the night, I threw the covers back and headed for the shower. The house had three bedrooms, two of which were spacious and had their own en-suite bathrooms. Never had I appreciated Mum's little touches of decadence more than I did then. I wasn't sure whether or not Paddy was still in the house, and I didn't particularly want to find out, not until I had at least showered, again.

Twenty minutes later, I stole across the landing, feeling clean and a lot livelier than when I had woken up. The door to the guest bedroom was closed so that I couldn't be sure whether or not Paddy was still around. For all I knew, he could have left ages before. I went downstairs as quietly as I could, hoping to find some clue as to Paddy's whereabouts.

I'm not entirely sure what I was hoping for as I crept to the sitting room window to look outside; I do, however, know that I felt an unmistakable thrill of excitement when I saw that Paddy's red Landrover was still there. The man was upstairs, and I was glad despite the unexpected regret of knowing that our affair was over before it had scarcely begun.

I looked back into the room for inspiration as to what I should do next. My eyes settled upon the hearth, where a turf fire laid waiting for the strike of a match to bring it to life. Picking up the box of matches that lay on the mantelpiece, I bent down, and in one irretrievable movement, lit the fire. Could the strike of a match have been compared to an instant between two people, a brief moment in time that sealed their fate forever? I believed so. I knew so. But in all cases, only time would tell what that fate was.

Forcing myself to abandon all philosophical musings for the sake of my sanity, I turned my thoughts to more practical concerns. Realising that I was in fact ravenous, I headed for the kitchen, remembering the chicken curry that I had left in the fridge two nights previously in preparation for our return the night before. That hadn't happened, but the dish would still be okay from the fridge. At that point, I was beyond caring about a little food poisoning; I could have happily eaten a dead badger! I placed the casserole dish in the oven and poured some water over a saucepan of rice, dragging it, and the kettle, on to the hotplate before calling Mum.

'Hi, Mum, sorry I've been out of touch for the last couple of days,' I said as casually as I could, 'I hope you weren't too worried.'

With any luck, she wouldn't delve too deeply into the matter of my absence.

'Worried, darling, why on earth would I have worried?' she protested. 'Emma kept me in the loop. Once I knew that you and Paddy were off on a little trip together, I knew that I had nothing to worry about!'

She paused briefly before continuing.

'How was it?' she asked meaningfully.

I hadn't counted on Emma being 'in the loop', and I knew full well by Mum's tone that the fact that Paddy and I had gone somewhere together, and alone, had been quite the topic of conversation! I felt a new level of weariness.

'It was fine, Mother. We got what we needed,' I replied, suddenly aware that my colour was rising; my remark was closer to the truth than I had intended.

Luckily for me, I was on the other end of a phone line and not having that conversation face-to-face with my mother, or so I thought.

'Really, Libby?' she asked, even more meaningfully.

'Really, Mother! And, Mum . . .,' I pleaded desperately, 'please try to remember that you are in fact my mother.'

Mothers and daughters were not supposed to have conversations that referred to either one of their sex lives! I believed in the perpetuation of the sugar-coated 'lie' that neither had, nor ever would, indulge in having sex. All conceptions were immaculate!

'Indeed, my girl, I have been well aware of that fact for some time now,' she declared indignantly, 'and that's one of the reasons why I know when you're being evasive! And it's because I'm your mother that I know what's best for you, even when you are not entirely convinced of it yourself!'

I knew when I was beaten, and I was in no fit state to take on my mother when she was in this kind of mood. Besides which, Paddy could have walked in on the conversation at any moment, and that was the very last thing that I wanted! I decided, on that occasion, that retreat was the better course of valour.

'Anyway, Mother, I just wanted to let you know that I am safe and well, and I shall talk to you tomorrow when I am not quite so tired.' My tone was intended to bring the conversation to a definite end.

'Okay, Libby, but you know it's always telling when you call me Mother,' she said knowingly. 'And, Libby, one last question before you go. . . .'

'Yes, Mum?' I enunciated the words deliberately.

'Is Paddy tired too?'

'Goodnight, Mum!' I said, ending the conversation once and for all.

Honestly, the woman had missed her vocation; she had a nose like a bloodhound and was as subtle as a brick! Why couldn't I have been blessed with a vague and trusting mother? I was already dreading meeting her face-to-face because I knew better than to think that that had been the end of the conversation! *Dog with a bone* was the phrase that sprung to mind when I thought about our mother and her tendency to fixate on things. But I knew that even Mum would have been surprised by how close she had come to the truth on that occasion!

Putting my mother firmly to the back of my mind, I made a cup of tea and settled down in front of the telly to watch *Grand Designs*, while the curry heated and the rice cooked. Kevin McCloud was in the middle of expressing his grave doubts as to whether 'the plan' would, or even could, work for the project in question when I heard *his* footsteps on the stairs.

All of a sudden, Paddy had become he, him, and his! At some point, he had managed to eclipse all the other men in my life to become the *royal he,* and I hadn't realised it until that very moment. I could only hope that Dan would arrive back in Ireland soon and that the sight of him would blow Paddy out of the water!

I struggled to imagine Dan standing in my kitchen and to recapture the feelings of lust that I had felt for him on that occasion. Unfortunately, that was impossible to do when the man responsible for giving me the night of my life filled the doorway of my sitting room, having already unlocked the door to my heart. I felt completely at sea as I acknowledged how easily my affections had shifted, but shifted they had, and I had to deal with the consequences.

Some time later, when Paddy had gone, I struggled to define my feelings for him. Good old reliable lust was definitely top of the list, and even I knew there had to be more to a relationship than that! My hormones had inexplicably gone into overdrive and had scrambled my brain. I reasoned that this was to be expected and that it was perfectly reasonable for a twenty-nine-year-old to have a healthy sex drive. Max and I had certainly enjoyed the pleasures of each other's bodies. *But not like that* whispered my conscience, *never like that!*

I went hot and cold remembering the carnal pleasures of the night before. Who would have thought that serious, conscientious Paddy O'Rourke would be such an expert and effortless lover? And what had that girl, Alyson, been thinking of when she cast him aside? The phrase *shit for brains* sprung to mind, and I blushed at my own profanity. Being a fantastic lover was hardly the most important thing in the world, but then reason had fled my world. Paddy O'Rourke could do things to a body that would make any woman forget her own name and that really was something worth considering!

Passing the door to the guest bedroom later that night, I fought the urge to visit the room where he had lain. I lost. The bedclothes had been roughly pulled back into a made position, and the towel had been replaced with care on the rail in the bathroom. Remembering Paddy's earlier haste to leave Willow Cottage after his 'nap', I dragged the sheets from the bed and gathered them together with the towel before bringing them downstairs to be washed. The sooner I forgot about 'Paddy O'Rourke the lover' the better! I would start by washing away the scent of him, the wonderful musky, manly scent of him. I buried my nose deep in the striped flannel of the stripped bedding. One last sniff and he would be gone forever in a whirl of detergent and fabric conditioner. That at least was the plan.

Dan

CHAPTER 37

New York, New York

J EFF'S DEATH CAME as a huge shock to all of us. It wasn't that Jeff was the epitome of good health, because he wasn't, we had just presumed that he was too young, and too spirited, to die. Jeff was almost two years younger than my sister.

We had celebrated his fiftieth birthday in style, in New York, the previous New Year's Eve. Jeff was a force of nature, and he and Hazel were two halves of a very sound whole. While Hazel freelanced successfully for various newspapers around the city, Jeff was a political lobbyist who excelled in his field and liked to play as hard as he worked. They had met while Hazel was working in Cape Cod as a student one summer. Jeff was a mature sixteen-year-old, driving around in his father's car, when cupid's arrow struck. He stopped to give my sister a lift, and the rest was history.

Jeff often told the story of how he had fallen in love with my sister's dark, mischievous eyes and her Irish brogue on that first car ride together. Hazel, for her part, hadn't taken their relationship seriously until two years later when he wrote to say that he was coming to Ireland to meet her family. Another three years passed before they were finally old enough to marry in the eyes of their parents, and the wedding took place in Ballyedmond.

Less than a year later, they were parents to twin boys, and the following year another set of twin boys arrived. Nobody had banked on a history of twins carrying through with such vigour into the next generation. Hazel and Jeff decided to call it a day; four boys under the age of two were more than enough for anyone!

Jeff was a giant of a man, reaching six foot seven in height he managed to dwarf my sister's six-foot frame. Hazel often said that one of the wonderful things about Jeff was that he made her feel delicate and feminine, things she had never felt before meeting him. On the other hand, Jeff also weighed in excess of thirty stone and had been warned by his doctors to lose weight. He hadn't taken their advice seriously and had continued to eat like a king.

His unhealthy lifestyle of stress and overindulgence ultimately led to his premature death from a massive heart attack, at the age of fifty-one.

Hazel got through Jeff's funeral displaying great pluck and fortitude, but once the formalities were out of the way and the house was quiet again, her courage disserted her. As the last funeral guest left the house, Hazel started to cry, and she continued to cry, more on than off, for the next two weeks. I realised that I was witnessing, for the very first time, the passing of a true love. I hadn't cried when Marie died.

People had advised me that it was 'good to cry'. I didn't bother telling them that I didn't want to cry, or even felt the need to, I simply didn't have any tears left for the woman who had, for all intense purposes, deserted me years before. With Marie gone, our home, not to talk of our marital bed, would be no colder than it had been for years. I felt released.

Jeff's death made me sit up and take stock of my own life and what was left of it. I didn't want to waste any more of it, not a second of it! Wooing the wonderful Libby was now at the very top of my to-do list. I wanted love and companionship in my life, and I wanted it with the right woman.

However, even Libby would have to wait. There was the small task of consoling my sister, in her hour of need, to be dealt with first. Her boys would all be returning to their lives by the week's end; I couldn't run back to Ireland and leave Hazel alone and struggling. Hazel had found it difficult enough to cope with the empty nest syndrome the first time round, even with Jeff's love and support; I could only imagine what effect the boys' leaving would have on her then. Head ruling heart, I had to stay with Hazel until I knew for sure that she would be okay.

Hazel and I spent the two weeks following the funeral crying and eating. Hazel cried, and I ate. The second of those two weeks involved even more crying and eating than the first, a direct response to her sons' departure. The third week saw us sorting through Jeff's personal belongings. This was something that I had strongly encouraged her to do because I knew that I wouldn't be leaving New York as long as Jeff's clothes still hung, untouched, in his wardrobe.

After a reluctant start, Hazel got stuck in and found that having a six-foot-seven, four-hundred-and-thirty-pound husband made this part of the grieving process surprisingly easy. There was nothing for it but to donate his entire wardrobe to goodwill because neither of us knew anyone else who could fill his clothes or his shoes for that matter! Their boys were tall, but even the tallest of them was a good three inches shorter than Jeff and thankfully weighed a whole lot less. Besides, Hazel figured that even if the clothes had fit any of them, they would have found the idea of wearing their dead father's clothes just a little too 'weird'.

Once Jeff's wardrobe had been taken care of, my sister took to her office and emerged four days later. She didn't look great, shattered, in fact, but she assured me that she would be fine and that it was time for me to leave, and for everyone and everything to get back to 'normal'. When her article entitled 'Jeff, My Rock' appeared two days later in the *New York Journal*, I knew that my sister would eventually find her way back to the surface of life. I didn't delay and booked my ticket home straightaway. I did, as it happened, have a few issues of my own to get sorted.

Libby

CHAPTER 38

I've Never Felt Like this Before

THE WEEK FOLLOWING the journey down south was marked by severe weather conditions. There was widespread flooding, and people everywhere seemed to be keeping a low profile. Paddy called early on the Tuesday of that week to say that he thought it would be best if work on Alice-Rose stopped for the moment, but that they would recommence as soon as weather conditions improved. The newly restored windows were ready to be fitted, and they would need a spell of dry weather to complete that part of the job. I readily agreed.

My conscience was all over the place once the initial tiredness, and the strange sense of exhilaration that lingered after Kinsale, had worn off. Paddy was friendly but businesslike over the phone, giving no impression that he even remembered what had taken place between us on that trip. He mentioned, in passing, that the salvage yard had called to say there would be a delay in delivery, but that they hoped to get to us the following week. He didn't miss a beat as he spoke, but my heart did, several.

I took the bad weather as a celestial sign that Paddy O'Rourke and I were definitely not meant to be. Left to my own devices, my emotions continued to swing wildly, and my imagination took a firmer hold. I began to worry about all sorts of thing! Was Paddy O'Rourke a serial womaniser? In my carelessness, had I managed to contract some virulent strain of a sexually transmitted disease?

The story about his last girlfriend's choice of contraception seemed highly unlikely once I had time to think about it. It was undoubtedly a total fabrication, a convenient lie concocted in the heat of the moment to allay my fears and thereby get me into bed. I decided to have myself tested for every pathogen known to man as soon as I could. That decision made me feel mildly better; I at least had a plan. Unfortunately, I also knew that one had to wait in excess of three months subsequent to the potentially infectious encounter before one could be accurately tested for HIV positivity, and I presumed that the same was true for most sexually transmitted diseases. I had no choice but to try to remain calm. In the meantime, if I developed any purulent symptoms, I would seek medical assistance immediately.

Of course, my decision to sleep with Paddy O'Rourke had other far-reaching consequences. Besides the worry of my own potential infection, I had the added burden of ensuring that I did not unwittingly infect anybody else. That 'anybody else' being, most notably, Dan Bryant, presuming that was that he ever showed up!

Another week dragged by without hearing from Dan or Paddy for that matter. Then on Wednesday, April the first, I woke up with an almighty hangover! This state of affairs would not have been good under normal circumstances, but the fact that I hadn't been drinking made it all the worse! I could not lift my head from the pillow; it was made of lead.

Rolling myself off the bed, I crawled to the bathroom on all fours. Then I crawled back again before entering a parallel world of night sweats and fevered dreams. Eventually, someone did show up to begin forcing liquid down my parched throat, and some days later, I discovered that my guardian angel was Mum. I had managed to contract the flu at a time when everyone else, including old-age pensioners and children, were well and truly over it!

It took me three weeks to recover from my first encounter with the seasonal virus, and I knew with certainty that it was my first because I would definitely have remembered it if I had ever had anything like it before! Unless you've been paralysed and relentlessly bathed in a bed of sweat, you haven't had the flu! I lost the will to live, and quite frankly, any sexually transmitted diseases that I might have contracted became unimportant in the grand scheme of things.

When I say that it took me three weeks to recover, I mean that it took me three weeks to even contemplate venturing outside again! My first venture forth could only have been to see Alice-Rose; it had been so long! After taking the best part of an hour to shower and dress, since everything was still in slow motion, I made my way to the Freelander. However, I only got as far as its door before I felt the familiar urge to throw up. A residual side effect of the illness seemed to be a dodgy stomach, and I strongly suspected that mine had been a strain of stomach flu.

At that point, I was beginning to get more than a little frustrated by my poor powers of recovery. Jules tried to console me by reassuring me that I would definitely be fully recovered by her wedding day, making the observation that while I was positively fading away, her happiness was giving her an almighty appetite! At the rate we were going, we would both be heading to the dressmakers beforehand: Jules to have her dress let out, and me to have mine taken in! Jules promised me that she was going to do her utmost to curb her appetite and urged me to rediscover mine.

It was late in the afternoon of that first day of recovery before I made it to see Alice-Rose. I hadn't expected to see much change because as far as I was concerned my illness had coincided with the world ceasing to rotate on its axis. It soon became clear, however, that while my earthly sphere had stalled, the rest of the world had gone into overdrive, and Alice-Rose was almost beyond recognition! More than three weeks had passed since my last visit, and in that time, Alice-Rose had become the proud bearer of refurbished sash windows and a newly erected wrap-around conservatory!

The amount of work that had been achieved in my absence was astounding! Paddy was like a man possessed and clearly happy to see me. Of course, I wasn't naive enough to take his joy personally; he was just happy to have a willing ear as he proceeded to effuse about 'the project'. In fairness to him, he did seem anxious to know what I made of 'the renaissance', his use of the term causing me to wonder if he had, at some stage, been speaking to my father. For my part, I thought every aspect of the house went far beyond my wildest expectations.

Paddy wasn't just excited about how well the house was turning out; he was excited about how quickly the work was progressing. He assured me that they were well ahead of schedule and that he envisaged the cost of the work coming in under budget. They would be 'out of my hair by the twenty-fifth of June'. This was all music to my ears, or would have been, a few months earlier.

Paddy was clearly anxious to get the work finished and to move on to other things. I reminded myself that Alice-Rose was, after all, just 'another job' and that Paddy had other clients. While his professionalism had made me feel, in one sense, that Alice-Rose and I were the only 'girls' in the world, I should have realised that this was only true for as long as the job lasted. As he was so clearly at pains to point out to me that day, Paddy had other 'pressing business' to attend to as soon as they finished the work on Alice-Rose. I looked around her magnificent rooms and wondered, not for the first time in recent weeks, how Alice-Rose and I would fare alone.

CHAPTER 39

Life After the Flu

PADDY HAD PHONED a few times during my *confinement*, but my fevered state meant that I was oblivious to his calls. Eventually, Mum intercepted one and enlightened Paddy about my illness. Much later, when I had regained lucidity, my mother was at pains to tell me that he had seemed very concerned about me and that she was certain that his interest in my wellbeing was more than just professional! According to Mum, he seemed much happier once she had promised him that she would have me call him as soon as my condition improved.

I felt oddly *non-reassured* by that news. Did Paddy really care, or did Mum just insist upon presuming that he did? Of course, regardless of everything that had happened between us, Paddy was bound to have some level of professional concern for my health. It was hardly in his interest for me to die while they were on the job, it would delay payday for one thing!

'Dan also called,' Mum said dismissively one day as she sat on the edge of my sickbed.

'Really? What did you tell him?' I enquired, irritated by her tone yet trying to assume an air of indifference.

'More or less the same thing,' she replied defensively.

'That was good of you, I know you don't approve,' I said, acknowledging the fact that my mother had acted against her better judgement.

'I don't, but then I didn't do it for him or for you for that matter. I did it for myself!' she said, sniffing the air as she was apt to do on occasion.

'For yourself! How so?' I asked, baffled by her statement.

'Libby,' my mother began solemnly, 'regardless of what I might think in relation to Dan Bryant and you, I try to remind myself that you are, after all, old enough to make up your own mind.' At this point, she took my hands in hers before continuing. 'And whatever your choice is at the end of it all, I want you to still love your old mother. Only a parents' love is unconditional.'

'Oh, Mum,' I said, throwing my arms around her, 'you're not old, and I'll always love you, no matter what!'

'Promise?' she asked, smiling.

'Promise!' I reassured.

After my excursion to Alice-Rose, the one that confirmed that my future did not lie with Paddy O'Rourke, I decided to give Dan a call to see if we could arrange to 'go out'. There was a new theatre opening in Dublin the following weekend, and I considered that somewhere like that would make for a memorable, but not too intense, first date. The opening performance was Madame Butterfly, and I could only hope that Dan shared my love of opera. He did. Things looked promising.

We made arrangements for Dan to pick me up the following Saturday. He said that he was really looking forward to it, and I tried to convince myself that I was too. If I could just shake off the after-effects of the flu, then I felt sure that I wouldn't find it quite so difficult to be wholehearted about our date.

I checked my conscience for feelings of guilt following my night of passion with Paddy O'Rourke, and I had to admit that I harboured traces of it. I tried to make myself feel better by reminding myself that it was, after all, the first time in my twenty-nine years that I had done anything so rash, not bad by some people's standards . . . *but abominable by others*, whispered my conscience. I went further still; I made a solemn promise to the Gods above that if they spared me the indignity, and potential life threat, of a sexually transmitted disease, that it would be the last! Surely, I didn't deserve to be punished for the rest of my life for one, albeit repeated, indiscretion. That unforgettable night in Kinsale would be my one and only guilty secret, forever!

I didn't bother factoring Paddy into the equation; I was pretty sure, judging by his behaviour, that he had forgotten the events of that night already. Even if he hadn't forgotten them, I felt confident that he wasn't the kind of guy to kiss and tell. My secret was in safe hands.

The following Saturday dawned bright and clear and warm. It heralded the arrival of summer, and I felt a certain excitement at the prospect of our date. Although I still wasn't feeling completely better, I was definitely on the mend, and I wanted to make an effort to look my very best for Dan. I arranged to meet Jules for an early lunch in town before going around the shops together. I wasn't stuck for something to wear, but I was interested in getting a new outfit if I saw one that grabbed my fancy. I had a hair appointment at four, and Dan was picking me up at Willow Cottage around six thirty.

Jules was sitting waiting for me in 'The Little Brown Jug' when I arrived. She looked so radiant that it might well have been her wedding day! I suddenly felt tired and shabby. Who in their right mind would want to go out with me? I was twenty-nine going on sixty-nine! I considered briefly the possibility that I should have been taking dietary supplements, or failing that, some form of medication. At my age, there was no way that I should have been feeling that poorly, regardless of the flu! I was permanently exhausted, and I didn't like it one little bit; in fact, I was beginning to loath my new lethargic self! 'Please, dear God,' I prayed, 'don't let this state of lassitude be a permanent feature of my life!' I had humanist ideals, but when the chips were down, I prayed like a catholic!

'Jules,' I said, taking my seat opposite her, 'how do you do it?' My tone resonated more of weary defeat than of admiration.

'Do what?' she asked, shovelling the last of a pre-lunch jam doughnut into her mouth.

'Manage to look so bloody healthy!' I said accusingly, eyeing up her full-cream cappuccino. I suddenly felt nauseous.

'Well, I haven't tangoed with influenza for starters!' she laughed.

'And?' I said.

'And what?' she asked.

'There's surely more to it than that?' I continued encouragingly, genuinely interested to know the secret of her apparent good health. '*You* don't usually start lunch with coffee and a doughnut!' Jules had the grace to look ever so slightly shamefaced.

'Well, apart from not having had the flu, I guess I'm just incredibly happy,' she said simply.

'No offence, but *is that it?*' I asked, disappointment dripping from my every word.

'Love gives a girl an appetite, you know,' she explained guiltily, licking her middle finger before using it to gather the last of the doughnut crumbs from her plate.

'If you say so,' I said, not entirely convinced.

Could the state of one's health, and appetite, really be governed by something as simple as love? If one was to follow Jules's line of reasoning, one's health and fitness were directed by the whims of fate, and I didn't like those odds. If at all possible, I preferred to take a more active part in the direction of my life! I hadn't sat back in the past and wondered about where my life would take me, and I wasn't going to start now. I had plans for my life and my health, they just had to be finalised.

Two cups of peppermint tea and a slice of brown toast later, I was ready for action, well, as ready as I would ever be without the use of intravenous drugs. I say intravenous because, as luck would have it, I didn't even have the stomach for a tonic. My one attempt at taking a flu remedy proved futile when it was followed by an immediate episode of projectile vomiting.

The doctor advised me that this was entirely normal under the circumstances and to take no further action other than to keep warm and hydrated. I guffawed inwardly at her throwaway enquiry as to whether or not I could possibly be pregnant. As far as I knew I hadn't been visited by any celestial beings, and so was unlikely to have had an immaculate conception!

I didn't express my innermost thoughts to the doctor, but I did go so far as to assure her that I definitely wasn't pregnant! Dr Áine Ginty didn't know anything about my demoralising history of infertility; I had arrived at her surgery newly returned to my home town and long past the highs and lows that each monthly cycle of my married life had brought. While I might have been infected with some horrible illness, I definitely wasn't pregnant! Nevertheless, I decided that if I wasn't feeling considerably better by the following Monday, that I would take myself along to her clinic so that she could attempt a diagnosis.

After lunch, Jules and I headed for Tina's House of Fashion. Tina was busy with a customer when we arrived, but he excused himself 'for a moment' when he saw us.

'Jules darling, gorgeous as ever!' he purred, taking her hand and twirling her on the spot. Then Tina turned his attentions towards me and studied me for what seemed like an age.

'Libby, where have you been, and what *have* you done to yourself?' he cried, throwing his hands up to his face in mock horror.

I felt too wretched to react.

'Is it that bad?' I asked. I was beginning to wonder whether or not I should cancel the trip to the theatre, after all. What would Dan make of my appearance? Tina must have been moved by my pathetic bearing because he hastened to comfort me, as only he could.

'Bad? Libby, how could it ever be bad with that bone structure? You are a beauty despite the flu's best efforts!'

Jules had obviously informed him that I had succumbed to the flu. I smiled wanly.

'Come to Uncle Tina,' he said, opening his arms to me.

I stepped into his considerable embrace, and it felt good, in a safe, comforting way.

'Now, dear Libby, let's see what *I* can do for *you*!' he said, pushing me from him and studying me intently as he tucked one supporting knuckle under his chin.

'Where are *we* going?' he asked in his familiar undulating tone, one that assured you that he was going to give your answer serious consideration.

Tina treated every occasion like it would be one's last.

'Ah,' he mused, raising his eyebrows in approval to my answer. 'I have *just* the thing.' And he did.

I left the shop with killer heels, killer clothes, and *to-die-for* accessories! As long as I remained moderately well, the outfit in the bag guaranteed that I would once again knock the socks off Dan. As it happened, my sense of wellbeing did increase somewhat during the day; this was partly due to the fact that I felt confident in Tina's choice of outfit for our date, and added to this, the magic wrought by Sandra on my sorely neglected locks. By evening, I almost felt as human as I looked!

CAITRÍONA LESLIE

CHAPTER 40

A Long Night at the Opera

DAN BRYANT PULLED his car up in front of Willow Cottage at exactly half past six. I liked that; I liked a man who wasn't afraid to show a girl that he was both interested and chivalrous. I, in turn, was ready when he called. Dan was well turned out in grey flannel pants and a dark grey sports coat. Underneath his jacket, he wore a crisp white shirt, left opened at the neck. He looked tall, fit, and very distinguished. He was any woman's fancy, and I didn't feel a thing. I reminded myself that I was still essentially sick and that I couldn't expect to get easily aroused in my weakened condition. I was quietly confident that Dan's appeal wouldn't seem so remote once I was feeling better!

Dan was warm and charming and unaffected. He was easy to be around, and I was soon feeling reassured that we were going to have a good time. Dan drove straight to the theatre, and after a leisurely drink in the patron's lounge, we made our way to the auditorium, blissfully unaware of the *complications* lying ahead. Our time together thus far had left me feeling optimistic about the chances of Dan and I becoming closer; I was thoroughly enjoying the permeating buzz of the theatre and the rediscovered pleasures of dating. But all that was about to change.

Just as I was bending into my seat, having at that point relaxed completely into the gaiety of the occasion, I caught sight of a very familiar head of tousled blond hair! There was no mistaking it; Paddy O'Rourke was sitting three rows in front of us! Oh dear God, no! Paddy was the last person I wanted to meet that night! I had completely forgotten about Paddy's musical talents. If I *had* remembered, I might have chosen a different venue for a date with *another* man. Of course it was probable that Paddy O'Rourke would frequent the opening of the latest, state-of-the-art, musical venue in his home town. I wanted to slap my head in frustration but refrained from indulging in such a public display of self-recrimination.

Please God, don't let him turn around, I pleaded silently.

It felt like an eternity passed before they dimmed the lights for the start of the performance.

It soon became clear that it was the mature woman sitting on Paddy's right that was his companion for the night and not the *leggy blonde* sitting on his left! But despite being enormously relieved by this small discovery, I still felt very ill at ease. I looked at Dan; he appeared completely unaware of the situation, and he smiled warmly in my direction. I was reminded that guilt was an emotion felt only by the bearer.

I sat anticipating the intermission with dread. Could I possibly get away with sitting through it, my head crouched and my face hidden in shame? I seriously doubted it. Dan would definitely think it strange, and if Paddy noticed me, he would think it stranger still. There was nothing for it but to take my chances. As the lights went up to herald a break in the proceedings, I fumbled for my bag in an attempt to delay the inevitable. If *we* were going to meet, the later that happened, the better!

Checking first, from my crouching position, that the coast was clear, I stood up and waved my bag triumphantly, indicating that I had been successful in my search for it. After all, it could have been anywhere within a two-foot radius! When we reached the foyer, I excused myself to go to the Ladies and left Dan to make his own way to the bar. I breathed a sigh of relief when I saw the queue for the bathrooms; my tactics meant that I was now near the end of a considerable line, and for once, I welcomed the delay.

However, I hadn't allowed for the state-of-the-art facilities that were designed to handle the numbers, and the line moved quickly. Before I knew it, I was thoroughly, and I mean *thoroughly*, drying my hands. I could no longer avoid the unavoidable.

Returning to the foyer from the restrooms, my hearted skipped a beat when I spotted Dan and Paddy chatting amicably together just inside the bar area. There was no sign of Paddy's *friend* anywhere as I made my way towards them. Show time!

'Ah, there you are,' said Dan, turning slightly to retrieve a soda water from a tall, dumb waiter. 'We were just talking about you,' he added, his tone clearly indicating that he was unaware that anything other than a business relationship existed between Paddy and me.

Of course, by that stage in the proceedings, he was basically right.

'All good, I hope,' I said glibly, trying to affect total ease in the situation that I now found myself in.

'The very best,' said Dan, leaving me, in effect, none the wiser.

CAITRÍONA LESLIE

Paddy was the *last* person I wanted to meet! How could I focus my attention on Dan with the oh-so-near distraction of Paddy? I drank in the sight of him as discreetly as I could. He was looking particularly tall and gorgeous, and I wondered how it was that he hadn't made an *impression* on me sooner. He wore denims and a dark navy blue shirt under an olive green corduroy sports coat. His thick curly hair was freshly washed, and he looked boyish and outright lickable . . . yes, lickable! Suddenly, Dan looked overdressed and a lot *less* appetising. I couldn't help it; right then, I wished with all my heart that I was the most fertile woman in Ireland and that I was attending the event on the arm of the gorgeous, and unobtainable, Paddy O'Rourke!

'Hello, Libby,' Paddy said evenly.

Try as I might, I couldn't detect even the smallest hint of jealousy in him upon encountering me out and about with another man!

Blast, blast, and double blast! I wanted to scream with sheer frustration at the God's and how they were managing my life. Of course, outwardly, I remained calm. I succeeded in delivering an Oscar-winning performance as the three of us chatted affably about things that, at that moment in time, I had absolutely no interest in. I was no longer amazed by how small Ireland was! I didn't care that the entire cast was Irish! I hadn't noticed how the venue was meant to resemble a ship! The blur of the conversation was kindly interrupted by the arrival of Paddy's companion.

'Ah, here's Mum now!' Paddy said, waving and smiling over my shoulder in a bid to gain his mother's attention.

I might have guessed it would be his mother!

This should be interesting, I thought, *you could tell a lot about a man by getting to know his mother*. Dan's mother was probably dead; I really had no idea, and what's more, I didn't care. On the other hand, I knew that Paddy's mother was alive and well and a musician. The only other thing I needed to know about her, at that point, was whether she was *naughty or nice*. Looking to my right, I saw a very pleasant-looking woman approaching us; she looked to be in her late sixties. Dan and I both stood back in order to allow her to join us.

She was neatly dressed in black pants and an emerald green jacket, which she wore, buttoned to the neck. She stood about five foot six inches tall in her patent pumps. Her short thick hair was steely grey, but the addition of a purple rinse gave it a softer look, and the overall effect was that of a woman whose well-maintained appearance was rather effortless. I liked her immediately, and as it turned out, the feeling was mutual.

Seeing that her son had met up with some people that he knew, she lovingly took his arm and smiled warmly in our direction. It was patently clear that she was of the absolute opinion that anyone who was a friend of her son's must be all right.

'Mum, I'd like to introduce you to . . .,' Paddy began.

Dan and I waited expectantly for our introductions, but that was as far as Paddy got.

'No need, Dear,' his mother interrupted gently. 'Would I be right in assuming that *you* are Libby?' she asked, reaching out her hand to take mine.

Her handshake was dry and firm, just like her son's. I nodded to confirm that I was indeed Libby.

'Lovely to meet you at last, my dear,' she said firmly, and I immediately felt completely at ease in her company.

'I'm Emily, and Paddy has told me so much about you!'

Paddy had the good grace to blush slightly.

'I *must* say that I absolutely *love* your outfit, very chic indeed!' Emily continued undaunted.

It was my turn to blush; I wondered guiltily what Emily would think of me if she knew about all the forbidden things that her son and I had done together, *and* to each other. Would she be impressed by the extent of my wantonness? Probably not!

'Well, it's lovely to meet *you*, Emily,' I said, pushing all guilt firmly to the back of my mind. 'Paddy has told me a little about you too,' I said, not wanting to appear too familiar.

'Don't you think that Libby looks lovely tonight, Paddy?' Emily persisted, and I was reminded of just how embarrassing mothers could be!

Paddy had the decency this time to blush deeply but agreed, nonetheless, that I did indeed look 'lovely'. I was beginning to wonder if Emily was aware of Dan's presence at all, when, as if reading my thoughts, she turned her attention towards him. Dan was standing back, the picture of benign amusement, and clearly enjoying the scene.

'And you must be Libby's dad!' she said, without a hint of irony.

I hadn't seen that one coming! I wanted the ground to open up and to swallow all of us whole! Dan wasn't looking quite so relaxed after her comment either!

'Eh, not exactly . . .,' replied Dan, straightening suddenly.

I could see that he was searching for the way forward. Eventually, it came to him. 'Although I can see how one could easily presume that,' Dan said kindly, attempting to recover the situation.

'My name's Dan. Libby and I are friends,' he explained, taking Mrs O'Rourke's hand and shaking it firmly. 'It's lovely to meet you, Emily,' he continued, sparing Emily O'Rourke any embarrassment.

I loved him for that small act of self-effacing kindness, and under different circumstances, it would have sealed the deal for me, but unfortunately, something undeniable had changed within me. By then I knew, without a shadow of a doubt, that Dan and I could only ever be friends. I felt sad, and suddenly very tired, as the public address system instructed us to return to our seats for the second half of the opera. The evening had now officially become an endurance test.

The second half of the performance passed in a distracted haze. I stared at the back of Paddy's head and wondered how I would extricate myself from the mess that I had once again created. I dreaded the end of the show, and yet I was eager for the evening to finish.

The thought of the journey home weighed heavily on me. I stared at the back of Paddy's head, willing him to turn around, willing him to give me some small signal that he cared, but he never did. In between staring at Paddy's head and stealing glimpses at Dan for inspiration, I studied the programme and prayed for a way out. None came to mind. As the performance drew to an end, I tried a new approach, and this time, I was ready with bag in hand to aid our escape. In fairness to Dan, he too was up and ready to go once the final bow was taken; he was probably as anxious as I was to avoid a further encounter with Emily O'Rourke. But despite our best efforts, we still fell at the last hurdle.

We exited the auditorium in the opposite direction to the one by which we had entered. I felt sure that this would give us a much better chance of missing the O'Rourkes on the way out. While it probably did increase our chance of avoidance somewhat, it didn't guarantee it. Dan and I were queuing to retrieve his jacket from the cloakroom when I felt a gentle tap on my arm. It was Emily.

'Libby dear, I just wanted to say how nice it was to meet you both,' she said gently. Well, that wasn't so bad. Unfortunately, there was more to come, and I was ill-prepared to deal with the request that followed.

'Paddy and I were wondering if you and Dan would join us for some supper across the road.'

I had definitely not been expecting this, and I suddenly felt like that fish again that found itself tossed up on to the riverbank. My mouth opened and closed a couple of times, but no sound emanated from my lips. *Help*, I screamed inwardly, *was there going to be no end to the night?* Apparently not!

I felt Dan catch me about my waist with one hand as he thanked Emily for the invitation and assured her that, as long as I was in agreement, 'a spot of supper would be lovely'. I had no real option but to comply.

Fifteen minutes later, we were all seated in a small Italian restaurant directly across the road from the theatre. Paddy had made reservations at Gino's earlier in the day for his mother and himself, and their booth, although cosy, was adequate to seat the four of us comfortably. I was feeling slightly less ill at ease by the time we reached the restaurant because Paddy had managed to catch my eye, as we were exiting the theatre, and had mouthed a silent 'I'm sorry'. I took this to mean that he was sorry that our night had been ambushed by his unabashed mother; I couldn't countenance the idea that he might have meant that he was sorry that he had ever laid eyes on me!

Gino's, like Cockles and Mussels in Kinsale, despite having an unassuming name, had a very presumptuous menu that delivered at every level. The wine list was impressive by any connoisseur's standards, and I fervently hoped that Dan wouldn't suggest, as I had done to Paddy weeks earlier, that we 'take a room' in order to sample some of Italy's finest vintages. He didn't.

Dan was gallant and insisted that I should enjoy a glass or two since he was driving. Men's insistence that I should indulge in alcohol was fast becoming something of a routine! I counter insisted that I wasn't fully recovered from the flu and that apart from having no desire for alcohol, I didn't think that I would benefit from it. However, if he was willing to entrust me with his car, I would be happy to drive us home. Dan agreed, and he and Emily ended up sharing a bottle of vintage red, while Paddy and I, the designated drivers, toasted the evening with a carafe of *house still*.

Under different circumstances, the meal at Gino's would have been the perfect end to a perfect evening. Emily and Paddy were excellent company; they clearly had a great fondness for one another, which made them very easy to be around. Dan, for his part, was genial and showed no signs that events had interfered with any plans that he might have had for us. Overall, the meal was seventy-five per cent successful. I was the missing twenty-five per cent.

Although neither Paddy nor I made any mention of our visit south, I felt it hang heavy in the air between us or rather in the air around me. Paddy, by all accounts, had entirely forgotten the encounter. From what I could gather, he was as relaxed as Emily and Dan; I, on the other hand, struggled to find the common ground so that I too could join the party. I felt like the third wheel, the bump on the log, a position that should have been reserved for Paddy O'Rourke! There were certainly times during the evening when I felt like I was having an out-of-body experience. I felt gauche, and I wanted the evening to end. And it did, eventually.

On the journey home, Dan chatted away, seemingly oblivious to the turmoil that raged within me. As time passed, I became increasingly anxious at the prospect of reaching home. On what note would the night finally end? Should I presume to drive to Dan's house? I was, after all, driving Dan's car, but I definitely did not want to end up in Dan's bed!

'You can drive us back to your house, Libby,' he said, intercepting my thoughts.

I hoped that Dan didn't expect to end up in mine.

'I'm sure I'll be well fit to drive home from there,' he continued. The man was a mind-reader.

'Are you sure?' I asked, surprised by the decision in his voice.

'I'm certain, Libby. I haven't had that much to drink, and I have eaten. I'm sure, all things considered, that I'll pose no danger to myself or to any other road users.'

His tone was warm but firm.

'Okay, Dan, if you're sure?' I said, still uncertain as to how *exactly* the night would end.

Fifteen minutes later, I pulled Dan's car to a stop in front of Willow Cottage. The lights glowed warmly in the hall of the little farmhouse, and it felt like days had passed since I lit them in anticipation of our homecoming. I had felt more confident then about Dan, or at least I had hope. Now I had very little hope left as far as Dan was concerned, and none at all left for Paddy and me.

'Will you come in for a coffee, Dan?' I asked, and I was surprised to find that I meant it.

'Thanks, Libby, but another time perhaps,' he said evenly. 'Frankly, you look like you could do with a good night's sleep, and I'm a little wrecked myself. We'll be in touch,' he said softly, before saying what seemed like a very final, 'Goodnight, Libby.'

'Goodnight, Dan,' was all I could think of to say, before easing myself out of the car and allowing him to take my place behind the wheel.

Nothing had been said, but we both knew where we stood. Somehow, Dan had sensed that he was suddenly and very firmly out of the picture, and somehow, I knew that he knew. Even the most avuncular of kisses would have been misplaced between us then.

I stood outside the front door and waited for Dan to reverse the car and drive away before turning the key in the lock and going inside. Closing the door firmly, I leant back against its sturdiness and began to cry. I cried for Max. I cried for Dan. I cried for Paddy. And lastly, I cried for myself. Now I knew what other girls meant when they said that I didn't understand the heartache of unrequited love. They had been right; I hadn't understood. But I did now.

CHAPTER 41

Where Is the Fat Lady and Why Hasn't She Sung?

THE FOLLOWING DAY was Sunday. It was usually one of my favourite days of the week; a day with endless possibilities as far as I was concerned. Most of my favourite things to do could be done very easily on a Sunday, and more importantly, most of my favourite people to do them with were free on that day. It was a day, weather permitting, for long country walks and late lunches with friends or with family or with both. On rainy days, long walks might be replaced by a classic black and white movie or a game of scrabble in front of a roaring fire.

Sunday mornings usually saw me up early and rearing to go. I say *usually* because there were the rare exceptions when Sundays found me suffering very badly from the after-effects of the night before. On those occasions where too much wine had been consumed, usually in the company of good friends, Sundays took on a whole different flavour.

On those days, I went into recovery mode, where very little was achieved, and the main aim of the day was to survive it and to wake up on Monday morning as little the worse for wear as was humanly possible. I didn't relish these Sundays but recognised them as collateral damage in an otherwise fairly blameless life. Despite my not having indulged in even a sip of alcohol the night before, the day after the opera was apparently going to be one of those Sundays . . . I had the energy of a dying cat.

After Dan left, I allowed myself to wallow in grief before eventually pulling myself together. Having the flu had definitely left me feeling vulnerable, and my emotions lurked very close to the surface, ever ready, given the least excuse, to bubble unhelpfully to the fore. I prayed that this particular side-effect, along with the chronic fatigue and nausea, would subside in due course and that I would be returned to my usual robust self! I went to bed feeling hopeful that everything would look brighter and clearer in the morning. It didn't. It just looked different.

Having tossed and turned for the entire night, as snakes and scorpions chased me in my sleep, I eventually rolled myself out from under the covers at twenty minutes past six in the morning and staggered downstairs to the kitchen, bouncing off the walls as I went. My head was thumping, and I was exhausted. I felt like someone who had drunk the pub dry the night before. I reminded myself, a little belatedly, that it was never a good idea to eat so late at night.

I set about brewing myself a pot of tea. It was my usual, fail-safe, hangover cure, but even I doubted its ability to put me right that morning. I toyed briefly with the notion of indulging in the *hair of the dog* that hadn't actually bitten me the night before. I was desperate! I had the makings of a Bloody Mary, but the very thought of vodka made me race for the downstairs' loo.

After several minutes of retching, I dragged myself into the sitting room and found the will to strike a match and light the fire that was set in the grate. I was grateful then that I hadn't had any use for it the night before. The log basket was full, and there were two bales of briquettes by the back door in the kitchen. That would be enough fuel to see me through the rest of the day or at least until I was feeling more human.

I wandered back into the kitchen and noticed that the message light was blinking on the landline. It was from Mum. She had called late the night before, inviting me to eat with them later that day. Mum and Dad were expecting Dad's parents, along with Dad's brother and his wife for dinner, and Mum was hoping that some of her children would be around to join them. Uncle Desmond and Auntie Sheila's family were our closest relations on Dad's side, living within twenty minutes' drive from us; the two families of kids had been inseparable growing up. Their daughter Patricia was home from London, and she was coming too.

Patricia and I had been born three days apart, and we were particularly close as children. She had married the year before, and I hadn't seen her since their wedding. Patricia and I had a lot of catching up to do, and I hoped that I would be feeling well enough to join the group.

Making my way back into the sitting room, armed with my pot of tea and the previous day's unread newspaper, I forced myself not to think about the events of the night before. It was pointless to try and make sense of it all, and I was only just beginning to realise how complex the human heart really was. I came to the conclusion that there were some things that one had very little control over, and the whimsical nature of one's heart was certainly one of them! It, therefore, made perfect sense, and was a great comfort besides, to decide that the best course of action now was to take none at all. Que sera, sera, and all of that! As events unfolded later that day, it emerged that truer words had never been spoken!

I spent the rest of that morning, and a good deal of the afternoon, in my pyjamas, wearing a path between the sitting room and the kitchen. My appetite for food, or lack thereof, didn't alter much over the course of the morning, but I did feel ever so slightly better as the day wore on. Earl Grey was my constant companion, and I was relieved that although I had felt nauseous on a couple of occasions, the sensation had passed, and I hadn't had to act upon it.

The grandfather clock chimed half past the hour, and I was aghast to realise that suddenly it was half past four and not half past three as I had thought. Dinner at Mum's was set for five o'clock, and I still wasn't sure if I was up to the task of getting washed and dressed, never mind actually *leaving* the house. There was no time to waste.

I decided to shower and see how I felt at the other end of what seemed like a gigantean task. It was after five when I struggled out of the bathroom, another half an hour saw me sitting quite dishevelled behind the wheel of the Freelander. Apart from the rudeness of arriving late, I didn't think that the rest mattered very much. After all; I wouldn't be eating. All that mattered at that point was that I would be catching up with family, and in my emotionally and physically challenged state, family seemed even more important than ever.

Uncle Desmond's 1967, lime green Mercedes was parked at the front of Mum and Dad's when I arrived. I continued to drive around to the rear of the house, preferring to steal in by the back door. Mum had potted up her tubs since my last visit, and the rest of her garden was in its usual impeccable order. The lawns were neatly mowed, with hedges and climbers trimmed and tidy. The early evening sun was warm, filled with the promise of a beautiful summer ahead. Despite the sun's best efforts, I couldn't shake off a sense of indifference and inexplicable dread.

As I observed the south-facing fig trees on either side of my parent's back door, I decided that there was nothing for it but to go to the doctor the following day. I was either depressed or dying. Worst possible case of flu aside, I should have been feeling well on the road to recovery by then and I wasn't, not by *any* stretch of the imagination!

I could hear everybody laughing and talking over one another as I passed through the kitchen on my way to the dining room. The conversation was lively as usual, and I felt my heart lift for the first time that day. I loved Uncle Desmond and Auntie Sheila; they were warm and easygoing, and like my own parents, they had a healthy appetite for life.

Uncle Desmond was Dad's eldest brother, and he had inherited the family farm; my grandparents still lived with them. Luckily, they lived in a very large house and had the benefit of 'the west wing' as we called it, where my grandparents happily resided. Although they were in their eighties, my grandparents enjoyed very good health and were rarely to be found at home. They busied themselves with all sorts of events ranging from coffee mornings to bridge evenings. It would be good to see them, and everybody else, again.

As I entered the dining room, the conversation came to a gradual but complete stop as one by one people turned to look in my direction. It was as if a ghost had entered behind me.

'Hello everyone,' I said, feeling strangely self-conscious, 'I'm sorry I'm late.'

No reply, just silence. Then my grandmother found her voice.

'Libby, whatever has happened to you?' my grandmother protested without restraint. '*You* look ghastly!'

'Hello, Gran,' I said, making my way towards her and bending to kiss her in greeting, 'I'm afraid I've had the flu, and I'm still feeling a bit under the weather.'

She drew back from me sharply, and I felt compelled to reassure her that I was no longer infectious.

'I'm not worried about catching the flu, Libby! We've had the jab!' she said stoutly. 'I can assure you that I'm far more concerned about your health than I am about my own!'

She was clearly appalled that I would presume such a thing.

'Take yourself off to the doctor first thing in the morning,' she advised, 'and find out what the devil is wrong with you!'

'Thanks, Gran, I will,' I said, grateful that the matter of my declining health had been dealt with so swiftly by my sprightly octogenarian grandmother! With any luck, we would all be able to enjoy the rest of the evening without the bother of second guessing 'what the devil' was wrong with me! All would be revealed in the fullness of time or, as it happened, by the end of that very evening.

Dinner proceeded as normal from then on. I picked at a plate of mashed potato and gravy, undisturbed by any questions from those around me as to why I wasn't eating properly. The conversation regained its momentum, and the news of the day was that Patricia and her husband Norman were expecting their first baby at the beginning of December, 'all going well'.

I was truly happy for them and for the baby waiting to be born. They would both make wonderful parents. Patricia was graciously underplaying the news, and I knew that it was out of a sense of concern for my feelings; I felt awful for her. I squeezed her hand and gave her a wink of reassurance that it was okay to be happy in my presence. She smiled her relief and touched her fingertips to her breastbone as a mark of true sympathy for me. We knew and loved each other *so* well.

I was feeling a lot better after dinner. I hadn't thrown up my feast of mash and gravy, and I had quite enthusiastically eaten three digestive biscuits with a cup of tea afterwards. I suggested to Patricia that we should take a drive so that I could show her Alice-Rose; the others could wait until the official unveiling. She jumped at the chance.

Giving vague reassurances that we wouldn't be long, we left like two teenagers on a covert mission to have some fun. With Patricia beside me in the car, I felt reassured and hopeful. Whereas Emma was my baby sister, Patricia was my peer and my confidant from earliest childhood. I knew and trusted her beyond measure, and now that she was back, I realised how much I had missed her.

Pulling on to the front avenue of Alice-Rose, Patricia gave an intake of breath that conveyed a true appreciation of what lay before her, and I, in turn, saw Alice-Rose with renewed regard through her eyes. Every aspect of Alice-Rose was truly remarkable in an organic, understated way.

'My God, Libby, it's wonderful!' she cried.

As we drove on, Patricia remarked on the impressive features that made Alice-Rose so special, starting with the giant, bifurcated oaks that lined the avenue. She reflected on things that would have been unremarkable in other settings but that were rendered exquisite in the surrounds of Alice-Rose, most notably the lawns and hedges in their generous proportions. I felt something resembling maternal pride swell within me.

'I didn't realise that you were this far on with the refurbishment,' Patricia said as we wandered around the house.

'You must be practically finished,' she continued, gazing through an upstairs window into the walled-garden below, where work on the glasshouses was gathering momentum.

'Yes,' I acknowledged.

'Your builder must be a rare one! The standard of work is exceptional!' she declared.

'Yes, Paddy has been great throughout,' I said, as non-committally as possible.

'I'd really like to meet him,' she said.

'*Really?*' I asked, somewhat surprised.

'Yes,' she said. 'Anyone who can do this to a house is definitely worth meeting.'

I felt myself beginning to blush, something that I was becoming increasingly good at. The thought occurred to me that I might, in fact, be suffering from early menopause.

'Have you been talking to Emma?' I asked suspiciously.

'No, but I have heard Auntie Sarah say a word or two in praise of the man!' she laughed. 'She thinks that Paddy O'Rourke is quite the catch and altogether perfect for you!' she continued playfully, pointing in my direction.

'My God, you *even* know his last name!' I said, exasperated. 'That woman is incorrigible!'

'*That woman* may be 'incorrigible', but you *have* to admit that she's usually on the money,' Patricia said, coming to my mother's defence.

'Not this time she isn't!' I insisted, a little too stoutly.

'So there is *no* chance of a love match between yourself and Paddy O'Rourke?' my cousin asked, clearly disappointed by my response.

'None at all, I'm afraid.'

'So you admit that you like him?' she said, as quick off the mark as a greyhound out of the traps.

'I don't admit to anything!' I said defensively.

'But there *is* somebody on the scene?' she probed, determined not to let the subject drop.

'Nobody at the moment,' I answered truthfully.

'Right . . .,' she said, appearing somewhat confounded.

'You seem surprised?' I said, bewildered by her slightly belligerent approach to the state of my love life. It wasn't like Patricia to be so persistent.

'Don't take this the wrong way, Libby,' Patricia continued gently, 'and please don't be offended, but when I saw you today, you reminded me so much of myself not so long ago.'

'How could I be offended by that?' I demanded.

Patricia shook her head, clearly baffled by something, but said nothing.

'You are, after all, "a true Finn", just like me!' I joked.

Patricia and I did indeed look remarkably alike. We were often mistaken for sisters, having inherited the tall, dark looks of the Finn side of our respective families.

'I don't mean in looks,' she explained, 'I mean more in appearance.'

I was left none the wiser by this statement and looked hard at Patricia, confusion clearly playing across my face. She took a deep breath before continuing.

'The appearance, that is, of a pregnant woman who is suffering from the most ferocious morning sickness!'

I felt the colour draining from my face as everything suddenly began to make sense. The pieces of the jigsaw puzzle finally slotted into place, and I rushed to the nearest bathroom to throw up, overcome by the enormity of its revelation. By the time Patricia reached me, I was shaking like a leaf, terrified by the possibility of what might actually be happening inside my body.

'Oh, Libby, I didn't mean to upset you, really I didn't . . . I shouldn't have said anything . . . I didn't mean to be so insensitive!' she apologised profusely, clearly horrified by my reaction.

'Its okay, Patricia. It's not *your* fault,' I tried to reassure her. 'I don't even know if there is anything to be upset about,' I said, trying to remain calm, while all the while fear and shock raged within me.

Patricia kept a protective arm around me and waited patiently for me to continue. Finally, I was able to.

'There is a very slim, and I mean *very* slim chance that I could be pregnant,' I said weakly.

'Dare I ask, by whom?' she queried tentatively.

'If I tell you, you must swear to bring it to the grave with you if necessary. You must promise me that you won't even tell Norman! Can you promise me that?' I asked desperately.

'I promise, Libby, anything for you. You know that,' she answered without hesitation, and I knew I could trust her.

'Paddy O'Rourke,' I admitted.

'Paddy O'Rourke, *the* Paddy O'Rourke?' she asked incredulously. 'For a minute there, I thought you were going to say Father Daly!'

'Why would you think that?' I laughed despite myself.

'Well, by the tone of your voice and the absolute need for discretion, I thought you were going to reveal some huge scandal!'

She laughed out of relief as much as anything else.

'Well, not quite a scandal of that magnitude admittedly,' I conceded, 'but a *massive mess* nonetheless!'

'How so?' Patricia continued.

'Well, apart from one night of incredible sex, Paddy O'Rourke has never shown one iota of interest in me!' I said.

'Not bad!' observed Patricia, settling into the story.

'Not bad?' I countered.

'Well, it's not like you forced him to have sex with you!' she said, coming to my defence.

'Well, no, that much is true. But,' I said slowly, trying to formulate my explanation.

'But?' Patricia said, urging me to explain.

'Well, when we didn't have any 'protection' and our mutual hormones were raging, I reassured him that I was infertile . . . as well as being free from all disease!'

I was relieved to finally have the gory details of our 'affair' off my chest.

'So you lied,' she said, and I could tell by her tone that she was completely bewildered.

'No!' I said, anxious to defend myself. 'I really believed that I was infertile! And since I'd only ever slept with Max, I presumed that I was disease free!'

'I think that was a fair assumption, under the circumstances,' Patricia acknowledged supportively.

'Anyway, we don't even know for sure whether or not I am pregnant,' I said desperately, grasping for a straw, that deep down I knew didn't exist.

'No, we don't,' Patricia said decisively, 'and there's only one way to find that out for sure.'

'A pregnancy test?' I asked feebly.

'Exactly!' Patricia said, taking me by the arm and linking me downstairs and out the back door to the Freelander.

We were sitting on my bed in Willow Cottage within the hour, having driven into Ballyedmond to get a pregnancy testing kit; luckily, Tesco was open until 9 p.m., and we made it just in time. With only minutes to spare, I waited in the jeep while Patricia ran in to purchase one. We had decided on the journey into town that even if Patricia encountered someone who knew her, it was perfectly reasonable for her, a well-married woman, to be purchasing such an item. And besides, the news that 'Patricia Finn' was expecting would be common knowledge around the town soon enough. Despite the fact that she had moved across the water to England, the locals of Ballyedmond would still have an interest in her; she was still one of their own.

On the other hand, if the news got out that I, Libby Finn, was seen buying the kit, the town gossips would think that all their birthdays had come together, and the news would spread like wildfire! That was definitely something that I didn't want, not yet anyway.

In the end, it didn't take very long to complete a pregnancy test. With the benefit of hindsight, I imagined that it took about as long as it did to get pregnant in the first place! As it turned out, despite everything that I had presumed to know about my body that fateful night in Kinsale, I did in fact know nothing!

'Are you going to tell him?' Patricia asked, breaking into my thoughts.

'No,' I said firmly.

'You'll have to at some stage,' she said reasonably, 'it's only fair.'

'I know, and I will,' I sighed wearily. 'Eventually . . . when the time is right,' I added, conceding to the inevitable.

'Good girl,' she said, squeezing my shoulder in an act of reassurance. 'Now take one of these,' she coaxed, handing me a small white tablet that she had taken from a pack in her bag.

'What's this?' I enquired, the word abortifacient flashing absurdly into my brain. Surely, Patricia wouldn't just *happen* to have something like that lurking at the bottom of her purse?

'It's vitamin B_{12} and folic acid,' she said, nudging me encouragingly. 'I presume that since this pregnancy wasn't planned, you haven't been taking anything on the off chance of becoming pregnant.'

'No,' I conceded, suddenly aware of something else that I had to start worrying about, neural tube defects! God, I was such an idiot!

'Relax, Libby,' Patricia said, reading my thoughts. 'Women have been having healthy babies for thousands of years without the benefit of all these things! But there's no harm in taking them just the same.'

'Thanks, Cous,' I said, taking the small round tablet from her and swallowing it.

'What do I do next?' I asked eventually, feeling the first tinges of excitement creeping into my spirit. I was going to be somebody's mother. I, Libby Finn, was going to be somebody's mother! Now that I had a chance to think about it; I couldn't quite believe it! Despite the less than ideal circumstances, *this* was a miracle! A wonderful, awful, and mixed-up miracle! And one way or another, I was determined that we would survive it! I was no longer me; I had finally become we. I knew that despite everything, this was the start of a love story that, for my part, would never end. My grown-up life had finally begun.

'First things first,' Patricia said, taking control of the situation. 'I think we should call home and let everyone know that I'll be spending the night at Willow Cottage.'

'I was hoping you'd say that,' I said, relieved to have Patricia's support as I embarked on a journey that I knew would be one of my most challenging so far. Looking at her then, I realised how much like our grandmother she was, and I was thankful for that.

CHAPTER 42

'Testing' Times

I T HADN'T BEEN difficult explaining the change of plan to our family. It was to be expected that Patricia and I would have a lot of catching up to do, as indeed we did, that and forward planning!

According to Patricia, it was vital that I knew the date of my last period in order to be able to accurately calculate my due date. I actually had this information readily to hand because I had, from an early age, formed the habit of recording the first day of my period in my diary. Initially, I started the practice for the sole purpose of avoiding embarrassing mishaps. However, in later years, this practice served another purpose when hope and expectation of a natural conception still reigned in our marriage. Habits are difficult to break, and despite my broken heart and broken dreams, the habit of recording those dates never died.

A brief referral to my diary revealed that March the tenth was the date of my last period. By adding on nine months and seven days to that date, Patricia, the gestational expert, calculated that Baby Finn would be due to arrive in or around December the seventeenth. Wow, wow, and double wow!

The following morning, after first making an appointment with my local practitioner, Dr Áine Ginty, I called the practice of Dr Joan O'Neill and asked to be put through to her. Joan O'Neill had been our family GP in Dublin, and she was our first port of call when it came to investigating the reason for our failure to conceive. Despite the tragic events that unfolded as a result of those investigations, the results of Max's semen analysis should still be on file. I hadn't looked for them before then; they were no longer relevant to me, or so I thought. And in any event, I had presumed to know the results.

'Good morning, Libby,' said Joan. Her kind, even voice was so familiar.

'Good morning, Joan,' I said, relieved to have been able to get through to her so quickly.

'How have you been keeping, Libby?' she asked.

'Good, all things considered. And you?' I replied vaguely, hoping that she would presume that I was referring to Max's death and not to anything else.

'Very well, Libby, thank you,' she said. 'Now is there anything I can help you with?' she asked, her tone indicating that she knew that I was anxious to get on with the point of my call.

'Yes, Joan. As it happens, I'm hoping that you might be able to help me with something. I was wondering if you ever got the results of Max's semen analysis back from the lab?'

'Libby, you must be a mind-reader,' she said. 'I actually came across Max's records yesterday, and I was going to contact you by post.'

Her tone revealed nothing. What was she going to tell me, and was I really prepared for whatever it might be? I reasoned that it could make very little difference to me now.

'I would have contacted you sooner,' she continued, her tone still even, 'but under the circumstances, I wasn't quite sure how the news would affect you.'

She paused, and the suspense continued to mount unbearably.

What did she mean when she said that she wasn't sure how the news would affect me? I began to worry then that she was about to tell me that Max's semen was normal and that I couldn't possibly be pregnant! Perhaps I had some malignant tumour growing inside me and not a baby, after all. I had read about hormone producing tumours that mimicked those produced in pregnancy.

'Go on,' I said quietly, trying not to betray any hint of my own anxiety.

'My notes indicate that Max wasn't on any medication or using drugs, including the excessive consumption of alcohol, at the time that this sample was taken,' she said very matter-of-factly.

'Yes,' I said.

I was surprised that Joan would even refer to such a thing! Max barely drank, never mind took drugs of any kind! We hadn't even stocked the usual supply of painkillers that others did; neither of us ever suffered from even the mildest of headaches. Friends and family were often surprised and frustrated by our lack of what they referred to as 'basic drug supplies'. I was confused.

CAITRÍONA LESLIE

'That's absolutely correct!' I continued firmly. 'Max was totally against *excess* of any kind! And as far as *we* knew, he was perfectly healthy, so there was no need for any form of medication.'

I'm sure Joan O'Neill heard the barely suppressed outrage in my voice because she continued along conciliatory lines.

'I don't doubt you, Libby, and Max probably was in excellent health,' she said, 'but I'm afraid that without further testing there is no way we can determine the exact reason for the results of his semen analysis.'

'What do you mean?' I asked.

'Well, I'm afraid the results were not promising,' she said, pausing.

By that point my heart was pounding so loudly in my chest that I felt sure that Joan must surely have been aware of it. After what seemed like an eternity, she continued once more.

'The tests reveal that Max's sperm count was reduced,' she said.

'I see,' I said, implying that I understood the implications, when in fact I did not.

'Reduced sperm numbers do not always result in an inability to conceive, but Max's were *significantly* reduced,' she said sympathetically.

I said nothing this time and waited for her to continue.

'I'm afraid that besides having reduced numbers, Max's sperm cells were, for the most part, morphologically abnormal, and their motility was reduced also.'

Silence. I didn't know what to say or think.

'Libby? Are you okay?' Joan's concerned voice carried down the line.

'Yes, Joan, sorry, I was just trying to digest the information,' I said truthfully.

I wondered what Max would have made of the news if he had been alive. I believed that he would probably have been devastated. It was one thing being supportive to a loved one who was infertile; it was an entirely different matter to be strong when you were the one with the problem.

It wasn't difficult for me to imagine how Max would have felt. For years, I had presumed that the problem had lain with me, and I had carried the burden of guilt, guilt that I would never be able to give Max a child of his own. I knew that Max would have carried that same lonely burden, just as I had.

'Basically, Libby,' continued Joan slowly, 'it would have been very unlikely that Max, given those results, would have been able to father a child.'

The fog cleared slowly as I processed the information that was being cautiously fed to me.

'Obviously, Libby,' she continued, 'if Max was still with us, we would insist on repeating the analysis on another sample. Despite it being very unlikely, there is always the concern that a sample mix-up could have occurred. One would always request a repeat sample when the results are not what one would expect.'

The silence between us was palpable.

'It makes sense, now,' I said eventually, as much to myself as to her.

'Sorry, Libby?' said the doctor, clearly bewildered by my comment.

'Joan,' I said firmly, remembering my vow to rejoice, 'I'm so pleased to be able to tell you that I am, in fact, pregnant! And despite less than ideal circumstances, I couldn't be happier!'

Dr Joan O'Neill wasn't the only one to be surprised by the news that I, Libby the infertile, was pregnant. Later that day, my general practitioner expressed mild surprise upon hearing that I was by then, almost certain that I was, in fact, "with child". This was quite a U-turn on my part, given my previous objections when she had suggested pregnancy as the possible cause of my symptoms. One small sample of urine later, followed by a five-minute wait, and the doctor was able to confirm my highest hopes and, to some degree, my greatest fears.

Dr Ginty's approach to my pregnancy was professional and no-nonsense. She bypassed any congratulatory expressions and got straight down to the business of taking care of her 'patients'. I had now officially become we! She estimated from my dates that I was approximately eight weeks pregnant. I should commence taking B_{12} and folic acid supplements immediately and iron supplements after my twelfth week of pregnancy, and not before it. A quick dipstick of my urine didn't indicate anything unusual, and she proceeded to take various samples of blood to send to the laboratory for analysis. My weight and blood pressure were fine.

Dr Ginty made a point of saying that I should ignore people who encouraged me to overeat. The old saying that urged pregnant women to eat for two was 'complete nonsense', considering that, as we spoke, the embryo was probably not much bigger than a raisin. The average baby weighed seven pounds at delivery, and there were 'no prizes for fat babies!' I should consume no more than two hundred extra calories a day, the equivalent of two Weetabix, and even then, only in my last trimester! Considering that I had probably shed the best part of a stone over the course of the previous month, I assumed that there was some room for manoeuvre around that particular target.

One of the great things about discovering that I was pregnant was the fact that my nausea now held no fear for me. That in itself was wonderful. Once I knew that it would pass, I concentrated on getting by, eating multiple small snacks throughout the day instead of the usual three substantial meals, a practice that did not go unnoticed by my mother. Over the course of the following month, Mum frequently cast an eye of suspicion in my direction, leading me to believe that while Sarah Finn might not actually smell a rat, she did at least get the whiff of a small mouse.

On the one hand, I felt absolutely dreadful, anticipating how she would react when I finally came clean, but on the other hand, I knew that I had no choice but to remain silent. Under normal circumstances, I would have told my mother the very second I found out that I was pregnant, but unfortunately, these were not normal circumstances. I couldn't tell another soul until Jules's and Noel's wedding was over, and Alice-Rose was no longer under the watchful eye of Paddy O'Rourke.

Mum wasn't the person that I was most concerned about when I thought about my condition and about those from whom I was keeping it secret, that was Paddy O'Rourke. I could barely think about Paddy without my chest tightening and my stomach twisting at the enormity of what I had to confess to him. I knew, even without Patricia's advice, that it was something that had to be done . . . just not yet.

Dear, sweet Paddy, who for some reason, was growing sweeter by the day despite his obvious desire to finish the job at Alice-Rose. It was only when I knew that he could never be mine that I realised just how kind he could be. His apparent surliness masked a dry wit and a burning ambition to achieve the highest standards for his clients.

Once, when I arrived on site, I fancied that Paddy had looked at me with an expression of absolute tenderness. Unfortunately, I couldn't really be sure; the moment was quickly lost when Mick arrived on the scene and jumped in with his size ten boots, oblivious to anything that might have been going on between us.

There again, maybe Mick knew something that I didn't know and had interrupted us wholly aware that Paddy's interests lay somewhere else. After all, wasn't I just grabbing at straws? Any displays of tenderness or intimacy were most likely imagined, and even if they weren't, I knew that once

Paddy discovered that I was pregnant, he would see me as nothing more than someone who had taken advantage of his trusting nature. Apart from the small grape of life growing inside me, the situation was an unmitigated mess and one that really didn't bear thinking about!

I longed to tell Jules about my pregnancy, but that was impossible for obvious reasons. Firstly, I didn't want to steal her thunder, and secondly, I didn't want to give her something else to worry about! Having said that, when I thought about it, Jules did seem unusually laid back all of a sudden, the control-freakishness that had become Jules since her engagement was totally gone, and an unusual calmness had descended upon her. This state of affairs would have been worrying was it not for the fact that it was such a blessed relief!

I wondered briefly if Jules was taking some kind of medication, and I considered tackling her about it *after* the wedding. A true friend would not ignore another friend's suspected drug abuse, but I allayed my guilt by reasoning that I wouldn't ignore it *forever*; I was just buying a little time.

In saying that, I wasn't particularly worried about eventually telling Jules. I knew that by then she would be tied up in wedded-bliss and far beyond caring about why I hadn't told her sooner. In fact, I knew without a shadow of a doubt that Jules would be one of my stoutest defenders. She would probably go so far as to insist to all and sundry that my pregnancy had been planned with military precision and that it had always been my intention to have a baby by the time I was thirty! I wondered how Dan Bryant would feel about that; I wondered how Dan Bryant would feel about it all. Not too badly, I hoped.

Dan

CHAPTER 43

Game Over

BEFORE I ARRIVED to take Libby to the theatre that fateful evening, I knew that she would look beautiful, as always. Even so, I wasn't prepared for the vision that met me at the door; Libby looked amazing! She wore a striking silk kaftan and matching pants, with a silver belt slung loosely around her hips. Silver sandals graced her slender feet, and a fine cashmere shawl was draped casually over one shoulder. Her hair was set thick and high on her head, and she smelled wonderful. I knew, without a shadow of a doubt, that I would be the envy of every other man in the theatre that evening. Unfortunately, it didn't take me long to discover that I was the envy of one man in particular, and to make matters worse, by the night's end, I was certain that his affections were not misplaced.

Initially, the evening started off well, although I sensed that Libby lacked a certain amount of her usual joie de vivre. The car journey to Dublin was spent in easy conversation, and we reached the theatre in plenty of time to have a drink before the performance. Libby declined a glass of wine in favour of tonic water, and I decided to join her, thinking that we could indulge in a bottle of wine together later. As we made our way to our seats before the start of the performance, I was already looking forward to dinner, and I felt sure-footed in pursuit of my goal to win her heart.

However, soon after taking our seats, it became apparent that all was not well with Libby. She became distracted and noticeably tense, and it was obvious to me that something in the status quo had shifted. I wasn't really sure what that was until I 'bumped' into Mr O'Rourke at the bar. He was quite relaxed at first, but then I disclosed to him who it was that had accompanied me to the theatre, and the colour seemed to drain from his face. He managed to recover himself by the time Libby joined us.

For her part, Libby maintained her cool to a large degree, but the chemistry between the pair was unmistakable. Heaven only knows why I jumped at the invitation to dine with Paddy and his mother; most would have seen it as an act of folly under the circumstances. I suppose that I was secretly hoping that I was wrong and that by buying more time in their company, I could return to Ballyedmond reassured that there was nothing going on between Libby Finn and Paddy O'Rourke. Unfortunately, this did not turn out to be the case, and by the end of dinner, my earlier suspicions were confirmed beyond any doubt.

I came away from the gathering certain that Libby and Paddy O'Rourke were destined to be together. It wasn't anything that was said between them, more that which wasn't! They were totally at ease with each other, and there didn't seem to be any effort required between them. The looks of absolute love and adoration that Paddy stole in Libby's direction, when he thought that no one was watching, were unambiguous. Libby was more restrained, but it was still obvious that she wasn't unaffected by his subtle charms.

Twenty years earlier, I would have given this young buck a run for his money and would have been confident of a fifty-fifty chance of victory. But at fifty-three years of age, I wasn't sure that I wanted to compete at that level. Loving Libby was a young man's game. Therefore, after a brief, but thorough, consideration of the situation, it became obvious that I had just two choices. I knew that both would lead to the same conclusion, with varying degrees of self-respect remaining at the end, and I decided to bow out gracefully while I still had some dignity left.

This I did as best I could, and I hoped that Libby would remember me as a better man because of it. As for Paddy O'Rourke, well, to be honest, I really didn't care what he thought! He was the victor; he was the one who had won the heart of the 'fair maiden', and he didn't need my goodwill on top of everything else!

CAITRÍONA LESLIE

Libby

CHAPTER 44

Revelations for Breakfast

I ALLOWED A WEEK to go by after finding out that I was pregnant before I thought about venturing up to Alice-Rose again. I knew that Paddy was perplexed by the fact that I was so conspicuously absent from the house just as the project was nearing completion. We corresponded by phone on a daily basis, and I reassured him that I would be up to inspect everything as soon as I could.

I worried constantly about meeting him again and wondered if he would suspect 'something' just by looking at me. I dreaded every conversation and agonised about when and how I would eventually break the news to him. I pictured his reaction, ranging from raging anger to hurt and bewildered disbelief, never delight and rapturous applause. I was, after all, merely pregnant, *not* delusional!

I awoke on the Monday of that week feeling surprisingly well, but instead of relief, I felt dread. I was only nine weeks pregnant and had not anticipated feeling any better until the end of my first trimester. If the library of pregnancy-related books that I had surreptitiously acquired over the previous week was anything to go by, I shouldn't expect to feel any improvement in my condition until at least then. The books sought to reassure me that nausea was perfectly normal in pregnancy and that many pregnant ladies experienced it to varying degrees throughout their entire pregnancy!

Putting two and two together and coming up with five, I deduced that if I wasn't yet twelve weeks pregnant, and I was suddenly feeling a whole lot better, there could only be one logical explanation. I had miscarried. I jumped out of bed and examined the bed sheets, nothing! No traces of blood, nothing! This brought slight but short-lived relief; I wasn't out of the woods yet! I raced to the bathroom and, without further ado, pulled down my pyjama bottoms to search for any signs of bleeding . . . again, nothing! I went to the toilet and, afterwards, examined the toilet paper, very carefully, for any traces of blood . . . nothing!

'Oh, thank you, God! Thank you, God!' I said aloud in the stillness of the bathroom.

'I promise that I will never, ever, have another doubt about this baby if you just let me keep it! Please let it be healthy and strong, and I promise to do my very best to be a good mother! Thank you, God!'

This was the start of my daily conversations with "The Man Above" and marked a significant turning point in my pregnancy. I resolved more firmly to revel in my condition as best I could; I didn't want my unborn baby picking up on any negative or ambivalent feelings that I might have felt obliged to have. What was done was done, and at least *I* knew that I had acted in good faith.

I also resolved to contact Paddy O'Rourke as soon as possible after Jules's wedding to inform him of my condition. I would make it absolutely clear to him that I wanted and expected nothing from him by way of child-support and that he could see our child at any time if *that* was what he wanted. It all sounded perfectly reasonable, in my head, but I suspected that the reality for Paddy would be rather different.

There was also the small matter of telling my family about the baby, that wouldn't be easy either! However, there was no point worrying about them until after I told Paddy; it was imperative that I tell him first. I could worry about everyone else later.

After establishing that I hadn't, in fact, miscarried during the night, I hurried downstairs in search of breakfast. Like Old Mother Hubbard, my cupboards were bare. Apart from some low-fat milk, a carton of out-of-date eggs, and a half pound of rancid butter, the fridge was empty, and my hopes for a pancake breakfast quickly vanished. I put the kettle on the hob and carefully considered my sudden craving for pancakes. It couldn't be ignored. I picked up the phone and called Jules.

'Any plans for breakfast?' I asked, when Jules finally answered the phone.

'What time is it?' she mumbled sleepily.

I had no idea what time it was. A quick check of the kitchen clock showed the time to be five past seven, a *little* too early for making, or taking, calls.

'Sorry, Jules,' I said, feeling almost contrite for having woken her at such an ungodly hour, even if it was a weekday. 'It's only five past seven. I forgot to check the time before calling you.'

'That's okay,' my friend said a little less sleepily, 'I was going to get up soon anyway. It looks good out there.'

'It's glorious!' I said.

'So . . . breakfast?' she continued, and I could tell that she was trying to gather her thoughts.

'Yes, breakfast!' I echoed enthusiastically. 'I woke up almost hungry this morning for the first time in absolutely ages!'

'Fantastic!' exclaimed Jules. 'I was beginning to worry about you. For a while there, I thought you had a touch of anorexia.'

'Thanks, Jules, I had the flu. Remember?' I said, a little too defensively.

It occurred to me that I had better ease up on all protests of indignation in light of the revelations that were to come.

'I know, I know,' she said soothingly. 'Anyway, now that you have your appetite back, what would you like to do for breakfast?'

'Well, I was thinking of pancakes at the Gourmet Deli,' I said.

'Sounds good. What time?' asked Jules, her voice indicating that she was clearly impressed by my choice.

'Could you make it for eight thirty?' I asked hopefully.

'Does a one-legged duck swim in circles?,' came her reply.

Just over an hour later, Jules and I were sitting at a small table, overlooking the Edmond River. It was the beginning of another glorious summer's day, and the early morning sunlight danced off the surface of the water, lifting even the most dubious of spirits, namely my own. Jules sat across from me, looking the picture of good health. Her already thick red hair looked even more lustrous, her skin was clear, and her eyes were bright.

'My God, Jules, you look amazing! I think I'll just order whatever you're having,' I said lightly, catching sight of Tracey Fitzgibbons approaching our table.

Jules paused and waited expectantly, a slight smile playing around her mouth, as Tracey readied herself with notebook and pencil. Only when Jules was sure that our waitress was well and truly ready to take our order, did she begin.

'Good morning, Tracey!' Jules said brightly, 'I would like a toasted sandwich of sliced Mars Bar and apple, with a helping of peanut butter on the side.'

The girl didn't flinch. It was as if she had taken this order before and was ready for it. I was not, and I felt the familiar twinges of nausea begin to stir once more. I forced myself to think of pancakes, and I began to feel better.

'Anything else?' Tracey enquired casually.

What in God's name would Jules's reply be to this, I wondered, already dreading the answer!

'Yes, thanks, Tracey. I'll have an extra-large virgin Bloody Mary with a twist of lemon,' she said, winking bizarrely as she said the word 'virgin', before snapping the menu shut and returning it into the girl's outstretched hand.

My stomach churned, and I began to sweat.

Now it was my turn, and Tracey turned her undivided attention towards me. But before I could utter a word, Jules intervened.

'Apparently, Tracey,' Jules said in a conspiratorial tone, 'Libby wants whatever I'm having. So I suppose you can just double that order.'

They both giggled at this, and I felt somewhat foolish because I clearly wasn't in on the joke.

'Ha. Ha,' I said slowly, completely bewildered by the events of the previous five minutes. 'On second thoughts, girls,' I said smiling determinedly, 'I'll choose my own breakfast *if* you don't mind.'

I hadn't bargained on Jules eclectic taste buds.

'Tracey, can I have an order of whole wheat pancakes with maple syrup and sausage?'

'Anything to drink?' Tracey enquired, resuming an air of professionalism.

'Yes, thanks. I think I'll skip the Bloody Mary, even a virginal one, in favour of a good old-fashioned pot of tea. Sorry to be so unoriginal.'

Taking the menu that I handed to her, Tracey turned on her heel and left. I looked at Jules waiting for the punchline, but Jules was giving nothing away.

'So I take it that you phoned in your real order, or did you just give it to Tracey on your way in?' I asked, curiosity getting the better of me.

'Nope!' she said.

'You're kidding, right?'

'Nope!' Jules said again, and I could see that she was waiting for some sort of a reaction from me.

Eventually, after what seemed like an age of expectation between us, the penny finally dropped.

'*You're* not!' I said, astonished.

'I am!' she said, giggling helplessly.

'Oh my God, Jules, when did you find out?' I asked, amazed by the coincidence that Jules, and Patricia, and I, could all be expecting babies around the same time.

'Last week!' she squeaked, leaning over the table towards me to assume a more discreet position. 'Can you believe it?' she continued breathlessly.

'Under the circumstances, I have to admit that I am well, and truly, amazed,' I said as quietly as I could.

'The circumstances being that I'm not yet married,' Jules mumbled, and I detected the ill-disguised hurt in her voice.

'Good God, no, Jules. Heaven forbid that I ever become that sanctimonious,' I whispered quickly, eager to put her mind at rest. 'I am simply amazed by the coincidence that you and I are pregnant at the same time.'

Jules's mouth literally fell open, and for the first time ever, I saw my best friend lost for words.

'Sorry, Jules, I should have broken that news to you a *little* more gently,' I said, realising just how abruptly I had spilled my secret.

'Dan?' she ventured tentatively.

'No.'

'Thank God,' she said without hesitation.

'But why?' I asked, genuinely taken aback by her reaction.

'He's not right for you,' she said firmly.

'Okay,' I said, not entirely convinced that she should be so sure.

'Who then?' Jules asked.

'It doesn't matter,' I said quietly.

'It does to me,' she insisted without apology.

'Paddy O'Rourke,' I whispered.

'Oh, thank God!' she whispered back, genuine relief flooding her voice.

'Why "thank God"?' I asked, unable to follow Jules's line of reasoning.

As far as I was aware, Jules barely knew Paddy O'Rourke, having met him on just a handful of occasions.

'"Thank God" because you two are *perfect* for each other, that's why,' she said, reaching for my hands and squeezing them.

'Oh, Libby, I'm so happy for *us*. I could cry!' she exclaimed under her breath. And then she did.

As I watched the 'tears of happiness' flow down Jules's slightly contorted face, I pondered her words. I was definitely happy for her; but I still wasn't entirely sure how I should be feeling for myself. Happy? Certainly on one level, but entirely overwhelmed on another! I had a lot of hurdles to clear before I could begin to unravel the threads of my complicated state of happiness and contemplate the future. As for Jules, she had all her threads neatly wound and ready for weaving, and for the first time in our lives, I *almost* envied the girl sitting opposite me. Her life seemed gloriously straightforward compared to mine.

Tracey returned with our orders, and we ate in silence, concentrating on our food as we considered each other's disclosures. I observed Jules in disbelief as she scoffed her strange combination of foods. I had to look away when my stomach sent out more warning signals; I didn't want my newfound appetite to vanish as suddenly as it had reappeared. Only when every morsel of my own food was eaten, and I was sure that Jules had eaten all of hers, did I return my full attention to our conversation.

'Jules, I think that we should suspend all talk of babies until after the wedding, what do you think?'

I hoped that she wouldn't see my reluctance to immerse myself in baby talk as an indication that I was resentful of her, near perfect, situation.

To my surprise, she readily agreed.

'As always, Libby, *you*'re absolutely right! After all, loose lips sink ships.'

She pressed her index finger against her pursed lips.

'And besides,' she added sensibly, 'I think we both have enough to think about until then!'

I presumed that she meant the final organisation of her wedding.

'*You* have a house to finish, and *I* have a wedding to attend!' she said laughing.

'*We* have a wedding to attend!' I said, unable to refrain from joining in her obvious excitement. Suddenly, Jules reached over and took my hand in hers again.

'Libby, I want you to enjoy every minute of your wonderful life. I just know it will turn out all right in the end.'

Jules and I parted company outside the delicatessen, after first arranging to meet there at the same time the following morning.

There was just over a fortnight left to the 'big day', and I felt slightly anxious that I had forgotten something, or everything!

I had one last site visit to make before I could remove myself from everything involving Paddy O'Rourke, that is, until after the twenty-fifth of June; Jules deserved my undivided attention in the run-up to one of the most important days of her life.

I had initially planned on wandering up towards Alice-Rose after lunch. However, after breakfasting with Jules, and having 'digested' quite a bit more than the food, I decided that the sooner I got this particular obligation out of the way, the sooner I could concentrate on all things matrimonial!

CHAPTER 45

. . . and a Cold Dose of Reality for Lunch

I T BEING A beautiful day, I decided to cycle up to Alice-Rose from Willow Cottage. Despite feeling decidedly better, I knew that my body was still in a weakened condition. Weeks of lying around the house, getting little or no exercise, had depleted my energy levels, and I presumed that I needed fresh air and exercise, every bit as much as nourishment. Therefore, I decided in my ignorance that a two-mile bike-ride to Alice-Rose was just the thing to kick start my eventual return to full health.

I set off from home at an optimistically steady pace, having loaded the bicycle's basket with a small bottle of spring water. One mile down the road and the water was gone. I began to wonder if I had imagined drinking it as my head was a mass of sweat, and perspiration trickled down my nose. Perhaps, I had unwittingly poured the water over myself instead? The sun was high in the sky, and I was already dreading the return journey.

You just have to make it as far as Alice-Rose, I reasoned, *and then you can call Mum to come and fetch you.*

When I finally reached my destination, some twenty minutes later, I was truly regretting my decision to cycle. I was out of breath, sweating, and my white linen shirt was clinging to my body in a way that left very little to the imagination, Paddy O'Rourke's imagination to be precise! As I puffed round the last bend of the front avenue, I almost ran him down. He was standing surveying the house in the sunshine, hands on hips, when my front wheel collided with the back of his left knee. Luckily, by that stage of the *marathon*, I was losing what little momentum I had so that our collision caused little or no damage to either of us, just a healthy helping of mortification for me.

'Jesus, Paddy, are you all right?' I exclaimed, as he jumped to one side in alarm.

'Holy mother of . . .,' he yelled more in fright than in anger, before seeing that it was only me, out of control on a bike, and not some maniac trying to kill him.

'God, Libby, you gave me a hell of a fright! I wasn't expecting to see you until later,' he explained.

I wondered whether it was the unexpected impact of the bicycle, or the appalling sight of me, that had caused him the most alarm.

'Sorry, Paddy,' I apologised. 'I decided to come a bit earlier if that's all right?'

He was laughing now and eyeing my bike in amusement.

'The bicycle seemed like a good idea at the time,' I justified ruefully, 'but I guess I'm a little out of shape.'

'Well, you haven't been well, and it is pretty hot today,' he acknowledged. 'I suppose both of those things play their part in . . ..'

He trailed off, and I could tell that Paddy O'Rourke was taking in every last ridiculous inch of me. I felt obliged to explain further.

'I really thought the exercise would be good for me, but I think I overdid it. Sorry, I must look a sight!'

'Indeed, you do, Libby Finn,' he said grinning from ear to ear, 'a sight for sore eyes!'

'Paddy O'Rourke, are you mocking me?' I said, relaxing slightly.

'I would never mock you, Libby Finn,' he said, and I thought that I detected that increasingly familiar tenderness in his voice again. I supposed that 'tenderness' came with getting to know someone; it didn't necessarily signify anything more than familiarity.

'Now how about a cool drink of water from your very own kitchen tap?' he asked, leading me into the house and through to the kitchen.

Once in the kitchen, I realised just how detached I had become from Alice-Rose over the previous couple of months. In that time, she had been transformed almost beyond recognition. When I first met Paddy, I had given him folders full of pages that I had torn from various country house and garden magazines. Those pages inspired me when I imagined what my ideal home would look like, and they were the images that I had aspired to in terms of how Alice-Rose would look when all work on her was complete.

Six weeks before, when I was unwittingly in the throes of early pregnancy combined with the flu, I had insisted to Mum that Paddy could and must carry on with all plans for Alice-Rose without me. I trusted his judgement entirely, and I didn't want the project held up on account of my illness, neither did I want the builders leaving loose ends to be tied up after their departure. After all, Paddy had all the contacts in the trade, and I was paying him top dollar for a job well done and, more importantly, completely finished. As I stood and looked around me in amazement, it was entirely obvious that Paddy had taken my ideas very much to heart. The kitchen of my fantasies lay before me, and I began to cry out of sheer relief and gratitude.

'You hate it,' he said, the disappointment lying heavy in his voice.

'I love it!' I cried, refraining from adding *and I love you*!

'You do?' he said, relief and delight changing his entire countenance.

'Of course, I do, you crazy man! What woman wouldn't love this kitchen?' I asked, stupefied that he could have mistaken my reaction as anything other than positive.

Then Paddy O'Rourke did something entirely unexpected, and with three long strides, he covered the distance between us, before scooping me up in his strong, manly arms and spinning me round like a small child. We were both laughing like kids when he eventually put me down, but unfortunately, what could have been a hallmark moment ended up being just a blip in his otherwise business-as-usual day.

I fought hard to hide my disappointment when Paddy released me and proceeded to showcase the kitchen as if nothing unusual had taken place between us. Paddy described the kitchen as a 'work of art', and I had to agree. The solid oak cabinets looked remarkably solid, and the plain in-frame doors and contrasting slate countertops suited the look and feel of the room perfectly.

The huge island-unit at the centre of the work area featured a gas hob and a double sink, complete with a waste grinder. There was an under-counter, pull-out bin, complete with sections for refuse, recycling, and composting. I was in heaven. The island also had a section for my cookbooks, generous cupboards for my baking ingredients, and a series of drawers where I could store my saucepans; I had mentioned in passing that I didn't like the idea of pans gathering dust while they hung from ceiling racks. I wanted a real kitchen with clean lines and unobstructed views across the worktops. Paddy had taken heed and delivered on every score.

'Aggie' was back in residence, looking totally revamped and sitting very comfortably beneath a newly sandblasted stone arch.

'I didn't know *that* was there!' I exclaimed, pointing to the arch in sheer amazement at the wonder of what had been revealed.

'I wasn't certain myself until I did some research of my own,' Paddy said modestly. 'As luck would have it, George Baxter had some old photos of the place, and one of them had been taken in the kitchen. It confirmed my suspicions.'

Further exploration of the house revealed that wood panelling had been completed to exacting standards, doors had been rehung, and that the new doors leading to the conservatory blended perfectly with the others. Although floors and surfaces were dusty, the walls and woodwork had been primed, and the overall effect was that of an exquisite painting just waiting for the master's finishing touches.

'So, Libby, what do you think?' Paddy asked at the end of our tour.

'Paddy, I think it's completely amazing!' I said, without hesitation. 'You have surpassed all my expectations in terms of vision and commitment!' I paused to draw breath. 'I'm so grateful to you for the fantastic job that you've done,' I continued, words failing to adequately convey my appreciation. 'It's obvious that you've put your heart and soul into Alice-Rose, and for that, I cannot thank you enough!'

Paddy shook his head, dismissing my need to express thanks, but I continued regardless.

'You've kept the momentum and enthusiasm going even when I couldn't. All I can say is thank you, thank you, and thank you again.'

Paddy was not as happy with my answer as I would have thought. He looked at me thoughtfully and hesitated before putting two fingers to his head as if to clarify his thought process. Then he continued along a more careful line of questioning.

'Libby, I hear what you're saying, or at least I think I do. But I'm not convinced that you're entirely happy with Alice-Rose.'

Paddy's brow was by then furrowed with obvious concern.

'You seem somehow distant from her. I suppose what I really want to know, Libby, is can you see yourself being happy here? Have I succeeded in making Alice-Rose your home?'

I wasn't expecting this from Paddy. It had never occurred to me that he would have such a level of concern towards his clients. I suppose I expected him to have a level of disregard towards me once he had delivered on the terms of the contract. He caught me unawares, and I blurted out an ill-conceived answer.

'Gosh, Paddy, yes! I'm sorry if I gave the wrong impression. You *have* created a wonderful home, and I'm sure that we'll be very happy here.'

'We?' he said sharply, my answer had taken him by surprise.

'Did I say we?' I stammered. 'I meant to say me, or I, or whatever the correct term is for the first person singular.'

I felt heat flooding my face, colour rising from my neck up.

'It's okay, Libby,' he said, shaking his head in a gesture of self-annoyance. 'If there is somebody else, I can handle it.'

He laughed, trying to make light of what he had just said. I didn't like it. I wanted him to care.

'There is someone else, but it's not a man. Well, it might be a man, but it's not what you think,' I stammered, making absolutely no sense at all.

'I see,' he said quietly, although it was quite clear that he couldn't see at all.

How could he? I was the pregnant one, and most days found me grasping for clarity in my newfound situation. I knew I was pregnant, but I didn't *know* . . . it was all so unreal! When Max and I had been trying for a baby, the effort had been intense. It got to the point where we presumed that making a baby must be incredibly hard work for everyone, and that every element of the universe had to be controlled and aligned in order for conception to take place. Then for one to discover that a baby could be made from the most casual and carefree of encounters hardly bore thinking about, it just didn't make sense.

'I'm sorry, Paddy,' I said finally, after what seemed like an eternity spent looking at his expression of barely concealed hurt and bewilderment.

Right there and then, I just wanted to take his finely chiselled face in my hands and gently kiss every part of it before allowing myself the pleasure of bringing my lips to rest on his. He looked suddenly vulnerable, and my heart broke with the thought of what lay ahead.

'I know that I'm not making any sense,' I continued slowly, 'but I've got a lot on my mind right now.' That was the understatement of the year if ever I had heard it. 'Would it be okay with you if we didn't meet again until after Jules's wedding?'

'Sure,' said Paddy, hesitating.

He was clearly confused by my request.

'I just feel that I've been neglecting her,' I explained, as much to myself as to Paddy. 'And there's all of this last-minute stuff to be seen to. I don't want to let her down.'

I stopped and waited, having no idea what Paddy would make of what I had just said. Here he was, getting ready to hand Alice-Rose back to me, and suddenly, I wasn't available for the next couple of weeks!

'Sure, Libby, I understand,' he said without reproach.

I felt a wave of relief wash over me; I had expected some form of protest, and yet there was none. I was released from the pressure of having to meet Paddy O'Rourke on a daily basis while guarding a secret that would inevitably have as much impact on his immediate life as it did on mine. Once Jules's wedding was safely out of the way, I would be in a better position to take on the world. My relief was somewhat premature because Paddy hadn't quite finished.

'I will, however, be finished here before then,' he said shortly.

I was taken aback.

'So I guess I'll drop the keys off at Willow Cottage before I leave for good,' he continued reasonably. 'I can post them through the letter box if you're not around.'

He sounded quite definite, and somehow I knew that even if he hadn't previously planned on finishing so soon, he would do so now. There was nothing to say that would change his mind.

'So that's it then?' I said, and I knew that I sounded wounded despite my best efforts. 'We won't meet again?'

'I'm sure we'll meet again, Libby,' he said, and I felt my spirits lifting at the mention of my name. 'Your building surveyor has to sign off on the final project before the last payment will be made. Having said that, I don't envision there being any problems.'

Paddy had offered me a glimmer of hope before snatching it back.

'So when *will* we meet again?' I asked, panicked by the vagueness of his 'reassurances'. I was at a loss to see any real opportunity to meet once he left Alice-Rose; the final payment could be posted on. Regardless of anything to do with the build, it was essential that I meet Paddy as soon as possible after Jules's and Noel's marriage, my mental health depended on it!

'Oh, I don't know, Libby,' he continued, far too casually for my liking, 'there are always weddings or the opera? We've met there before. It's not beyond the bounds of possibility that we could meet there again.'

I didn't like those odds, and besides, the next time we met, I did not want it to be in the company of his mother! I scrabbled around wildly in my head for clues as to what I was supposed to do next. I could just let him go, I reasoned, that might be the kindest thing; I was sure there were lots of men in the world who were blissfully unaware that they'd accidentally fathered children.

I forced myself to confront my true emotions and asked myself what it was that I really wanted from this man. Was I merely seeking an opportunity to tell him the truth before releasing him from all burden of responsibility? Or was I secretly hoping for a happy-ever-after that included him? I honestly didn't know. But whatever it was, it wasn't the uncertainty of wondering when I might get a chance to reveal his parental status to him! While uncertainty reigned, one thing was indisputable; I would have to figure it all out later, after the wedding.

'Great, Paddy, I look forward to meeting your mother again,' I said rather bizarrely.

I had no idea why I had said such a thing, and by the look on his face, neither had he. 'Till then,' I said, taking his hand and shaking it firmly.

'Till then,' he said.

And that was it; we parted company on the most ludicrous of notes. I turned on my heel and made my way outside, fighting the tears of self-pity that were threatening to overcome me. Reaching my bicycle, I turned it around and, having mounted it, peddled furiously away from Alice-Rose, and from Paddy O'Rourke.

The rest of the day passed in a haze. I forced myself to visit home, knowing that if I didn't, Mum would suspect that something was wrong and would relentlessly pursue the 'root of the problem'. The last thing I needed right then was Mum fussing about me; there would be plenty of time for that after the wedding. I couldn't even begin to imagine what her reaction would be when I finally told her that I was pregnant.

Dad would be an even bigger deal. He would probably be crushed by the news that his 'darling girl' was pregnant and husbandless, and somehow, I didn't think that *dead husbands* would count under the circumstances. I realised the full extent of my moral courage when I found myself deciding to allow Mum to break the news to him when the time came; it wasn't impressive. I toughened my resolve to deal with the situation in hand with courage and conviction once the wedding was over.

CHAPTER 46

From This Day Forth

S ATURDAY, THE TWENTY-FIFTH of June, dawned bright and clear and beautiful! Jules and I were awoken early by Felicity urging us to 'look lively'! Pulling on our dressing gowns, we made our way down to the Mahon kitchen and the heavenly smells of their housekeeper Nora's cooking. We were both clear-headed, and I was by then blissfully free from all forms of morning sickness; Jules never having had to endure that unfortunate aspect of pregnancy!

According to the eight-day clock hanging to one side of the range, the time was half past eight, give or take ten minutes. The clock had hung there all my life, and I knew its vagaries well. Ten minutes was neither here nor there that early in the morning; we didn't have to be at the hairdressers until ten thirty, so there was plenty of time to enjoy the first meal of the day.

Jules and I were the only ones properly seated for breakfast that morning. Although family and friends popped in to wish the bride well, for the most part, visitors were transient. Occasionally, having playfully snatched a rasher hot from Nora's pan, someone would straddle a chair for a few minutes while they gulped down a mug of coffee or chewed on a bacon butty. The Mahons were busy people, and taking time off, even for a loved one's wedding, required careful planning and a great deal of hard work. While events unfolded, a wedding photographer worked away in the background and was to shadow us for the rest of the morning.

Jules, Felicity, and I left the house at ten fifteen and drove the five-minute journey to Ballyedmond's Hair and Beauty Salon. We were alive and fully charged on sunshine and eager anticipation. I was determined to make the most of the day and to suspend my cares until the following one.

Sandra met us at the door of the salon with a huge smile and an unopened bottle of champagne. Much to her surprise, we all insisted that it remained so, and we settled for tea instead. An hour and a half later, we emerged from the salon looking considerably more elegant than when we had arrived. Our hair was coiffured, our faces were polished, and our nails were buffed to exacting standards. There was nothing left to do, except slip into our dresses and hope that the cars would arrive to get us to the church on time. Jules had been explicit in her wishes; she did not want to be more than ten minutes late for the church. She had no desire to keep Noel waiting on that day, of all days!

It was no surprise that Dad arrived in his Jaguar in plenty of time. He had been well-warned, and Mum had hired two locum vets to ensure that every emergency was covered. My brother Philip, having borrowed Uncle Des's 1960s Mercedes, arrived shortly thereafter. It was Philip's job to ensure that Felicity and I got to the church before the bride.

Philip drove away from the Mahon house at twenty past one exactly and delivered Felicity and I to the church just before half past the hour. Crowds of people were still gathered outside in the sunshine when we arrived, chatting and eager to catch a glimpse of Jules. Eventually, the wedding photographers managed to hunt the guests inside, allowing only those required for the pre-wedding shots to linger. Jules and Leo arrived shortly thereafter, and once all of the photographs were taken, adults and children disappeared within, leaving Jules, Leo, and I to face the music, alone.

Upon entering the church, which had been transformed into a basilica of exquisite blooms, our arrival was heralded by the joyous strains of 'Tabhair Dom do Lámh'. Walking up the aisle ahead of Jules and Leo, I became mildly curious about the identity of the musicians. I had forgotten to ask Emma, the musical director for the day, who else, apart from Dad and herself, would be playing. It didn't really matter because whoever they were, the sound was truly amazing.

The wedding proceeded without a hitch. The music throughout was inspiring, the operatic tones of a trained soprano lending an extra special dimension to the proceedings. As we exited the church to Handel's Hornpipe from Water Music, I looked up towards the gallery, and instead of catching Emma's eye, I caught the knowing eye of Emily O'Rourke! Emily, of all people, was playing the flute! My heart skipped several beats, while the musicians missed none.

If Emily was in the church, could Paddy be far away? Who was playing the organ? I hadn't planned on meeting Paddy O'Rourke's mother so soon again and at Jules's wedding of all places! Then I remembered that Paddy had hinted that we might meet again at a wedding.

There was no immediate opportunity to accost Jules about her little deception because the bride and groom stood to receive every last guest exiting the church. It took forever! Knowing all that she knew about Paddy and I, how could she possibly have neglected to tell me about the music arrangements?

Finally, when every last guest's hand had been shook, including Paddy and Emily O'Rourke's, I managed to corner her discreetly on the pretence of straightening her veil.

'You never told me that the O'Rourkes would be here!' I hissed through gritted smile.

'You never asked,' she answered innocently.

'I didn't think I had to!' I countered. 'It never occurred to me that you would choose *them* of all people!'

'I didn't,' she said. 'I left the music in Emma's hands, and by the time I knew the arrangements, it was too late!'

'*Oh, really?*' I said, not entirely convinced that Jules hadn't, in fact, planned it all from the start.

'*Really*, Libby,' she insisted. 'You have to admit though the music was wonderful!'

'Yes,' I admitted reluctantly. 'But . . ..'

'But nothing,' interrupted Jules. 'Given that you're heavily involved in the wedding, it should be easy enough to avoid *them* without causing any offence.'

'Gee, thanks, Jules, I feel better already,' I whined sarcastically.

My sarcasm, however, was lost on Jules; she just patted my arm before returning her attention to her new husband.

I breathed deeply, and feeling like there was somebody watching me, I turned around sharply and caught Paddy O'Rourke's unsuspecting eye. He was chatting in a small group of people; I waved briefly in his direction before following the bridal party back on to the steps of the church for another photo call.

I was camera weary by the time we eventually got seated for dinner, smiling on queue was more tiring than I remembered. Jules and Noel had decided to have the wedding speeches before dinner; they were short and sweet, with an emphasis on the latter. I wasn't a fan of public speaking myself, but even so, given the occasion, I felt moved to say a few words on my friend's behalf. Once my contribution was over, I made a conscience decision to relax, and I began to enjoy myself. There was no point worrying about the O'Rourkes; I had managed quite easily to avoid them thus far, and I felt confident that Michael Quigley, as Noel's best man, would keep me busy on the dance floor for the best part of the evening. In between times, I could occupy myself by flitting tables, feigning the skills of a social butterfly.

Jules and I were in one of the hotel's restrooms, taking a break from the proceedings, when Emma rushed in to tell us that we were needed in the marquee for the first dance. My heart sank. Even though I was relying on Michael Quigley to keep me busy on the dance floor, I wasn't looking forward to a repeat performance of our toe-crushing routine from the Hallowe'en Ball; there would be no Dan Bryant to rescue me this time. Jules had sent an invitation to him, but he had politely declined on the basis of a 'previous commitment'.

As Jules and I made our way back into the marquee, we were met on the edge of the dance floor by Noel and Michael. As per the custom, Jules and Noel took to the floor first, Michael and I waiting in the wings to join them for the second song. All too soon we were bopping alongside them, Michael and I doing our best not to look too amateurish but failing miserably. Two songs later and I was already beginning to lose the will to live. I was toying desperately with the idea of developing a headache for the rest of the night when our 'dancing' was interrupted by somebody tapping Michael's shoulder. I looked up to see Paddy O'Rourke.
'May I?' he asked, brokering no refusal as he directed Michael into the arms of another woman.
'Well, yes, I suppose . . .,' Michael agreed reluctantly, clearly not as charmed by the vision of Emily O'Rourke as he might have been.
'Alone at last,' Paddy sighed, before expertly whisking me to the other side of the dance floor. *Alone at last . . .* I must be hearing things!
'Sorry?' I asked, unsure of what else to say. Maybe I had missed a question.
'I thought we'd never get to this point,' he answered, leaving me none the wiser.
'This point being?' I continued, determined now to get to grips with the gist of our conversation.
'The point where you and I no longer have a business relationship,' he said, obviously not in the least bit worried about offending me.
'I didn't realise it was that bad,' I said, stunned by his bluntness.

'It wasn't,' he said.

Silence.

'Don't you see?' he asked, sensing that I misunderstood his meaning. 'I would never have asked you to dance if I was still your employee.'

It still didn't make any sense to me. This man had taken me to bed and had given me the most wonderfully intimate night of my life, while he was still my 'employee', but asking me to dance would have been crossing the line? Then suddenly I remembered something, part of a conversation that had taken place on the road back from Kinsale.

'Paddy, now that we are in fact *dancing*, I seem to remember you saying that you couldn't dance,' I said, surprised by the lightness of his step which was a blessed relief after Michael Quigley's clodhopping.

'Don't dance, not, *couldn't* dance. There's a difference.'

He smiled as he rocked me gently to the strains of 'It had to be you'.

'Mind you, now that I've finally got you in my arms like this, I'm beginning to reconsider my former reluctance to take to the dance floor.'

I was speechless, and at a loss as to what to say next. This was not the Paddy O'Rourke that I knew. The Paddy O'Rourke that I thought I knew couldn't dance and would never make a fool of himself over a girl! Of course, just because Paddy O'Rourke wanted to dance with me didn't mean that he wanted to spend the rest of his life with me or, more importantly, have a baby with me. I had to get out of that cosy situation as fast as I could.

'Paddy,' I said, 'there's something that I have to tell you but not now.'

'Not bad news, I hope,' he said quietly.

'Not exactly, but it might come as a shock to you all the same,' I said.

At that point I had no idea what to say, yet I wanted to give Paddy some indication that all was not necessarily well.

'Please don't tell me that you're in love with Dan Bryant,' he whispered into my ear.

'God, no!'

My response was automatic, and I pulled back from him slightly. I wanted him to be absolutely certain of that fact at least, and I looked him squarely in the eye to make sure of it. I felt him tightening his grip on me, and I allowed him to pull me close to him again.

'Thank God for that! *He* had me worried,' he said, and I knew that he was telling the truth.

'He had? Why?' I asked. I needed to know.

'Because I love you, Libby Finn,' he whispered urgently.

'You do?' I countered, stunned beyond belief.

'Always have and always will,' he said.

It was now Paddy's turn to pull away from me and to look deep into my eyes.

'I know it's not the right time to tell you this, but I've been waiting so long for the right moment, and it never seems to come.'

'Have you been drinking?' I asked accusingly.

The thought suddenly occurred to me that we were, after all, at a wedding and that it was very likely that Paddy had been drinking. I didn't want to wake up the following morning to discover that he had made a mistake.

'Not a drop, I swear to you,' he replied, and I wanted to believe him.

I looked hard into his eyes for reassurance, and I found it there.

'Is my loving you so impossible to imagine?' he asked, his voice full of pain and longing. 'Have I got it all wrong, Libby?'

'No, darling Paddy, you've got it all right, as always,' I said, anxious to reassure him.

'I love you too, but there's something else to be considered,' I continued, seeing the joy that my revelation brought to his face but knowing that he needed to know the whole truth.

'Can we go outside?' I asked, beginning to feel more than a little uncomfortable, conducting our conversation on the dance floor.

Holding my hand, Paddy led me outside into the garden and across the lawn to a bench, which stood to one side of a summer house. It was not yet eight o'clock, and there was still some heat left in the evening sun. Despite this, I began to shiver uncontrollably. Paddy removed his jacket and placed it around my shoulders before sitting down beside me.

'What's wrong, Libby?' Paddy asked urgently. 'You're not seriously ill, are you?'

'Not ill, no, though I have as you know been feeling unwell and that's part of what I have to tell you.'

Paddy hugged me to his side in an effort to control my shivering, but it was pointless. My teeth began to chatter with the enormity of what I was about to reveal to him.

'Remember Kinsale?' I said, trying to break the news of my pregnancy to him gently.

'How could I forget?'

'Remember how I thought then that I couldn't have children?' I probed cautiously.

'Is that what this is all about? I don't care about babies any more!' he said, jumping to the obvious conclusion.

'You don't?' I chattered.

'No.'

'I'm pregnant,' I said simply, unable to beat about the bush any longer and finding it altogether too hard to go on amid my chattering teeth.

I watched silently as the information sunk into the depths of Paddy's being.

'Seriously?' he asked, clearly stunned by the revelation.

'Seriously,' I promised. 'I wouldn't joke about something like that.'

Silence.

'I didn't lie to you. I just hadn't figured on the problem lying with Max,' I explained.

I would have gone on to apologise further, but there were tears cascading down Paddy O'Rourke's face, and I felt pretty sure that they were the proverbial tears of joy. Rising to his feet and standing in front of me, Paddy pulled me into a standing position. He held out my hands and surveyed me before bowing to place his own on my still flat stomach. It was as if we were suspended in time as I lovingly sunk my fingers into the thick curls at the nape of his neck and clung on for dear life. We were together at last. We were a family. 'Thank you, Alice-Rose.'

EPILOGUE

I KNEW THAT I was in trouble the instant that Libby Finn crashed into my world. 'Crashed' might *seem* like too strong a word to describe the moment, but that's how it felt when she first walked into my office, full of life and beauty! My heart took flight, and all my carefully arranged emotions broke loose in chaos. I was lost to her, and straightaway, I felt the cold, familiar hand of fear.

My immediate instinct was to protect myself by dissuading this girl from wanting anything to do with me. To achieve this end, I chose the previously tried and tested method of ill-disguised hostility. As it turned out, I needn't have bothered going to such lengths. Since allowing myself to love and be loved, I've realised just how far out of synch my life was with my deepest, heartfelt desires. I had buried them deep within me where no one but Libby Finn could reach.

I met Alyson on the street today, and the Garth Brooks' song 'Unanswered Prayers' came to mind. After a brief chat, I shook her hand, and I wished her well. I meant it. I didn't tell her that I was now in love for the first time in my life because that would have been childish and cruel, but I was thinking it. Neither did I tell her about my two girls, she didn't need to know, and I didn't need her to.

As it happens, I was on my way to collect my girls, to take them home to Alice-Rose, when we bumped into each other. Alyson was leaving the National Maternity Hospital just as I was going in. We didn't refer to each others reasons for going there; there didn't seem to be any point; we had both moved on.

Lucy Emily O'Rourke, the light of our lives, was born two days ago at the National Maternity Hospital, Dublin, weighing seven pounds, four and a half ounces, precisely. Lucy was pipped at the post by Cecily Kinsella, who was born two weeks ago 'weighing in' at a whopping nine pounds and seven ounces!

Since the birth of our daughters, I have become aware of a streak of competitiveness in Noel Kinsella that I hadn't previously known existed. It must be the Mahon influence because suddenly a lot of racing terminology is creeping into our conversations. It appears that Cecily is the winner so far, in terms of being the first to cross the *finish line* and in terms of the *weigh-in*. Personally, I am still in some disagreement about the latter; I've always been lead to believe that a light jockey is preferable to a heavy one! As for who the real winner is? Of this, I am certain. That would be me. 'Thank you, Alice-Rose.'

THE END

CAITRÍONA LESLIE